Praise for the Work of

For St. *Francis Soci*

"Noblin's books are known for ~~...~~, and the animals are present here. . . . Despite some heavy subject matter . . . the story is funny and light. Readers will bond with Maeve and her sweet disposition."

—*Booklist*

"Feel-good fiction at its finest. Annie England Noblin has crafted an utterly entertaining tale of unexpected chances and small-town secrets, and it's as sweet and comforting as a hand-knit sweater and a warm puppy in your lap."

—Susan Wiggs, *New York Times* bestselling author

"I was immediately enchanted! Lively and heartfelt, the characters—both human and four-legged—in Annie England Noblin's *St Francis Society for Wayward Pets* come alive. I adored it."

—Lori Foster, *New York Times* bestselling author

"Noblin's masterful touch hits the sweet spot of humor and tragedy in this heartfelt book about the truest meaning of family, friends, abandoned dogs, and love amidst a weave of plot-twisting heroics."

—Jacqueline Sheehan, *New York Times* bestselling author

"Annie England Noblin is an incredibly gifted storyteller. *St. Francis Society for Wayward Pets* is heartfelt, charming, and funny."

—Meg Donohue, author of *You, Me, and the Sea*

For *The Sisters Hemingway*

"For anyone who loves a family drama, with wit and heart to go around. Recommended for fans of Susan Mallery."

—*Booklist*

"Combining sibling rivalry, romantic story lines . . . a strong cast . . . and a realistic, colorful Ozarks setting, this well-paced story will appeal to those who enjoy family dramas. Its warm, engaging tone and happy ending for all will appeal to readers of Susan Wiggs or Mary Alice Monroe."

—*Library Journal*

Christmas
in
Blue Dog Valley

Also by Annie England Noblin

Maps for the Getaway

St. Francis Society for Wayward Pets

The Sisters Hemingway

Just Fine with Caroline

Pupcakes

Sit! Stay! Speak!

Christmas in Blue Dog Valley

A Novel

Annie England Noblin

AVON *An Imprint of HarperCollinsPublishers*

P.S.™ is a trademark of HarperCollins Publishers.

CHRISTMAS IN BLUE DOG VALLEY. Copyright © 2022 by Annie England Noblin. All rights reserved. Printed in the United States of America. No part of this book may be used or reproduced in any manner whatsoever without written permission except in the case of brief quotations embodied in critical articles and reviews. For information, address HarperCollins Publishers, 195 Broadway, New York, NY 10007.

HarperCollins books may be purchased for educational, business, or sales promotional use. For information, please email the Special Markets Department at SPsales@harpercollins.com.

FIRST EDITION

Designed by Diahann Sturge

Illustrations throughout © VeraDominica; GreenPlate; Faenkova Elena; Kimleva; MOSAIC; La Puma; AnastasiaSonne / Shutterstock

Library of Congress Cataloging-in-Publication Data has been applied for.

ISBN 978-0-06-304019-9

22 23 24 25 26   LSC   10 9 8 7 6 5 4 3 2 1

For Jude—
the best Christmas present I've ever received.

Christmas
in
Blue Dog
Valley

Prologue

Dr. Gene Saltzman, the seventy-year-old veterinarian at Valley Veterinary in Blue Dog Valley, Wisconsin, was just closing up for the night when he noticed the red pickup truck pulling into the parking lot.

He sighed heavily but waited as the man behind the wheel parked, got out, and walked up to him with an expression that was something akin to anger but not quite.

Not yet.

"Evening, Cohen," Dr. Saltzman said. "What can I do you for?"

"I heard a rumor," Cohen said. "Word is that you've sold the clinic to a woman vet in California."

Cohen Gable didn't like surprises, and, boy, had he been surprised when Ruby down at the diner told him Dr. Saltzman was selling the clinic to some *outsider from Los Angeles* and moving himself down to Florida to retire. Cohen had to go right over and find out for himself if it was true.

In the truck, Cohen's cairn terrier, Peanut Butter, yipped

through the cracked window, begging to be let out. Peanut Butter didn't like anybody having a conversation without her.

"That's not a rumor," Dr. Saltzman replied patiently. "It's fact, and she'll be here sooner rather than later." Dr. Saltzman had known Cohen the boy's entire life, and he'd always been serious—too serious for his own good. "She's going to be a great addition to this town. She'll liven the place up."

"We don't need livening up," Cohen said. "We need a reliable vet."

"And you'll have one."

"How do you know?" Cohen asked. "Do you know her?"

"I know her enough," Dr. Saltzman replied. "I have all the confidence in the world that she will settle right in."

"How do you reckon a vet from L.A. is going to settle into the valley?" Cohen asked. "She can't possibly understand us here."

"About as good as that dog of yours settled in on the farm—in time. You need to have some faith, my boy," Dr. Saltzman said. "I'm counting on you to make sure she feels welcome."

Cohen snorted.

"I'm serious," Dr. Saltzman said. "I'm also going to need you to pick her up from the airport in Milwaukee."

"That's a two-hour drive, one way!" Cohen said.

"Then I suggest," Dr. Saltzman said, patting Cohen on the back, "you learn how to drive and talk at the same time."

Chapter 1

Goldie McKenzie watched the pet carrier circle around on the conveyor belt and disappear into the bowels of the Milwaukee airport. There was a cat inside the carrier. She knew that, because she'd watched a man—probably about her age, in his forties—walk up beside her as she waited for her luggage, chattering into a Bluetooth headset attached to his ear like it was 2004.

"What am I looking for?" he was asking. "A *cat*? You've got to be frickin' kidding me, Brenda. A frickin' *cat*?"

The first time the carrier passed by them, the man did not make a move to pick it up. Instead, he folded his arms across his chest, listened for a moment, and then said, "You didn't tell me nothin' about pickin' up a frickin' cat."

The carrier made another trip around the belt.

"Well, if you don't even want this frickin' cat, why am I here to pick up a frickin' cat?"

Goldie looked down at her phone, pretending to read an email while she listened.

"I can't believe I paid to park just to pick up a frickin' cat," the man continued. "Cost me ten bucks. Why didn't your sister tell you she was sendin' your dead mother's cat on a frickin' airplane? Of all the ridiculous . . . What? No. I don't want the frickin' cat."

By this time, Goldie had picked up her own bags, the carrier was nearly the only thing left on the belt, and a crowd of people had come and gone. She only had two suitcases; the rest of her belongings would be arriving later, sent to her new home in Blue Dog Valley, Wisconsin, once she got settled.

Next to her, the man sighed. "If I leave it, won't they just send it back?"

Goldie flicked her eyes up to the man. Surely, he wasn't just going to leave the cat at the airport. Was that even a thing a person could do?

Apparently, it was something a person could do, because the man turned around and walked away, vanishing into the thick onslaught of people who'd already claimed their luggage. All around her, people were hustling and bustling, meeting loved ones, embracing, and grabbing their suitcases, until it was just Goldie and the cat and the low hum of the belt as it continued to circle.

She stood there so long that it must have started to look suspicious, and she jumped when she felt a tap on her shoulder. Behind her, there was an airport security guard, and he looked concerned.

"Everything all right, ma'am?" he asked. "You need help with something?"

Goldie blinked. Did she need help? She didn't even know where to begin. For starters, she was in *Wisconsin*, which was an entire solar system away from Los Angeles, where she'd spent nearly her entire life. And then there was the small matter of that life, the one she'd left behind, which was currently in total shambles.

Obviously.

Because why else would anyone come to Wisconsin on purpose? Clearly, she was having a complete and total breakdown, and she doubted very much that the pubescent security guard could help her with that.

"Ma'am?"

"What?"

The security guard cleared his throat. "Are you all right? Can I call someone for you?"

"Oh," Goldie replied, shaking her head. "No, no, I'm fine."

"Are you sure?" He didn't look convinced. "That your pet taxi there on the belt?"

Goldie turned her attention toward the cat. "Uh, well . . ."

"I swear to Father Christmas, if that's another abandoned animal, I'll lose my crackers," the guard said. "That's the third one this month."

Goldie tried not to laugh. So far, she hadn't heard a single curse word uttered since landing in the Midwest. She wondered if the people here were physically incapable of using bad language. As she'd been exiting the plane, she'd heard the flight attendant mutter "cheese and rice" under her breath when the businessman who'd been flying next to Goldie in coach asked the flight attendant for her number.

When the security guard reached out to grab the pet carrier, Goldie stopped him. "No," she said. "No, it's my cat. I'm sorry. I'm just tired. It's been a long day."

"Cat?" The guard bent down and peered inside the carrier.

"It's one of them hairless cats? Lady, you need to get that cat a sweater. Do you know how cold it's about to get here in the city?"

Goldie hid her surprise at finding out that this was a hairless cat—a Sphynx cat to be exact—and said, "Well, I guess it's lucky I'm not staying in the city."

"Oh yeah?" the security guard asked. "Where you headed?"

"Uh, Blue Dog Valley?" Goldie replied, annoyed that her response came out as more of a question. "Have you heard of it?"

The guard lifted up his stocking cap to scratch his head, looked Goldie up and down, and then said, "In that case, I think you're both gonna need to be wearing more than a sweater."

Chapter 2

Blue Dog Valley, Wisconsin, had not been in Goldie's five-, ten-, or even fifteen-year plan. At no point when she was growing up in suburban Los Angeles or attending the University of Southern California or, later, veterinary school at UC Davis, did Goldie envision herself as a forty-year-old West Coast transplant in the Midwest.

In fact, if anyone had told her even a month ago that she would be holding an abandoned cat carrier and standing at the entrance of the Milwaukee International Airport waiting for a ride from some farmer in a red pickup truck, she would have laughed.

But right now Goldie wasn't laughing. She was shivering in the jacket she'd thought would be warm enough and cursing herself for making rash decisions like buying a crumbling veterinary clinic, sight unseen, after a night of one too many bottles of wine.

"You should have left him a long time ago," Goldie's best friend, Alex, had said to her when Goldie showed up at her apartment in tears, mascara streaming down her face, holding the broken heel of her favorite pair of pumps. "I mean, like ten years ago."

"He gave me my first job out of veterinary school," Goldie replied, pushing past her friend and flailing onto Alex's couch. "I was grateful."

"So you repaid him by wasting a whole decade on his narcissistic ass?" Alex replied. "That hardly seems fair."

"I wasted a decade on him because I loved him," Goldie said, trying her best not to wail. Alex hated when she wailed. "The job was just a perk."

"Yeah, for him," Alex said. She sat down beside Goldie. "You deserve better."

Goldie rested her head on Alex's shoulder. "I know," she replied. "I know, but I just kept thinking it would all work out."

"That's always been your problem," Alex reminded her. "You're way too optimistic for L.A."

"I'm so over L.A.," Goldie said.

"You can always come with me to Kenya," Alex said. "They need veterinarians as much as they need doctors."

Alex was a top-notch dermatologist and something of a celebrity after a video of her draining a Guinness World Record–breaking cyst on an elderly patient went viral on YouTube. Now Dr. A, as Alex was fondly known, had her own YouTube channel with three million subscribers worldwide. For the past several years, she'd been making the trek to Kenya with her film crew to shine a spotlight on the dangerous infestation of a sand flea that burrows into human skin and lays eggs. She'd saved thousands of lives and raised countless donations for the families she helped.

It was a noble cause, and Goldie admired her.

"I can't just uproot my entire life and run off with you to East Africa," Goldie replied. "Besides, when do you leave? I don't have time to get my passport and everything ready."

"Not for a little while," Alex said. "You can stay here as long as you want." She stood up. "You know, Goldie, your whole life doesn't have to be here if you don't want it to be. Los Angeles isn't the center of the universe."

"I won't tell anyone you said that," Goldie replied, giving her friend a genuine smile. "I don't think the other natives know."

Alex laughed. "Don't answer his calls."

Goldie nodded. She had no intention of answering *his* calls. Deep down, she knew that he probably wasn't going to call her, anyway. When he did, it would be about dividing the contents of their house and to nicely, condescendingly tell her that she needed to find another job.

Dividing their stuff wouldn't be so hard, Goldie knew. They were already sleeping in separate bedrooms, and she and her fiancé of nearly a decade, the veterinarian Brandon Burrows, were living entirely, absolutely separate lives.

They had been for a long time.

Everyone else knew it, too, although they were at least polite enough to talk about it behind Goldie's back. They had an unspoken agreement, she and Brandon. He cheated on her as often as he liked, and Goldie pretended not to notice. She didn't like the fighting and the making up and the broken promises to never do it again. It was easier to act like everything was fine. It was easier to ignore it, to go on with life as it was, and Goldie didn't know what happened that changed it all, what broke inside of her.

Well, actually, she did know. It was that damn bulldog, Brutus.

The back end of Brutus the bulldog was much less adorable than the front end. The front end of Brutus was the famous face of one of California's most expensive and gourmet dog foods, even though Brutus routinely rummaged through the trash and would eat anything put in front of him. When this happened, Dr. Marigold McKenzie was responsible for handling whatever happened at the back end of Brutus.

Brutus the bulldog was a millionaire, and Goldie was his ass doctor.

"Okay, Brutus," Goldie said, pulling on a latex glove and snapping it against her wrist. "You know the drill."

Brutus snorted as Goldie lifted his little corkscrew of a tail and cleaned underneath it. Sometimes she thought that if she had one wish, it would be to never see another tail pocket as long as she lived. But that would mean not seeing Brutus, and she had to admit, she did love him, despite his snorts and farts and wrinkles that needed constant cleaning.

Goldie motioned to the wide-eyed vet tech standing next to her. "Have you ever expressed a dog's anal glands before?" she asked. "It's gross, but it's a fairly simple procedure."

The vet tech shook her head. "No," she replied.

"All right." Goldie threw the cloth she'd used to clean the tail pocket into the trash and motioned for the vet tech to come closer. "I'll walk you through it."

The vet tech, whose name was Romy, was hired by Brandon as a temporary employee while one of their regular vet techs was on maternity leave. Goldie knew that Brandon was sleeping with Romy. They hadn't even tried to hide it.

It was pretty brazen, though, even for Brandon, to bring one of his other women to work with him. Goldie wondered just how stupid he thought she was. She knew it was maybe a little vindictive to make Romy express anal glands, but in Goldie's own defense, it *was* what she'd ask any vet tech to do.

Just not for Brutus.

He had a bit of a temper.

And now he was starting to get restless. He gave a little growl to voice his displeasure.

Goldie was about to announce that she'd do it herself when Romy stepped forward, gloved and ready to go. "Okay," she said. "Okay, I can do it. Show me."

Goldie moved out of the way so that Romy could take position behind Brutus. "Now," Goldie began, "lift his tail just a little and put the paper towel I'm going to hand you over his backside while placing your thumb and forefinger at four and eight o'clock."

Romy did as she was told.

"Gently squeeze. You'll know when it expresses."

Romy closed her eyes.

"Don't close your eyes," Goldie said.

Reluctantly, Romy opened her eyes. She squinted. "I can't tell that anything came out," she said.

"Squeeze just a little harder," Goldie replied. "Not too much."

As she squeezed, Romy bent down to get a better look.

"No!" Goldie said, gasping. "Don't put your face so close to his—"

But it was too late, and Goldie watched, as if in slow motion, as Romy recognized her mistake seconds after the stream of liquid shot out onto her face.

Romy stumbled back, knocking into Goldie, who reached out

toward the stainless-steel table where Brutus was standing. When Goldie's hand grazed Brutus's backside, he let out a disgruntled bark, no doubt already irritated from the injustice he'd just endured, and leaped off the table and skittered out into the lobby.

"Brutus!"

Goldie ran after him. For a bulldog, he was fast. He ran past his unassuming handler, and in a split second, he was out the front door, which at the moment was being held open by Mrs. Griswold, an elderly woman who'd once been a chorus girl during Hollywood's Golden Age, married quite rich, and now regularly brought in her Lhasa Apso, Benjamin, to be seen for depression, PTSD, and general anxiety disorder.

"Dr. Goldie!" Mrs. Griswold gasped, tightening her grip on Benjamin's leash. "What is this ruckus?"

"Sorry, Mrs. Griswold," Goldie said, rushing out the door after Brutus. "I'll be right back!"

"Benjamin can't handle this much excitement!" Mrs. Griswold called after her.

At that very moment, Goldie wished she were taking the same medication she'd prescribed to Benjamin. Instead, she was chasing after a renegade bulldog that was heading south out of the veterinary parking lot and straight for the busy street in front of them.

"Come back here!" Goldie screeched. "Your toenail is worth more than my life!"

Brutus paused for a split second to glance back at her, and Goldie could have sworn she saw him smirk. Just before he was within reach, he took off again, right through the crosswalk at the stoplight, causing a man on a Vespa to swerve out of the way, just missing a woman in a convertible who had her music up so loud that she didn't even notice.

Goldie could feel her black pencil skirt straining against her stride, and it was a relief when it finally gave way and ripped, allowing her more room to run. It was an impractical work outfit, anyway. She just liked the way the skirt looked with her favorite pair of red heels, which were, at this very moment in time, *incredibly* impractical.

Brutus, deterred by neither Vespa nor person, continued on until he got to the construction site of a new hot yoga studio. Several men in orange vests watched as Goldie came barreling onto the lot, tripped on a pile of gravel, and went flying through the air, nearly doing a somersault, and landing prone right in front of Brutus.

Goldie wished the earth would just swallow her up whole. That would be preferable to whatever fresh hell was awaiting her when she finally willed herself to get back up.

There was a chorus of concerned voices hovering above her.

"Hey, lady, are you all right?"

"Do you think she's knocked out?"

"Maybe she's dead."

"Nah, she's breathin'."

"Mumphulump," Goldie replied. And then, turning herself over with a groan, continued, "Don't let that dog get away."

"He ain't goin' nowhere," one of the construction men said. "Reggie is givin' him some beef jerky."

Another one of the men helped her to her feet and sheepishly handed her one of her heels. "I think you lost this, ma'am."

"Of course," Goldie said, staring down at the mangled shoe. The heel was hanging on by a thread. "Thank you."

"You don't look too bad. I guess you're all right," the first man said. "That your dog? He get away from ya?"

In the distance, Goldie could see Brandon running in her direction, waving his hands in the air, and shouting something.

"This dog look familiar to you?" said a man who Goldie assumed was Reggie from the metric ton of beef jerky he was holding in one of his hands. "I coulda sworn I seen him somewhere before."

"*Dogapalooza 4*," Goldie replied automatically. "He wore a pink tutu through most of it."

"Oh, no shit?" Reggie asked. "Wow."

By this time, Brandon was nearly to where they were, a look of concern tinged with anger on his face. Goldie sighed. "Don't give him any more jerky," she said to Reggie. "He's a vegan."

"He ain't vegan," Reggie said, shoving the jerky into his back jeans pocket. "What kind a dog is vegan?"

"The celebrity kind," Goldie replied. "If my fiancé sees you feeding that stuff to him, I'll never hear the end of it."

Brandon jogged up to them, the tails of the white lab coat he insisted on wearing every day flapping behind him. "What in the hell happened?" he asked, looking first to Brutus and then to Goldie. "Mrs. Griswold is beside herself, Romy may need to go to the ER, and Brutus's handler thinks you're trying to steal him."

"I'm fine, thanks," Goldie muttered, shoving her broken shoe into Brandon's chest. She turned her back on him and gave a small smile to Reggie, who released the grip he had on Brutus's collar and sidled away with the rest of the construction crew. "Obviously, I'm not trying to steal the dog. He escaped through the front door, and I had to chase after him. We're both lucky we weren't run over in the process."

Brandon leaned down in front of Brutus and clipped a leash onto his harness. When he straightened up, he turned his attention back to Goldie. "Did you roll around in a dirt pile?"

Goldie thought she might strangle him right there, in front of God and yoga. "I tripped," she said through gritted teeth. "Trying to save this dog *and* our asses."

"Romy said you made her do the gland expression," Brandon continued, as if he hadn't heard her. "What were you thinking, Marigold? You know better than to have a brand-new vet tech anywhere near Brutus on expression day."

Goldie touched her tongue to the roof of her mouth and tried to remain calm. "I'm sorry," she said, finally. "I didn't know we were calling your twenty-year-old girlfriend a vet tech."

A flicker of shock passed over Brandon's face before he regained his composure and replied, "That's not fair."

"Fair?" Goldie snatched the leash away from Brandon and kicked off her remaining heel. "You want to talk about what's fair?"

"What's gotten into you?" Brandon asked. "Don't make a scene, babe. Come on. We can talk about it later. *In private.*"

Goldie stared at him. "You want to talk to me about being private, when you literally brought the woman you're sleeping with into our clinic?"

"It's my clinic," Brandon replied, looking away from her and toward the construction workers, who were pretending not to be listening to their argument. "You just work there."

Goldie felt as if she'd been punched in the gut. For nearly the past decade, she'd been a part of every single decision made at the clinic. She'd been there during the hard days and late nights. She'd sat with clients after their pet died and they needed comfort. She'd not taken a salary for a year after they'd been sued by a client angry about the untimely death of their cat, because most of the money was tied up in lawyers. She'd celebrated with Brandon when they'd won the suit, largely in part due to her father's connections.

But as far as Brandon was concerned, she just worked there. Goldie guessed she'd known it all along.

"Here," Goldie said, returning Brutus's leash to Brandon. "I don't work for you anymore." She turned around and began to walk back toward the clinic, trying to keep both her dignity and her one working shoe intact.

Brandon stood there for a moment processing what she'd just said. After a few seconds, he started off after her, but Brutus wouldn't budge. Brandon pulled on Brutus's leash for a second before sighing and picking him up.

"Goldie," Brandon called after her, breathless after a few seconds of carrying the weight of the sixty-five-pound Brutus. "Goldie, come on. Wait. You know that's not what I meant!"

Goldie pretended not to hear him. She knew if she turned around and looked at him, she'd go back. She knew if she said another word to him, she'd go back. She didn't want to go back. It was too late to go back to anything—to Brandon, to their relationship, to the life she'd thought they shared.

It was over.

It wasn't until much later that evening, after ordering more wine than she needed for herself alone at Alex's house, when Goldie saw it—a listing for a veterinary clinic for sale. It had been posted in one of the veterinary groups she'd joined on social media. There were veterinarians from all over the world, sharing stories and pictures from their lives spent working with animals.

Even now, she interacted with people from all over. She had virtual friends in nearly every area of the United States and a good friend in Belize with whom she exchanged Christmas cards and birthday gifts. Brandon hated it, but Goldie liked the internet.

She always had. As a teen, back in the early nineties, she'd gotten a computer as a birthday gift one year from her bewildered parents. Even as neurologists who regularly used technology in their practice, they still didn't understand Goldie's need for the bulky and expensive computer. But Goldie, who was chunky (*sturdy*, her mother called her) and full of pubescent acne, found solace in the anonymous early days of the World Wide Web. It was also the only place where her parents weren't keeping track of what she was doing. They simply didn't know enough. So Goldie made friends and pen pals, and she posted regularly to message boards and spent entirely too much time in chat rooms where the first question was always *A/S/L?*

Goldie didn't spend nearly as much time as she used to on the internet. For one, until very recently, she'd had a job, and a fiancé, and a life. Right now, however, what she had was the veterinary group, and as she scrolled through the latest postings, she stopped when she saw one posted by a friend, an elderly veterinarian in the Midwest—in Wisconsin, to be exact.

Dr. Gene Saltzman was a seventy-year-old third-generation veterinarian, and he really didn't understand much about how social media worked. He tried, though. He'd recently gotten a smartphone, and he was forever taking pictures of the animals he worked with and posting them in the group, even though half of the time his thumb was covering the shot. He also posted funny captions with them, like *Merry Pugmas!* or *I asked this cow to mooooove, but she wouldn't.*

Goldie's personal favorite was an alpaca named Alice, who loved donning a cape and visiting the local nursing home as a therapy pet. She didn't know alpacas could be therapy animals, but she had to admit, she'd not spent much time around alpacas. Most of her experience was with small animals. It was rare that the clinic was ever called to assist with anything much bigger that a potbellied pig whose owner had been ill-advisedly told that it would stay small. She had to deal with their shock when they awoke one morning to realize that their "micro-pig" was roughly half the size of a pony. Once in a while, they'd take on a bigger animal like a horse at a stable or another barnyard animal on the set of a movie, but in general, it wasn't Goldie's specialty. She couldn't exactly call herself a veterinarian to the stars, but she did have a few famous four-legged creatures on her client list.

She'd struck up a friendship with Dr. Saltzman when she'd been the first to correctly identify a mystery diagnosis he'd posted to the group. Dr. Saltzman had been impressed, especially for a city doctor, as he often called her. They sent messages back and forth to each other, and Goldie got the feeling that maybe Dr. Saltzman was a little bit lonely. He'd spoken more than once about missing his sister. She'd moved to Florida years ago, and his practice in Blue Dog Valley kept him too busy to visit. He was a lifelong bachelor, and Goldie got the impression that he had been a bit of a rugged mountain man in his earlier days. She pictured him as being a little bit like Paul Bunyan, even though by the time Goldie met him, Dr. Saltzman was nearly seventy. Goldie didn't identify with being a mountain man, but she certainly identified with being lonely. It was an odd feeling, Goldie thought, to have a life full of people and still feel alone. But Alex was gone all the time for work, Goldie's parents were busy enjoying their retirement, and Brandon . . . well, even when he was home, he wasn't really home. Despite the age difference and distance, Goldie considered Dr. Saltzman to be one of her closest friends.

Which was why she was surprised to see what the older veterinarian had posted earlier that day—that he was selling his clinic and retiring to Key West.

After reading through the comments on the post, Goldie sent Dr. Saltzman an instant message.

Are you really selling? Goldie asked. How come you didn't tell me?

I meant to, Dr. Saltzman replied. But I was afraid if I said it out loud, I might back out.

Congratulations, Goldie typed back. Blue Dog Valley won't find another vet like you.

You should buy the place, Dr. Saltzman replied a few minutes later. You'd love it here. It's quite the change of pace from Los Angeles.

Goldie began to type a reply about how she couldn't possibly buy his veterinary clinic but then stopped herself. Why couldn't she? Alex's words bounced around in her head like a beach ball. L.A. wasn't everything. In fact, at the moment, it was absolutely nothing. Maybe she wasn't going to Kenya, but Wisconsin didn't require a passport.

She emptied her second wine bottle and thought about it. Then she typed a reply.

How much are you asking?

By the time Goldie was so drunk she'd passed out on the couch, she'd somehow managed to talk her way into her very own Wisconsin vet clinic.

By the end of the conversation, Goldie and Dr. Saltzman had worked out a deal. It was a gentleman's agreement, as the older veterinarian explained, a trial run. Goldie would arrive in November and have until the new year to decide if she truly wanted to buy the veterinary clinic, and Dr. Saltzman would hold off on the sale until then. It made Goldie feel good to know that Dr. Saltzman trusted her so much. In L.A., there weren't very many, or any, gentleman's agreements. Well, at least she'd never made any. Pay up front. Sign a contract. Always have lawyers present.

So when Goldie woke up in a panic after her wine-fueled discussion, she called the veterinary clinic in Wisconsin, thinking the whole agreement had to be part of a fever dream. The receptionist, a woman named Tiffany who did *not* live up to the bubbly nature that her name promised, informed Goldie that Dr. Saltzman had sold the clinic to "some bimbo from California."

Goldie did not tell Tiffany that she was, in fact, the bimbo from California, and merely asked if Dr. Saltzman was available to speak.

Dr. Saltzman, for his part, wasn't the least bit surprised to be receiving a panicked call from Goldie.

"I was wondering when you'd call" was all he said.

"I didn't sign anything, right?" Goldie asked. "I mean, virtually. You didn't send me any paperwork?"

"No, of course not," the older man said. "We have a gentleman's agreement."

"I don't know what that means," Goldie replied. "Did I buy your clinic or not?"

"Not quite," Dr. Saltzman said. "We agreed that you'd give it a trial run first."

Goldie rubbed her left temple with her free hand. "A trial run?"

Dr. Saltzman, who had every right to be annoyed by Goldie's questions, merely chuckled. "We agreed you'd take over through the new year, and if you've decided that Blue Dog Valley suits you, well, then we'll make it official."

Goldie stood up and walked into the kitchen and opened the refrigerator, where she knew Alex kept an abundance of coconut water. Grabbing the first can she saw, she cracked it open, took a swig, and then said finally, "Dr. Saltzman, forgive me, but I just have to ask . . . why are you doing this?"

"Doing what?"

"Why are you giving me a trial run?" Goldie asked. "Why are you doing anything for me at all? I know your practice is successful, and you and I both know you could sell the clinic before the end of the year if you wanted to."

There was a pause, and then finally Dr. Saltzman said, "It seems to me that we both need a change of setting. We can help each other."

"I do need a change of setting," Goldie admitted, picking up the Advil that were placed next to a sticky note that read, "Take me," in Alex's handwriting.

"Do you think I'm the right person for the job?" Goldie asked.

"I think," Dr. Saltzman replied, a fair amount of humor in his voice, "that you are most certainly the only person for the job."

Goldie's parents, Cynthia and Marshall McKenzie, were the kind of people who'd had a child, one child, because they believed it was their patriotic duty. In fact, they did everything out of patriotic duty, even practicing medicine, which they'd both done for nearly four decades.

They were, more than anything else, absolutely in love with their child. But they were also bewildered by her. Marigold Malinda—Goldie for short—was nothing like they'd expected her to be. Cynthia and Marshall were both tall and striking and quietly thoughtful, with dark hair and dark eyes. Neither had been able to figure out Goldie, who had been born nearly six weeks early, with white-blond hair and the widest blue eyes, squalling as if she was deeply offended to have been evicted from the womb. She hadn't shut up since.

Marshall, who'd always gone by the name Shelly, used to say that when Goldie was little, she'd been dropped off as an infant by the faeries, but a quick look into the family photo album revealed that she was actually the spitting image of her great-great-grandmother on her father's side, a woman for whom Goldie was named but who had died long before Goldie was born.

Cynthia, for her part, told Goldie that, from the time she was born, she'd never met a stranger, a phrase Goldie didn't realize hadn't quite been a compliment until she was well into adulthood. Still, despite being loud where her parents were reserved, and despite being the apparent black sheep of the family, Goldie always felt loved.

However, the news that she was moving to the middle of the

country where there was—*shudder*—snow did not exactly elicit a congratulations from either one of them.

"Wisconsin?" her mother asked. "Why?"

Goldie shrugged, even though her mother's back was turned to her as she fought with the Keurig. The woman could read a brain scan, but she couldn't work a coffee machine. "I don't know," Goldie said, finally. "I think I just need a change."

"But does it really have to be *Wisconsin*?" her father asked. "It's so cold there."

"You want me to go back to the clinic and beg Brandon for my job?"

"Oh, God no," her mother replied. "He's a snake."

"I've always thought that," her father said. He shuffled over to help his wife. "Honey, you have to fill up the water first."

Goldie smiled. She liked the way they helped each other—both in and out of their medical practice. "I've lived in California my whole life," she said.

"And what's wrong with that?" her mother asked, turning her back on the coffee machine to face Goldie.

"Nothing!" Goldie said, exasperated. "I just want to take a chance on something new. You know what I mean?"

Her mother, in fact, did not know what she meant. Her parents had lived in the same modest home for decades, despite recently retiring from their practice and selling it for a mint. They shopped at the same grocery store. Bought the same groceries every week. Traveled to the same resort every six months like clockwork, and they'd driven the same kind of car—a sensible Mercedes sedan, factory model only—ever since Goldie could remember.

"Never mind," Goldie said.

Goldie's parents both sat down across from her at the kitchen table. "We support you, one hundred percent," her father said. "Don't we?" He looked expectantly at Goldie's mother.

Goldie's mother made a face but finally relented and replied, "Of course we do."

"That's a relief," Goldie replied. "Because I'm going to need your help packing up."

Eventually, Goldie's parents and Alex and everyone else came around to the idea of Goldie moving to Wisconsin, even if they were still confused about how a California girl like her was going to fit in, in the Midwest. Goldie had to admit she was more than a little concerned herself, especially because it was nearly November by the time she'd packed up her life, settled her affairs in L.A., and passed the licensing exam to practice veterinary medicine in Wisconsin.

Chapter 3

Goldie wished she'd worn a warmer coat. It hadn't felt that cold at first, standing near the automatic doors in the airport, waiting for her ride to arrive. But now she was starting to shiver. She set the pet carrier down and squatted to look at the cat inside. It hadn't made any noise at all, and Goldie hoped it was okay. She'd have to examine it the first chance she got.

"Are you all right in there?" Goldie asked.

Two huge eyes stared back at her.

"I'm sorry you're having such a bad day," she continued. "Believe it or not, this isn't my best day, either."

The cat scrambled to the back of the crate when Goldie tried to stick a finger inside.

"I know," Goldie said. "Kinda wish I could hide in a crate right now, too."

The cat inched a bit closer this time and sniffed Goldie's finger.

"It's just that my life is really complicated right now," Goldie continued, encouraged by the finger sniff turning into a lick. "It's less *complicated* than it is a *complete disaster*. Don't get me wrong, it's not as bad as being stuck on a luggage belt or anything. It's just that, well, maybe I *was* stuck on a luggage belt, but now I'm freezing my ass off in an airport, so who knows."

Somewhere off in the distance, someone cleared their throat, and Goldie looked up to see a man standing just inside the double doors so that they were closing and reopening and closing and reopening.

She stood up, too startled to be embarrassed by the conversation she'd been having with her feline companion. He was just standing there staring at her, his hands shoved down inside the pockets of a faded pair of jeans.

When he didn't say anything, Goldie broke the silence. "Uh, hi?"

"Sorry, didn't want to interrupt," he said.

Goldie looked around. This part of the airport was practically empty. For a fleeting second, she wondered if she ought to be afraid. It wasn't yet dark outside, but it was beginning to be. Maybe he'd mistaken her for someone else.

Goldie said, finally, "I'm waiting for . . . for someone."

"Yeah," he said. "Me. You that L.A. vet?"

His tone reminded her of Dr. Saltzman's vet tech, and Goldie bristled just a bit. "I'm Dr. Marigold McKenzie, if that's who you mean."

"Great," the man said, taking his hands out of his pockets and rubbing them together. "Let's load up."

Goldie stared at him. Surely, he didn't expect her to *go* with him, just like that. He didn't look like a serial killer or anything, but then again, neither had Ted Bundy. Maybe he'd killed Dr. Saltzman in the parking lot and was getting ready to knock Goldie over the head and drag her back to his white van.

Goldie shook her head. "I've got to stop listening to true crime podcasts," she said. Accidentally. Out loud.

"What?"

"Nothing," Goldie said. "Never mind. Listen, I'm not going anywhere with you."

The man took off a faded Milwaukee Brewers cap to reveal a head of wavy, dark hair. Then, almost as if he didn't quite know what to do with it once he took it off, he put the cap back on again. "Well," he said. "It's going to be an awful long walk to Blue Dog Valley."

"I'm waiting here for Dr. Saltzman," Goldie said. "He said he'd pick me up."

"He sent me," the man said. "He had to catch a flight this morning to Florida. Guess there was some issue with his new house. I don't know. The doc said he called you."

"I haven't checked my phone," Goldie admitted.

"Go ahead," the man said. "I'll give you a minute."

Goldie reached down into her carry-on and fished out her phone, switching off airplane mode. Her phone began to chime furiously, alerting her to messages from both her mother and father, Alex, and, finally, Dr. Saltzman.

"So you're . . ." Goldie said, trailing off.

"Cohen," the man said. "Cohen Gable."

Goldie tried not to feel embarrassed about the way she'd acted. Upon second examination, the man didn't look at all like a serial killer. Or Ted Bundy. He looked a little bit more like Clark Kent at home on the farm with his parents—a little grimy, but underneath, well . . .

"So, are you ridin' or walkin'?" Cohen asked. "It's a two-hour drive from here, and I'd like to get on the road, and I've got Peanut Butter waiting in the truck."

"Right," Goldie replied. She had no idea what a jar of peanut butter had to do with anything, but she guessed maybe he didn't want it to get cold. "Yes, of course." She stepped out of the way to allow him to grab her two rolling suitcases.

"Truck's in the lot," he said to her, nodding his head at the security guard who'd reappeared to watch their interaction.

"Better get that woman a coat," the guard said to Cohen. "She ain't from around here."

"No kidding," Cohen replied, turning around slightly to look at Goldie before continuing on, out of the airport.

"You could have told me your name up front," Goldie said, hurrying after him. He was walking at quite a clip.

"Would that have mattered?" Cohen asked. "You thought Doc was coming after you."

Goldie gritted her teeth. This was not the first impression she'd wanted to make. She was also starting to panic a little bit about the fact that Dr. Saltzman wouldn't be there to show her the ropes over the next few days. He'd promised to find someone to help integrate her to daily life if for any reason he couldn't be there to do it himself. She doubted very much that this man, who seemed ambivalent about even *driving* her to Blue Dog Valley, was going to be doing any of that.

Cohen stopped when he reached a red Chevy pickup in the

short-term airport parking lot. He threw both of her bags up over the side and into the bed of the truck. He turned and took the cat carrier out of her hands before she could protest.

"Hop on in," he said to her, opening the driver's side of the pickup. "The passenger's side door is a little tricky. It'll be easier if you just slide through. Watch out for Peanut Butter. It's a good thing this cat's in a carrier."

"Peanut Butter is a . . ."

"Dog," Cohen said, sighing. He pointed to the window, and as if on cue, there was a yipping sound from inside the truck. "You going to get in or not?"

Goldie stood there for a second, trying to figure out the best way to "slide through," seeing as how she'd never actually done it before, and the truck was higher up off the ground than she'd thought it would be.

"You need a boost?"

"No," she replied, even though a boost would have been helpful at that very moment. Instead, she grabbed the steering wheel and pulled herself up, plopping down onto the bench seat with a hyperbolic "oomph." She slid all the way over to the far side of the truck feeling much less dignified than she had ten seconds earlier.

Cohen's lips twitched just a bit, but he didn't laugh. He simply loaded the cat carrier into the truck and pushed it into the middle before swinging himself up into the driver's seat. He didn't say anything as he paid for parking and left the airport parking lot, falling into line with the rest of Milwaukee traffic heading north along the interstate.

Goldie felt a little cramped among Cohen, the cat carrier, and the small, brown dog that was now staring at her from Cohen's lap, growling.

"She won't hurt you," Cohen said to Goldie, taking one hand off the wheel to pet the dog's head. "She just doesn't like strangers. Or cats."

"She's cute" was all Goldie could think to say. In reality, the dog was so ugly that there was no other way to describe her except as cute. "How old is she?"

"Twelve," Cohen said. "She's mostly deaf, but she still sees okay, and she's a good farmhand, aren't ya, girl?"

Goldie smiled. At least this man seemed to like his dog.

She focused her attention out the window, trying to ignore the fact that the cab of the truck smelled faintly like a barnyard animal she couldn't quite identify. She guessed she was going to have to get used to those smells, where she was going. And it wasn't like she didn't have any experience with farm animals, although it was mostly from working with the animals on some movie sets. Still, she knew she could do it. Surely, she could do it. She'd just planned on Dr. Saltzman being there to make the transition a bit easier.

The buildings and traffic melted away behind them, and eventually, the freeway became a two-lane road stretching out in front of them. Buildings disappeared and were replaced with long stretches of land with a few houses here and there. Goldie tried to pay attention to the markers as they passed, but it was useless. She had no idea where she was, and she'd never seen so much open space in her entire life.

"It turns from city to nothin' pretty quick," Cohen said, breaking his silence. "That's the Midwest for ya."

"I've never been to the Midwest," Goldie admitted, unable to tear her eyes away from the window. "Well, that's not true. I was in St. Louis a few years ago for a conference, but I didn't leave the city."

"St. Louis is all right," Cohen said. "They've got the Cardinals and Budweiser."

"I toured the brewery," Goldie replied. "One of the other veterinarians I was with got so drunk, he tried to climb in with the Clydesdales."

"I don't imagine that went over too well."

Goldie shook her head and turned to face him. "It did not," she said. "He is not welcome back. I don't know if he's even welcome back inside the state of Missouri."

"You can't mess with the Clydesdales," Cohen said, chuckling.

"He's lucky they caught him in time," Goldie replied. "I can't imagine getting kicked by one of those things. It would knock you senseless."

"It'd do more than that," Cohen said. "Doc said you had a small-animal clinic in California. Do you have any experience with animals the size of horses? We've got a lot of them in the valley."

Goldie sat up a little straighter and fidgeted with the seat belt. "I have a little," she said. "I did some intern work at a couple of stables." She wondered if she should mention the potbellied pigs. Did they even count?

Cohen shook his head. "That's not exactly the same thing as a farm, though, is it?"

"No," Goldie said. She squinted into the relative darkness of the truck. It had gotten a lot darker a lot faster once they were out of the city. "But Dr. Saltzman said that his practice was about seventy-five percent small animals."

"There aren't nearly as many farms as there used to be," Cohen replied.

"How come?"

"They built a bypass outside of town," Cohen said. "About fifteen years ago. People didn't stop in the valley as much on their way to Milwaukee. We lost a few businesses. People moved off."

"That's sad," Goldie replied. "Dr. Saltzman didn't tell me about any of that."

"Of course he didn't," Cohen said. His tone had shifted from friendly to polite. "I just wish I knew what he'd been thinking, moving off and selling his business to an outsider."

Goldie stopped fidgeting with her seat belt and looked up. She wasn't sure what she'd said to elicit that kind of a response. She'd thought they were having a pleasant conversation. She willed herself not to respond, to just turn her head and look out the window. They'd been on the road for a while. They had to be getting close to Blue Dog Valley by now. Still, she couldn't stop the words from tumbling out of her mouth.

"Well," she replied. "Maybe Dr. Saltzman didn't know anyone else capable of taking over."

Cohen didn't hesitate. "Couldn't find anybody sucker enough, is more like it."

For the first time all evening, the cat inside the carrier between them let out a soft mew, and Goldie bit down on her tongue so hard she nearly tasted blood.

Fine. It was fine that this guy, this one person, didn't seem to particularly like her, for whatever reason. She was sure she didn't appear to be anything like what he'd been expecting, and that was a reality she was accustomed to. People often underestimated her.

It was her greatest weapon, most of the time. She'd walk into an examination room, and a client would wonder who the pixie was in front of them, with her short, blond hair, wide, blue eyes, and five-two frame. She worked hard to look professional in heels and tailored clothes, but the truth was, her face gave her away. Every emotion played across it as if it were her first day on earth.

They nearly always came to respect her and her capabilities as a veterinarian . . . in time.

The problem, of course, was that Goldie didn't have a patient bone in her body, and this was new territory. She hadn't a clue how to charm her way out of this one, because what she really wanted to do was to tell this stranger, this unwilling taxi driver, that he could absolutely go fuck himself.

Instead, she clamped down on her tongue once more and turned her entire body away from him for the remainder of the drive, which was, much to Goldie's dismay, much longer than she'd hoped.

Chapter 4

One stop at a Dollar General for cat supplies and two dirt roads later, Cohen pulled up to a small, saltine-box-shaped building with a gravel parking lot. The truck's headlights shone on a fading, antique sign that read, "Saltzman Animal Hospital, est. 1955."

"This is it," Cohen said. "The cabin is just behind it, 'bout half a mile."

"Cabin?" Goldie asked. She'd assumed the "stately living quarters" Dr. Saltzman had described were where she'd be staying. She'd seen pictures of the clinic, but not pictures of the house.

"Please tell me that old coot told you he lived in a one-bedroom cabin on the same property as the clinic," Cohen said. "Saved all that money for retirement, I reckon."

In fact, Dr. Saltzman hadn't told her, but she wasn't about to let Cohen know. "He did," Goldie replied breezily.

"Good," Cohen said, putting the truck into reverse. "I'll drive you down. It wouldn't be gentlemanly to make you walk."

Goldie doubted very much that Cohen bothered with being a gentleman, but she was grateful he hadn't abandoned her right there with her luggage, even though it sure seemed like that's what he would have preferred.

"I do have a key," Cohen continued. "If that's something else Doc neglected to provide you."

"I've got one," Goldie said. "I've got keys to the house and the clinic."

"*House* is pushing it," Cohen said, cutting the engine in front of a weather-beaten structure that looked slightly lopsided. "Here we are. Casa de Saltzman."

Goldie tried to keep her face impartial as she got out of the truck. There was a little front porch, and the light was on, but Cohen left the truck lights on while he fished her bags out of the back and followed her up to the front door.

The door was already slightly ajar when she went to put the key into the lock, but Cohen didn't act as if that was anything unusual, so Goldie stepped inside. The cabin smelled clean enough, sort of like a mix between old leather and lemon.

It was furnished, as Dr. Saltzman had promised. There was a tiny kitchen off to the left with what had to be appliances from the 1970s. Everything was avocado-colored. A slightly larger room, the living room, was to the right. There, Goldie found a large, leather chair with an ottoman, a table by the window, and a very new, large flat-screen television set hanging on the wall above a fireplace.

Down the hallway in front of them had to be the bedroom and the bathroom.

"This isn't so bad," Goldie said, not realizing she'd spoken out loud.

"He's done some work since the last time I was in here," Cohen replied. "Patched that hole in the roof, for one." He pointed up at the ceiling.

Goldie looked up. "Well, I guess I can check that off my list," she said.

Peanut Butter was also out of the truck, prancing around the cabin, sniffing everything, including the cat carrier. The dog did a little scuttle backward when a low hiss emitted from between the metal slats in the front, and Goldie, in that moment, couldn't have identified any more with that damn cat.

"Anyway, I . . . uh . . . guess you'll be all right here by yourself?" Cohen asked. He made a hand motion toward Peanut Butter, and she went right to his side and sat down.

"I'm fine," Goldie said. She wasn't entirely sure she would be fine, but at this point, all she wanted to do was fall into a bed, any bed, and sleep for a hundred years. "Thanks for the ride."

"There's a letter for you from Doc on the table in the kitchen," Cohen said. "Wanted me to make sure I told you."

"Thanks."

Cohen nodded to her and turned on his heel, leaving her in the house alone. Goldie watched him go. What a strange man. He couldn't have been any older than she was. In fact, she got the distinct impression that he was probably at least a little bit younger. But he had this dark, brooding force lurking about his face that made him look . . . *troubled* was the only way she could describe it. Not dangerous, but not entirely safe. She wasn't sure why Dr. Saltzman had asked someone like him to pick her up from the airport, when surely there had to be other, more obliging people in town.

She hoped, anyway.

Goldie nearly jumped out of her skin when the cat meowed from the cat carrier. She'd nearly forgotten that she *had* a cat.

"Oh, I'm so sorry!" Goldie said. She made sure the cabin's front door was shut and locked and then walked over to the carrier and knelt down, unlatching the metal gate.

The cat stared at her, and its eyes, Goldie realized, were two different colors. One was a striking blue and the other, gold.

"Well, aren't you the strangest-looking thing I've ever seen." Goldie reached her hand very slowly into the crate, careful not to get too close. She wasn't in the mood to have her hand ripped to shreds by what she was sure was probably an unvaccinated cat.

The cat sniffed her hand and then turned, rubbing the side of its hairless body across her fingertips.

"There you go," Goldie whispered. "See, it's not so bad."

Goldie stood back up and went to retrieve the litter box, litter, and cat food she'd purchased at the dollar store. It wasn't the best, but it would do for now. It didn't take long for the cat to wander out of the carrier and inspect its new surroundings.

Goldie tried to watch from a safe distance. It looked healthy enough, maybe a little skinny. She wasn't entirely sure how much a Sphynx cat should weigh. She'd seen a few at the clinic in Los Angeles, but there weren't any regular clients who owned one. She made a mental note to do some research as soon as she could.

The cat found its food first, sniffed it, and then looked up at Goldie as if to say, *Really? You want me to eat this?*

"Sorry," Goldie said, shrugging. "I'll get you something better tomorrow."

Goldie sat down at the kitchen table and picked up an envelope with her name on it. Inside, there was a one-page letter, scrawled in black pen.

* * *

Dearest Marigold,

I am so very sorry that I was unable to meet you today at the airport. There is an urgent matter I must attend to immediately in Florida. I have entrusted your care to one of my closest friends, Cohen. He is not as bad as he seems, I promise. I am certain he will become a friend in time.

As for the clinic, I have instructed Tiffany to meet you tomorrow morning promptly at 8 A.M. The clinic will remain closed for the next two days (or longer if you'd like), so that you may make yourself familiar. All of the records are in the storage room, should you need the history of an animal, although I assure you that Tiffany is better than any file. She knows every person and every animal. She is <u>invaluable</u>.

I hope you find the cabin to your liking. I have installed a new bed with a mattress and sheets, and left the pantry full of nonperishable foods. There is a shed out back with wood for the fireplace, but there is central heating. I left it on for your arrival. In the shed you will also find a rudi-

mentary vehicle for driving around town. It is especially good for snow, and there will be snow. The keys are in the ignition. Finally, there is whisky under the sink, should you need a nightcap.

Please make yourself at home. I will be in touch, and after the new year, we shall revisit the terms of our agreement. I have a feeling that you will come to love the valley as much as I do.

Yours truly,
Gene Saltzman

Goldie sat the letter down and leaned back in the chair. She should take her suitcases back to the bedroom and unpack them. She should shower. She should familiarize herself with the house. She should call her parents and Alex to let them know she'd arrived safely. There were so many things she knew she needed to do that, instead, she fished around the cabinets for a glass and poured herself a shot of whisky from the bottle underneath the sink.

If someone had told her two months ago that by the beginning of November, she'd be sitting in a shabby cabin in Wisconsin, drinking whisky alone out of a John Deere mug, she would have laughed hysterically. No, California was her home. That lovely apartment with its clean lines and stainless-steel kitchen. That handsome, stupid veterinarian who'd been in that apartment increasingly less and less, until they'd become invariable strangers to each other, two people sharing a bathroom in the morning, sharing a bed at night. Brandon had given her a weekend to get her things out of the apartment. Alex had come and helped her, and Goldie managed to keep it together until she looked around one final time at the half-empty apartment and realized that it looked a lot like her half-empty life. She'd left him a note on the kitchen counter that she would be out of state for the foreseeable future. He hadn't called to ask about where she was going, and Goldie figured that if she'd been on the fence before, his silence said all that it could have said.

She took another sip. The whisky burned all the way down, but she didn't flinch. She hoped that it would cleanse something inside of her, that it would cure the deep ache she felt every time she allowed herself to think about her life.

Or what was left of it.

The cat jumped up onto the table and sat back on its haunches. Goldie held out her hand, and the cat allowed her to stroke its head, eventually getting close enough to rub up against her, and then jumped into Goldie's lap.

"So you're a girl," Goldie said, as the cat turned round and round until finding an acceptable position. "Do you have a name?"

The cat looked up at her.

"Okay," Goldie replied. "You're right. New life, new name."

Goldie finished the whisky and leaned back in the chair, closing her eyes. There were just so many things to do. So, so many things . . . but she was tired. Maybe if she just sat there for a few minutes longer and rested her eyes, she'd find the energy to get up and unpack. The rest of her belongings were being delivered later, so she'd have to buy a few more items of clothing—warmer clothing—and she'd have to wash her clothes. Was there a washing machine? She hadn't seen one. Maybe it was farther back in the cabin. Where? The bathroom?

Goldie felt herself dozing off, lulled by the whisky and the comforting weight of the cat on her lap. A nap wouldn't be so bad, she thought . . . Just a few more minutes, and then she'd get to work. Yes, a few more minutes. That's all she needed.

Chapter 5

Goldie had never been a very good sleeper. At least, that's what her mother told her repeatedly. She'd had colic as a baby, and after that, it was always something keeping her awake, until her mother finally gave in to Goldie's nocturnal nature and quit trying to force her to sleep at night. If Goldie had her way, she'd stay up until three A.M. and sleep well past noon every day of the week. Of course, there hadn't been many careers that catered to that kind of a habit, and Goldie did her best to adhere to a strict schedule once she graduated from veterinary school and got a job.

Brandon was the opposite, preferring to turn in early and get up early to go for a run or head to the gym for a morning cycling class. Nothing seemed worse to Goldie than an early morning cycling class, but she'd made concessions for Brandon, who encouraged a healthy lifestyle. Los Angeles, in general, was full of opportunities to have a healthy lifestyle, and the young couple had their pick of activities.

At first, Goldie chafed against the early morning runs, and Brandon left her in bed alone while he met his running group at the park for a quick 5k twice a week. It wasn't until a few months into their relationship, just after they'd moved in together, that Goldie finally gave in and got up, complaining, to go with him.

That was the first time Goldie noticed the way other women looked at Brandon. Rather, it was the first time she noticed the way *he looked at them*. Brandon was a flirt. It's what had drawn her to him in the first place. He was outgoing and funny and unafraid to ask for what he wanted. He was confident, and Goldie liked that. He hadn't asked her to tone herself down for him the way other men had. He took pride in having her on his arm, in the way she, with her small stature, was often underestimated until it was too late and the spitfire lurking beneath her sweet smile came out and devastated those in Goldie's path. He didn't challenge her. He simply accepted who she was.

It was like that at first, anyway.

Then the clinic started to take off, primarily *because* of Goldie and her rapport with the clients. They liked her. They trusted her. Most of them appreciated her honest assessment of their pets, even if it was sometimes hard to hear. But Brandon didn't always appreciate her. He began to ask her to dress more professionally or keep her professional opinion to herself when they had a more famous or powerful client in the examination room. He broke away from her at parties to carouse with attractive admirers, and eventually, he stopped waking her up in the morning for runs.

Goldie felt herself shrinking back, always in the background of the action, never in the middle like she'd used to be, and at some point, that life became comfortable.

It was easier, at least.

There wasn't anything Goldie could have said to Brandon to provoke a fight. No matter the accusations of cheating or her desire to take more control over the clinic or anything else—her grievances were met with a shoulder shrug or a calming, "Let's just talk about this later."

Even in the midst of their breakup, after the initial confrontation in the construction lot, Brandon maintained his distance. He never asked her to reconsider. He let her take whatever she wanted from the apartment and had even made sure to be gone while she collected her belongings. It was as if their lives had been separate for so long that it didn't matter. They shared nothing, not even, it pained Goldie to realize, love.

Alex told Goldie from the beginning that she hadn't liked Brandon—hadn't trusted him. She thought his personality was too easily swayed by the people around him. He could be whatever it was that people wanted in a moment, and that, Alex declared, was not the kind of man that Goldie needed. Secretly, Goldie thought Alex hadn't liked him because he'd made fun of her YouTube channel when she'd started it, wondering aloud why anyone would want to watch another person's skin being picked at, and then later, when her channel was successful, asking Alex to run ads for the veterinary clinic for free.

Goldie had wondered as she was preparing to leave Los Angeles if she would have kept on going with Brandon forever if not for the afternoon Brutus escaped. She still didn't know what part of her had broken, and she still didn't know if she'd made the right decision. Starting from scratch at forty years old didn't seem like the best plan. Maybe she should have fought a little harder for what she had before she left it behind to pursue a do-over in a cold, Midwestern state where she didn't know anyone.

Being unemployed and living with her parents would have been humiliating, sure, but she was a good veterinarian. She could have started her own business and taken half of Brandon's clients with her. She doubted very much any of them were going to catch a flight to Blue Dog Valley, Wisconsin, to see her.

Was it still cute to have no life plan at her age?

Was it still cute to still be worried about being cute?

Why did it still feel like she was playing in the shallow end of the pool while the adults took turns going off the high dive?

Why did her head feel so heavy?

Why couldn't she sit up?

Wait, where was she?

Goldie opened her eyes. Her head did, indeed, feel very heavy. It felt like something was sitting on top of her. She was freezing everywhere except for the top of her head, where the weight was. Panicked, she sat up, only to have whatever it was on her head *dig in* and *stay there*.

"Ow!"

Goldie reached up and grabbed a handful of hissing cat.

In her confused, half-asleep state, Goldie stood up, realizing that she was still at the kitchen table in the cabin, but now there was daylight shining in through the thin curtains hanging in front of the windows.

The cat, for her part, refused to budge, hanging on to the top of Goldie's head like some kind of furless Russian kubanka. She was hissing and spitting and digging her needle-sharp claws into Goldie's scalp.

"What is wrong with you?" Goldie yelped, wriggling around the kitchen. "Get off!"

That's when Goldie saw it. The huge, gray lump collapsed on the floor near the fireplace in the living room. At first, she thought it had to be a rug or something, but when it started moving, Goldie realized that the rug was alive, and it wasn't a rug at all—it was instead a huge Bergamasco shepherd.

The cat on Goldie's head hissed louder and held on tighter, and Goldie didn't know which animal to deal with first. If she tugged on the cat any harder, she feared her scalp might come off, too, and just when Goldie was starting to think that this just might be the end of the line, the moment she collapsed in a heap on the kitchen floor, the front door swung open and a woman three times the size of the shepherd appeared. Her dark hair was pulled up into a ponytail so tight that any wrinkles on her face had been pulled up with it; in turn, her scowl made her face appear skeletal. She cut a terrifying figure.

The woman took one look at Goldie and then turned her attention to the dog. *"Kevin!"* she bellowed. "Get out of here! You know the rules!"

She pointed toward the door.

The dog cocked his head to one side.

"You heard me," the woman said. "Go on."

The dog shook himself, his long, dreadlocked coat swaying

with him. He took one more look at the woman before trotting out the front door and disappearing outside.

Goldie stood there, frozen to her place. She'd somehow managed to lose her shoes in all the commotion, and she could feel the cracks in the old linoleum floor with her bare feet. She tried not to think about how she must look, in various stages of undress, with a scared hairless cat on top of her head.

The cat, realizing that the dog had gone, jumped off Goldie and shot past both women down the hallway.

The woman's scowl did not soften. She placed her hands on her hips and looked around the kitchen, her eyes settling first on the bottle of whisky and empty glass still sitting on the table and then on Goldie, who was currently trying to decide which linoleum crack she could disappear into.

"You're late," the woman said. "I waited until eight oh five before I decided I better come down here and make sure you weren't dead."

Goldie blinked. "Tiffany?" she asked.

"Yup."

"I'm so sorry," Goldie said. She hoped her scalp wasn't bleeding. "I must've fallen asleep last night at the table. I got here late, and I just meant to sit down for a minute."

"Uh-huh" was all Tiffany said.

"Just give me ten minutes," Goldie continued, scrambling to grab her abandoned suitcases in the hallway. "I'll be right up."

"I'll just wait right here, if it's all the same to you," Tiffany replied. "I don't want to take any chances that you'll get spooked by a squirrel."

Goldie opened her mouth to speak but thought better of it.

"Go on," Tiffany said, using the same tone that she'd used to remove Kevin the dog from the living room. "I don't have all day to wait."

Goldie nodded and turned to find the bathroom, wishing like hell she could take the bottle of whisky with her.

Chapter 6

Tiffany clearly wasn't at all interested in hearing any excuses Goldie had to offer by the time they began their trudge up the hill to the vet clinic. Goldie alternated between being irritated that she'd been chastised by someone who technically worked for her and embarrassed that she'd been caught looking so ridiculous by someone whom she desperately needed to keep on staff.

"Did you know the dog in the living room this morning?" Goldie asked when she could no longer stand the silence. "He was just lying there when I woke up, like he lived there."

"That's just Kevin," Tiffany replied. "He's the valley's worst sheepdog."

Goldie quickened her step to catch up. Her heels were sinking down into the soft mud on the trail. "That doesn't explain what he was doing in my house."

"Doc's house," Tiffany corrected her. "Technically, he belongs to one of the farms down the road, but he spends most of his time roaming around looking for a place to sleep. Doc used to find him asleep by the fire all the time. That front door doesn't lock quite right. Kevin knows how to get in."

"Great," Goldie replied.

"Nobody except Kevin is going to bother you," Tiffany said as they reached the clinic doors. She pulled out a ring full of keys from the pocket of her scrubs. "This isn't California."

"Trust me," Goldie replied. "I am well aware of that."

Tiffany went inside, and Goldie followed. She watched as Tiffany turned on the lights and went about preparing for the day as if Goldie weren't even there.

"Do you want to sit down and have a little staff meeting to get to know each other?" Goldie asked. "We could make coffee, and you can tell me about yourself and the clinic."

Tiffany screwed up her face in disgust. "No, I don't want to have a *little staff meeting*. I just want to do my job and go home."

Goldie bit her bottom lip. This was not how she'd pictured her first day going—already having a disagreement with the only other employee at the clinic.

"Well, it would really help me if I know what your job is," Goldie replied. "I know you're the vet tech, but are you the receptionist, too?"

"I *can* answer the phones," Tiffany said. "Doc and I took turns. He liked to speak to everyone personally. It was his thing."

"I'm not great on the phone," Goldie admitted. "It would probably be a lot better if you just did it from now on."

As if on cue, the phone began to ring. Tiffany and Goldie

stared at each other, neither one making a move to answer it. Goldie wondered if Tiffany was going to hike up her leg and pee on the front desk to assert her dominance.

"Doc promised me he wasn't going to leave me with a mess," Tiffany said, not taking her eyes off Goldie. "And what's he done? Gone off and left me with a mess."

"The place looks pretty clean to me," Goldie replied.

"I'm not talking about the clinic."

Goldie heaved a sigh and moved past Tiffany to answer the phone, but when she got to it, she promptly forgot the name of the clinic and just said, "Hello?" The line went dead. "They hung up."

Tiffany looked as though she wanted to laugh, but she couldn't quite get it out. She was older than Goldie, probably in her mid-fifties. She was wearing sensible black scrubs and black shoes. The only way Goldie could think to describe her was *sturdy*.

"People have been calling and canceling their appointments since they found out Doc was leaving," Tiffany said. "There's not but one appointment left on the books for this entire week."

"Look, if you want to quit, just go ahead and do it now," Goldie replied, sitting down in the chair behind the desk.

"I'm not going to quit," Tiffany replied. "Why would I do that?"

Goldie gestured vaguely around the clinic. "It's clear you don't like me, and it's clear you don't want to be here."

"Doc's been the veterinarian in the valley for nearly four decades," Tiffany said. "And then he up and sells to you—some person we don't even know, some Doc Hollywood. He should have known better. That's all. He just should have known better."

"I'm from Los Angeles," Goldie replied. "And I ran a successful clinic for years before coming here."

"Like I told you earlier," Tiffany said. "This isn't California, but that's not your fault, is it? It's Doc's."

"So you aren't going to quit?"

Tiffany rolled her eyes. "No. I'm not going to quit. I've got to work, don't I?"

Goldie glanced around the clinic. It looked like any other clinic. It could use a little updating, but it was clean and cheerful. The white walls were lined with pictures of animals, many of them with the older veterinarian in them. There was a wall of cat and dog food and a rack of collars and leashes for sale. Behind the reception desk, flea and tick and heartworm medications were stacked. The small examination room looked similar to the one Goldie had back in L.A., besides a few archaic contraptions Goldie didn't think she'd ever seen outside of a veterinary history textbook, but she was clearly out of her element. The only thing that really stuck out was the fact that it was scarcely November, and already the office was decorated entirely for Christmas.

"Why are Christmas decorations already up?" Goldie asked. "Isn't it a little early?"

Tiffany made a face. "Didn't you come through town last night?" she asked.

"Yeah," Goldie replied. "But it was late and it was dark."

"Well, we decorate for Christmas early here," Tiffany replied. "November first, we're decorating. Christmas is the valley's favorite holiday, and you won't get too far around here if you start insulting that love."

"I . . . I wasn't insulting Christmas," Goldie replied. "I'm sorry. I'm just nervous, I guess. And worried about the clinic if people aren't going to show up."

"People don't know you," Tiffany said. "That's all that matters. They don't know you, and they don't trust you."

"Maybe I should find a way to introduce myself," Goldie said. "Do you think that would help?"

"No," Tiffany said. "Why would that help?"

"If I can introduce myself, maybe I might be able to make them more comfortable," Goldie replied. "They can see for themselves that they can trust me with their animals."

"That's not how it works here."

Goldie pushed the palms of her hands against her eyes. "Okay, fine. Just tell me what you think I should do."

For a moment, Tiffany's face softened, and Goldie wasn't sure if she found that more or less terrifying than the scowl.

"Doc would tell you to be patient," Tiffany said. "He'd tell you people will come around, especially after they realize the closest vet is twenty miles away and charges double."

"Really?" Goldie asked. "They charge double?"

"I don't know," Tiffany replied. "But that's what Doc would say."

"What would you say?"

Tiffany's scowl returned. "I'd tell you to go back to California," she said. "But then I'd be out of a job before Christmas, and I've got grandbabies to take care of. So I guess we're both stuck listening to Doc. Plus, the clinic is closed for a couple of days. Nobody would call to make an appointment, anyway."

"Where would you *or* Doc tell me to get some coffee?" Goldie asked. "Because if either one of us is going to survive the day, I'm going to need it."

"Ruby's," Tiffany said without hesitation. "First left off the dirt road will take you straight into town onto Main Street. You can't miss it."

"Okay," Goldie said, gathering up her jacket and purse. "I guess I'll just . . . walk?"

"It's three miles," Tiffany replied. "Just take the Jeep that Doc left you."

"I forgot about that," Goldie said. "Thanks."

"I take my coffee black with two sugars," Tiffany called after Goldie as she left.

In short order, Goldie found the Jeep in the shed with two large tarps covering it. Goldie was surprised to find not the Jeep Wrangler she'd been envisioning but instead an early-1990s-style Jeep Wagoneer, complete with wood paneling on the side. It smelled faintly of cigar smoke, but otherwise, the inside of the Jeep was in good condition, the keys were in the ignition, and it started up with no problem at all.

Driving down the road, especially in the idyllic countryside of Blue Dog Valley, felt a little bit like being in one of those TGIF family comedies she used to watch as a kid. She hadn't seen the town in the daylight. As she entered the city limits, there was a road sign that read:

Welcome to Blue Dog Valley
Home of the Fighting Elk
Population 3,411
The Town That Loves Christmas

Goldie sincerely hoped that the "fighting elk" was Blue Dog Valley's school mascot and not actual fighting elk. After the morning she'd had, though, she wasn't going to bet on it. Tiffany hadn't been wrong about the town being serious about Christmas. Every streetlight and storefront was decorated for Christmas. Goldie reminded herself not to make any comments about Christmas decorations unless it was to say how pretty they were. If a town has an ode to Christmas on their welcome sign, then it must be pretty serious business.

There was a little bit of a light mist in the air, and the windshield wipers on the Wagoneer didn't work the best, but Goldie had no trouble finding Ruby's Daylight Diner, nestled between an auto parts store and a funeral home on what she guessed was the town's main strip.

The place was busy, and Goldie tamped down her anxiety as she got out and walked up the steps and in the diner's entrance, past a dozen old men drinking coffee, reading the newspaper, and arguing loudly among one another. There were other people, too, filling out the diner's booths.

They all looked up at her, their conversation stalled as she seated herself at the diner's blue Formica countertop. Goldie tried to ignore the fact that there were eyes on her back and instead concentrated on the glistening cinnamon rolls stacked on top of each other inside a glass case.

"Those are the best cinnamon rolls in three counties," a voice said.

Goldie tore her eyes away from the cinnamon rolls to look at the woman standing behind the counter in front of her. She had frizzy, red hair and glasses much too large for her face. She was smiling at Goldie, and Goldie thought she might cry just looking at her. She seemed so . . . *friendly*. Nobody had smiled at her since yesterday at the airport.

"I'll take one," Goldie said. "Actually, better give me two."

"Anything else? Some candy cane cocoa maybe?"

"Oh yes," Goldie replied. "I need two coffees. One black with sugar and one just black. To go, please."

"On it." The waitress winked at Goldie and then scurried off to place two giant cinnamon rolls into a white paper bag.

"Here you go," she said. "Let me just get those coffees. I guess you're taking one of them to Tiffany down at the clinic. Two sugars. Am I right?"

"That's right," Goldie replied, trying not to appear any more confused than she felt. "How did you know?"

"She won't drink it," the waitress continued. "She never does. That woman wastes more coffee than what should be legal. But don't tell her I said that."

"I won't tell her." Goldie reached down into the paper bag to tear off a piece of cinnamon roll. "I'm pretty much afraid to say anything to her."

The waitress giggled. "I don't blame you there. Her bite is every bit as bad as her bark."

"Great," Goldie replied. "Oh my God, this *is* the best cinnamon roll in . . . what did you say? Three counties?"

"Should have been four," the waitress replied. "But that ridiculous woman over in Cobb County beat me out last year for the title."

"It must have been a rigged contest," Goldie said. She tore off another piece. "Because this is heaven."

"I'm Ruby," the waitress said, setting two cups of coffee with lids down in front of her. "The one with the white lid is the one with sugar."

"I'm—"

"Dr. Marigold McKenzie," Ruby finished for her. "I know who you are. Everybody knows who you are."

"Am I wearing a nametag?" Goldie asked.

"The valley is a small town," Ruby said, grinning. "Doc nearly had to call a press conference to announce his retirement. It was only a matter of time before word got out that you were his replacement."

"I don't think anyone is too excited about me being the replacement," Goldie muttered. "Every single appointment Tiffany had on the books for the next week has already canceled."

"Aw, honey," Ruby said. She put one of her hands on Goldie's. "Be patient. Folks'll come around."

Goldie resisted the urge to jump up, reach over the counter, and hug Ruby. "Thank you," she said. "I needed to hear that."

"No problem." Ruby walked over to the cinnamon roll case, grabbed one, and stuffed it down into Goldie's bag. "It's on the house today." Then she leaned in and whispered, "You better scoot before these codgers alert the old-boy network that you're here."

"That sounds ominous," Goldie replied, standing up and wondering how many more old boys there could be—they all seemed to be sitting right in front of her.

"It's not really," Ruby said. "But they'll have eight thousand questions for you all the same."

"I'm leaving!" Goldie called over her shoulder, a piece of cinnamon roll sticking out of her mouth.

She felt better driving back to the clinic. Ruby seemed nice. At least there was one person in town who didn't absolutely hate her. Still, Goldie felt like a real idiot for not taking a more proactive approach in a new practice. She knew from experience that it would have been good business to introduce herself to the town *before* moving to Blue Dog Valley. She could have created a website, sent out a welcome letter, or something, anything at all, really, to warm people to the idea of her, before she showed up with an offensive "California Native" sign on her back. But there really hadn't been time, and she had wanted to leave L.A.—and Brandon—as quickly as possible.

Sometimes she wondered how her parents could both be such rational, even-tempered people and still manage to create someone like her. Moving here, sight unseen, was impulsive and reckless, even if it was on a trial basis.

She had to figure out some way to get into the good graces of the community.

As she neared the clinic, driving, thinking, and eating what was left of her second cinnamon roll, she didn't notice at first that Tiffany was standing outside waiting for her.

"What took you so long?" Tiffany asked as soon as Goldie got out of the Jeep.

"I didn't know I was on a schedule," Goldie replied, handing Tiffany her coffee.

Tiffany waved it away. "We've got a house call," she said. "Mayor Rose has a horse with an abscess."

Goldie stared at Tiffany. "Who is Mayor Rose?"

"The mayor of the valley, of course," Tiffany replied, exasperated. "Didn't Doc tell you anything?"

"Sorry, no," Goldie said. "He clearly did not."

"Well, we've got to get out there ASAP," Tiffany said. She held up a black medical bag. "Here."

Goldie set the coffee down on the small table on the porch of the clinic and said, "The mayor called us? Even after everybody canceled?"

"He couldn't get the farrier on the phone, and the vet the next town over doesn't do house calls all the way out here," Tiffany replied. "Now, are you going to keep asking questions, or are we going to go?"

"Okay," Goldie said. She could feel adrenaline and excitement pumping through her. "Let's go."

"I'll drive," Tiffany replied. "I don't trust that death trap Doc left for you."

"Thanks for telling me that *after* I'd already driven it all over town," Goldie mumbled, sliding into the front seat of an old-model Chrysler that didn't look any safer than the Jeep.

"I've been telling Doc for years we need a vet van," Tiffany said, trying and failing twice to start the Chrysler before the engine finally got going. "But he said it was too gimmicky, and he didn't think people in town would go for it."

"We had two company cars at my old clinic," Goldie replied. "We didn't use them much, though. We rarely made house calls."

"Lots of house calls around here," Tiffany said. "Mostly barn calls, I guess, like today, but you know what I mean."

Goldie looked out the window, feeling more nervous than ever. Sure, she'd treated horses, more than a few horses, but they were the kind of horses that were kept in stables in the city. She doubted that where she was heading would resemble the Los Angeles Equestrian Center. She hoped she hadn't made a huge mistake.

After what felt like forever, but was probably no more than about fifteen minutes, Tiffany turned off the highway and onto a winding, gravel driveway. At the top of a hill stood a brick, ranch-style house, and beyond that, there were acres and acres of farmland.

"This farm has been in the Rose family since before the Civil War," Tiffany said.

"Wow," Goldie replied.

"You'll want to impress him," Tiffany continued. She parked the car next to a rusted metal cattle gate. "He's not the mayor for nothin'."

Goldie got out of the car and looked around. She'd never seen so much open land in one place.

"Are you coming?" Tiffany asked, already trudging far ahead of Goldie. "What are you staring at? Hurry up!"

Goldie hobbled after Tiffany, realizing with an increasing pit in her stomach that she was absolutely not dressed for a farm, a barn, or a horse. "I wish you would have let me go back to the cabin and change clothes," she called to Tiffany.

"Do you have anything in that fancy suitcase of yours that is well suited for horse shit?" Tiffany yelled back.

"Not really," Goldie replied, catching up to her. "But I could have found something better, I'm sure."

"Let me offer you some free advice," Tiffany said, turning to give Goldie a good once-over. "You should dress every day like you're going to get cow placenta all over your Gucci shoes."

"My shoes aren't Gucci," Goldie said, secretly pleased that Tiffany would even think that. "They're Everlane."

"I have no idea what that means," Tiffany said. "Please don't tell anyone what brand your shoes are once we get inside this stable."

There were two men waiting for them. One of them, younger and clearly a farmhand, stepped aside as they approached. The other man, older and much, much taller, nodded to Tiffany.

"Hey, Tiff. Thanks for getting here on short notice," the older man said.

Goldie stared at him. She couldn't help herself. He looked like a cowboy. He was wearing a snap-up western-style shirt, well-worn jeans, and boots. His face was ruddy, like he'd spent nearly every day for the past seventy-odd years in the sun.

Goldie figured there were plenty of Hollywood screenwriters who could probably use this man for reference.

"Mayor Rose, this is the new doc, Marigold McKenzie," Tiffany said, gesturing to Goldie. "Goldie, this is Mayor John Rose."

Goldie resisted the urge to say *howdy* and stuck out her hand instead. "It's nice to meet you," she said.

"Likewise," replied Mayor Rose. He looked hard at her. "You have a lot of experience with horses?"

"I would say I have an adequate amount of experience with horses," Goldie replied.

"Adequate, huh?"

"Adequate," Goldie repeated. "I won't lie to you and say horses are my specialty, but I can drain an abscess. Of course, if you'd rather wait for your farrier, I understand. I can stay and make sure the wound doesn't need live-tissue debridement, or see if sedation is necessary."

Mayor Rose squinted at her.

Goldie met his gaze. She knew how she must look to him,

to all of them, and she didn't really blame them for judging her based on how unprepared she appeared for a farm and, well, Wisconsin in general. They might be right in that regard, but that didn't mean she wasn't damn good at her job. She could treat a horse in kitten heels any day of the week.

"You better let her take a look, boss," the younger man said, finally. "Large Marge ain't happy."

"All right," Mayor Rose replied. "Since you're already here."

"I'll show you back," the younger man said. "I'm Teddy, by the way."

"It's nice to meet you, Teddy," Goldie said. "When did you first notice . . . Large Marge, was it? How long has she been lame?"

"We had her trimmed up last week," Teddy replied. "I think the farrier trimmed her too short, and she's not been right ever since."

"Is this the farrier you called today?" Goldie asked.

"No." Teddy turned around to see that Tiffany and Mayor Rose were some ways off behind them, talking between themselves, and then he said, "The boss man's grandson is training to be a farrier, and he trimmed her up. He didn't do a very good job."

"Ah," Goldie replied. "I won't mention that, then."

"I'd appreciate that," Teddy said. "I think he mighta been a little drunk, too."

Goldie bit her lip to keep from laughing. "So, you think it's an abscess, or have you seen it for yourself?"

"The boss and me did a hoof test to check her," Teddy said. He stopped in front of the stall of a chocolate-brown quarter horse with one of the most beautiful manes Goldie had ever seen. "We put her right back hoof in a vise to check for tenderness, and I'll be a son of a bitch if ol' Marge didn't about take my head off."

"Did any pus come out?" Goldie asked.

"Couldn't get her to be still long enough to see," Teddy said. "But I've been handling horses for a long time, and I think it's an abscess."

"Okay," Goldie replied. "If she wouldn't let you look at her hoof in the vise, we might need to sedate her before we do anything else."

"I don't think that will be necessary" came a voice from behind them.

Goldie and Teddy turned around to see Cohen Gable standing there, farrier bag in hand. And right beside him, there was Peanut Butter. She seemed to be less interested in growling at Goldie this time, and she trotted up and sniffed Goldie's shoes. Before Goldie could offer her a hand to sniff instead, two Australian shepherds barked a command, and Peanut Butter ran over in their direction.

"Oh hey, Cohen," Teddy said, waving at him. "I guess you finally got my voice messages."

"Yep," Cohen replied. "I was out at the Rogers' farm, and I don't get any cell reception. I didn't see the missed calls until I got back into town."

"You're the farrier?" Goldie asked.

"Last time I checked."

"Four hands are better than two," Teddy said. "We could use the extra help. Marge is not happy today at all."

"Did that hack of an excuse for John's grandson do this?" Cohen asked, moving closer to Marge. "I could have told you hiring him was a mistake."

Teddy opened his mouth to reply, but promptly shut it when Mayor Rose and Tiffany approached.

"I told Cohen the new vet was here to take a look," Mayor Rose said.

"I'm glad you were available," Cohen said to Goldie. "But I think I've got it under control now."

"You don't even know the problem," Goldie replied. She looked over at Tiffany, who shrugged. "The horse is lame from a possible abscess. Teddy says she's agitated and she may need to be sedated."

"I've never had to sedate a horse," Cohen said. He set his bag down on the ground. "Especially not Large Marge."

"You've probably never clipped a hoof too close," Goldie said. "I'm sure your work is impeccable, but as I told Mayor Rose, if she needs live-tissue debridement, you'll be out of your depth."

Next to her, Teddy cleared his throat.

"You debride a lot of live tissue in Los Angeles?" Cohen asked. He crossed his arms over his chest. "Can't imagine you get too many lame horses in the city."

"They're not uncommon out west, especially in the desert, since that's a natural environment for a horse," Goldie said.

"I appreciate the veterinary lesson," Cohen replied. "You're welcome to stay if you want, but like I said, I've got it covered."

Goldie stepped out of the way and motioned for him to move past her. She turned back and looked at Tiffany, who was still standing next to Mayor Rose. They were both watching her and Cohen, as if they were spectators at a prize boxing match. She wondered if either of them had placed their bets on her. She doubted it.

Cohen entered the stall, followed by Teddy.

"Hey there, gorgeous lady," Cohen said to Marge. He reached up and stroked her neck, and Marge nuzzled him slightly.

If Goldie hadn't been so annoyed, she would have found their clear fondness for each other adorable. As it stood, however, she half wished Marge would bite him.

"Back right," Teddy said to Cohen, as Cohen eased himself to the rear of Marge. "Are you sure you don't want to sedate her first? She's not going to like you messin' with that hoof."

No sooner had the words gotten out of Teddy's mouth than Marge began to make her displeasure known. She backed up slightly, moving to the left, kicking out her injured hoof, narrowly missing Cohen's ribs.

Goldie waited for the two men to make it safely out of the stall before she reached down into the bag Tiffany had packed and found the sedation gel. She tried not to smile when she handed it to Cohen.

* * *

IT HAD TAKEN Goldie, Cohen, Teddy, Tiffany, and nearly a pouchful of treats to get Marge to take the sedation, but she'd eventually relented, and forty-five minutes later, Goldie watched as Cohen expertly vented the abscess in the hoof wall. The fluid drained for several seconds, and then he applied a drying salve, taping it to the hoof.

"I've always soaked the hoof," Goldie said. She studied Cohen's work carefully. She hated to acknowledge it, but he was good at his job. "Why are you using the salve instead?"

Cohen looked up at her.

"Honest question," Goldie continued. "I'm a veterinarian, but I'm not a farrier. I'm not a horse expert. I've dealt with maybe five abscesses in my whole career."

For a moment, it seemed as if Cohen were going to reply to her sarcastically, but instead he said, "Like you said, horses aren't native to the Midwest. It's wet here, especially this time of year. That's half the problem already. I don't like to make it worse by soaking. I think the salve works better."

"Okay," Goldie replied. "That makes sense."

"Come here," Cohen said, motioning for her to come closer to where he stood behind Marge. He pulled out a roll of duct tape and ripped a piece off with his teeth. "See, I've put this pad in here, which is already precut, to draw out the infection. Then, if I tape it, like this"—he put the duct tape over the pad—"we don't have to get her to stand still for half an hour in a soak. It's easier for everybody, including Marge."

"Duct tape," Goldie murmured to herself.

"It's nothing fancy," Cohen replied. "But it gets the job done."

"I can see that," Goldie said.

"I appreciate you both," Mayor Rose said. "I reckon you'll both be sending me a bill."

"You ought to make your knucklehead grandson pay it," Cohen replied, removing his gloves. "He's the whole reason you're in this mess."

"You know him as well as I do," Mayor Rose said. "Which means you know that's about as likely to happen as me taking Large Marge out for a ride this afternoon."

Cohen turned his attention to Goldie and said, "It was convenient you were here."

"Yes, it was." Goldie packed up what was left of the tranquilizer into her bag and continued, "But I think the phrase you're looking for is *thank you*."

Again, Teddy cleared his throat.

"Yes," Cohen said, a semblance of a smile appearing on his face. "Thank you."

"With any luck, ol' Marge will be leading Santa's sleigh in the parade this year," Mayor Rose said, smiling broadly. "It would hurt her feelings something awful if she couldn't be Rudolph."

Chapter 7

Tiffany seemed to believe that their encounter with Mayor Rose and Large Marge would be good for the clinic, even if Cohen had ended up doing most of the work. "The mayor owns the biggest farm in the valley," she said to Goldie on the drive back to the clinic. "The rumor was that he was going to call in one of his large-animal contacts from Milwaukee after Doc left."

"Why would he do that?" Goldie asked. "That would have to be incredibly expensive, not to mention impractical when we're less than twenty minutes away."

"It's like I told you," Tiffany said. "You aren't going to get business unless people trust you."

"Well, I'm not sure how I can earn their trust if they won't allow me to actually earn it," Goldie replied. "Especially if my competition is Cohen Gable."

"Just for hoof work," Tiffany said. "And he's the best there is."

"I'm not especially fond of hoof work, anyway," Goldie said. "I'm honestly kind of glad he showed up."

"You and me both," Tiffany said. "I hate horses."

"You hate horses?" Goldie asked, surprised. "How can you live here and hate horses?"

"Did you love absolutely everything about Los Angeles?" Tiffany asked. "I just don't like them. They're big, and they're shifty, and I don't trust them."

"I wondered why you didn't offer to help with Marge until I asked," Goldie said. "I thought maybe you were secretly hoping I'd mess up."

Tiffany rolled her eyes. "I already told you I need this job. Besides, the valley can't afford to lose another business. We're shrinking enough as it is. Losing the clinic would be devastating to the community."

"A clinic they can't even decide that they want to use?"

"It's you they're undecided about," Tiffany reminded Goldie. "Not the clinic."

"That argument doesn't make any sense," Goldie said. "Without me and without you, the clinic is just a building."

"I didn't say it was rational."

When Goldie returned to the cabin at the end of that first day, she felt exhausted but hopeful. Maybe the town didn't trust her, but it was just the first day. She had a lot of time to prove herself to everyone, and certainly, today at the Rose farm couldn't have hurt.

She wished she'd had time to go over the records of the animals on the farm before she'd been hurried out there to see about Marge, but her ignorance hadn't hurt much, since Tiffany knew nearly everything already. Tiffany was prickly, but she was clearly going to be an invaluable partner in this . . . well, whatever this was that Goldie thought she was doing.

No sooner had Goldie gotten inside and settled than her phone rang. It was Dr. Saltzman.

"Hello, Goldie," he said when she answered. "How did your first day in the valley go?"

"Well." Goldie chewed on her answer for a moment. "I guess it went both better and worse than I expected."

"How do you mean?"

"You didn't do a very good job of preparing me for this town," Goldie said. "In fact, I don't feel prepared to handle anything at all."

"So, everyone canceled their appointments, and Tiffany wasn't very nice to you," Dr. Saltzman replied.

"You knew this would happen?" Goldie asked. "Why didn't you warn me?"

"Would you still have come if you knew?"

Goldie didn't know how to answer that. It wasn't as if she thought she'd waltz right into a brand-new state, town, and clinic with immediate fanfare, but she had assumed that she'd waltz into an established clinic with clients who at least pretended to be happy to have a vet. As it stood, she didn't feel any more welcome than a bag of trash left over after a holiday party.

"Goldie?" Dr. Saltzman asked. "Are you still there?"

"I'm here," Goldie said. "I'm here, and I guess it doesn't matter whether I would have come or not, because I'm here now.

"That you are."

Goldie sat down in one of the kitchen chairs and sighed. "The guy you had pick me up last night . . . Cohen? Well, he wasn't at all happy to see me at the airport. That should have been my first clue that this was going to be trickier than I thought."

"Cohen is a bit of a bear," Dr. Saltzman said.

"That's an understatement."

"He's a little bit like the town," Dr. Saltzman continued. "He might seem unwelcoming, but that doesn't mean he's not worth getting to know."

"How can a town that loves Christmas as much as this one does be so unwelcoming?" Goldie asked. "There's even a slogan about Christmas on the welcome sign!"

"They're not unwelcoming," Dr. Saltzman replied. "They're cautious. But they're also charitable and kind, once you get to know them. Word to the wise, decorate the cabin for Christmas ASAP. It'll make them feel like you're getting into the spirit."

"Why did you pick me?" Goldie asked. "I know you had other offers. I know you could have found someone more local to take your place. Why me?"

"You asked first," Dr. Saltzman replied, his voice cracking with laughter.

"This isn't an eBay auction," Goldie said. "This is my life."

"You make the decisions in your life," Dr. Saltzman said. "I didn't force you to move to Blue Dog Valley."

His tone was patient. It was clear that he wasn't even the least little bit annoyed with the way Goldie was talking to him, which made Goldie feel terrible. She'd been spoiling for a fight.

"No," Goldie said. "You didn't. I just thought it would be easier, that's all."

"So you want an easy life. Is that it?" Dr. Saltzman asked.

"I want some things to be easy," Goldie said. "I would have at least liked for someone in this town to welcome me."

"Ruby didn't welcome you?"

"How did you know I met Ruby?" Goldie asked. She looked around the cabin for hidden cameras.

"All roads lead to Ruby and her cinnamon rolls," Dr. Saltzman said, laughing again. "It was only a matter of time."

"She was very nice," Goldie conceded. "And I met the mayor today, too. He wasn't nice, exactly, but I did help with his lame horse, and so I guess he probably doesn't hate me."

"Which horse?"

"Large Marge," Goldie replied, smiling a little at the name. "She had an abscess. Cohen got there late, and she ended up needing to be sedated. It worked out all right."

"Did he let his fool-headed grandson trim her up?" Dr. Saltzman asked.

"Okay," Goldie replied. "I'm going to need you to send me a list of things you know that I don't."

"That would take years," Dr. Saltzman replied. "But I'm here anytime you want to talk. I promise that I wouldn't have given you free rein over my clinic if I didn't believe you were the best person for the job. I never had any children. That place is what I loved most."

"I hope I'm up to the job," Goldie replied, honestly. "Although I don't think free rein will ever happen as long as Tiffany is in the building."

"Truer words have never been spoken," Dr. Saltzman said. "Have a wonderful evening, my dear."

"Wait," Goldie said, standing up, just now remembering that morning's chaos. "There was a dog in the cabin when I woke up this morning."

"Kevin."

"Yes," Goldie replied. "Tiffany said he was your dog? Well, not your dog, but he was a dog that sometimes stays here?"

"Kevin belongs to no man," Dr. Saltzman said. "But he wanders in and out on occasion. I'm sorry. That much I meant to tell you. There is a bag of dog food in the top left cupboard."

"So should I just let him in and out?"

"If you like," Dr. Saltzman replied. "It won't matter whether you invite him or not. He does what he pleases. He's the—"

"Worst sheepdog in Blue Dog Valley," Goldie finished for him.

"See?" Dr. Saltzman replied. "You know some things already."

"He scared the life out of me and my cat this morning," Goldie said. "I'm going to have the scars from cat claws to prove it."

"I didn't know you had a cat."

"Me, either," Goldie said. "Until yesterday."

"Goldie," Dr. Saltzman said.

"Yes?" Goldie asked. "What is it? More dogs? A giant Santa Claus lawn ornament?"

"It sounds like you're going to be just fine," Dr. Saltzman replied. "Have a little faith in yourself and the town, and be patient."

"I'll try," Goldie replied. "At least until the first of the year."

"That's all I ask," Dr. Saltzman said. "Have a good night."

"You, too," Goldie replied.

She pressed the END CALL button and plopped back down into the chair, wondering how she was going to find the energy to get up and find the cat . . . or anything in the house for that matter. Maybe she'd just sleep in the chair again.

Or, on second thought, maybe not. Her head was still tender

from that morning. Instead, she rattled off a few *I'm doing all right.*
Don't worry about me texts to her parents and Alex, and then, with
much effort, pulled herself out of the chair and dragged her tired
body back to the bedroom, falling asleep for the second night in
a row in all of her clothes.

Chapter 8

It was time for Goldie to get down to business. Tiffany showed her all of the patient files, and Goldie suggested they update their computer software, so Tiffany didn't have to go back to the filing cabinet every time she needed to find information. Tiffany was in favor of the idea, so long as she got to pick what program was used.

At lunchtime, Goldie went back to the cabin and rounded up the cat into her carrier for vaccination. She'd noticed the night before, when the cat was asleep on her back, that she had a tiny tattoo on her stomach, which alerted Goldie that she'd at least been spayed. At some point, Goldie knew, this cat had been loved.

"What are you going to name her?" Tiffany asked once she'd heard the story of how the cat had come to be in Goldie's possession.

Goldie shrugged. "I don't know. I can't think of anything, which is sort of unlike me. I'm pretty good at naming animals. I've been thinking about calling her Airport, since I found her there."

"That's worse than Large Marge," Tiffany said with a slight grin.

"I feel like that name is kind of mean," Goldie replied. "Marge can't help it if she's a little . . . large."

"Cohen named her," Tiffany continued. "She stepped on his foot and broke three toes."

"Probably served him right," Goldie said.

"It usually does," Tiffany said. "He's not so bad, though, once you get to know him."

"That's what Dr. Saltzman said," Goldie replied. "But I don't know him, and I'm not sure I want to *get* to know him."

"He's been that way since he was a kid," Tiffany said. "I used to babysit him when I was a teenager. He was always very serious, with those big eyes. You could always tell when he was about to do something ornery, because his eyes would just dance around, even though he tried so hard to keep a straight face. He's still like that."

"I didn't know he was a farrier," Goldie said. "I wish I had known. I could have asked him more about the animals in town when he picked me up at the airport. Instead, we spent most of the ride in silence, when he wasn't chastising me about being an outsider."

"Like I said," Tiffany replied, "give him a chance. He'll grow on you."

"No, thanks," Goldie said. "I can't believe we haven't had anyone call for an appointment today. I guess the mayor wasn't as impressed as we thought."

"You really are the most impatient person I've ever met," Tiffany said. "And that's saying something, considering I've got a teenage granddaughter at home."

Goldie considered telling Tiffany about her conversation with

Dr. Saltzman the night before, but she already felt ridiculous for being so petulant. She might not be much better than a teenager, now that she thought about it. Her behavior hadn't been very professional, and Dr. Saltzman was a business partner, not her father. It wasn't his job to console her or to make her feel better about her life decisions.

"I just really want this place to be successful," Goldie replied. "I don't want to go back to L.A. with my tail between my legs."

"So you've got an ex back home that you want to make believe you're successful without him," Tiffany replied knowingly. "I get it."

"More like I don't want to go back to Los Angeles and be forced to beg for my job back," Goldie replied, trying not to sound bitter. "He was—is—a vet, too. We worked at the same practice for years. His practice, I guess, but for a long time I thought it was ours."

"And it wasn't?"

"Not so much," Goldie admitted. "I don't hate him or anything. We should have ended things long before we did, but that still doesn't mean I want him to know I've failed at something he's managed to stay very successful at."

Tiffany nodded. "And you thought Wisconsin was the way to get your groove back? Don't people like you go to someplace tropical to do that?"

"People like me?"

"Yeah," Tiffany replied, motioning toward her with one hand. "You know, rich West Coast gals of a certain age."

"I'm not rich," Goldie replied. "And I'm not in a rom-com."

"Los Angeles to Wisconsin seems more like a tragedy to me," Tiffany said.

"It's not that, either." Goldie scratched the cat behind her left ear. "It was just far enough away, that's all."

"I've never been out of the state," Tiffany admitted. "My ex-husband always said he was going to take me to Hawaii for our twenty-fifth wedding anniversary, but we just made it to fifteen."

"A month ago, I would have gasped at that," Goldie said. "The never-having-been-out-of-the-state part, not the divorce part. But now I don't know, I don't have that much good to say about any-where."

"This place will either kill you or save your life," Tiffany said. "There ain't no in-between."

* * *

THEY FINISHED OUT the day with hardly any disagreements, and Goldie decided she was going to count that as a win. She was re-lieved to find that there was no enormous sheepdog lurking in the cabin when she got home. She figured the cat was relieved, too, and Goldie let her out of the kennel as the cat meowed pitifully. She hadn't enjoyed being at the veterinary clinic. It made Goldie wonder if the cat had ever been vaccinated or regularly seen a vet in her entire life, which, as far as Goldie could tell, had been about five years.

"Come on," Goldie said to her, refilling the cat's empty food bowl. "I'm sorry I'm late. I'll try not to make this a habit."

The cat began to eat, and Goldie searched the pantry for some-thing to feed herself. She knew she was going to have to get to the grocery store eventually, but Dr. Saltzman had left a stash of crackers, and there was cheese in the refrigerator that looked fresh, as well as several cans of Coca-Cola. Goldie couldn't remember the last time she'd had a soda, so she sat down happily to her meal, feeling only slightly paranoid that Alex would somehow know and soon be calling to scold her for drinking liquid cancer.

It was kind of nice, Goldie thought, sitting in this small kitchen with only a cat for company. There was nothing in particular she needed to do, no people she had to see. She could shower and then spend the rest of the night curled up reading a book or watching television. She could go to bed early and get up in time to walk over to the clinic before Tiffany got there. Then she could spend some time learning about the animals and the humans they belonged to. She had to figure out a way to get them to come back, to make them trust her as a veterinarian, and if that was going to happen, she would need to make a better impression than she had on Cohen Gable, that was for damn sure.

She still didn't understand what she'd said or done to offend him.

There sure seemed to be a lot of rules for living in such a small town.

Goldie had just popped the top to her second can of Coke when her phone rang. She didn't recognize the number, and so she let it ring for a few seconds while deciding whether to answer. The continued noise sent the cat heading straight for the bedroom, so Goldie answered.

"Hello?"

"Goldie? Goldie, can you hear me? It's Alex!"

"Oh my God, Alex!" Goldie stood up and brushed the cracker crumbs from her skirt. "I didn't think I'd hear from you for weeks!"

"I was worried about you," Alex said, her voice barely above a whisper. "I just wanted to make sure you were doing okay. Your text had no exclamation marks. That's a bad sign."

"Why are you whispering?" Goldie asked. "What time is it there?"

"It's five A.M. in Nairobi," Alex said. "I borrowed a volunteer's phone. International calling isn't working on mine yet. So . . . are you all right?"

"I'm fine," Goldie said. "Everything is fine."

"Are you sure?"

"Yes, I'm sure," Goldie replied. "Don't I sound fine to you?"

"I can't really tell," Alex said. "The connection is really shitty."

They both laughed, and then Goldie said, "It's different, but that's what I said I wanted. So I'm trying to make the best of it."

"Any cute guys?" Alex pressed.

"Alex, I've been here less than forty-eight hours."

"So?"

Goldie rolled her eyes, even though Alex couldn't see her. "I'm not looking for cute guys. I'm trying to salvage my career. Anyway, why are you awake at five A.M.?"

"I haven't been to sleep yet!" There was a pause, followed by laughter and something in another language Goldie didn't understand, and then Alex said, "I'm sorry, I've got to go. I love you!"

"I love you, too," Goldie got out before the line went dead.

She sat down and put her phone on the table. It sounded like Alex was having quite the adventure. Maybe she should have taken her up on the offer to go with her to Africa. Goldie remembered a holiday movie she'd watched with her mother a few years ago. The title escaped her, but it had been about a newly divorced veterinarian who went on an African safari and ended up with Rob Lowe.

Goldie couldn't see a downside to that.

From the hallway, the cat stuck her head out and looked around.

"Nobody's here," Goldie said to her. "It's just us. You spook too easily, you know that?"

Goldie made her way back to the bedroom to change into her pajamas. The shower would have to wait until the morning. She was too tired. The little bedroom was off to the left-hand side of the cabin, next to the bathroom. It was the only room in the whole place that had carpet. The yellow seventies shag was a bit worn but still in pretty good condition for its age. There was a double bed in the middle with heavy, wooden bedposts, a matching nightstand, and a small dresser in one corner.

For now, all of her clothes were still in the two suitcases she'd brought with her, but she'd get around to hanging them up once she really had time to focus and make room. Goldie wasn't sure what she'd do with the rest of her clothes when they arrived or the six boxes of items she hadn't thought she could live without while away from Los Angeles.

She allowed herself to wonder, just for a minute, what the apartment she'd shared with Brandon looked like now. What of hers had he replaced? Had he even noticed she took half of the coffee cups or the knit blanket that was always at the end of their bed? Was he wandering around in search of the electric toothbrush charger or that lotion of Goldie's he used when his elbows got dry? How many times already had he called the building super to ask about trash day or what went in which recycling bin? Would he realize that his protein shakes didn't magically appear in the refrigerator after every one of his workouts?

How long before he forgot the name of a client and went to

turn to her for a reminder only to realize she was no longer standing beside him?

Goldie sat down on the bed and hoped that this change of scenery, of circumstance, was the palate cleanser that she'd wanted it to be. It certainly was *different*.

The cat jumped up on the bed and rubbed her head against Goldie's arm, and Goldie reached out to pet her.

"Listen," Goldie said. "You can't be jumping up on my head anymore. It makes both of us look ridiculous, and I'm having a hard enough time fitting in as it is. We are both going to have to get a grip."

The cat looked up at her, fixing Goldie with her mismatched eyes.

"Sure, you like me now," Goldie continued, "because I'm feeding you."

The cat, predictably, did not reply.

"Come on, Airport," Goldie said, standing up again. "Let's go see what we can find to watch on television. Maybe we can find that African safari movie. If you thought that sheepdog was big, just wait until I introduce you to elephants."

Chapter 9

Goldie felt like she was making progress inside the clinic. She'd rearranged the waiting room and familiarized herself with the records, sterilized nearly every surface, and she'd even convinced Tiffany to help her send out a postcard to each person with a pet on record, offering a free office exam for the first visit. Still, they hadn't had any takers. Nobody called to reschedule their appointments. Nobody called at all.

Kevin, it seemed, was their only visitor. He'd show up randomly throughout the day, and Goldie couldn't help but develop a soft spot for him. He seemed to be just as lost as she was, staring up at her with his big eyes, and he was just so sweet. She figured having a dog like him around, even if he was the worst sheepdog to ever walk the earth, was good luck.

"If I have to get a job at the Gas n Go because you've run this place into the ground, I will fill your shower with bees," Tiffany said to her one morning as Goldie set down a bowl of water for Kevin. "My ex-husband works at the Gas n Go."

"Then why would you get a job there?" Goldie asked. "That doesn't sound like a very good idea."

"He's the only person in town who still likes me enough to hire me!" Tiffany replied. She stared down at the phone, dejected.

"Is it because you filled everyone else's showers up with bees?"

"No," Tiffany said. "It's because—"

She stopped talking when both women heard a car door slam outside. Goldie jumped up and ran to the window.

"I think there's someone here!" she whispered. "Come look!"

Tiffany joined Goldie and squinted through the blinds. "Oh no," she said. "Nope. No. I'd rather work at the Gas n Go with Roger Dale."

"What are you talking about?" Goldie asked. "We've got a client!"

Tiffany backed away from the window and Goldie. "What you've got is crazy Delores Watkins and her Crypt Keeper cat, Milton."

"She doesn't look crazy," Goldie replied. She watched as a tiny woman with a silver bob got out of her car, one hand wrapped tightly around a battered kennel.

"Turn the lights off," Tiffany hissed. "Pretend we aren't here."

"Don't be ridiculous," Goldie said. "We can't afford to pretend we aren't here."

"Do you see this?" Tiffany demanded, holding up her pinky finger. "Do you see the way it tilts to the left like that? That's because of *Milton*. He latched on like a snapping turtle and wouldn't let go. Eight stitches! *Eight!* That cat doesn't even have any teeth!"

Goldie opened the door for Delores and tried not to look too eager to see someone, anyone, at the clinic.

Delores rushed inside and shoved the kennel into Goldie's hands, her eyes wild and panicked.

"Oh, help me. I think he's dyin'!"

"Now, Ms. Delores, that's what you said last month," Tiffany said before Goldie could answer. "And it only turned out to be a little indigestion. You haven't been feeding him your bean burrito casserole again, have you?"

"No, no, it's not that," Delores replied, wringing her hands. "I don't know what it is, but I know he's dyin'. Oh Lord in heaven, I'm not ready to lose my baby!"

"It's all right," Goldie said, finding her voice. "You have a seat right here, and Tiffany and I will get him checked out for you. Sit down and take some nice, deep breaths."

Delores looked at Goldie as if seeing her for the first time. "Dr. Saltzman said I could trust you with my Milton," she said.

"I am going to take very good care of him," Goldie said. "You just wait right here and concentrate on your breathing."

Goldie turned and followed Tiffany back into the examination room. She set the crate up on the steel table and then leaned down to look inside.

And inside was a *very* irritated, very old, gray-and-white tiger-striped cat. Goldie didn't think she'd ever heard a hiss so visceral.

"Okay," Goldie said, going over to the sink and washing her hands. "Here's what we're going to do. I'm going to distract him by taking the top off the carrier, and you're going to wrap him up in a warm towel. Then I'm going to sedate him."

Tiffany nodded and left the room to grab the towel from the warmer in the back, while Goldie busied herself preparing a small syringe of diazepam.

"Are you ready?" Goldie asked when Tiffany returned.

"Let's do it," Tiffany replied.

As soon as Goldie lifted the top, the smell filled the room, and both women were stunned into silence. Milton, realizing it was his opportunity for escape, took it, and tried to scramble out of the crate.

Tiffany got to him just in time, and Goldie managed to inject the sedative as Milton struggled, confused by the blanket.

"Not today, Satan," Tiffany whispered. "Not today."

"That cat is very much alive," Goldie said, catching her breath. "But that smell means something is wrong."

"He's alive, but he smells dead," Tiffany agreed. She placed the now sedated Milton down onto the tabletop. "What do you think it is?"

"I'm not sure," Goldie replied. She unwrapped Milton and began to examine him. "But I have an idea about what it could be. Did you notice the hair loss on his tail?"

"Yeah," Tiffany replied. "As soon as I laid him down."

Goldie carefully lifted up the cat's tail. "That's what I thought," she said. "Poor Milton. He's got stud tail. That sebaceous gland is working overtime."

"I knew I recognized that smell," Tiffany said. "We had a cat in here last spring with the same problem."

"It's not as common in neutered cats," Goldie said. "But Milton is pretty old, so that might've contributed to the problem. I can clip away some of this hair and get him cleaned up. You can tell Delores he's going to be fine. We'll send her home with a medicated shampoo and some antibiotics. She'll just need to watch him to make sure it doesn't flare up again and get out of control. He'll feel a lot better when he comes to."

Tiffany hesitated.

"What is it?" Goldie asked. "Would you rather clean him up than go tell Delores?"

"No," Tiffany said. "It's just, well, she won't be able to pay you."

"That's okay," Goldie said. "We can just send her a bill, can't we?"

Tiffany shifted uncomfortably from one foot to the other. "I mean, she can't pay you today, and she won't be able to pay you next week. She's going to *say* she'll pay you, and in a couple of weeks, she'll come in with freezer jam or fresh bread or a scarf she knitted, and that will be payment."

Goldie considered this. She hadn't been in charge of billing at her other clinic. They had a host of receptionists to take care of that. Nobody told her when a bill was late. She knew of a few instances when a client attempted to barter with Brandon for an expensive procedure, but it wasn't with freezer jam . . . whatever that was. Still, there was no way she was going to refuse Delores or Milton treatment. It wouldn't be right.

"Well, I don't know what freezer jam is," Goldie said, finally. "But I could use a scarf. Tell Delores to give me about fifteen minutes."

Tiffany smiled just a little, and Goldie had to hide a laugh. A smile, even a small one, looked so foreign on her face, and when Goldie emerged later with a very groggy Milton, she found not just Delores and Tiffany in the lobby, but three ragamuffin children as well.

"Here you go," Goldie said to Delores, handing the carrier with Milton in it to her. "He's going to be a bit out of it for another hour or so, but he's going to be fine. In addition to the antibiotics and cream, I'm also going to send you home with a pill that will relax him for his next visit. I'd like you to bring him back in two weeks so I can make sure he's healing all right."

Delores set the carrier down and embraced Goldie in a hug that showed surprising strength for a woman of her age and stature.

"Thank you so much . . . Dr. . . . Dr. . . ." Delores trailed off.

"Dr. Goldie is fine," Goldie replied. "And you're welcome."

Delores turned her attention to Tiffany. "Send me a bill, Tiff," she said. "You know I'm good for it."

"I'll do that," Tiffany replied.

"That lady is so weird," the oldest of the children, a teenager, said once Delores was out of earshot. "I don't know how you deal with it, Granny."

Goldie raised her eyebrow and looked over at Tiffany. "Granny?" she said.

Tiffany rolled her eyes. "They insist on calling me that. These are my grandkids." She pointed at them individually. "This here is Kaitlyn, then this here is Trevor Junior, and the youngest down here is Lakelyn."

"Hi," Goldie said. "It's nice to meet all of you."

"Is this your new boss?" Trevor Jr. asked. "She looks way younger than you, Granny."

"We're colleagues," Goldie said quickly. "Your granny has been teaching me a lot over the last few days."

"I thought you said you couldn't teach her anything," Lakelyn said, and then promptly squealed, "Ow!" when Kaitlyn stepped on her foot.

"We just stopped by for some cash so we can grab dinner," Kaitlyn said. "They both want McDonald's."

"We have food at home," Tiffany replied.

"It's all gross," Trever Jr. said. "Come on, Granny. If we have to stay home alone with *Kaitlyn* while you go out and have a good time, then we need McDonald's."

"I'm not gonna be gone all night," Tiffany protested. "I'm just going to watch your grandpa Dale's band play a couple of songs."

"I bet Pop would buy us McDonald's," Trevor Jr. grumbled.

Tiffany sighed. "Fine," she said. "But if I get one call from anyone in the neighborhood that you're acting like hooligans, you won't be able to sit down for a week. You hear me?"

Trevor Jr. gave Tiffany a mock salute, and all three of the grandchildren followed Tiffany around the reception desk and waited as she dug through her purse.

Kaitlyn leaned down and whispered, just loud enough for Goldie to hear, "You should invite her to go with you, Granny."

"Shhh," Tiffany hissed.

"She doesn't know anybody," Kaitlyn continued. "You made me invite the new girl to my birthday party last year, remember? You said I had to be *charitable*."

Goldie excused herself to go back into the examination room and clean up. She was already embarrassed that a teenager could feel the desperation oozing out of every single one of her pores. She couldn't help it. Her ears had perked up at the very mention of actual human interaction. She supposed she could go without Tiffany, but that also meant she would have to find out the name of the place and then show up without being invited. That sounded worse than spending the night alone with Airport eating crackers and drinking Coke, which she'd actually come to enjoy.

In L.A., she had gone out to dinner several nights a week,

and sometimes the night took her elsewhere. Goldie was both reveling in her newfound alone time and absolutely *dying* for a night out.

She was bagging up the trash when Tiffany stuck her head into the room and said, "I'm going to head out."

"Okay!" Goldie said, inwardly cringing at her attempt at fake cheerfulness. "Have a great weekend. I'll see you on Monday."

Goldie waited for the front door to slam before she set the bag of trash down on the floor and laid her head down on the cool, steel exam table. She'd have to sanitize again, but she didn't care. If she could just focus on the good things—she'd actually seen a patient today. She'd helped someone. Maybe Delores, no matter how strange she was, would tell other people in Blue Dog Valley, and they would make appointments. She didn't care if she had to accept food and knit clothing for a month. She would do it if she had to. She didn't have to make friends. She didn't have to be invited places. She just needed to survive.

She was outside the clinic locking up when Tiffany pulled back into the parking lot and rolled down her window.

"I'm going to be at the Bushy Beaver down on Main Street at nine P.M.," she said. "I'll wait for you out front if you want to come."

"Oh, that's all right," Goldie replied. "I've got a lot to do at the cabin, and I'm sure you don't need me tagging along."

"I'm not going to offer twice," Tiffany said. "Take it or leave it. Doesn't matter to me."

"Okay," Goldie said. "Nine P.M.? I'll be there."

"Do you have some jeans to wear or something?" Tiffany asked.

"What?"

"Do you have something that's not quite so pretentious?" Tiffany pointed at Goldie's pencil skirt.

"I don't know what you mean," Goldie said, confused. "I got this skirt on clearance."

"Let me put it to you this way," Tiffany replied. "Do you want to fit in with the locals or do you want to stick out like an expensive sore thumb?"

"Definitely fit in," Goldie said.

"Jeans," Tiffany continued. "T-shirt. Casual shoes."

"Okay."

"Don't be late."

"I won't," Goldie said. "And, Tiffany?"

"Yeah?"

"Thank you for inviting me."

"Don't thank me yet," Tiffany said, shifting her old, white Chrysler into reverse. "Let's make sure you survive a night at the Bushy Beaver first."

Goldie looked around for Kevin, but he'd wandered off again, and so she walked herself back to the cabin to get ready for her first night out in the valley—a much different kind of valley than California had to offer.

Chapter 10

Goldie did, in fact, own a pair of jeans. She owned several. Of course, she hadn't packed any except one pair—an old, oversized pair of Brandy Melville jeans. She loved them because they were so comfortable, but she didn't ever wear them for a night out. They were more for trips to the farmers' market on Saturdays or for making a quick visit to the bodega down the street from her apartment, where she knew everybody and everybody knew her.

Tonight, despite Tiffany's instructions, she didn't want to look like a slob.

"This is fine," she said out loud, as she pulled the jeans up above her hips. "This is cute. I'm going to look cute."

From her lounging position on the bed, Airport stared at her, clearly uncomfortable with the flurry of activity during what was usually their quiet time.

"Don't judge me," Goldie said to her. "I'm doing my best."

Goldie padded into the bathroom and opened up the dryer. She pulled out a blue classic Paul Frank baby tee with Julius the

Monkey on the front that she'd had since college. She'd worn it out all the time as a freshman at UCLA, because it showed off a now-regrettable lower-back tattoo that she'd gotten on a whim during a night out with Alex. Like so many other elder millennials, Goldie had fallen victim to the "tramp stamp."

Alex had long since had hers lasered off, but Goldie thought getting the tattoo itself had been painful enough. She didn't want to suffer through having it removed. So she covered it all the time, unless she was at home. Her Paul Frank shirt was old and worn and comfortable. She wore it to sleep.

When she looked at herself in the mirror twenty minutes later, she felt like she should be wearing butterfly clips and sparkly eye shadow just like she did when she was in college.

Airport sat at the end of the hallway as Goldie pulled on her black peacoat, the only coat she'd brought with her, and buttoned it up.

"I'll be back," Goldie said to her. Then, feeling guilty, she went to the cabinet and pulled out a can of wet food she'd taken from the clinic and scraped its contents into the cat's bowl. "There. Now you can't be mad at me."

Goldie made it two steps out of the door when a rush of cold wind hit her in the face so hard, she nearly fell back into the house. A coat. She was going to need a real coat. The problem was, she didn't have one. She had a couple of sweaters, but those weren't going to do the trick. She went back inside, briefly thought about draping Kevin around her shoulders. Instead, she rummaged through her suitcase again. That was when she remembered seeing a winter coat of some sort in the hallway closet.

Goldie wasn't really sure whether it was a coat that she found or just a very large wool blanket with armholes, and it smelled like something she couldn't quite put her finger on, but it was better than freezing. Goldie accidentally shut the coat in the door two times before she managed to pull the entire thing into the Jeep and start out toward the bar.

She was so engrossed in her thoughts about being warm that she nearly missed the sign for the Bushy Beaver. In fact, if there hadn't been a giant wooden beaver statue out front, she would have missed it altogether.

The bar was at the end of Main Street, several storefronts past Ruby's Diner. It wasn't attached to any other store like the rest of the businesses on the street that shared a common wall. The parking lot came first, and behind the parking lot sat the long Bushy Beaver building.

The sign above the door read, "The Bushy Beaver. Come for the Beer. Stay for the Bushiest Bush in Wisconsin."

Tiffany was waiting for her out front, just beneath the sign.

"You're late," Tiffany said.

Goldie looked down at her phone. "Just five minutes."

Tiffany squinted at her. "What in the hell are you wearing?"

"A coat," Goldie said, looking down at herself. "It's arctic here. I don't know how you stand it."

To Goldie's surprise, Tiffany began to laugh. It was a loud, open-mouthed laugh that caused Tiffany to nearly double over.

"I don't think I look that bad," Goldie said, offended.

"That's Doc's cow-birthin' coat!" Tiffany gasped.

"It's his *what*?"

"His cow-birthin' coat!" Tiffany repeated, standing up. "That's the coat he used to wear when it was cold and he was called out about a heifer having complications with delivery. I bet there is still some placenta on it."

"Oh my *God*!" Goldie squealed, wriggling out of the coat.

"You can just leave it out here over the railing," Tiffany said, wiping away a tear that was rolling down her cheek. "Trust me, nobody is going to steal it."

Goldie followed Tiffany inside, and she grinned when she saw Ruby at a table by the bar, waving furiously at them with one hand, a pitcher of beer in the other.

"Hi!" Ruby squealed when Goldie and Tiffany sat down. "Tiff told me you were coming tonight, and I'm so glad you did!"

"Me, too," Goldie replied. "It was nice to be invited."

Tiffany rolled her eyes and tapped her empty mug on the table, prompting a refill from Ruby.

"You want some?" Ruby asked, holding up the pitcher. "It's Coors. It's not my favorite, but it's just one dollar a pint on Friday night."

"Yes, please," Goldie replied.

"See?" Ruby said, turning her attention to Tiffany. "I told you she'd drink it."

"Why wouldn't I?" Goldie asked.

Ruby filled a mug for Goldie and said, "She thinks you're too fancy."

"I live alone in a cabin with a hairless cat," Goldie replied. "I have eaten nothing but crackers and drunk nothing but Coke for a week. I'm not too fancy for anything."

Ruby giggled and clinked her glass against Goldie's. "Here's to not bein' fancy!"

Nearly all the tables, as well as the bar stools around them, were full. There was a stage up front, where a few men were set-ting up. They were all dressed as Santa Claus to varying degrees. One of the men kept looking over in their direction and stroking an off-white elastic beard.

"Roger Dale keeps looking over here," Ruby said, elbowing Tiffany. "Didn't he know you were coming tonight?"

Tiffany shook her head. "Nope. And if he asks, I'm going to tell him I had no idea his stupid band was playing tonight."

"I was with you at the Gas n Go last week when he told you!" Ruby replied. "Roger Dale is an idiot, but he's not stupid."

"Did you forget he was once arrested for a DUI twice in one night?" Tiffany asked Ruby.

"Okay, so he's a little bit stupid."

"He also cheated on me with my sister."

"Okay, fine!" Ruby exclaimed. "He's a lot stupid, but the point is that he keeps lookin' over here!"

"You can have him," Tiffany said.

"No way," Ruby said. "I remember what you did to your sister."

"Was it bees in the shower?" Goldie asked.

Ruby shook her head. "No," she replied, her voice solemn. "It was snakes."

"He looks stupid in that beard," Tiffany said, raising her mid-dle finger to Roger Dale the next time he glanced over at her.

"You can't flip the bird at Santa!" Ruby gasped in mock horror. "You'll be on the naughty list!"

"He wishes," Tiffany grumbled.

"I bet you think it's weird everything's all decorated for Christ-mas already, huh?" Ruby asked Goldie.

Goldie glanced over at Tiffany and then back to Ruby. "No, not at all. Of course not," she said.

"She thinks it's totally weird," Tiffany said.

"I do not!" Goldie protested.

"It's okay," Ruby said, waving her off. "I think it's weird, too. But I can charge a little extra at the diner for Christmas-themed pastries, so I don't complain."

Goldie leaned in closer to Ruby and whispered, "Why does the town love Christmas so much?"

"It's been that way ever since I was little," Ruby replied. "It used to be a real big deal. We used to have a carnival and everything. Back then, the town was a lot bigger. Gosh, I can't even remember the last time we had a carnival. It must've been when I was a teenager."

Goldie turned around in her chair when the front door swung open, and she saw Cohen step inside. He stood there for a second scanning the crowd, and when he caught Goldie's eye, he looked away and to the bar, where a large man in a green John Deere hat was calling his name.

Cohen walked over to the bar and bent down to scratch the ears of a sleeping Labrador retriever before addressing the man behind the bar, and Goldie turned back around, focusing her attention on the stage. The lights dimmed a little, and a cheer erupted.

Tiffany wasn't cheering, but she *was* watching the stage with interest, and Goldie wondered just exactly what was going on between her and her ex-husband. It was clear that it was something.

"So did your week get better?" Ruby yelled to Goldie over the throb of the intro to a song Goldie knew but couldn't name. "I hope the cinnamon rolls helped."

"I've had dreams about those cinnamon rolls!" Goldie yelled back. "I need a truckload of them!"

"Come by any time!" Ruby said. "I'll set a few back for you!"

"Thanks!"

"I love your shirt!" Ruby continued. "My sister used to go to a Paul Frank store in Milwaukee all the time when we were teenagers."

"I got this one at Delia's," Goldie replied. "It was my favorite store in the nineties."

"I loved that catalogue!" Ruby exclaimed.

"We had a store in L.A.," Goldie said. "My mom would take me on the weekends, and I'd just stay there for hours."

"I'm so jealous," Ruby replied. "Was it wonderful growing up in Los Angeles?"

"It was pretty great," Goldie said.

"Well, if you don't mind me asking—why did you come here?"

Goldie took a drink of her beer and considered how to answer the question. There were plenty of acceptable answers she could give, and she was almost sure Ruby would accept any one of them. Still, she found herself wanting to be completely honest with her new friend.

She leaned across the table and yelled, "My fiancé was cheating on me with a teenager, and it was either move here or run over him with my car!"

It was right then, just as she finished speaking, that Goldie realized the song was over and she'd been yelling to Ruby loud enough for the entire bar to hear. Everyone, including Tiffany, had turned and was looking at her.

Goldie was frozen in her seat. She wondered if she could crawl to the door without anyone noticing.

After a few tense seconds, Tiffany grabbed the pitcher of beer and said, "Well, hell. That calls for another round!"

There was more cheering, and Roger Dale's band began another song as Tiffany poured the rest of the beer into each of their glasses.

Goldie gave Tiffany a grateful smile, and Tiffany almost smiled back.

"Are you hungry?" Ruby asked. "This place has great food."

"Really?" Goldie replied. "I didn't think a place called the Bushy Beaver would have food at all . . . let alone anything good."

"It's a secret," Ruby said with a wink. "They don't even have a menu, but they'll make whatever you ask for in the back."

"It's true," Tiffany said, not taking her eyes away from the stage. "Last week some woman was in here. I guess she took a wrong turn on her way to Milwaukee, and she asked for a Cobb salad. Randy in the back whipped one up for her in five minutes."

"Does that happen a lot?" Goldie asked. "People getting lost on their way into the city?"

"No," Ruby said. "It used to happen a lot more, but on purpose, before they built the bypass. Now it's mostly just locals."

"The Beaver had the best menu in the state," Tiffany interjected. "There were bands from all over in every weekend when Brian's dad used to own the place." She pointed to the bartender, who was still carrying on a conversation with Cohen. "The bypass ruined all that. It looks like a hole-in-the-wall now, but it was legendary in its day."

"People just stopped coming?" Goldie wanted to know. "Because of the bypass?"

"Not at first," Ruby said. "But after a while, the traffic stopped, and Brian's daddy died. Brian is a great guy, but he couldn't keep it up. It was too much work."

"Is that why you don't have the Christmas carnival anymore?" Goldie asked.

Ruby nodded. "It's just not worth it when people won't come."

"That's sad," Goldie said.

"You know what's not sad?" Tiffany asked, as the song finished and Roger Dale announced that the band would be taking a twenty-minute break to "throw back a few with the boys."

"What?" Goldie asked.

"Their Jamaican jerk wings," Tiffany finished.

"With ranch!" Ruby said. "All the ranch."

Tiffany started to pull out her wallet and Goldie said, "I'll get it."

"All right," Tiffany replied, shrugging. "Tell Brian you need at least—what?" She looked at Ruby. "Fifteen?"

"At least," Ruby said.

"Okay," Goldie replied, standing up. "Do we need more beer, too?"

"Definite yes," Ruby said.

Goldie stood up and took her debit card out of her wallet, thought better of it, and grabbed cash instead. She walked to the end of the bar, opposite where Cohen stood, and waited for Brian the bartender to notice her. After a few minutes of nothing, she turned around to Tiffany and Ruby, who both motioned for her to walk to the other side of the bar.

Goldie sighed and walked halfway over. She sat down at the only empty bar stool. Surely someone would help her there. In L.A. she'd rarely had trouble getting the attention of a bartender. Of course, she'd never been wearing ratty jeans and a twenty-year-old T-shirt, either.

Brian moved down the line of people at the bar and finally reached Goldie.

"What can I get ya?"

"I need . . . uh . . . I need at least fifteen Jamaican jerk wings and a whole bunch of ranch," she said. "Oh, and another pitcher of Coors."

Brian squinted at her. "You're sittin' over there with Ruby 'n' Tiff, right?"

Goldie nodded. "Yes."

"You that doctor from L.A.?"

"I'm a veterinarian," Goldie replied.

"Same thing."

"Well," Goldie began, and then she decided against it. "Okay."

"A vet isn't the same thing as a medical doctor, Brian," Cohen said. He slid in next to Goldie and leaned against the bar. "You know that, man."

"Whatever," Brian replied, shrugging. "I'll go tell Randy to fix up some wings. He ain't gonna be happy about it, though."

Goldie immediately wished she'd let Ruby or Tiffany come up and order instead. She took a deep breath and then mustered enough courage to look over at Cohen and smile. The least she could do was *try* to be friendly, considering everyone said he wasn't as bad as his first impression.

"I didn't think I'd see you here," Cohen said after a beat. "Did Ruby invite you?"

"Tiffany did," Goldie said, feeling oddly proud of that fact. "I think she was relieved that she didn't lose a finger to a toothless cat named Milton at the clinic earlier, so she probably felt obligated to invite me."

"Delores's cat is still alive?" Cohen asked, his tone incredulous. "He's been on his deathbed for at least five years."

"He's a marvel of modern medicine," Goldie agreed. "I read his file. But aside from the teeth and having a bit of a tail issue, he's healthy."

"I was a teenager when she got that cat," Cohen said. "She caught him in our barn when he was a kitten. He's always acted like he's got a burr in his saddle. Tiff's lucky she didn't lose her whole damn arm."

"Like he's got a what?" Goldie asked.

"A burr in his saddle," Cohen repeated. "It just means he's mean."

"Oh," Goldie said. "Then yes, that's an accurate assessment."

Cohen glanced down at the scarred bar countertop and then looked back up at her, a grin on his face. This time, it looked as if it was a little less painful for him. When his eyes caught hers, he held her there for just a second beyond what would have been considered polite, and Goldie suddenly wished she were wearing something better than a shirt she usually slept in.

"Hey, Cohen?" came a voice from around the bar.

For a split second, Cohen hesitated, holding Goldie's gaze before he turned away to address whoever it was calling his name.

"Yeah, Mo, what's up?"

"Have you seen Brian?" An older man with salt-and-pepper hair stood at the end of the bar, concern written all over his face.

"He's in the back talking to Randy. Why?" Cohen turned fully away from Goldie. "Everything all right?"

"I dunno, brother. His Layla isn't looking too great." Mo pointed down to where the Labrador lay on the floor, a fresh pile of vomit next to her. "Is she sick?"

Goldie followed Cohen over to the dog.

"I asked Brian when I got here if something was wrong with her," Cohen said. "He told me she hadn't been feeling great today, said she was panting and threw up once or twice. He figured she caught a squirrel or something, and it made her sick."

Goldie bent down to look at the dog. She was, in fact, panting and also drooling. She was overweight—Goldie could tell that just from looking at her—but she had a sinking feeling that Layla's stomach might be enlarged for another reason.

Gingerly, she reached out and applied a bit of pressure to the dog's abdomen, which caused the dog to whine and attempt to shift away from her.

"What's going on?" Brian asked, when he emerged from the kitchen and saw the three of them huddled there.

Goldie stood up. "I think your dog is very sick," she said. "Specifically, I think she might have bloat, but the lighting in here isn't great, and I can't tell for sure. I think we should take her into the clinic so I can examine her."

"Naw," Brian replied, waving her off. "I've got an appointment Monday morning with the vet over in Ridgedale. She'll be fine until then."

"I'm not sure she'll make it to Monday," Goldie replied. "She needs an examination now, and she might need emergency surgery if it is what I think it is."

A wave of panic and then anger passed over Brian's face. "Cohen, tell your little girlfriend here that I don't need her help, and I don't need her advice. If I wanted it, I woulda made an appointment with her."

Cohen opened his mouth to speak, but Goldie cut him off. "I'm nobody's girlfriend," she said. "Do you have a veterinary degree from UCLA? Do any of you? If your answer is no, then I suggest you listen to me when I tell you that your dog is going to die if you don't do something *now*."

"I'd listen to her, Brian," Mo said.

By now, Tiffany was up and out of her seat. Goldie didn't even have to say anything to her. She took one look at Layla and said, "I'll get my keys. Dr. McKenzie, you can ride with me."

"I'll bring my truck around front. Brian, I'll help you carry Layla out," Cohen said. "Mo, you go on and tell Randy he's going to have to come out front for a while."

"Will do," Mo replied. He clapped Brian on the back. "It'll be okay, brother. Just listen to the lady."

Brian nodded. "Okay. Okay, fine."

Goldie hurried back over to the table to explain the situation to a bewildered Ruby.

"I'm sorry," Goldie said. "I hate to cut the night short, but I'm afraid the bartender's dog is really sick."

"Go!" Ruby replied. "I'll help Randy out for a while, just so he doesn't get overwhelmed."

"Thank you!" Goldie called over her shoulder.

She could feel everyone in the bar staring at her as she went, but she didn't have time to think about it right then. She was too busy worrying about Layla, hoping that it wasn't bloat, and if it was, praying that they'd caught it in time.

Tiffany was waiting for her in the car, and she waved to Goldie when she saw her, motioning for her to get in.

"I told you not to thank me too soon for inviting you to the Beaver," Tiffany said, as she pulled out of the parking lot. "The valley may be the smallest town for fifty miles, but I tell ya what, Doc, there ain't ever a dull moment."

Chapter 11

It didn't take long for Goldie to diagnose Layla, the chocolate Labrador, as having bloat. The X-ray showed that Layla's stomach was badly twisted, which was what had caused the swelling, and Goldie worried that if they didn't take care of it quickly, Layla would go into shock from lack of blood flow to her heart.

"Can you fix it?" Brian asked.

"We can try," Goldie replied. "We're going to have to release some of that pressure, and then Layla will need surgery to untwist her stomach. I'll have to derotate her stomach and tack it to one wall of her body to keep it from happening again. Can you tell me how long she's been like this?"

Brian furrowed his eyebrows and thought about it. "Maybe an hour or so before we got to the bar," he said. "Then we were at the bar—I don't know—maybe two hours before you saw her?"

"Okay," Goldie replied. "I need your permission before I can do anything, and I'll need you to sign a form. Tiffany will have it ready for you in a few minutes, if you agree."

"Do whatever you can, Doc," Brian said. "Whatever you can."

"Brian, I need to tell you that while I think I can save her, this is a serious condition. I want you to understand up front that just about thirty percent of dogs die from the surgery. I'm not saying this to scare you, but it's important that you know the risk."

"She'll definitely die without the surgery, though, right?"

"Yes," Goldie said, nodding. "She will."

"Then you've got to do it."

"You can go back to the bar, and I can call you when we're done," Goldie said. "We'll get started right away."

"Can I wait?" Brian asked.

"You'll have to stay out here in the lobby," Goldie replied. "You have to promise me that you won't interrupt."

"I'll stay with him," Cohen said. He'd been standing silently beside Brian, his hands stuffed into his jeans pockets. "Let's go up to the Gas n Go and get you a pop and some of those powder donuts you like. Then we'll come right back."

"I think that's a good idea," Goldie said. She smiled gratefully at Cohen. "We'll leave the door unlocked for you."

Goldie retreated to the back to prepare for Layla's surgery. In some ways, she was glad it was happening at night. There was something calmer about the clinic after dark, and it put her at ease. If she had to perform a surgery like this, calm was what she needed.

"They're gone," Tiffany said. "Poor Brian's a wreck."

"Are you sure you're all right to stay?" Goldie asked. She checked Layla's breathing. The fluids and pain medication she'd already started seemed to be helping. "We should be ready to start soon."

"The kids are fine," Tiffany replied. "Doc and me have had some late nights before. Kaitlyn knows the drill. I left Roger

Dale a message to go by and check on them after he leaves the Beaver."

"Tell Kaitlyn I appreciate it," Goldie said.

"She's a responsible kid," Tiffany continued. "She's been watching after her brother and sister for longer than she shoulda had to. My daughter, Beth, is a marine. She's been deployed for eight months. The time before that was a year."

"Wow," Goldie said. "That must be tough."

"It would be easier if Beth hadn't inherited my shitty taste in men," Tiffany said, pulling on a pair of latex gloves. "But we're suckers for blue eyes and fast cars."

Goldie laughed. "No judgment. As it turns out, I don't have the greatest taste in men, either."

"Could do a lot worse than Cohen Gable," Tiffany said.

"I'm not doing anything with Cohen Gable," Goldie replied.

"Suit yourself."

After Goldie shaved a patch of skin on Layla's stomach, Tiffany handed her a bloat trocar, which was basically a fancy term for a fourteen-gage needle that Goldie would have to insert into Layla's stomach to release some of the gas trapped inside.

"Have you done this before?" Tiffany asked. She placed one of her arms under Layla's neck and one on top. "Doc did plenty, but we lost a few along the way."

"A few times," Goldie replied. She inserted the needle and, almost immediately, there was a low hissing sound of gas being released.

"Jesus, that smells," Tiffany said, wrinkling her nose. "I never get used to that smell."

"We had a client with a beautiful pair of Harlequin Great

Danes," Goldie continued. "Sisters. When we spayed them, I told the client that I thought it might be a good idea to go ahead and do a preventative gastropexy, since giant breeds are prone, but she refused. Both dogs ended up getting bloat about a year apart. I saved the first one, but I couldn't save the other."

"Let me guess," Tiffany replied. "She blamed you."

"Naturally," Goldie replied. "She got another Dane puppy from the same breeder a few months later, and when she brought her in to be spayed, I said I wouldn't do it unless she agreed to the gastropexy."

She put her ear down to the trocar and listened.

"Yep," Goldie replied. "There." She removed the needle. "I think we're good now. It's amazing how this works."

"All right, old girl," Tiffany said, petting the top of Layla's head. "Let's get you fixed right up."

Chapter 12

Everyone was exhausted but relieved when Goldie announced that Layla had come through the surgery and seemed to be doing well.

"I'll need to keep her for at least forty-eight hours to monitor her," Goldie said. "I'm going to stay with her through the rest of the night for observation, and Tiffany will come back in the morning. She's not totally out of the woods, but she did great with the surgery, and that is a good sign."

"Thank you," Brian said. He was clutching an empty grape-soda bottle. "I don't know how I'll ever be able to repay you."

"Actually, paying is all you need to do," Goldie replied. "But let's not worry about that right now. Go home and get some rest. You can call tomorrow morning, maybe about nine, if you want to check on her."

"Come on, man," Cohen said. "I'll take you back to the bar so you can pick up your truck."

"Yeah, okay," Brian replied. "Thanks, Tiff. Layla and I appreciate you both."

"I'll be sending you a bill," Tiffany replied. "Count on it."

Goldie walked over to the shelves of dog food and bent down to grab a few cans of wet food. "Let me go ahead and give you these, just so you don't have to worry about it when you pick her up on Monday," she said. "Layla will need to eat soft, bland food in small amounts for a week or so."

"Dr. Goldie?" Brian asked.

Goldie stood up, several cans of food in her arms. "What?"

"Was that a, I mean, did I just see a . . ."

Goldie sighed. She'd forgotten all about the tattoo and how it would be visible without her coat. "Yes," she said. "It is."

"A tramp stamp!" Brian said. Then he turned around and lifted up his shirt to reveal a faded tribal design along his lower back. "I got one, too! It ain't as pretty as yours, though. Got it one night in Milwaukee at a house party."

"You're lucky you didn't get blood poisoning," Cohen interjected.

"I was real drunk," Brian said, grinning. "You were there, Co! You remember."

"Unfortunately, I do."

"I wasn't drunk," Goldie admitted. "I wish I could use that excuse."

"Well, yours is prettier," Brian replied. "'Course, you're prettier'n me, anyway."

"No argument there," Cohen said. "Let's go, Brian, before that new girlfriend of yours has my hide for getting you home so late."

Goldie saw them to the door and locked it behind them. "It was nice of Cohen to stay with Brian," she said.

"They've been friends since elementary school," Tiffany replied.

"Cohen was the best man at Brian's first wedding, and his second, and his third."

Goldie laughed. "I don't know if that's funny because I'm tired or if it's just funny."

"Cohen's loyal, I'll give him that," Tiffany said. She shut off the computer and walked out from behind the desk. "But Brian was there for Cohen when . . ." She trailed off. "When he needed him, so I understand why he puts up with Brian's bullshit."

Goldie sensed there was something Tiffany wasn't telling her, but she didn't ask, afraid she'd break the tenuous connection they'd built by being nosy. She remembered what Cohen said about asking too much about a person's business.

"You sure you're all right to stay?" Tiffany asked.

"I'm fine," Goldie replied. "I wouldn't sleep, anyway, if I went home. I just want to make sure Layla makes it through the night."

"I'll be back in the morning." Tiffany unlocked the door and stepped outside, and she shuddered when a blast of cold air rushed in. "You left your coat at the Beaver," she said.

"I'll go by and get it in the morning," Goldie said.

"You're going to need a warmer coat," Tiffany replied. "Go down and see Ashley at the Horse Trader. She'll get you fixed up."

"I will."

"You did good tonight," Tiffany said. "Word will get out."

"So my shower is safe from bees?" Goldie asked, only half joking.

"I didn't say that," Tiffany said. "Bees are always a strong possibility."

Chapter 13

Goldie thought it might be a good idea to go and get a very strong coffee that morning after Tiffany came in to relieve her. She was half asleep on her feet. Layla was getting along just fine. The night before, Goldie had tried to sleep on the exam table, covered up by a few towels, but she'd been too worried to sleep. At the clinic in Los Angeles, they'd had someone come in for overnights when there was a critical patient, usually a trusted tech who wanted the extra hours. They had a rollaway specifically for that purpose.

It occurred to Goldie that, since she was the only vet in town, the only vet in a twenty-mile radius, there was no emergency clinic for people to take their animals to. If there was an emergency in the middle of the night—she was going to get the call. She had the number to the clinic forwarded to her cell for the weekend. She hoped Layla would be the only emergency for a while, although she was happy to have any patients at all.

She wanted to get some sleep, absolutely, but she also needed to be awake when the majority of her things from Los Angeles were delivered that afternoon to the clinic. She hadn't known the exact address of the cabin when she'd scheduled the delivery. When she'd asked Dr. Saltzman for it, he'd simply said, "Oh, it's a hop, skip, and a jump from the clinic."

Goldie doubted very much that the delivery people would be able to deliver to that location.

So, instead of going home, she went to Ruby's for coffee and a cinnamon roll. Okay, two cinnamon rolls. She'd gotten there early enough to beat the morning rush, and she'd stayed just long enough to be introduced to a few of the regulars, including two elderly men named Jack and Elvis, who were friendlier than most and had offered her a seat at their booth. She'd politely declined, citing exhaustion, and headed back to the cabin to prepare for the rest of the day.

She didn't even notice as she rounded the corner to the clinic that the Wagoneer was beginning to lose power. It wasn't until it actually started sputtering and came to a stop that Goldie looked down at the dash and realized that the Jeep was completely out of gas.

"That's perfect," Goldie said aloud, resting her forehead on the steering wheel. "Just absolutely perfect."

After willing herself not to burst into tears right there on the side of the road, Goldie got out of the Jeep and steeled herself for what was sure to be a humiliating experience of calling Tiffany, who was just down the road and literally the only person in Wisconsin whose cell phone number she had saved into her phone.

She'd started to search through her contacts, when she heard the ominous crunch of tires on gravel behind her.

It was Cohen.

He pulled up alongside her and rolled down his window. "You havin' technical difficulties?"

"No," Goldie replied. "I just thought it would be fun to park way off and walk to my house in forty-five-degree weather."

"Forty-five degrees isn't cold," Cohen said.

"It is to me," Goldie said. "I think my fingers may be frozen to this steering wheel."

"Maybe you should wear warmer clothes."

"And maybe *you* should mind your business."

Cohen sighed. "You ran out of gas, didn't you?"

Goldie shook her head and started looking through her cell phone again. "I did not."

"Yes, you did," Cohen insisted. "That damn gas gauge hasn't worked in years. Doc should have told you."

Goldie stopped and turned to face the truck so quickly that she nearly lost her balance. "There seem to be a lot of things Doc *should have told me*."

"Agreed," Cohen replied. "Come on. Hop in. I'll take you back into town, and we can get you some gas for that hunk of junk."

"I'm fine, thanks," Goldie said. "I'll figure it out later."

"How exactly are you going to do that?" Cohen wanted to know. "Tiffany is at the clinic, and I know you don't want her to leave Layla to help you."

Goldie gritted her teeth. "Fine."

Cohen cut the engine and got out, leaving the driver's side open for her to climb in. "Are those Ruby's cinnamon rolls in that bag?"

"There's one left," Goldie said, handing him the bag before she got into the truck. "You can have it for your trouble."

"I just came from Ruby's," Cohen replied. "She told me she was out, but she wouldn't tell me who the culprit was. Now I know."

"Yes, I'm sure when word gets out, I'll be even less popular than I am now," Goldie said, sighing heavily. "If you eat that, you'll be implicated."

Cohen let out a laugh as he started up the truck. "Wouldn't be the first time."

Goldie let his laugh wash over her. It felt like warm honey—rich and sweet, and maybe a little bit raw, like it wasn't something he did very often.

It was disarming.

"Where are we going?" Goldie asked, when Cohen kept driving down the gravel road past the clinic. "I thought we were getting gas?"

"Gotta pick up a gas can," Cohen replied in between bites of the cinnamon roll. "I don't suppose you have one lying around?"

"Do I look like someone who would have one of those lying around?" Goldie replied.

"Nope."

A couple of minutes later, Cohen turned left onto a paved driveway with a metal archway with GABLE FARMS emblazoned across the top. Both sides of the driveway were fenced, and off in the distance, Goldie could see a white house coming into view.

It was the kind of house Goldie hadn't really ever seen except on television. Sure, there were old houses in California, but not in *her* part of California, and this house was *old*. It looked like it

ought to be blanketed in snow and covered in Christmas lights—
a postcard house.

Greetings from Wisconsin!

"Is this your house?" Goldie asked.

"I live here" was all Cohen said. He parked the truck. "I'm going to run into the barn just over there and grab a gas can. I'll be
right back."

Goldie sat in the truck and waited. She wondered what this
farm looked like in the spring and summer, when everything was
beginning to wake up from its winter slumber. She found that she
was excited to experience all four seasons of the year, instead of a
mild fall and winter that eventually turned into a scorching spring
and summer.

She wondered if Cohen lived in the house alone. She hadn't really considered the fact that he might be married or have a family.
She'd been too annoyed with him at first. Goldie still felt pretty
annoyed, but she was thankful that he'd stopped. She really
hadn't wanted to go in and tell Tiffany what she'd done.

The house didn't look like it was occupied by a family. There
were no toys in the yard, no minivan parked off to the side. There
was an older green Ford truck parked over by the barn, but it appeared to be stuck in the mud or, at the very least, not to have
been driven in a while. Still, Goldie had a hard time believing
that someone who *looked* like Cohen Gable could be unattached.
Maybe other women found his personality as off-putting as she
did, but she doubted, in a town as small as this, that he could be
single without something being terribly, terribly wrong with him.

Goldie's attention began to wander away from Cohen and to

the field on the other side of the house. She couldn't really see much in the distance—there weren't cows that close to the house, but it looked like there was something out there grazing.

There were several of them.

Goldie squinted. Whatever they were, they were fluffy. And brown, mostly. She knew she ought to stay in the truck. Cohen hadn't demanded it, but he hadn't exactly told her to get out and explore, either. She looked back over to the barn, and when she didn't see Cohen, she got out and walked over to the fence.

The closer she got, the clearer it became to Goldie that what she was seeing was a herd of alpacas. Well, maybe not a herd. There were about a dozen or so roaming on the grass. A few of them looked up as she drew nearer to the fence, and they separated just enough that Goldie could see a bright white spot in the center of the brown thicket. It, too, was an alpaca, but it was much smaller than all the rest. When it looked up and saw her, it began to trot over on slightly wobbly legs.

Goldie nearly squealed with delight when she realized that the alpaca was not just any alpaca, but it was *Alice the Alpaca*. The very same alpaca she'd seen posted so many times in the veterinary group she was in with Dr. Saltzman.

"Oh, hello," Goldie cooed when Alice got close enough for her to touch. "Aren't you the cutest thing in the entire world? I can't believe it's you!"

Goldie knelt down slightly to examine Alice's feet. She remembered from pictures that Alice had a type of deformity on her two front feet that caused her to be polydactyl. It was fascinating. Alice in general was fascinating, because, in addition to being a white, blue-eyed alpaca, she was also deaf. She was a tiny thing, but Goldie knew from Dr. Saltzman's posts that she had a big personality.

Peanut Butter came barreling out of the house and ran right up to Goldie, barking. Goldie hoped she wasn't about to get the shit bitten out of her for roaming around uninvited on what she was sure Peanut Butter thought of as *her* farm. Of course, Goldie realized, it *was* Peanut Butter's farm.

Peanut Butter didn't bite her. Instead, she wriggled through the fence and stood in front of Alice protectively, her tail sticking straight up.

"I'm not going to hurt either of you," Goldie said to the dog. "I promise. I'm a good guy."

Peanut Butter ticked her head to one side and studied Goldie. She took a step closer, and Goldie stuck out her hand, which Peanut Butter promptly licked.

"There you go," Goldie said to her. "See? I bet I taste better than an alpaca."

Peanut Butter hedged closer, but before Goldie could stroke her head, Cohen began walking toward them, and Peanut Butter reverted to barking at Goldie.

"I won't tell him you secretly like me," Goldie whispered.

"I see you found Alice," Cohen said. He had a red gas can in one hand. "I didn't figure you'd stay in the truck long after you noticed her. Nobody does."

"I didn't know Alice belonged to you," Goldie said. "She's one of my favorites."

At first, Cohen looked confused, and then he nodded in

understanding. "Oh, that's right. I forgot Doc used to post her picture in those vet groups he was in. I heard she was a big hit."

"Oh, she is," Goldie agreed. She reached out to give Alice a scratch. "It's a wonder she survived. You must've taken really good care of her."

"She almost didn't," Cohen said. "For the first year or so, we just weren't sure. She's healthy now, though."

"Where did you get her?" Goldie turned to face Cohen.

"I bought her at an animal swap," Cohen replied. "I took a few chickens down for the first-Saturday-of-the-month sale a couple of towns over, and some guy had her there. She was just a baby. Looked pitiful. I drove all the way home and couldn't stop thinking about her, so I went back and got her. Took her to Doc right away."

"Did he know what caused her mutations?" Goldie asked. "Most crias with all of her issues probably wouldn't survive that long without serious medical intervention."

"Inbreeding, probably," Cohen replied. "Or maybe just poor breeding. Doc didn't know for sure, and the guy I bought her from didn't tell me anything. Hell, I didn't even know anything about alpacas before I got Alice."

Goldie couldn't help but grin. "And now look at you," she said, gesturing to the field in front of them. "You're a regular alpaca whisperer."

Alice nudged Cohen, and he gave her a playful scratch. "She was lonely without friends," he said. "She lived in the house for a while, but once she got to feeling better, she wanted to go outside and be a regular farm animal."

"I'm sure the others help keep her safe," Goldie replied. "And Peanut Butter, of course."

"Oh, she can fend for herself," Cohen said. "She may be deaf and lame, but she's not scared of anything."

Goldie opened her mouth to respond, but just as she was about to speak, the door to the farmhouse swung open and a man appeared. He stood there for a few seconds, staring at the two of them, and then he broke into a broad grin and ambled down the steps toward them.

"Son, I thought you were headin' into town for feed," the man said. "I might not be the sharpest tool in the barn, but it sure does look like you've come home with a woman instead."

"Dad, this is Dr. Marigold McKenzie, Doc Saltzman's replacement," Cohen said, not looking at Goldie. "Marigold, this is my father, Alfred Gable."

"Call me Alfie, please," Cohen's father said, sticking out his hand to Goldie. "Pleasure to meet you, Dr. McKenzie."

"Call me Goldie," she replied, taking his hand. "It's a pleasure to meet you, too."

"I'm sorry my errant child didn't have the decency to invite you inside," Alfie said. "I've been trying to teach him manners for the last thirty-two years, and, well, he's a bit of a slow learner."

Goldie laughed. "It's okay. I know I've disrupted his morning. I ran out of gas on the way back to the clinic from town, and he stopped to help me."

"And we should really get going," Cohen interjected. "I do still have to buy feed."

"Son, you didn't tell me she was a looker," Alfie continued, ignoring Cohen. "How are you finding Blue Dog Valley, Goldie?"

"It's great so far," Goldie said, trying to smile. "I'm very happy to be here."

Alfie squinted at her. "Nonsense," he said. "Tell me the truth now, Goldie. I'm an old man, but I can take it. The locals givin' you trouble?"

"I'm sure people will come around eventually," Goldie said, smiling weakly. "At least that's what Dr. Saltzman said. It's only been a week."

Alfie rocked back on his heels and then leaned forward to whisper conspiratorially to Goldie, "Don't let 'em run ya off. Most of 'em don't have the sense God gave a goose."

Goldie laughed. "I think I'm going to like you, Alfie."

"Dad, we really need to get going," Cohen said, beginning to walk back toward his truck.

"All right, all right," Alfie replied, waving them off. "Don't be a stranger now, Goldie." He bent down and picked up Peanut Butter. "You're staying here with me, old gal."

"It was nice to meet you!" Goldie called over her shoulder as she ran to catch up with Cohen.

Once they were away from the farm and back bouncing along the gravel road, Goldie said, "Your dad seems nice."

"He is," Cohen agreed. "He's nice to everyone."

"Even outsiders like me," Goldie replied.

When Cohen didn't reply, Goldie continued, "So you live with your dad, then?"

"Yep," Cohen answered.

"Just the two of you?"

"Yep."

"Have you always had the farm?"

Cohen nodded. "Been in the family since 1910."

"My great-grandparents owned a farm in Tennessee," Goldie said. "But they sold it decades before I was born, when my mom was a kid. I've never even been to Tennessee. My grandfather was in the military, and he was stationed in California. He met my grandmother, and I guess he never went back."

"My dad was in the service, but he came back home. He was already married to my mom, though," Cohen said. "I guess he had a reason for coming back other than breaking his back on the farm."

"My grandfather used to say that the military was a piece of cake compared to the farm," Goldie replied. "It does seem like a lot of work."

"It's a lot of work for an old man and his son," Cohen agreed. "We have some seasonal help in the summer and fall, so I try not to complain too much."

"Are you an only child?" Goldie asked.

They pulled in to the gas station, and Cohen got out to fill up the gas can without answering her question. He didn't attempt to answer it when he got back inside the truck, either, so Goldie busied herself with finding enough cash in her wallet to pay for the gas.

"I don't want your money," Cohen said to her after he'd filled up the Wagoneer.

"But you paid for the gas," Goldie argued. "I didn't see how much it was, but surely this will cover it."

"Do you want some friendly advice about how you can fit in better in the valley?" Cohen asked. He was looking at her fully, his eyes set intently on hers, in that stormy way he'd done the night before.

"Yes," Goldie answered honestly. "I do."

Cohen threw the empty gas can into the back of his truck, and for a moment it seemed like he'd changed his mind. He looked down at the ground and kicked the tires of the Jeep and then said, "You don't offer to pay a neighbor for a friendly favor. It's insulting. Nobody around here is going to appreciate it."

"Okay," Goldie said. She shoved the money down into her purse. "Is that it?"

"Don't ask personal questions," Cohen replied. "People don't like it. It makes you look nosy."

"Are you sure these are tips for living in this town or tips for interacting with you?" Goldie asked.

"Both," Cohen said. "Maybe where you're from—"

"I'm from California, not from Mars," Goldie said, cutting him off. "Stop acting like I should have had my intergalactic passport stamped to be here."

One side of Cohen's mouth ticked up, but he didn't smile. "Might as well be Mars," he replied. "Blue Dog Valley isn't an experiment to see how well you can acclimate to the hillbillies. This is an actual town with actual people who aren't inclined to trust anyone not from here."

Goldie crossed her arms over her chest. "Then I'd suggest you stop acting like a hillbilly, if you don't want me to treat you like one."

"Like I said," Cohen continued, "it's just a bit of friendly advice."

"Doesn't seem too friendly."

"On second thought," Cohen said, "I think I will take your money, after all."

"Too late," Goldie replied, jumping into the Wagoneer and

starting it up. "Just some friendly advice from me to you—I'm not ever going to offer twice."

With that, Goldie pulled away from the curb and turned down the road toward the clinic, leaving Cohen standing there, hands shoved down into his pockets, watching her go.

Chapter 14

Business at the clinic was picking up. Goldie had it on good authority that Mayor Rose had told everyone at the feed store that Goldie was worth calling, at least in an emergency. Brian had also sung her praises at the Beaver, according to Tiffany. Layla was doing well after her surgery and had eagerly resumed her bar-guarding duties. Goldie considered going over to check on her and have a beer or two, but she felt awkward about going there alone. Business picking up at the clinic didn't necessarily translate to friendship, even though she secretly considered Tiffany her friend.

"This has been a long-ass day, huh?" Tiffany asked.

"I think the woman with ten puppies about did me in," Goldie admitted.

"I keep tellin' Connie she can't rescue every dog she sees, but she can't help it," Tiffany replied.

"Well, I'm glad she saved them," Goldie said. "If she hadn't, I'm not sure how they could have made it. They were . . . what was it you said? *Ate up* with mange."

"It sounds weird when you say it," Tiffany said.

Tiffany looked down at her watch for what felt to Goldie like the hundredth time that day. "Do you have a hot date tonight or something?" Goldie asked.

"What?" Tiffany looked up. "Uh, no. It's nothing like that, but since we don't have anything on the books for the rest of the day, do you care if I head out early?"

Goldie shrugged. "Sure, I guess not."

"Thanks," Tiffany said, hurrying over to the coatrack beside the door. She yanked at her coat so hard the rack tumbled over. "Sorry!"

"It's fine," Goldie said. "Why are you in such a rush? Where are you going?"

"Nowhere!" Tiffany replied. "I mean, I'm going somewhere, but it's nowhere, really. Anyway, I gotta go. See you later!"

Goldie stared after her, utterly confused. Tiffany had been acting strange all day. Although she wasn't a paranoid person, Goldie was starting to wonder if Tiffany was headed out to see someone or do something that she didn't want Goldie to know about or didn't want to invite her to. Maybe Tiffany felt like, since she'd invited Goldie out once, she had to do it every time.

Goldie wanted to tell her that wasn't true. She didn't expect to be included in Tiffany's social circle every time she went out. Of course she enjoyed being included, but they were all adults. Her feelings weren't going to be hurt. At least, she wasn't going to admit that they might be hurt.

As she busied herself cleaning up for the day, Goldie realized that Kevin was nowhere to be found. Usually by this time, he'd wandered up, let himself into the clinic, and would be following her around, leaving muddy paw prints where she'd just mopped.

Now Kevin was avoiding her, too?

Goldie finished up, then sat down at the front desk. There was still time left in the workday, but she doubted anyone was going to show up. She pulled out her phone and called Dr. Saltzman. He answered after the fourth ring, when Goldie was just about to hang up.

"Goldie!" he said. "How lovely to hear from you. How are things going over that way?"

"Pretty well," Goldie replied. "That's why I'm calling you. Business has picked up. Though I don't think I've convinced everyone to come back."

"Well, not even I could get everyone," Dr. Saltzman replied. "I heard about Layla."

"You did?" Goldie asked.

"Cohen called," Dr. Saltzman said. "He said you did a wonderful job. He said you saved that dog's life."

Goldie smiled to herself. "I'm just glad we caught it in time," she said.

"It seems like you're fitting in and making friends," Dr. Saltzman continued. "I had no doubts about it, just in case you were curious."

"I don't know about all of that," Goldie said. "I think saying I have friends is pushing it a little bit, but I'm getting along all right, and I wanted you to know."

"Thank you for telling me so," Dr. Saltzman replied. "You have a good night, Goldie."

"You, too," Goldie said, pressing the END CALL button.

Goldie let the crisp, evening air bite at her as she walked back to the cabin. She was cold, but not as cold as she expected to be, and there was something invigorating about the way the air felt.

As she walked, she heard voices coming from the direction of the cabin. She couldn't make out what they were saying, but there were a lot of them. So many, that by the time she rounded the corner, she'd convinced herself she was being robbed by some kind of rowdy theater group. What she saw instead were a crowd of townspeople gathered around the cabin. They were laughing and joking. They were on ladders stringing up lights. They were hanging a Santa wreath on her front door, roasting marshmallows around a makeshift fire pit, and when they saw her approaching, her mouth hanging open in surprise, they greeted her with a rousing, "Hey, Dr. Goldie!"

"What is all this?" Goldie asked. She walked closer to the cabin to get a better look.

"We're decorating your place!" Tiffany said. "What do you think?" She spread her arms wide and gestured to the cabin. "It was Brian's idea."

Brian waved from the roof of the cabin. On the ladder, directly below him, was Cohen, cursing to himself as he untangled a mass of Christmas lights that Ruby had handed him.

"This is amazing!" Goldie said. She reached out and impulsively hugged Tiffany. "Thank you."

Kevin, followed closely by Layla, padded up to Goldie, their tails wagging in excitement. "I wondered where you were," Goldie said to him, letting go of a very uncomfortable Tiffany. She reached down to give both of the dogs scratches.

"I was afraid you'd get suspicious and walk down here before we could get started," Tiffany said. "Especially when I couldn't get Kevin to go up to the clinic."

"You were acting really weird," Goldie said. "But I thought it was because you had plans you didn't want me to know about or something."

"I mean, I kind of did," Tiffany said, grinning.

"I don't even know half of these people," Goldie replied, looking around. "How did you convince them all to come out here?"

"I didn't have to convince anyone," Tiffany said. "Nobody says no to a little Christmas decorating around here, and besides, some of us, uh"—Tiffany cleared her throat—"we feel bad about not being as welcoming as we should have been."

"Some of us?" Goldie asked.

"Not me," Tiffany said. "I'm always welcoming."

"Oh, of course you are," Goldie agreed.

"But, you know, Cohen and other people."

"Cohen?" Goldie asked. "I don't see him feeling bad about anything."

"You'd be surprised," Tiffany replied, a sly smile playing at her lips. "Come on, let's get you over to the bonfire. Alfie's got a Tom and Jerry with your name on it."

"What's a Tom and Jerry?" Goldie asked.

"Wisconsin's finest holiday drink," Tiffany replied.

Alfie unscrewed the lid of a beat-up metal thermos and poured her a drink. "Here ya go," he said. "It'll warm you up in no time."

Goldie took a sip. "Wow," she said. "That's very . . . alcoholic."

"You're welcome," Alfie said, with a wink.

"I'll take one of those, Dad," Cohen said, heaving a sigh. "I cannot untangle another set of lights that don't even work. Brian's been on that damn roof over an hour."

"Is he still up there?" Goldie asked, twisting around to look at the cabin.

"Nah, he's taking a break," Cohen replied.

"Thanks for doing this," Goldie said. "I mean, helping decorate."

"It was Brian's idea," Cohen said. "I'm just following orders."

"Is that something you do often?" Goldie asked. "Follow orders?"

Cohen took a long drink and then said, "I reckon I follow orders just about as well as you do."

"Still," Goldie said. "You didn't have to."

"No, I guess I didn't," Cohen replied. "But I wanted to."

Goldie stared out into the encroaching darkness, and she didn't move away when she felt Cohen take the smallest step closer to her. She turned to look at him, but the moment was interrupted when Teddy approached them.

He was holding a child in a red stormtrooper costume.

"We better be heading out," he said to them. "It's way past Addie's bedtime."

"How long have you been wearing that getup, Adeline?" Cohen asked the little girl.

"Since Halloween," Teddy whispered. "We only take it off to wash it."

"It's not dirty!" Addie shrieked, taking off her helmet and thrusting it out toward Cohen.

Cohen caught it and put it on his head over his baseball cap. "How do I look?"

The little girl, who Goldie guessed was probably about four, stuck out her bottom lip. "That's mine."

"I thought you were giving it to me," Cohen said.

"No," Addie replied. "Give it back."

Cohen obliged, and Addie put the helmet back on her head.

"It looks much better on you," Goldie said to her. "You're the perfect stormtrooper."

"More like Darth Vader," Teddy mumbled. "Anyway . . ." He waved at Goldie and Cohen. "I better get on out of here before she falls asleep in this thing for the third night in a row."

"It's not dirty!" Addie yelled, over and over, until she and Teddy were completely out of sight.

"She's a pistol, that one," Cohen said. "Got a whole lot of opinions."

"Good," Goldie replied, finishing off what was left in her cup. "That will serve her well in life and, as she's already figured out, fashion."

Chapter 15

Goldie woke up the next day to the sound of her phone ringing in her purse, on the kitchen table. By the time she realized what was going on, she'd missed the call. Her mother, of course, called right back minutes later.

"I'm sorry," Goldie said without even saying hello. "I was asleep."

"It's the middle of the day," her mother replied. "Long night?"

"You could say that," Goldie said. "We had a Christmas decorating party at the cabin, and people didn't leave until after midnight and then I couldn't get to sleep for the longest time after."

"I can call you back later," her mother said.

"No, it's okay." Goldie padded back to the bedroom and began to rummage around for clean clothes. "I need to head into town and go by a store there to get a warmer winter coat. It's freezing here."

"I told you," her mother replied. "I still can't believe people live there willingly."

"It's not so bad," Goldie said. "I mean, it's cold, but the people, I don't know. I kind of like them."

"That's an improvement from the last time we spoke."

"How is everything going?" Goldie asked. "How's Dad? I've texted him a few times, but he never replies."

"He's never been very good at texting," her mother said. "I'll tell him to check his messages."

"I'll call him this week," Goldie replied.

"I'm sure he would like that."

There was a pause in the conversation, and Goldie thought for a minute that maybe her mother had accidentally ended the call.

"Mom?"

"Hmm?"

"I was just checking to see if you were still there."

"I'm still here," her mother said. "It's just, well, I don't want to upset you . . ."

"What is it, Mom?" Goldie could feel her voice rising with alarm. "Are you sure Dad's okay?"

"Honey, he's fine."

"Okay, then what is it?"

"I just miss you," her mother said. "And I know it's early to be asking, but your dad and I were hoping that you might make plans to come home for Christmas, even for a couple of days."

"Of course I'll come home for Christmas," Goldie said, aghast. "What would make you think that I wouldn't?"

"We know you're busy," her mother replied. "And I know you won't be here for Thanksgiving, since you very nearly just left."

"Not too busy to come home for Christmas," Goldie said. "I still have to talk to Tiffany about it, but I think we'll close up on the twenty-third and reopen again on the twenty-seventh. I know that's not a lot of time, but I've still got control of the clinic until the first of the year, so it's my responsibility."

There was another pause on the other end, and then her mother said, "And have you decided what you'll do after that?"

Goldie shrugged, even though her mother couldn't see it. "I don't know. I like it here, Mom, I really do. I'm just not entirely sure that this place likes me."

"I don't believe that for a second," her mother replied. "I can't imagine one person not liking you, let alone a whole town."

"And I love you for that," Goldie said, an intense wave of homesickness washing over her.

"I love you, too, my darling," her mother said. "Don't forget to call your father this week."

"I won't," Goldie said. "Talk to you soon."

"Talk to you soon."

Goldie sighed and lay back onto the bed, clutching her phone. She missed her parents. Her mother hated to go shopping, but she would have gone with Goldie if she were here. She would have spent the entire time telling Goldie she didn't really "need" anything but one good winter coat and a few warm pieces of clothing she could match with what she already had, and it would have been solid advice that Goldie would completely ignore. Maybe, if she decided to stay, her parents could come for a visit, and she could show them around town and introduce them to everyone . . . even Cohen. That thought made her flush, and all she wanted to do was shake it off. The best thing to do, she figured, was to head right on out into the afternoon air and forget she'd ever considered it.

* * *

THE HORSE TRADER was on the opposite side of town from the diner and the bar, and Goldie had a little bit of trouble finding it. It was the newer side of town, Goldie could tell for sure, across the street from the grocery store.

There were quite a few people milling about, walking in and out of stores in a hurry, bundled up. Goldie wished she had a coat that didn't have cow placenta all over it, if for no other reason than because people were going to think she was ridiculous, jumping out of the Jeep and running inside without so much as sleeves to cover her arms.

The shop itself was warm inside and brightly lit, with clothes every color of the rainbow for sale. The woman behind the counter smiled at Goldie as she entered.

"Hello," the woman said. "Come in, come in, you must be freezing!"

"That's why I'm here," Goldie replied. "I've been instructed to buy a winter coat."

"I can help with that," the woman said. "I'm Ashley."

"Goldie," she said. "It's nice to meet you."

A look of recognition passed over Ashley's face, and she said, "Oh yes! I've heard all about you. I guess you wouldn't have much need for a winter coat where you're from."

"I'm never going to get used to that," Goldie replied, touching the sleeve of a puffy Columbia jacket. "Living in a place where everyone knows who you are before you've met them."

"It's small-town charm," Ashley replied. "Well, that's what we tell each other, anyway. Besides, the mayor is my father-in-law, so that's where I heard about you."

"I'm not sure Mayor Rose was very impressed with me when

we met," Goldie replied, trying not to make a face. "But I think his horse was grateful for the sedative, at least."

"Oh, he's never impressed with anyone," Ashley said, waving her off. "But he told me you didn't take any lip off Cohen, and I sure liked to hear that."

Goldie grinned. "Well, in Cohen's defense, I think I was encroaching on his territory."

"He thinks this whole town is his territory," Ashley said.

Ashley was tall and blond, with a sleek ponytail and blunt-cut bangs. She looked like every single one of Goldie's childhood Barbie dolls, although her smile was genuine and not at all plastic. If Goldie had seen her on the street in Los Angeles, she would have pegged her for a native, her skin was so tan and her nails so well-manicured.

"I don't really know what I need," Goldie said, turning Ashley's attention away from Cohen and back to clothing. "I know I need a coat and maybe a few other things. What do you recommend for the winter here?"

"Well, seein' as how it's November now . . ." Ashley put a finger to her mouth and tapped. "Hmmm . . . a coat for sure, and boots. You'll want some snow boots and maybe just a pair of warmer boots to wear around when it really gets cold. A hat, some gloves, a scarf or two. Do you have any sweatshirts or long pants that aren't dressy?"

Goldie looked down at her black slacks. "I have several pairs of yoga pants, but I'm guessing they won't work."

"You'll need some sweatpants, then. And maybe some long underwear."

"Do you have all of that?"

Ashley nodded. "I have everything. It's just me and the Walmart, as far as apparel goes, so lots of people come here to buy their clothes."

"Great," Goldie replied. "That makes everything a lot easier, knowing I can get it all in one place."

"Why don't you have a look around?" Ashley said. "I'll go back and get one of the dressing rooms cleared out for you. We had a rush earlier today, and my help left early. I haven't had a chance to clean them out yet."

Goldie began to go through the racks and stacks of clothing. There was a lot for such a small store.

"Whatever I don't have in your size, I can order for you," Ashley called out from the back. "Just set anything you want to try on the counter."

"Okay!" Goldie replied, picking up a cherry-red sweatshirt with a "Life Is Good" logo across the front. It was so soft, she wanted to put it on right that second.

The store reminded her of a much smaller version of REI—a sporting goods and outdoor store she'd sometimes visited with Alex in Los Angeles. Goldie had always wanted to buy things at REI, but she had never known where she'd wear them. She didn't go hiking or camping the way Alex did. She'd gone a few times with Alex when they were in college, but she wasn't nearly as proficient. Now, however, seemed like the perfect opportunity to indulge the desire to at least *appear* outdoorsy. She set the red hoodie and a pair of lined Bearpaw snow boots on the counter.

"Those boots will be good for when you want to go out and still look cute," Ashley said. "But you'll need at least one pair of Muck Boots if you're going to visit anyone with cattle this winter." She set a pair of Muck Boots on the counter. "They're not sexy, but they're waterproof, warm, and they'll stay on your feet even in the mud."

"Okay," Goldie said, nodding her head. "I need a size seven."

"Do you want tall, like these, or short?"

"Maybe both?"

"Good choice," Ashley replied. "I've got a couple colors in your size. I'll go get them."

In the end, Goldie picked two pairs of Muck work boots and a pair of short lace-up Muck Boots in bright yellow. She had no idea where she was going to wear *those*, but she had to have them. She also purchased several pairs of lined yoga pants, sweatpants, two sets of long underwear, long-sleeve shirts, socks, gloves, hats, and a goose-down North Face parka.

"You're a true Wisconsinite now," Ashley said, beaming.

"Well, I've certainly paid the price for it," Goldie replied, handing over her credit card. "Thank you so much for your help, though. I really appreciate it."

"What are you doing later?" Ashley asked, taking Goldie's card and sliding it through the credit card machine. "We're having a town hall meeting at seven. If you want to see a true representation of the valley, you should come."

Goldie looked down at her phone. "That's just half an hour from now," she said.

"I know," Ashley replied. "We close at five, but I didn't have the heart to tell you that, what with you coming in dressed for summer and all."

"I'm so sorry!" Goldie replied. "I wasn't even paying attention to the sign. I should have looked first."

"It's fine!" Ashley replied, waving her off. "My husband has the kids. He's a teacher at the high school, so he doesn't work on Saturdays. He and the girls spent the day at his dad's farm."

"Still," Goldie replied, signing the receipt, "I promise to pay more attention next time."

"Come to the meeting," Ashley said. "We're having a vote on the Christmas parade. Last year, Delores Watkins insisted on making her cat baby Jesus in the Nativity scene, and he about took Mary's eye out."

"I've met Delores and her cat," Goldie said. "I can't imagine anyone liking him enough to gift him frankincense and myrrh."

"Might make him smell better," Ashley said with a laugh. "So you'll come? We could really use some fresh ideas. The old coots on the city council just keep doing the same thing every dang year, including my father-in-law."

"I'll try," Goldie replied. "I need to take these clothes home first and change."

"Pick something out and go change in the dressing room," Ashley replied. "You can follow me out. It just takes a minute or two to get there. Everything in this town just takes a minute or two to get there."

Goldie ran to the back and changed into the red sweatshirt, a pair of lined yoga pants, socks, and, seizing the opportunity, the yellow Muck Boots. They made her just a little bit taller, so she didn't look quite so short next to a gorgeous gazelle like Ashley.

By the time they emerged from the shop and were on their way to the high school gymnasium, where the meeting was being held, Goldie was thankful for her new clothes. It was even colder than it had been, and she wasn't quite sure that the heat in the Jeep worked very well.

The gym parking lot was packed. There were people walking in and out of the big double doors, smiling and greeting each other.

Ashley waved to a man with a military-style buzz cut sitting in one of the many rows of bleachers. He was sandwiched between two blond tweens who looked exactly like Ashley.

"Mom!" they said in unison when they saw her.

Ashley motioned for Goldie to follow her over to them. "Hey, babe," she said, leaning down to give the man a quick peck. "Cal, this is Dr. Goldie McKenzie." She raised an eyebrow at Cal, a gesture Goldie didn't quite understand.

Cal stood up and held out his hand. "Nice to meet ya," he said. "You don't look like a fancy Los Angeles vet to me." He leaned in and whispered, "That's a good thing around here. I see my wife got ya all fixed up."

"Oh my *God*," one of the girls said. "You're from L.A.?"

"Morgan!" Ashley exclaimed. "What have I told you about using the Lord's name in vain?"

"Sorry," Morgan mumbled. "But, *Mom*! She's from *L.A.*!"

Ashley laughed. "Dr. McKenzie, these are my daughters, Morgan and Kelsey."

"It's nice to meet you both," Goldie said, taking her cue from Ashley and sitting down beside her. "They look just like you, Ashley."

"Act like her, too," Cal replied.

Morgan and Kelsey both rolled their eyes, and Goldie had to stifle a chuckle. Just then, Mayor Rose walked up to the podium and tapped the microphone. It squelched, and the crowd collectively groaned.

"I heard you met my father a few weeks ago," Cal said. "Large Marge is his pride and joy. She is the most cantankerous horse this side of Wisconsin."

"She wasn't in a very good mood when I saw her," Goldie agreed. "Of course, if I had an abscess in my foot, I wouldn't be in a very good mood, either."

"My brother's kid did that," Cal said. "He thinks he's a farrier, but he's really just pretty stupid."

"Cal!" Ashley replied, using the same scolding tone she'd used with her daughter. "Be nice."

"I can be nice, or I can tell the truth," Cal said, shrugging. "But I can't do both."

Goldie laughed. She liked Ashley and Cal.

"Let's get started," Mayor Rose said, the mic finally adjusted. "We have some short business to discuss before we get to the parade. I know many of you have ideas, but please hold on to them for a few minutes."

Goldie sat there and listened to a heated conversation between the mayor and a man who looked more than a little bit like Tom Selleck about potholes, when her mind started to wander. She glanced around the crowded gym and caught Tiffany's eye from a few bleachers away.

She mouthed to Goldie, "What are you doing here?"

Goldie shrugged. She didn't know. It seemed like a good idea at the time, but she felt out of place. At least she looked like everyone else.

"We'll take a vote on the pothole issue at the next council

meeting," Mayor Rose said, interrupting Goldie's thoughts. "If you'd like to speak on it before the vote, please attend that meeting. Details will be forthcoming. Now"—he cleared his throat—"we need to discuss the matter of the Christmas parade. We've had several community members remind us not to use the same Saturday or time as any surrounding towns, which we will try to accommodate as we learn those dates and times. What we need to decide tonight is theme."

"Winter wonderland!" someone in the crowd shouted.

"No, you dummy! We did that two years ago!" someone else replied.

"Wait, wait," Mayor Rose said, holding out his hands. "If you want to speak, please stand up, and we'll get to you in a timely manner."

"I heard there isn't any prize money for winning floats this year!" one woman shouted, standing up. "The prize money goes down every year. Now there won't be *any*?"

"Lois, please," Mayor Rose replied. "Wait your turn!"

"Well?" Lois asked, placing her hands on her hips. "Is it true?"

Mayor Rose pulled out a white handkerchief from the breast pocket of his overalls and wiped it across his forehead. "First prize will be a fifty-dollar gift certificate to use at the chamber of commerce bake sale in the spring," he said.

"What a load of crap!" Lois replied, to cheers from the crowd. "How can businesses be expected to spend money on a decent float when there is no reward?"

"Nobody from any other town will enter their float and pay the fee if they aren't going to win anything," a man sitting beside Lois said. "Float entry fees pay for the damn potholes!"

Ashley turned to Goldie and whispered, "First prize for the winning float used to be five hundred dollars. Our Christmas parade was huge. Since the bypass was built, the parade keeps getting smaller and smaller. Bob said the town just doesn't have the money to pay that much for first prize anymore."

"We hope to have more money for next year," Mayor Rose continued.

"What about *this year*?" someone who was not Lois shouted. "Half of our businesses are dang near bankrupt, and you want us to—what?—spend money on a float and then eat some cookies?"

Goldie shifted in her seat and said to Ashley, "I heard you used to have a Christmas carnival. Why couldn't you try something like that again?"

"The city can't afford it," Ashley replied. "We can't even afford to give about fifty dollars for a dang float prize."

"But if everybody volunteered their time and worked together, it wouldn't cost the city all that much, would it?" Goldie asked. "It might be worth it if people showed up."

"I don't know if they'll go for it," Ashley said. She looked over at Goldie. "But maybe if someone like *you* suggested it, they'd listen."

"Why me?" Goldie asked.

"You're an outsider," Ashley said.

"Isn't that supposed to be a bad thing?"

Ashley shrugged. "I don't know. Let's find out." She stood up. "Mayor Rose!"

The mayor turned his weary eyes to his daughter-in-law. "Yes, Ashley, what do you have to contribute?"

"It's not me," Ashley said, reaching down and pulling Goldie up by the arm. "It's our new veterinarian, Dr. Goldie McKenzie. She has a really good suggestion!"

Goldie shook her head back and forth, even as she stood up. Everyone in the gymnasium, which had to be nearly everybody in Blue Dog Valley, was staring at her.

"Go on," Ashley said. "Tell them."

"Uh, well . . ." Goldie trailed off. She hadn't had time to fully form an idea yet. All she'd done was have a thought and tell Ashley about it. She looked over at Ashley, who smiled at her encouragingly. "I heard that Blue Dog Valley used to have a Christmas carnival every year."

"Yeah, a hundred years ago!" Lois shouted.

"That would make you a hundred and fifty!" someone behind Goldie shouted.

Goldie cleared her throat. "I know it was a long time ago, but why couldn't the community try it again? Instead of the city being in charge and bearing the burden of the cost, maybe the citizens of this town could come together."

"How are we going to do that?" Lois asked.

"Everybody has something they're good at," Goldie said. "Surely, you've got people who make arts and crafts who could have a booth set up. We've got people who are good with food and games. There are plenty of places to set up both inside and outside. Maybe even here in the gym?"

"I make popcorn balls," Lois replied, chewing on Goldie's suggestion. "Delores makes cat-hair Christmas ornaments." She jabbed her thumb at Delores, who was sitting a row ahead of her.

"Well, that's a start," Goldie said. "Anyway, it's just an idea."

"It's a good idea," Ashley said. "I think we could have the carnival during the day and end the night with the parade. I bet we could get some businesses from out of town to participate, too, if they thought they'd make money."

"If we charged a booth fee, a small one, that might get the money for the float prize," Goldie said. She was starting to feel a little buzz of excitement.

"I could rig up a hayride," one man sitting in the front row said. "That old tractor is just takin' up space, anyway, now that we ain't farmin' no more."

"Don't let Roger Dale drive it!" someone else hollered, and everyone began to laugh.

"I like these ideas," Mayor Rose said. "But it would be a lot of work to plan. It's already November."

"I'm sure Dr. McKenzie would help us, wouldn't you?" Ashley asked.

"Of course!" Goldie said enthusiastically.

"Mayor Rose is right. There isn't enough time," said a voice behind Goldie.

She didn't even have to turn around to know who it was—Cohen Gable.

"Now hold on," Mayor Rose said. "I didn't say there wasn't enough time. I said it wouldn't be easy."

"Having people in town for the parade is one thing," Cohen continued. "But are we sure we want a whole bunch of people setting up shop in our town for a whole day? We shouldn't have to compete with them for business."

There was a murmur of agreement throughout the gym, and Goldie finally turned and fixed her gaze on Cohen.

"Why would it need to be a competition?" she asked. "If we advertise well enough, people might come from all over the state to the carnival—Milwaukee isn't that far. People traveling could stop if they saw signage on the bypass."

"This isn't Los Angeles," Cohen said. "People don't just stop off here. Not anymore."

"I don't see why that couldn't change," Goldie replied.

"You haven't been here long enough to see much," Cohen said. "There's a reason we stopped having the carnival, and most of us who are *from here* know that."

Goldie put her hands on her hips. She couldn't figure him out. He'd been so pleasant the night before, and now here he was, standing up in front of the whole town and insulting her.

"You're right, *Mr. Gable*," Goldie said. "I haven't been here very long. But it's pretty obvious to me that this town is full of wonderful people who care about their town and want to see it thrive. My only real question is, why don't you?"

Cohen's jaw flexed, and his eyes darkened. Goldie realized she might've taken it a step too far, but she was too angry to apologize. For the life of her, she couldn't figure out why he seemed to dislike her. Her idea was good. He had to know it was good. Even Tiffany had given her a thumbs-up.

Before Cohen could reply, Mayor Rose spoke up. "Now, Dr. McKenzie, I think you've got yourself a fine idea here, and, Cohen, we all know how much you love this town. We can all work together, don't you think?"

"Of course," Goldie said.

At the same time Cohen said, "I've said my piece." He sat back down.

"Wonderful," Mayor Rose replied. "The city council will have a chat about it tonight after the meeting, and we can put it to a town vote."

"We don't need a vote!" Lois said. She'd been standing up the whole time. "This carnival is a fine idea."

"Even so," Mayor Rose said, wiping his forehead again, "we'll put it to a town vote." He put the handkerchief back into his pocket and then pulled out a pocket watch. "It's time to git, folks. They're callin' for sleet tonight."

And with that, to Goldie's surprise, the meeting was over. Everyone began to get up and filter out of the gymnasium. Goldie followed Ashley and Cal into the gym lobby.

"Thanks for inviting me," Goldie said to Ashley. "Do you really think the town will go for a Christmas carnival?"

"I don't see why not," Ashley said. "I think people are pretty much willing to try anything to get some traffic our way. Christmas used to be such a festive time for the valley, and over the last few years, it's just been more sad than anything else."

"It's a good idea," Cal said, herding his girls farther out of the gym while they tried to talk to a few of their friends. "I think nearly everyone will support it."

"Cohen will come around," Ashley continued. "He's just a stick in the mud."

"He doesn't like me very much," Goldie replied. "I'm not sure why. I haven't put bees in his shower or anything."

"Now, I wouldn't say I don't like you." Cohen appeared in front of them. "I just disagree with you."

"You could have disagreed with me in private," Goldie replied.

"I'm trying to run a business here, and I need any support I can get from the town."

"This town isn't responsible for making your business work," Cohen replied. "And it's not your business. It's Doc's business. You're just filling in."

"Oh, is that what he told you?"

"That's what he told me."

"Hey, Cohen," Ashley said, cutting into the conversation. "What are you doing here? You never come to these things."

"Dad asked me to come," Cohen replied. "He couldn't make it, because he's got some business in Milwaukee, so I had to be here to report back to him."

"Business?"

Cohen sighed. "You know what I mean."

Goldie, however, had no clue what he meant.

"How is your dad?" Ashley continued. "Staying out of trouble?"

"He's fine. You know, the usual amount of trouble. Same old Dad."

Ashley smiled, and Cohen smiled back. For a second, Goldie saw something pass between the two of them that she recognized but couldn't quite place, but it was familiar, whatever it was.

"We better get going," Cal said. "Our driveway will be a nightmare if we don't beat the sleet. It was nice to meet you, Dr. McKenzie." Then he turned to Cohen and nodded. "Cohen."

"Cal."

"Bye!" Goldie said, waving to them. "Well." She looked up at Cohen. "I guess I should be on my way, too."

Cohen didn't move out of her way immediately, and Goldie

stood there for a second, trying to decide if she should just go past him or attempt to make conversation.

"I see Ash got you looking like a local," Cohen said. "I was wondering how long it would take."

"You were wondering about my clothes?" Goldie asked. "That's weird."

One side of Cohen's face ticked up, and he shoved his hands down into the pockets of his jeans. "I don't think it's that weird."

"Goodbye, Cohen," Goldie said, stepping past him. "Watch out for potholes."

"Hey, now, you're not mad about that little debate in there, are you?" Cohen asked, following her out. "I just think you're wrong about it, that's all."

"You made that pretty clear already," Goldie replied. "And you looked pretty mad to me, especially while you were insulting me about not being from here."

"I wasn't trying to insult you," Cohen said. "I was just telling the truth. You haven't been here very long, and you aren't from here, and you're biting off more than you can chew."

Goldie turned around so fast, Cohen nearly knocked into her. "You don't know how much I can chew," she said. "You don't know anything about me at all."

"Can you come out to the farm and have a look at Alice for me in the morning?" Cohen asked, ignoring Goldie's reply. "She cut herself this morning on a piece of downed fencing. I patched her up, but I don't want it to get infected, especially with this weather."

"You're a farrier," Goldie replied.

"And you're a veterinarian," Cohen said. "Phew, glad we got that out of the way."

Goldie eyed him. "Okay," she said, finally. "What time?"

"I'll be up by five thirty," Cohen replied. "So any time after that is fine."

"I will not be up by five thirty," Goldie said. "I'll be there by nine."

"Not much of a morning person?"

"Right now," Goldie said, "I'm not much of a person-person. I've had about four hours of sleep."

"That explains your ridiculous idea about turning this town into a Hallmark movie for Christmas," Cohen said. "Lack of sleep."

"This town could never be the setting of a Hallmark movie," Goldie said, turning around to leave. "Not with you in it."

"For the record, I live outside the city limits," Cohen called after her.

"Great," Goldie replied, as she walked toward the Jeep and the first droplets of sleet began to hit her face. "When the vote passes, and Blue Dog Valley hosts its new and improved Christmas carnival, you can stay there."

Chapter 16

The first time Goldie hosted a Christmas celebration at the vet clinic in L.A., it had been wildly successful. Goldie sent out fancy invitations to all of their clients, and nearly everyone who'd been invited showed up; a couple of clients came and brought their pets. The next year, they did the same thing, and more people showed up, including the paparazzi, who hoped to get cute Christmas pictures of celebrities and their pets for their glossy covers. Eventually, the neighboring businesses got involved, and the celebration became one of Goldie's favorite nights of the year.

As it turned out, she was pretty good at organizing events. Sure, she'd never helped organize an event for an entire town, but Blue Dog Valley was small, and most of the residents, with the exception of Cohen, seemed eager to be involved. If the vote passed, and she was asked to help, it would be good for the clinic, too.

Goldie rolled over from her stomach onto her back, pulling the comforter up over her head. As she did so, she heard two disgruntled protests at the foot of the bed and sat up to see both Airport and Kevin staring back at her. She'd tried to get Kevin to leave when she'd gotten home earlier that evening, but he was having none of it, and Goldie couldn't bring herself to leave him out in the sleet. So she'd trudged back up to the clinic, grabbed a bag of dog food, and fed him alongside the cat. She was pretty sure he was never going to leave now.

Besides, he was keeping her feet warm.

She unplugged her phone from the charger and looked at it. It was still so early.

She could go back to sleep for another couple of hours if she wanted, but she'd been tossing and turning for at least an hour. Goldie knew there was no hope of any more sleep. She might as well get up, shower, and go over to Cohen's farm to take a look at Alice.

Goldie left the dog and cat in bed and got up, stretching. It occurred to her that it might be a good idea to start yoga again. She felt like it had been months since she'd done any kind of exercise, and she was starting to feel it. Instead of opening YouTube and doing some Yoga with Adrienne, she went to the bags she'd left on the kitchen table and pulled out a sweatshirt and another pair of lined yoga pants, taking them back to the bathroom with her as she went.

In her old apartment, she'd had a huge walk-in closet. It was one of the perks she dearly missed. Before she'd gone to bed every night, Goldie had pulled out the clothes she planned to wear the next day so that they were ready for her in the morning. It was an old habit from high school that she'd never quite been able to break, and it saved her at least an hour of indecision each day.

She'd not been doing a good job of staying organized since moving to Blue Dog Valley. At some point, she was going to have to hang up her clothes and do some laundry.

Taking a shower and getting dressed had been the easy part. Going outside in the cold and starting the Jeep took sheer willpower. It was at least above freezing, and none of the sleet from the previous night had stuck, which just made for a lot of mud and wet. Goldie wasn't yet a big fan of this Wisconsin weather. She wasn't sure that she would ever be.

Once the Jeep was at least warmer inside than it was outside, Goldie backed out of the yard, careful not to get herself stuck in the process. The Gable farm was less than two miles down the road.

She took a slight detour through town to scope out the area with fresh eyes—eyes that were now set on hosting a Christmas carnival. There seemed to be no lack of vacant buildings with "For Rent" signs posted inside. She hadn't noticed this before. It was clear, even to an outsider like her, that the town really had fallen on hard times. It made sense, at least a little, why the residents of the valley might be skeptical of an outsider, especially when outsiders had come in and built a road that bypassed the entire town. Still, she thought that, should the carnival go ahead, they could use the bypass to their advantage. If they posted signs along the highway, that would give them advertisement, and maybe they could even work something out so advertisements for the town stayed up year-round.

It couldn't hurt to try.

By the time Goldie got to the Gable farm, it was after seven

A.M., and the sky was beginning to light up just a little. She parked the Jeep a little way from the house, but she could tell that there weren't any lights on inside. Maybe Cohen hadn't been up as early as he said he would be.

She looked around for Alice, but she didn't see her. Just as she was about to get back into the Jeep to go home and wait until closer to nine, she saw a light coming out of the cracks of the barn door. As she crept closer, she could hear music. It sounded like *Una Mattina* by Ludovico Einaudi, and Goldie stood there, just outside the door, listening for a few seconds before she leaned forward and peered inside.

Cohen was there, his back to her, holding up glass bottles of a yellowish liquid to the light. Each time he set a bottle down, his hands moved along with the music. Every once in a while, Cohen would close his eyes and just listen, and as Goldie watched him, watched his chest rise and fall beneath his white T-shirt, it was all she could do not to reach out to him so that she could feel it, too, whatever it was that he was feeling.

She'd never seen anything so raw, so personal, and she knew without a doubt that she wasn't supposed to be there, shouldn't be bearing witness to this moment that was supposed to belong to him alone, and yet she couldn't make herself look away.

Peanut Butter, who must've been outside the barn sniffing around, found Goldie's feet. Goldie knelt and put out her hand, and the dog allowed her to rub her head. Goldie felt a sense of triumph that she'd managed to win Peanut Butter over and made a mental note to put this newfound friendship on display when she made her presence known to Cohen.

The song ended, and in the silence, Peanut Butter began to bark. Cohen turned around. Goldie, betrayed, tried to back away. Instead, she tripped over Peanut Butter and fell backward, right smack on both her ass and her dignity.

She was still sitting on the ground when Cohen came out to check on the commotion.

"Well," he said, reaching out a hand to help Goldie up. "What have we here."

"I think your dog is trying to kill me," Goldie said. She grudgingly took his hand. "I got here earlier than I thought, and I saw the light on in the barn . . ." She trailed off.

"So you were spying on me?" Cohen asked.

"No," Goldie said. "I wasn't spying on you. Not exactly." She followed him inside the barn. "Well, okay. Maybe I was spying on you a little, but I wasn't doing it on purpose."

"How exactly does one spy accidentally?" Cohen held up one of the glass bottles she'd seen him with earlier. "Here," he said. "Take a drink. It'll make you feel better."

Goldie allowed him to give her a drink and then another. It was delicious. "What is that?" she finally managed to say.

"It's cider," Cohen replied, setting the bottle down.

Cohen began to clean a machine that was directly in front of them. It was wooden, with two barrels and a large iron wheel with a handle on it.

"What is that?" Goldie asked after watching him for a few minutes.

"It's a cider press," Cohen replied. He pointed to the bottle Goldie was holding. "For making hard cider."

"Ooooh, so that's what you were doing."

"Yes, until I was rudely interrupted."

Goldie took another drink from the bottle and then set it down next to her. "I really am sorry."

"Do you like that one?" Cohen asked. "It's my newest batch."

"It's delicious," she said. "But I shouldn't drink any more. I haven't had anything to eat this morning."

Cohen stopped cleaning and went over to a table next to the cider press. He opened a plaid piece of fabric and pulled out a thick slice of bread and slathered it with honey. "Here," he said.

Goldie had to force herself not to devour it. "Is this how you spend every morning?" she asked, her mouth half full.

"Mostly," Cohen said. "Once I'm finished with the morning's chores, I head to the barn and stay here for an hour or two."

"I don't ever want to leave here," Goldie replied, polishing off the last of the bread.

Cohen chuckled. "It gets pretty damn cold at night once I turn off the heaters."

"It's too late to change my mind," Goldie said, grinning. "I'm going to fall down outside your barn every morning, just so I can eat and drink and . . ." She trailed off, because what she almost said was *watch you*.

"That's not fair," Cohen said. "My barn never did anything to you."

Goldie sighed and stood up. Her ass still hurt. "I guess I do need to see about Alice."

"I almost forgot," Cohen replied. He wiped his hands off on his jeans. "Listen, I'd really appreciate it if you didn't tell anyone about this."

"About the cider or the Einaudi?" Goldie handed him what was left of the bottle of cider.

"Both," Cohen said. "Mostly about the cider. Not everyone knows about my . . . project. I'd prefer to keep it that way."

"No problem," Goldie replied. "Your secret is safe with me."

A wave of relief passed over Cohen's face. "Thank you."

"I don't know why you don't want people to know, though," Goldie continued. "It's really good. Incredible, actually."

"I just don't want people in my business," Cohen said. "It's no-body's business but my own."

"I said I wouldn't tell," Goldie replied. "And I won't. You have my word. Now come on. Let's see about your alpaca."

They set out for the pasture, and Peanut Butter was on their heels as they walked.

"Traitor," Goldie whispered to her.

* * *

ALICE WAS GRAZING with the herd when they found her. Goldie could see, even from a distance, where she'd cut her leg.

"We're a pair, me and you," she said to her once they got closer. "We both seem to be clumsy."

Goldie bent down to inspect the leg while Cohen kept Alice still with a piece of apple. It wasn't a deep wound, but it was going to be hard to keep clean. She could see where Cohen had tried to keep it covered, and the gauze had already been torn off.

"It doesn't look infected to me," Goldie said, opening up her case and pulling out a cleaning solution. "But I'll start her on a round of antibiotics just in case."

"She won't keep a wrap on it," Cohen said, scratching Alice's head. "She kept pulling it off yesterday."

"I really think it'll be fine," Goldie replied. "I could glue it, but I don't think that will be necessary. Just try to keep it clean. I'll leave this antibacterial wash here with you. Maybe clean it again tonight."

"You hear that, Alice?" Cohen said. "I reckon you'll live."

Goldie packed up her travel kit and stood up. "Dr. Saltzman used to post pictures of Alice in a cape. He said she was a therapy alpaca." She laughed. "I'd never heard of anything like that, not even in L.A."

"In the summertime, I take her downtown and let the kids pet her," Cohen said. "Once in a while we go to the nursing home a few towns over. Mayor Rose gave her the key to the city a few years ago."

"She's quite accomplished."

Cohen nodded, beaming. "She's a good girl. Her personality is different than most of my other alpacas'. My dad and I think it's because she lived in the house with us at first, since she was so sick."

Goldie reached up to give Alice a scratch, and Alice leaned into her. "I think she'd be a real draw to the Christmas carnival," she said. "Maybe she could wear one of her capes."

"If there was going to *be* a Christmas carnival, I might agree with you," Cohen said.

"You don't think the town will vote for it?" Goldie asked, following Cohen away from Alice and toward the house.

"Not if they know what's good for 'em."

Goldie trudged behind him, her feet occasionally sticking in the thick mud from the previous night's rain. "I don't understand why you're so against this," she said. "What does it even matter to you? It's a good idea. It would be good for the town."

"You've been here eighteen days," Cohen replied. "Don't lecture me about what's good for the town."

"You're keeping track of how many days I've lived here?" Goldie asked, grinning.

"I'm keeping track of how many days you've been a goddamn thorn in my side," Cohen grunted.

Goldie ran in front of him, jumping up onto the bottom porch step so that she was at eye level. "Well, I think it's probably time *somebody* is a thorn in your side," she said.

"And you think you're the person to do it?" Cohen asked. "I hate to break it to you, Dr. McKenzie, but better women have tried."

Goldie crossed her arms over her chest. "There is no woman better than me, Mr. Gable."

"Is that right?"

"That's right."

Cohen took a step closer to her, so close that they were nearly touching.

Goldie thought about taking a step back, or rather a step up, so that she could keep her distance, but she realized too late that she didn't want to, and before she could react or say anything else, Cohen reached out and lifted her up so that she was flush against him for a split second before he set her right back down onto the ground next to him.

"Send me a bill," he said to her, bounding up the porch steps two at a time. "Save your lecture for when the vote fails."

He didn't look back at her as he went inside, and Goldie was left there in the mud, bewildered, as he shut the door behind him.

Chapter 17

Goldie couldn't stop thinking about the way Cohen had picked her up off the porch steps. She knew she ought to be annoyed by it. It was clearly a show of brute strength, and Goldie really wasn't a fan of that kind of machismo. At least, she didn't think she was. She'd always preferred men who were, well, not timid, exactly, but she preferred men who didn't feel the need to show her all the time that they *were*, in fact, men. She knew Cohen was a man.

Yep, she knew it, all right.

But when he'd picked her up, all she could think about were his hands on her and the incredible disappointment she'd felt when he'd let go of her seconds later. She didn't like that, and she really didn't like the bruise on her rear end that hurt any time she tried to sit or wear pants.

She and Brandon had never had what anyone would have called chemistry. They didn't fight or make love with force. But they worked well together, at home and at work, and that was good enough. At least, it had been for a long time. She always thought there was something to be said for partnership, even if they weren't crazy about each other the same way other couples were. That kind of feeling couldn't last forever, anyway. Could it?

Goldie and Brandon made a nice-looking couple—she with her short, blond hair and big eyes, her open face, and him with his not-entirely-handsome but confident profile. Brandon was the kind of man who didn't have to prove how intelligent he was. People could see it written all over him. Goldie liked that. She felt happy most of the time, lucky even, to be with him. He'd taught her so much about veterinary medicine, about what it meant to be dedicated to his craft. She found it attractive, even if she wasn't necessarily attracted to him.

Alex often chided Goldie for her lack of confidence, but confidence wasn't the issue. Goldie knew she was smart. She knew that even if she wasn't beautiful, she was eye-catching. There was something about her demeanor that pulled people toward her. She had charm, and she'd usually gotten by with it. Now that it wasn't working in Blue Dog Valley, she'd been feeling more whiny than anything else, first complaining to Dr. Saltzman about how running the clinic hadn't come as easily as she thought it would, and then complaining to Tiffany when clients hadn't appeared in droves after she'd done virtually nothing to encourage them to trust her. She knew it was a bad habit, just expecting success. Maybe she'd relied on Brandon to be the steady hand for too long.

Still, that charm had counted for something most of her life, although she also knew she had a tendency to be reckless, to make decisions before she thought them out, to be headstrong, and she just didn't trust herself to be with someone she was head over heels in love with. She wanted to be with someone who made her feel secure.

"Why are you selling yourself short?" Alex asked, after Goldie and Brandon had been dating a few months. "You could do so much better than *him*."

"I like him," Goldie replied, searching for a way to explain herself so that Alex could understand. "He's got a good job, and he's—"

"He's got the same job as you!" Alex interrupted. "That's not a reason to be with someone, and you know it."

"Fine," Goldie said, leaning back onto Alex's couch. "Why don't you tell me what *is* a good reason to be with someone, and why don't you also tell me why you're the authority, seeing as how you don't even have a boyfriend right now."

"That was a low blow," Alex replied, getting up off the couch and walking into the kitchen. "Even for you."

Goldie sighed. Alex was right, not just because she was nearly always right, but it was also because Goldie knew Alex had terrible luck with men.

"I'm sorry," she said, following Alex into the kitchen. "I didn't mean it."

"I know," Alex said. "If I thought you meant it, I'd be mad, but I just don't get it, Goldie. Why Brandon? He's nothing special."

"Can't you just be happy for me?" Goldie asked. "Please?"

"Fine." Alex rolled her eyes. "But I can't promise I won't say that I told you so when this ends badly."

The one thing Goldie did know was that the moment she'd been free of him, she'd made the most reckless decision of her life— moving to Blue Dog Valley on a whim to escape her problems—

and now she was standing in her tiny cabin with a bruised ass, shivering because even though the heat in the house worked, she just wasn't used to the outside being quite so cold. She went to the shed and grabbed some of the firewood Doc mentioned in his letter and one of the starter logs she'd bought at the grocery store on her way home from Gable Farm, along with, she was a little ashamed to admit, a twenty-four pack of Coke. She'd also purchased a lighter, bags of dog and cat treats, a dog bed big enough for both Airport and Kevin, and enough food to feed a small army. It hadn't been the best idea to shop while she was hungry.

"Okay," she said, rubbing her hands together. "Let's try this one more time."

She grabbed the thick fireplace gloves that were sitting by the iron fire stoker and put them on. She'd watched no fewer than a dozen YouTube videos about how to start a fire in a fireplace and sworn the animals to secrecy that she had to resort to such methods.

Goldie cleaned the fireplace and checked to make sure the flue was open. After a couple of attempts, she got it, and she plopped down right in front of the fire in relief. Airport, who had been nuzzled next to Kevin, got up, stretched one of those strange cat stretches, and ambled over to Goldie, rubbing herself up against her human.

"Oh, so you haven't traded me in for a canine?" Goldie asked her, stroking her back. "I guess I'll have to keep feeding you, then."

Kevin, sensing he was missing out on something very important, got up and lumbered over to Goldie, positioning his large body on her other side. They sat there and watched the fire for a while, and Goldie felt a kernel of happiness begin to pop inside of her. They were, the three of them, a strange mix. Goldie, who was very much out of her element in the freezing Midwest; Airport, who'd been abandoned in an airport; and Kevin, quite possibly the worst sheepdog to have ever lived.

There were still quite a few things she'd yet to figure out about life, that was for sure, but in this moment, Goldie was warm, and she was loved, and that was, in her opinion, more than enough.

Chapter 18

There was going to be a vote in Blue Dog Valley, and Goldie knew for sure it was happening, because the phone at the clinic had been ringing off the hook since the announcement that the town would vote to decide if a Christmas carnival was going to take place, or if, as Delores described it, "the town was going to sink down into the depths of a hellish financial despair."

Goldie thought that might be overstating it a bit, but many townsfolk seemed to agree, and they were telling Goldie as much. Every single phone call was about whether or not Goldie *really* thought they could pull off a carnival and if she *really* thought it might bring more people to the town. There were also a staggering number of people willing to make pie.

Honestly, Goldie wasn't entirely sure if the carnival would help. It certainly wouldn't fix all of the valley's financial woes, but she thought it was a good start, regardless of what Cohen thought.

She told everyone it *would* help, though, and gave them her grand idea as she saw it—they could use several of the vacant buildings, with the owners' permission, for distinctly inside activities, such as crafts and food. If the weather permitted, they could use the town square for other activities, like the petting zoo idea she and Tiffany had been tossing around.

She'd been amused that Tuesday morning when she got to the clinic to find Alfie Gable waiting on her, his hands shoved deep into the pockets of his brown coveralls, his wind-burned face expectant.

"Good morning, Alfie," she said. "What brings you to the clinic so early? Is Alice okay? That scratch on her leg didn't look so bad, but I can prescribe something . . ."

"Oh, she's fine," Alfie said, waving her off. "She's doing just fine."

"Okay," Goldie replied. "Then what can I do for you?"

"Well," Alfie said, "I wanted to tell you I think this carnival idea of yours is a good one."

"It wasn't entirely my idea," Goldie confessed. "It was Ashley's, mostly."

"I've known her all her life," Alfie said. "That doesn't surprise me."

Goldie smiled. She wasn't sure what Alfie wanted, but whatever it was, he didn't seem to be in a hurry to say it.

"I was wanting to tell you that I support the carnival," Alfie said again. "And I might have someone who could help with advertising."

"Oh!" Goldie exclaimed, just as Tiffany pulled in to the gravel driveway. "That would be wonderful. I mean, if the vote passes."

"Of course," Alfie said, with a wink. "If it passes."

"So who is your contact?"

"My stepson," Alfie replied, eyeballing Tiffany getting out of her car. "But see, the thing is, I'd appreciate it if you'd keep that to yourself for now. At least until I ask him."

Goldie tried not to look shocked. She had no idea Alfie had any children other than Cohen. Nobody in town had ever mentioned it, least of all Cohen. And if Alfie had a stepson, did that mean he had a wife somewhere that nobody ever talked about, either?

"Good morning," Tiffany said, walking up to the clinic doors where Goldie and Alfie stood. "You're out early, Alfie."

"Just thought I'd stop by on my way to the feed store and tell Dr. McKenzie here how much we appreciate her patchin' up Alice's leg the other day. She's practically healed."

"It wasn't anything at all," Goldie said.

"I best be on my way," Alfie said. He tipped his hat to the both of them. "I'm sure we'll talk soon, Doc."

"It was nice seeing you!" Goldie called after him.

Tiffany unlocked the door to the clinic. "What was that all about?" she asked.

"I guess he just wanted to thank me for helping Cohen out with Alice," Goldie said. She hoped her lie was convincing enough. At that moment, there was nothing she wanted to do more than ask Tiffany how in the hell Cohen had a stepbrother and nobody had mentioned it.

"Because of a damn cut?" Tiffany asked.

Goldie shrugged. "Cohen thought I should take a look at it, just in case it was worse than he thought."

"He's a farrier, and he's been workin' on a farm since he was a kid," Tiffany replied. "He's gonna know if the cut is bad enough to require a vet."

"I guess it was."

Tiffany fixed Goldie with a stare Goldie hadn't seen on a person since high school when she lied to her mother about spending all night in a chat room when she was supposed to be studying for a geometry test.

"What's really going on?" Tiffany asked.

"Nothing," Goldie replied. "I swear."

"Why is your neck red?"

"It's hot in here."

"My ass," Tiffany said. Then her face softened. "Ooooh, I understand now. Cohen and you have a little thing going on."

"We do not!" Goldie said a little *too* emphatically. "I don't even think we're friends. We certainly don't have a *thing*."

"Mmm-hmm."

"I swear!"

"You're swearing to a lot of things this morning," Tiffany said. "Besides, I wouldn't tell anyone if you did have a thing. Cohen is a good guy. He deserves some happiness with a woman."

Goldie checked to see if the message light was blinking on the office phone, and then said, as casually as she could, "So has Cohen ever been married before?"

"Lord, no," Tiffany said. "As far as I know, he's only ever had one serious girlfriend his whole life."

"Who was that?"

For a moment, it seemed as if Tiffany wasn't going to respond. Then she sighed in resignation and replied, "Ashley."

"Ashley Rose?" Goldie asked. "As in the Ashley who owns the Horse Trader and is the mayor's daughter-in-law?"

"The one and only," Tiffany said.

"That explains the weird way they were looking at each other at the town meeting," Goldie mumbled, more to herself than to Tiffany.

"It's a shame it didn't work out," Tiffany said. "But she's happy with that Rose boy, and they have two adorable girls. They're happy, which is more than I can say for Cohen."

Goldie's mouth felt very dry all of a sudden. "Is he unhappy because they broke up?"

"If he is, he needs to go to therapy," Tiffany said. "They were just kids. Cohen was in college. It was other stuff, and that other stuff is what caused the breakup. It isn't just Ashley."

"What other stuff?" Goldie asked.

"Now you're asking too many questions," Tiffany replied.

"You gave me the third degree about a sick alpaca," Goldie said.

"That was a work question," Tiffany said.

"It was not."

"Speaking of work," Tiffany began. "Let's close up early this evening so we can go vote."

"I don't think I can vote," Goldie said. "I don't technically live here."

"Well, you can go with me to vote," Tiffany replied. "People are expecting to see you there."

"Why?"

"This whole thing was your idea!" Tiffany said, exasperated.

"It was not," Goldie said. "This was Ashley's idea."

"Well," Tiffany said. "Everyone thinks it was your idea, and if they see you there, they're more likely to vote yes."

"Okay," Goldie said.

"This could be really good for the town," Tiffany continued. "Maybe it'll even bring some music back to the Beaver."

Goldie wanted to giggle at "the Beaver," but she didn't. Tiffany was right. It could help the town, and she did want to be a part of that. Even if it didn't work out at the clinic and she was back in L.A. by January, she still wanted to help.

"I hope it passes and it does help," Goldie said. "I also hope that we can pull it off in less than two months."

"Don't worry," Tiffany said. "I already told Mayor Rose that you and I would be on the planning committee. We can't chance it being handed over to Delores or Brian or . . . both of them."

"You told the mayor we'd be on a committee for an event that hasn't even been approved yet?" Goldie asked. "And you didn't ask me?"

"Did I need to ask you?"

"Nope," Goldie said. "I would have volunteered."

"That is," Tiffany replied with a wry smile, "exactly what I thought."

Chapter 19

Goldie was surprised to see so many people filing into city hall to vote on the measure to hold the Christmas carnival. Tiffany had to park on the street, because the parking lot was already full.

"I told you people were excited to vote," Tiffany said. "Mayor Rose said they've been comin' in steady all day."

"When did you talk to the mayor?" Goldie asked.

"He called while you were down at the cabin for lunch," Tiffany replied. "I forgot to tell you."

"Is everything okay with Marge?"

"She's good," Tiffany said. "In fact, that's why he was calling. He wanted to tell you thank you for doing such a good job. Actually, what he said was, 'Tell that girl she's a keeper for puttin' up with Marge and Cohen at the same time.'"

As they approached city hall, Goldie saw Delores sitting in a lawn chair and holding a handmade sign that read, quite simply, "VOTE YES!"

"Hey, Delores," Goldie said, when Delores noticed her.

"I'm one hundred feet from the entrance!" she yelled. "I'm following Wisconsin law! I checked!"

"I wasn't even going to mention it," Goldie replied. "Besides," she continued, leaning in conspiratorially, "I'm not a voter, anyway, so you can't electioneer me."

"Everyone has voted yes," Delores said. "I've asked."

"I don't think you can do that," Tiffany said.

"You sound like the mayor," Delores replied, rolling her eyes. "Go vote, and when I ask you how you voted, you better say yes."

"Yes, ma'am," Tiffany said, pulling Goldie inside with her. "When she gets arrested later," Tiffany whispered to Goldie, "we want to be as far away from her as possible."

Goldie waited at the front while Tiffany went behind a white-and-red-striped curtain to vote. She recognized a few people from the bar and the town meeting, and there were a few friendly smiles and waves from people who'd come to decorate the cabin.

Mayor Rose sat officiously at a large folding table with paper ballots, along with two older women Goldie thought she'd seen sitting up at the front of the town meeting. Another two women were standing at the far end of the building, handing out paper cups of hot chocolate and napkins full of sandwich cookies.

"Let's go get some hot chocolate," Tiffany said when she emerged from around the curtain a few minutes later. "Voting makes ya thirsty."

They'd no sooner gotten their hot chocolate when they heard elevated voices coming from outside.

"What's going on out there?" Goldie asked a man wearing a large cowboy hat who was blocking the exit. "Are people fighting?"

The man turned around. "They're about to be, Doc."

Goldie didn't have time to enjoy the fact that a man she didn't even know had called her "Doc," because as she and Tiffany edged around him and outside, she realized that at least half of the screaming was coming from Delores.

She was standing up, hands on her hips, shouting at a woman in front of her, who Goldie realized, as they got closer, looked an awful lot like Delores herself.

"Oh no," Tiffany said. "Oh. No."

"What?" Goldie asked. "What is it?"

"Come help me break them up," Tiffany said, ignoring Goldie's question. "Or Delores really will get arrested."

Goldie hurried along behind Tiffany while a crowd formed, seemingly out of thin air, around them.

"Get outta my face, you old *hag*!" Delores was shrieking. "I'm a hundred yards away! *I am one hundred yards away!*"

"That's not nearly far enough!" the other woman yelled back. "And your sign is stupid!"

Delores bent down and picked up her sign, advancing on the other woman. "How would you like me to shove my stupid sign right up your ass?!"

"I'd like to see you try it!"

Tiffany ran around to one side of Delores, and reached out her hands, blocking an incoming blow to the other woman with her palms.

"Delores," Tiffany said, after the sign had bounced out of Delores's hands and landed safely on the ground. "Go sit back down and take a few deep breaths before the mayor sees you and calls the sheriff."

"That old bastard isn't going to bother us," the other woman said. And then to Goldie's utter amazement, the woman spat on the ground what looked like an absolutely huge wad of tobacco.

"And, *Maxine*," Tiffany said, a sharp warning in her voice, "what are you doing here?"

"I'm doin' what everybody else is doin'," Maxine replied. "I'm votin'."

"You better vote yes!" Delores shot back.

"I was gonna, but now I won't, just to spite *you*!"

Delores began to advance again, but this time, Goldie flanked her other side. "Come on, Delores," Goldie said, gently taking her arm. "Let's go get some hot chocolate and cookies. It's so cold out here."

"No!" Maxine said. "*I'm* going inside."

"Maxine," Tiffany said again. "You promised after the last time, you wouldn't come within ten feet of your sister. Remember?"

Goldie wondered what had happened the last time. These women had to be nearly eighty. What on earth could they have been arguing about that would make them come to blows? Knitting? Pie baking?

"What are you, my mother?" Maxine asked. "I used to wipe your ass when you were a baby. You can't tell me what to do."

Tiffany fixed Maxine with the meanest look Goldie had ever seen in her entire life.

"Who do you think will be wiping your ass in a few years?" Tiffany asked, her teeth clenched. "Take a walk, Maxine."

"Fine," Maxine said. "But when I come back, she better be gone!"

"I'll leave when my Lord and Savior takes me!" Delores called after her.

To Maxine's credit, she did not turn around to respond.

"That's your sister?" Goldie asked Delores, once Maxine was out of sight. "Like, your actual sister?"

"Older by two years," Delores replied. "And she's never let me forget it."

Chapter 20

Despite the upheaval outside city hall, the vote to host a Christmas carnival in Blue Dog Valley was successful, and Goldie and Tiffany had both made good on Tiffany's promise to Mayor Rose to help organize the event.

"I cannot believe I got myself into this," Tiffany said on Friday, as she pored over a map of the downtown area of the valley. "I don't know where we're going to put everything. We've got at least fifteen vendors from other towns coming in."

"There are several empty buildings downtown," Goldie said. "Maybe we could use those."

Tiffany looked over at her. "You know who owns all those buildings, right?"

Goldie shook her head. "How would I know?"

"I guess you wouldn't," Tiffany admitted.

"So who owns them?" Goldie asked. "Surely, if it's someone local, they'll jump at the chance to help out the town, especially if the carnival ends up getting those buildings rented."

"Mrs. Lucretia Duvall owns them," Tiffany said. She looked at Goldie as if that answer should provide all the information Goldie needed.

"Okay . . ." Goldie replied. "So let's ask her."

"*You* can ask her," Tiffany said. "I'm not asking that old witch anything."

"You drop a house on her sister or something?" Goldie asked.

"Ha-ha-ha," Tiffany replied. "*No*, but I'm not gonna go inviting that woman's criticism, either."

"Well," Goldie replied, "I can't believe there is someone in this town who intimidates you, Tiffany."

"That isn't gonna work on me," Tiffany said. "You can't trick me into talking to her. If you want to go asking her for favors, you'll need to head on up to Hill House. She's there. Been there since she was born, I reckon."

"Where is that?" Goldie asked.

"Take Main Street all the way out of town and up the hill," Tiffany said. "It's a giant blue house. You can't miss it."

"Fine," Goldie said. "I'll ask her. No big deal."

"In other news, Cohen Gable agreed to bring Alice to the petting zoo," Tiffany said, changing the subject. She raised her eyebrow. "All Roger Dale had to do was tell him how much you would appreciate it if he helped out."

"I doubt that very much," Goldie replied. "The last time I spoke to him, he told me in no uncertain terms that he thought the carnival was a bad idea."

"Well, maybe he's had a change of heart," Tiffany said, shrugging. "He and his dad are going to rent a heated tent for a few of the animals."

Goldie stood up straight and crossed her arms across her chest. "I do not understand him," she said. "Why all the hassle over the carnival if he was just going to jump in with both feet?"

"That's just Cohen's way," Tiffany replied. "He always makes a fuss."

"Why?"

Tiffany folded the map up and then turned her attention back to Goldie. "He's had some hardships, Goldie," she said. "It ain't my place to tell 'em, but he's had 'em."

Goldie considered telling Tiffany about her conversation with Alfie, but she didn't want to betray his trust. She didn't want to betray anyone's trust, but she hadn't heard anything from Alfie since their conversation, and she wasn't sure if she could count on the advertisement he'd mentioned. Maybe she should call him.

Just then the doorbell jingled, and a woman and a little boy walked through the door, the boy holding something wrapped in a blue towel.

"Hi," Goldie said, trying not to frown at the towel. Things wrapped in towels were never a very good sign. "What have you got there?"

"P-P-Patrick," the little boy said, stuttering through tears.

"And who is Patrick?" Goldie asked, looking to the woman standing beside him.

"His guinea pig," the woman replied. "He's not acting right. He won't eat."

"Okay," Goldie said, reaching out for the blue towel. "Let's go take a look at him."

The little boy held back, afraid to hand his friend over to Goldie.

"It's okay, Colin," the woman said. "Let the nice lady have a look at him."

Goldie knelt down a bit and said to the little boy, "I'm a veterinarian. Do you know what that is?"

The little boy nodded his head yes.

"Then you know it's my job to help Patrick," Goldie continued. "But I need to look at him to help him."

Reluctantly, Colin handed Patrick over to Goldie.

"Would you and your—" Goldie began.

"Grandma," the woman interjected.

"Would you and your grandma like to come back to the exam room with him?" Goldie finished.

Colin nodded again, and the two followed Goldie back into the exam room, where Tiffany was already setting up.

"Hey, Zelda. Hey, Colin," Tiffany said to them. "Is Mr. Patrick not feeling well today?"

"He's sick," Colin replied. "He could die."

"Oh, well, we'll try to make sure that he doesn't," Tiffany replied. She glanced worriedly over at Goldie, who was unfolding the towel to reveal a very lethargic guinea pig.

"How long has he been like this?" Goldie asked.

Zelda shrugged. "I don't know," she said, somewhat sheepish. "Colin keeps the dang thing in his room. I really don't pay much attention unless it's time to change his cage."

"Has he had diarrhea?" Goldie asked Colin. "I know it's yucky to talk about, but I need to know."

"Yes," Colin said. "A little."

"We thought that was because we changed his food a little,"

Zelda replied. "That's happened once or twice before. I didn't think anything of it."

"That's okay," Goldie said. "Sometimes it's hard to tell if they're really sick or if they've just got an upset tummy." She smiled encouragingly at Colin. "What's important is that you brought him in today."

Goldie checked the little creature over, noting his rough coat and slightly swollen feet.

"Is he going to die?" Patrick asked after a few minutes.

Goldie looked over at him and smiled. "Not today," she said. "But your guinea pig does have scurvy."

Zelda screwed up her face. "Scurvy? How in the hell did our guinea pig get scurvy? Isn't that the thing sailors get?"

"What's scurvy?" Colin asked.

"It's really just a fancy word for a vitamin C deficiency," Goldie explained. "See, guinea pigs are a little bit like people—their bodies don't make their own vitamin C, so it's important for them to have it in their diets, just like it is for us."

"Well, I'll be damned," Zelda replied. "Can you fix it?"

"I can," Goldie replied. "I'll give him a shot of the vitamin today, and I'll send you home with some liquid vitamins, and Tiffany will tell you how and when to administer them before you leave. He should feel better in a few days."

"Can he go home with us today?" Colin asked, already reaching out for Patrick.

"Absolutely," Goldie said. "Have you been giving him vitamin C tabs at home?"

"We didn't know we should be," Zelda replied. "We just got

him a few months ago, but he was fine when we brought him in to see Dr. Saltzman."

"The oral solution will be fine for now," Goldie said. "And then once that's gone, you can get vitamin C tabs from the local pet store, or you can come here to get them. It's also important for you to give Patrick some fruits and vegetables along with whatever else you're feeding him."

Colin held Patrick while Tiffany put a dropper into Patrick's mouth.

"I feel like a real dumbass," Zelda said. She pulled a cigarette out of her back pocket and went to light it before she realized where she was and stopped. "Sorry. It's been a stressful morning."

"Guinea pigs can be tricky," Goldie replied. "He's going to be all right, just as long as you remember the drops. Lots of people get these little guys and don't even notice that they're feeling poorly until it's too late. You both did the best thing you could have done by bringing him in."

With that, Zelda relaxed. "Good," she said. "Colin loves this thing, and I don't know what we would have done if something had happened. I never could have forgiven myself."

"Do we have any pamphlets on guinea pig care here?" Goldie asked Tiffany.

"I don't think so," Tiffany replied. She handed a bottle to Zelda. "But I can print something off this afternoon and run it by to you after work. Give him thirty-two milligrams a day. It shows how much right here on the dropper."

"Thanks, Tiff," Zelda replied, taking the dropper. "Thank you both."

"Would you like to take home a bandana for Patrick?" Goldie

asked Colin. "They're really for dogs, but we have some tiny ones that I think might fit him. You can pick the color."

Colin's eyes lit up. "Yes! Please!"

"What do you say?" Zelda asked him.

"Thank you!"

"Maybe if he's feeling better by the day of the Christmas carnival, Patrick can come to the petting zoo," Tiffany said. "We need more animals."

"He can wear his bandana," Goldie added.

"Everyone in town is awful excited about this carnival," Zelda replied. "My husband works over at the feed store, and he told me Mayor Rose came in asking for enough hay for three hayrides."

"Hayrides!" Tiffany exclaimed. "That's what I forgot! We need a route for the hayrides!"

"Pop said I could help him drive the tractor," Colin said. "But I bet he won't let Patrick drive."

"Well, his legs aren't long enough to reach the pedals," Zelda said. "Come to think of it, neither are yours."

"I can steer," Colin said, his tone very serious. "Pop's feet can reach the pedals."

"Wait'll we tell your pop that your guinea pig has scurvy," Zelda said, chuckling. "He's going to think we've both lost our damn minds!"

Chapter 21

Two things were clear from the look of Hill House when Goldie arrived at the top of the hill and at the giant iron gate that surrounded the house and the yard—Mrs. Lucretia Duvall was very, very rich, and she was also very, very old. The only thing that kept Hill House from looking like it had come straight out of a horror movie was that the grounds were immaculately kept. Still, there were a few signs that the once-grand house wasn't all that it used to be, like the way the gate squeaked—loudly—when Goldie opened it, and the way the porch steps were slightly soggy in the middle when she went up them. The brass door knocker was green with age, and the mailbox attached to the front of the house was hanging on by a single screw.

Goldie hesitated for just a second before knocking, and in that hesitation, the door swung open and a little woman appeared in the doorway, dwarfed by the sheer magnitude of the house.

This won't be so bad, Goldie thought to herself, taking in the woman. She looked like a sweet, old grandmother, not the wicked witch Tiffany had described, with her snow-white hair swept up into a bun and her floral housecoat.

"What do you want?" Lucretia asked sharply, shattering Goldie's daydream. "I'm not buying any Mary Kay or whatever it is you gals are selling these days."

"N-n-no," Goldie faltered. "No, I'm not selling Mary Kay."

Lucretia squinted—well, it was more of a glare—at Goldie. "Whatever it is, I don't want it."

"I'm not here to sell you anything," Goldie said, her words coming out in a rush as Lucretia attempted to shut the door in her face. "My name is Goldie McKenzie, and I'm the new veterinarian in town . . ."

"Who told you to come here?" Lucretia wanted to know. "I did what the city said I had to do—I keep my cat inside. He's not out there terrorizing the precious children. What more do you want?"

"I didn't even know you had a cat," Goldie said, surprised. "I'm not here about that."

"My patience is wearing thin, child. Out with it."

"We're having a carnival," Goldie said. "I mean, the town is."

"I'm a little old for acrobatic work," Lucretia said, the smallest hint of a smile playing on her thin lips.

"No," Goldie replied. "Uh, I mean, it's a Christmas carnival, and I heard you owned some of the empty buildings downtown, and I wondered if you might be willing to allow the town to use them."

For a moment, Goldie thought the old woman might shut the door in her face, but, instead, she took a step back and motioned for Goldie to come inside.

The inside of the house was clean, if a little dusty. Goldie followed Lucretia through the foyer and into a large sitting room where everything, absolutely everything, was covered in plastic.

Lucretia eased herself down into a flowered chair that was nearly too tall for her and motioned for Goldie to sit down on the matching floral couch.

Goldie sat with a slight crunch. From the corner of her eye, she saw a fat orange cat peering at her from behind Lucretia's chair. She averted her gaze when Lucretia cleared her throat and said, "So, what do you want with my buildings?"

"Well," Goldie said, swallowing. She'd be lying if she said the way that cat was looking at her didn't make her nervous. "You might have heard about the Christmas carnival that's being planned."

"I've heard a little," Lucretia said. "Didn't vote on it, but I heard about it."

"I'm kind of in charge."

"Kind of?" Lucretia asked. "Or are you in charge?"

"I am," Goldie said, straightening her spine. "And I noticed several buildings downtown are vacant. I asked Tiffany, my, uh, vet tech, about it, and she said they belonged to you."

Lucretia nodded. "They do."

"I thought maybe you might be willing to let us use them for the carnival," Goldie said. "For . . . free."

"And why exactly would I do that?"

"Civic duty?" Goldie tried.

Lucretia laughed. It was more like a cackle, and Goldie was reminded again of Tiffany's description of the old woman.

"It would really help the town," Goldie continued. "And it might help get those buildings rented eventually."

"Eventually," Lucretia echoed. "And why didn't Mayor Rose or anyone else from town come and ask. Why did they send you?"

"Nobody sent me," Goldie said. "I guess I just volunteered."

Lucretia leaned forward conspiratorially. "They're all afraid of me," she said. "Every last one of them."

"Why is that?" Goldie asked.

"Oh, I'm a witch, you know," Lucretia replied. "Or maybe just an outsider, which to them is close to the same thing, I guess. Makes sense they'd send another outsider to come and talk to me about it."

"Nobody sent . . ." Goldie paused. "Another outsider? What do you mean?"

"You're from California," Lucretia said. It wasn't a question. "I don't hear much anymore, but I hear some. I'm from New York. My husband brought me here in 1962, and Lord, I thought he'd brought me straight to the ends of the earth."

Now it was Goldie's turn to laugh. "I guess I thought pretty much the same thing when I got here," she said.

"And now?"

Goldie shrugged. "I don't know; I kind of like it."

The fat cat behind Lucretia slunk around the wooden legs of her chair and, in an act of athleticism Goldie found more than a little shocking for a cat with such girth, jumped up and landed squarely on Goldie's lap.

Goldie gasped, surprised at first and then all at once delighted. "Oh, hello," she cooed. "Aren't you handsome."

"That's Amos," Lucretia said, beaming. "He's such a good boy. He doesn't usually show it, though. Not to strangers."

Amos, sensing he was being discussed without his consent, turned around three times in Goldie's lap and promptly fell asleep.

"When was the last time Amos saw a vet?" Goldie asked, stroking the cat's head.

"He doesn't like car rides," Lucretia replied. "So we made a deal. I promised to never take him in the car, if he promises to kill every mouse he sees."

"He must see a lot of them," Goldie said.

"He could lose a few pounds," Lucretia admitted. "But he's a difficult cat to reason with."

"Most of them are," Goldie replied. "I tell you what. If you'll consent to letting us use your buildings during the carnival, I'll come out here for his veterinary care, so that Amos doesn't have to ride in the car anymore."

Lucretia opened her mouth to protest, but Goldie held up her hand.

"Free of charge," she finished.

Lucretia considered this.

"I'll agree to those terms," she said, finally. "On one condition."

"And what is that?" Goldie asked.

"You," Lucretia said, pointing a gnarled finger at her, "have to stay for tea."

Chapter 22

After a phone call to Tiffany to tell her about her success with Lucretia Duvall—and taking great satisfaction in Tiffany's astonished reaction—Goldie spent her time poring over maps of the town and calling vendors in other towns to ask them if they'd like to come to Blue Dog Valley for the carnival. Most of them expressed interest, but only a few agreed to come. So far, she'd gotten three food trucks, a woman who knitted Christmas stockings out of that thick, chunky wool that was all the rage, and two overzealous and out-of-work circus clowns. They'd promised to make balloon animals for the kids and paint faces, which Goldie thought sounded fun. She wasn't technically in charge of entertainment, but she didn't think anyone would mind a couple of extra clowns.

By the afternoon, she was overworked, starving, and out of groceries, so she decided to take a trip into town to grab something to eat at Ruby's. She liked that Ruby's was open seven days a week until ten P.M. Most places in the valley were closed on

Sundays entirely, and throughout the rest of the week, the town went dark by seven P.M.

But not Ruby's.

When she stood up, stretched, and began to look around for her coat, Kevin perked his ears up and watched her. He'd been with her in the living room all day while Airport napped in the bedroom by the heating vent on the floor. Kevin got too hot doing that, and so he nestled himself beside Goldie, and she fed him bits of leftover food. Now there was no food left, and he was clearly just as hungry as she was.

"Do you want to go with me?" Goldie asked him.

Kevin tilted his head.

"Go?" Goldie asked.

Kevin got up and shook himself, then trotted over to Goldie.

Goldie opened up the front door, and Kevin went out and scampered right over to the Jeep. Goldie wondered if Dr. Saltzman had ever taken Kevin for a ride, and she made a mental note to ask him about it the next time they spoke. She pulled the hatchback open, and Kevin jumped inside and barked at her until she shut it. She couldn't help but laugh at the image of the massive dog in the back of the Jeep. He sure was a sight.

The drive was quiet, minus Kevin's panting. The daylight was fading, but the weather was mild, so Goldie rolled down her window a little bit. She stuck her hand out and let the wind blow through her fingers.

There was no traffic. There were no honking horns, no angry motorists. No radios playing. There was nothing except the wide expanse of the Wisconsin countryside rolling out before her, and she wondered how she'd gone four decades of her life without knowing what this felt like, what it meant to actually hear quiet.

Ruby's, however, was fairly busy. There were at least a dozen cars in the parking lot, and Goldie noticed Cohen's red truck right off. She kept the window cracked for Kevin and promised him something yummy once she got back.

"Goldie!" Ruby said when she saw her. "We were just talking about you!"

"Was it good or bad?" Goldie asked. She saw Cohen at one end of the counter sitting on a bar stool.

"Good!" Ruby replied. "Cohen said Alice is going to be in the petting zoo, and I asked him how you managed to convince him to do it—ya know, seeing as how he was such a stick in the mud about the carnival."

"I never said I wouldn't participate," Cohen replied. "I just said I didn't think it was a good idea."

Ruby rolled her eyes. "So, anyway, what can I get ya?"

Goldie shrugged. "Uh, are you out of cinnamon rolls?"

"You can't eat cinnamon rolls for every meal," Ruby replied. "Well, you can, but I don't recommend it."

"Have the burger," Cohen said, getting up and walking over to where Goldie stood.

"Okay," Goldie said. "That sounds great, actually."

"Fries or onion rings?" Ruby asked.

Goldie screwed up her face and thought about it. "Can I have both?"

"Absolutely."

"Oooh, and a chocolate shake."

Ruby scribbled Goldie's order on a little blue pad, tore the page off, and stuck it onto the counter behind her for the cook. "It'll be about ten minutes."

"Okay," Goldie replied. "Are you sure I can't have a cinnamon roll?"

"Let me see what I can do, sugar," Ruby said with a wink.

Goldie turned when she felt Cohen staring at her. "What?" she asked.

"Nothing," Cohen replied, putting his hands up in the air. "I'm just impressed, that's all."

"With what?"

"Your order," Cohen said. "I wish I'd thought to order a cinnamon roll and a chocolate shake."

"I'm not sharing," Goldie said, smiling a little.

"Well, how about we share a booth instead?" Cohen asked, returning her smile.

Goldie wasn't expecting this, and she wasn't exactly sure how to respond. "I can't," she said, finally. "Kevin is in the Jeep. I don't want to leave him out there alone too long. It's freezing out."

"He's a sheepdog," Cohen replied, snorting. Then he turned to Ruby and said, "Ruby, holler at us when the food's done. We're going to eat outside. Throw in a plain burger for that mutt of Goldie's."

"We're going to what?" Goldie asked.

"It's a nice night," Cohen said. "We can sit on my tailgate and eat."

"Oh," Goldie said. "You can eat on a tailgate?"

Cohen eyed her. "Do you even know what a tailgate is, Dr. McKenzie?"

Goldie thought about it. "I think so."

"What is it?"

"If you already know what it is," Goldie said, "why should I have to tell you?"

Cohen laughed. "Okay, fine, city slicker. Come on."

Goldie followed Cohen outside to his truck. They walked around to the back, and he pulled the tailgate down.

"That's what I thought it was."

"Jump on up," Cohen said, patting the metal.

Goldie touched the metal of the tailgate and shuddered. "Why is everything so cold?"

Cohen rolled his eyes. "You're going to have to get used to this," he said. He opened the truck door and pulled out a brown Carhartt jacket. "Here," he said.

"What about Kevin?" she asked, taking the jacket.

"I'll go get him," Cohen said. "Is the Jeep unlocked?"

"Here," Goldie said, handing him the keys. "He's in the very back."

Cohen returned with a very excited Kevin at his heels. Cohen snapped his fingers, and Kevin jumped right up into the back of the pickup.

"I don't know where he learned to do that," Goldie said. "I didn't teach him, but he jumped right into the Jeep, too."

"It's innate for some dogs," Cohen replied. "Farm dogs, especially. I think they're born knowing how to load up."

Goldie gave Kevin's shaggy head a pat. "He's a pretty good boy."

"No wonder he stays," Cohen replied. "I don't think anyone has ever called him a good boy."

"Well, that's sad," Goldie said.

"Not for the world's worst sheepdog, it isn't."

"I don't think he identifies as a sheepdog."

"Well, whatever he is, he's yours now," Cohen said.

Ruby waved to Cohen from one of the diner windows, and he hopped off the tailgate and went inside to retrieve their food. A few minutes later, he returned with two chocolate shakes, two Styrofoam boxes, and two small paper sacks—one with a cinnamon roll for Goldie and one with a plain hamburger for Kevin.

The minute Kevin smelled the food, he began to nose around them, and he ate his hamburger in one bite. Goldie was both impressed and horrified.

"You shouldn't let him get used to that," Cohen said, taking a bite of his own hamburger. "He'll expect it every time you leave the cabin."

"Well, he's going to be sorely disappointed when his next trip is to the clinic to be neutered," Goldie replied.

"Sorry, buddy," Cohen said to Kevin.

Goldie dipped a giant onion ring into a blob of ketchup, took a bite, and audibly sighed. "I think this is the best food I've ever had in my entire life," she said, once she was finished chewing. "I don't blame Kevin for eating so fast."

"Ruby's has the best food in Wisconsin," Cohen agreed. "Maybe even the Midwest."

"Maybe the whole damn country," Goldie said.

They ate in silence for a little while, and Goldie wondered if she could spend every Sunday night with her feet dangling off the back of a pickup truck while she enjoyed a chocolate shake. There were a few movie drive-ins in L.A., but she'd never been to one, although she couldn't imagine any of them compared to Ruby's Diner.

"You know," Cohen said after a while, "I guess I have to give you some credit. You've acclimated well. Better than I thought you would the first night I met you."

"You'd already made up your mind about me before we met," Goldie reminded him, slapping his hand away from what was left of her french fries.

"You were talking to a cat."

"I'm a veterinarian," Goldie replied. "That's what we do."

"Let me rephrase that," Cohen said, managing to steal a fry and pop it into his mouth. "You were talking to a cat, and you were wearing heels that set you up a good six inches off the ground. You looked like you just stepped off a movie set."

"You've clearly not been to very many movie sets," Goldie said.

"I was wrong, all right?" Cohen said.

"Could you say that again, but louder and slower?" Goldie asked, grinning.

"Hold this," Cohen said, handing her his shake. Then he jumped up on the bed of the pickup truck and said, his hands outstretched, "I was wrong, oh Lord! Please forgive me!"

"Shut up!" Goldie said, laughing. She threw an onion ring up at him. "People are staring."

"Not until you accept my apology."

Kevin began to howl.

"Fine!" Goldie replied, as two teenage girls turned around from their positions on the diner steps to look at them. "I accept! You're forgiven!"

It was dark, and around them, people were beginning to finish their food and leave the diner. Goldie shivered in the chill of the evening, and she didn't even notice that Cohen had jumped out of the bed of the truck until he returned with a blanket and handed it to her.

"What's this for?" she asked.

"You looked cold," he said, simply. He sat back down next to her.

"Thanks," Goldie said. She spread it out over the both of them. "Do you always keep a blanket in your truck?"

Cohen nodded. "A blanket, a flashlight, and some water, just in case I get stuck out of town somewhere and can't get back for a while. I bet if you checked the back seat, you'd find the same thing in the Jeep."

"I hadn't even thought of that," Goldie replied.

"Okay, maybe you haven't totally acclimated."

"Hey," Goldie said. "I'm working on it."

"I guess Wisconsin would be a shock to the system, huh?" Cohen asked.

"A little," Goldie admitted.

"Which do you like better?" Cohen wanted to know. "L.A. or the valley?"

"That's not a fair question," Goldie replied. "I lived in Los Angeles pretty much my whole life. It's my home."

"I get that," Cohen replied. "But can you see the stars in Los Angeles?"

"Not really," Goldie said. "Not the ones in the sky. I don't know that I ever tried."

Cohen lay back onto the bed of the truck, his hands behind his head. "Well, you can see them here."

Goldie lay back beside him and looked up into the night

sky. There were stars everywhere. She couldn't believe she hadn't thought to look up at them before now. "They're lovely," she said, a little breathless.

"That one there," Cohen said, pointing up, "is Cassiopeia. And then that bigger one to the right is Cepheus."

Goldie looked over at him. He was staring straight up, lost in the sky. His dark hair was tousled slightly from the wind, and she had to squeeze her hands together to keep from reaching out and smoothing it, because she didn't want to disturb his quiet concentration.

Most of the time, when she was near Cohen, he was a force—a white heat that was barely contained by his body. It felt like at any time he might combust and burn her up. But right now, lying beside her in the bed of his pickup truck, Goldie felt him relax.

"I think I could stay here all night," Goldie said, not even realizing that as she spoke, she was inching toward him ever so slowly.

"We could," Cohen said. "Of course, we'd have a lot of explaining to do tomorrow morning when the breakfast crowd showed up."

"It might be worth it," Goldie replied.

From underneath the blanket, Cohen's hand found hers, and she unfurled her fingers and let him trace constellations in the palm of her hand as he pointed each one out to her.

Goldie wasn't really sure how long they stayed like that, but it was pitch black by the time they heard the screeching of tires off in the distance that pulled them out of their private moment and back into reality.

"What was that?" Goldie asked, sitting up. "Was there a wreck?"

Cohen untangled himself from her and hopped out of the bed of the pickup. There were headlights heading toward them at a frightening speed, and over the music blasting from the speakers, there was a *lot* of screaming.

Goldie thought the car was going to hit them, but it ground to a halt in front of the diner. The passenger-side door flew open, and a teenage girl shot out, her eyes wild.

"You're an asshole, Robbie Young!" she yelled. "I hate you!"

Robbie, who Goldie could only guess was the person driving the car, did not reply. Instead, as soon as the girl slammed the door closed, the car took off again, shooting like a bullet down the two-lane road.

The girl let out another string of curse words and then took off her shoe, throwing it in the direction of the car as it sped off.

Goldie got out of the truck, followed swiftly by Kevin, who was not at all happy about being woken from his slumber. He barked his annoyance first at Goldie, then at Cohen, and finally at the girl, who, as she got closer, Goldie recognized as Tiffany's eldest granddaughter.

"Kaitlyn?" Goldie asked, jogging up to her. "Are you all right?"

Kaitlyn turned to look at Goldie, her face stained with mascara and tears. "I'm fine," she spat, kicking at the ground with her shoe-less foot.

"You don't look fine."

Kaitlyn glared at Goldie, but her rage didn't last, and she instead dissolved into a puddle of tears.

"Shhhh," Goldie said. She reached out to Kaitlyn and pulled her to her shoulder. "It's going to be all right."

"What's Robbie done now?" Cohen asked.

After a few seconds, Kaitlyn looked up. "Well, he's drunker than a skunk for one thing," she said, sniffling. "And he's meaner than . . . well, I don't know what. But I hate him."

"What were you doing in the car with him?" Cohen asked.

"I didn't *know* he was drunk when he picked me up," Kaitlyn said. "He's had me locked in the car for the last hour."

"I'll call the sheriff," Cohen said. "It looked like Robbie was headed home, so I'll head out that way and see that he makes it without killing anyone."

"Don't call the sheriff," Kaitlyn said, alarmed. "My granny will kill me when she finds out."

"She'll kill Robbie first," Cohen replied. "Goldie, can you . . ."

"I've got it," Goldie said, waving him off. "Go on."

By this time, Ruby, who was the only one left at the diner besides the three of them, had come outside.

"What's all this noise?" she asked as Cohen drove off. "Kaitlyn, where did you come from?"

"Robbie Young's stupid Mustang," Kaitlyn muttered.

"I thought you were banned from being inside Robbie's Mustang," Ruby said.

Kaitlyn began to cry again.

"Okay," Ruby said with a sigh. "Come on in. I'll fix us some hot cocoa, and you can tell us all about it."

Goldie and Kaitlyn followed Ruby inside, and Kevin trailed after them. He waited patiently at the door while they went inside, and Goldie reached down and gave his head a scratch. "Good boy," she said.

Ruby switched the diner sign to CLOSED and turned off the front lights.

Kaitlyn slunk down onto one of the bar stools and buried her head in her arms.

Goldie, who was having trouble pulling herself out of the quiet loveliness of the evening and into what had just happened, sat down beside her.

"So," Goldie asked, "is this Robbie your boyfriend?"

Kaitlyn looked up at her. "No," she said. "Kind of. Maybe. I don't know."

"Robbie," Ruby said, setting down two mugs in front of Goldie and Kaitlyn, "is trouble."

"You sound like Granny," Kaitlyn replied, sniffling.

"But do I sound wrong?" Ruby asked.

"Sometimes he's real, real nice," Kaitlyn replied.

"He should be real nice all the time," Ruby said. "I know your granny taught you that."

Kaitlyn made a face. "She still loves my pop, and he cheated on her with half of this town."

"Is she still married to him?" Ruby asked.

"No."

"Well, then," Ruby said, "she ain't puttin' up with his shit. She might love him, but that's not the same thing as allowing a man to treat you bad."

Kaitlyn looked up at Ruby. "Is that why you're not married?"

"I guess," Ruby replied with a shrug. "It's more that I've just never found anyone I love enough to marry."

"What about you, Dr. McKenzie?" Kaitlyn asked, turning to Goldie. "Have you ever been married?"

"No," Goldie said. "I did come close once, but it didn't work out."

"Did he cheat on you with your sister?"

Goldie laughed. "No, but that's probably only because I don't have a sister."

"You're young," Ruby continued. "You've got plenty of time to find someone to marry, if that's what you want. There's no need to settle for someone like *Robbie Young*."

"I don't love Robbie," Kaitlyn said, wiping her eyes with the sleeve of her sweatshirt. "I'm not even sure I *like* him."

"That's okay," Ruby said. "Nobody does."

About that time, there was a loud knocking on the door of the diner, and they all three turned to see Tiffany standing outside. She did not look amused.

Ruby hurried over and unlocked the door, letting Tiffany inside just in time for Tiffany to say, "Kaitlyn, what in the *hell* were you thinking?"

Kaitlyn got up from her seat and ran over to her grandmother, embracing her as tightly as she could. Tiffany looked over Kaitlyn's head at Goldie and Ruby, a mix of confusion and amusement playing on her face.

"Don't ask me," Ruby said.

"I'm sorry, Granny," Kaitlyn said, pulling away from Tiffany. "I know I'm in trouble, but I'm really, really sorry."

Tiffany let out a breath she'd clearly been holding, all of the anger melting away from her. "We'll talk about it when we get home, sis," she said. "I'm just glad you're safe. I heard over the scanner Robbie was out for a joy ride, and I went to your room to check on you. You weren't there. I thought you were in the car with him until I ran into Cohen and the sheriff on the side of the road.

The sheriff was putting Robbie in handcuffs. That boy had nearly flipped his car trying to turn around when he saw the law coming. Cohen told me where you were."

"If his parents would stop buying him a car every time he crashes the old one, we'd all be a lot safer," Ruby said.

"Don't think his mama and I won't be having a talk at church next week," Tiffany replied. "If I talk to that woman anywhere but the house of the Lord, we might both end up in handcuffs like her son."

"Don't tell Mom," Kaitlyn said.

"I won't," Tiffany replied. "She'll think I can't handle you, but I learned my lesson with her. I'm locking you in your room until you're thirty-two."

"Right now, I'm okay with that," Kaitlyn said, half smiling.

"Thanks for keeping her safe for me," Tiffany said to Goldie and Ruby.

"Any time, Tiff," Ruby said.

"I'll see you tomorrow morning," Goldie said to Tiffany.

Tiffany waved at them and ushered Kaitlyn out of the diner.

"You want another cup?" Ruby asked Goldie, collecting what was left of Kaitlyn's mug of cocoa.

"No," Goldie replied. "Thanks, but I better get home. I'm sure the cat thinks Kevin and I are both dead."

"Yeah, it's pretty late," Ruby said. "What *were* you and Cohen doing out there for so long?" She raised an eyebrow.

"Looking at the stars," Goldie said. "Really, that's about it."

"Mmm-hmm," Ruby replied. "You know, Cohen is a good man. He's nothing like Roger Dale or that seventeen-year-old high school dropout Robbie, or even half of the men around here. Or anywhere, for that matter."

"I know," Goldie said. "I mean, I guess I don't know him very well, really."

Ruby leaned forward on the counter. "Well, I've never seen him spend hours outside with a woman lookin' at the stars," she said.

Goldie tried to hide her grin. "Well," she said, "I guess there's a first time for everything."

Chapter 23

"What do you mean you're having a Christmas carnival?" Alex asked Goldie on the phone that morning as Goldie rushed around to get herself ready for work. "Like, with clowns and stuff?"

"That's a circus," Goldie replied. She tried to smooth her hair down in the back to no avail. She desperately needed a haircut. "This is a carnival. You know, with crafts and games for the kids and stuff. And there's a parade at the end."

"Ooooh," Alex said. "Okay, I get it. But why are *you* having it?"

"I'm not having it," Goldie said, beginning to feel exasperated. "The town is having it, and I'm helping."

"I guess that means you're settling in," Alex said. "Does this mean you're never coming home?"

"It means I'm helping the town have a Christmas carnival," Goldie replied. "I haven't decided anything past January yet."

From her perch on the bed, Airport stared at Goldie. It was like the cat could read her mind. Goldie held her phone away from her face and said, "Stop looking at me like that!"

"What?" Alex asked.

"Not you," Goldie replied. "I was talking to . . . Oh, never mind. Anyway, I'm excited about it. You should be excited that I'm excited. That's what best friends are supposed to do."

Alex harrumphed. "Fine, fine. I'm excited for you . . . Is that better?"

"Not really," Goldie said. "You don't mean it."

"Take what you can get," Alex replied. There were some muffled whispers and a loud clanging noise, like metal on metal, and then Alex continued, "Oh shit. I gotta go. We'll talk later!"

"Okay. Bye!"

"Bye!"

Goldie set her phone down on the bed next to Airport, hoping that what she'd heard on the other end of the line wasn't anything too serious. Usually, with Alex, it wasn't. She had a habit of making everything sound more dramatic than it really was—like her insinuation that Goldie was *never coming home again*.

Of course, if all nights were like last night, maybe she wouldn't. Goldie wondered when she might see Cohen again, even though she told herself that what had happened the night before could have been more her imagination than anything else. They hadn't been on a date. They hadn't even kissed. Still, there had been *something*—something that neither of them was ready to admit, and if Goldie was being honest, it scared her just a little.

"I don't have time for this right now," Goldie said to Airport, who'd begun batting at Goldie's phone. "I have to go to work, and you . . . well, you have an entire day of sleeping ahead of you. We'll talk about it when I get home."

Airport looked up at Goldie, yawned, and then knocked Goldie's phone right off the bed.

* * *

THE INSIDE OF the clinic looked like a giant, concrete storage unit. Goldie couldn't quite figure out how so much *stuff* could fit inside, and she especially couldn't figure out why the entire town somehow believed that everything for the Christmas carnival ought to be stored there.

"The mayor did this," Tiffany said savagely, picking her way through a vast ocean of Christmas blow-up decorations. "It looks like a church rummage sale in here."

"Why would Mayor Rose tell people to drop things off here?" Goldie asked.

"Well," Tiffany said, "I might've mentioned to him that we had a storeroom in the back that wasn't being used. But I didn't think he'd tell the entire town to drop off their entire garages' worth of Christmas decorations."

"Oh, so this is your fault," Goldie replied. "That makes much more sense."

"What are we going to do with it all?" Tiffany asked, pained. "We can't see animals with all this shit in the way."

"Let's put what we can in the back room," Goldie replied. "We can store some in the cabin, and maybe we can find a place for what's left over."

"We can put it at Roger Dale's," Tiffany said. "He's got a whole trailer on his property that he's not using right now."

"Great," Goldie said. "Let's get started."

Just as Goldie picked up a giant, bedazzled Santa hat, the phone rang.

"I'll get it," Tiffany said, leaping over a box of what had to be Delores's cat-hair ornaments. "Hang on. I'm coming! I'm coming!"

Goldie, not knowing what to do with herself for the moment, sat down on the scrap of floor that was still showing and looked around, completely overwhelmed.

"Animal Hospital," Tiffany said. She picked off a ball of cat hair from her blue scrubs. "How can I—Oh, hey, Maxine."

"Maxine?" Goldie mouthed to Tiffany.

Tiffany waved her off. "What? How did that—Oh, okay. We'll be there in fifteen minutes." She hung up the phone.

"What?" Goldie asked. "What happened?"

"Maxine has a goat stuck in her kitchen," Tiffany said. "Those damn goats, I swear."

"Are we the people to call when there's a goat stuck in a kitchen?" Goldie asked. "I have to admit, that's not a problem I've ever encountered."

Tiffany grabbed her purse and car keys from the reception desk. "She said the goat cut its fore flank, and she's afraid to move it around too much, so we better get out there."

"Okay," Goldie said. "Let me go grab my kit . . . Is this the same Maxine that was screaming at Delores outside of the town hall? The kind of . . . crazy one?"

"Listen," Tiffany said, following Goldie back into the examination room. "Do not, under any circumstances, mention Delores."

"Why would I do that?" Goldie asked. "Do I look like I want to get stabbed today?"

"They hate each other," Tiffany continued. "I mean *hate*. They have for at least as long as I've been alive . . . maybe longer."

"Why?" Goldie asked.

Tiffany shrugged. "Nobody knows, really. And anybody who did know is probably dead by now."

"Nobody knows? Seriously?"

"Most people are probably too afraid to ask," Tiffany replied. "I know I am. They had a falling-out when they were really young, and they've hated each other ever since."

"Was it over a man or something?" Goldie asked, hating herself just a little for wondering. Surely there were other things sisters had to fight about, but at the moment, she couldn't really think of any.

"Neither one of them has ever been married," Tiffany said. "So I doubt it's that. But I guess it could be. Maxine is the town seamstress. She has been for as long as . . . well, I guess for as long as she and Delores have hated each other. She made every single one of my prom dresses. And Delores was an English teacher at the high school for years and years. Before that, she was a beauty queen. She was first runner-up for Miss Wisconsin in 1961."

"You know," Goldie replied, "I can kind of see that."

"You're the only one," Tiffany said, picking off another pile of cat hair. "We need to go. Do you have everything you need?"

"I think so," Goldie said. "I need to get some gauze from the back. I used it all up last time on Alice."

"Speaking of Cohen . . ." Tiffany began.

"I wasn't speaking of Cohen," Goldie said. "I was speaking of Alice."

"Same thing," Tiffany replied, ushering Goldie out the door. "Were you on a *date* with him the other night at Ruby's?"

"No," Goldie replied, willing herself not to blush. Damn her near-translucent skin. "We were just both there at the same time."

"In the bed of his pickup truck?"

"How did you know we were in the bed of his pickup truck?" Goldie asked.

"Kaitlyn told me," Tiffany said. "She's told everyone else in town, too. It's all anyone can talk about."

"For Christ's sake!" Goldie exclaimed. "We were not on a date. We just happened to be at Ruby's at the same time and got our food at the same time and then we sat together while we ate it."

"I don't think Christ approves of comingling in the bed of a pickup truck," Tiffany said. "Besides, that sounds an awful lot like a date to me."

"Are we leaving to help Maxine and her goat or not?" Goldie asked, standing in front of Tiffany's car, waiting for her to unlock the door. "You acted like this was an emergency, and now you're giving me the third degree about my non-date."

"Oh yes," Tiffany replied. "Yes. And remember, whatever you do, *do not* bring up Delores. Don't even *think* about Delores, because if you do, Maxine will know."

"Well, now that's *all* I'm going to think about!" Goldie said, throwing her hands up into the air. She closed the top of her travel kit and said, "Where does Maxine live? How far out of town?"

"She doesn't live on one of the farms," Tiffany replied. "She keeps those damn goats right in the middle of town. I bet half the valley has heard the commotion by now."

"Can you keep goats in town?" Goldie asked.

"City ordinance says you can have six."

"How many does Maxine have?"

Tiffany opened the car door, motioning for Goldie to get in. "Last time I counted, twenty-eight."

"Hang on a minute," Goldie said to Tiffany. "I think I'm going to need more gauze."

Chapter 24

When Tiffany said that Maxine lived in the middle of town, Goldie hadn't anticipated the woman *living right in the actual middle* of town. But when Tiffany pulled up to the two-story Victorian house, which had been painted bright purple, Goldie realized that it hadn't been hyperbole. She'd driven past that house quite a few times. How she missed all the goats, she wasn't sure.

The place looked like something right out of *Alice in Wonderland*, with its purple-painted wood and imposing black steepled roof. Its size and ornateness set it quite apart from the other, quainter houses surrounding it. A little woman stood on the porch waving her arms back and forth. Goldie again noticed immediately that she looked nearly identical to Delores. The only real difference was that Maxine had long, flowing hair that looked as if it hadn't been brushed since at least 1983.

And there were Tennessee fainting goats everywhere.

"Oh, thank the Lord," Maxine said when Goldie and Tiffany parked and got out of the car. "Edgar is just beside himself. He keeps fainting, poor thing."

"What happened?" Tiffany asked.

"Well, the girls were all being cantankerous today, and I had a rush order out of Milwaukee for a tutu, and I had to get it done. So I grabbed Edgar, and he was just fine while I was taking measurements, but after I'd finished and was putting it on him to see how it looked, he just freaked out," Maxine said, her words coming out close together and breathless. "He tried to get away from me, and when I tried to grab him, he got scared and ran right through the screen door. Took the whole thing with him for a few steps before he fainted."

"Where is he now?" Tiffany asked.

Goldie looked from Maxine to Tiffany. She was having trouble digesting the conversation, and she couldn't believe that Tiffany wasn't standing there with her mouth hanging open the way she was. A goat in a tutu? What was happening?

"He's out back," Maxine said, a sigh of defeat shuddering through her. "He's stuck in the door, and it looks like he's cut himself, and I don't know *what* to do."

"Let us take a look at him," Tiffany said, motioning for Goldie to follow.

Goldie gripped her travel kit and walked behind the two women to the backyard, where a goat was stumbling around with an entire screen door up around his neck and a hot-pink tutu around his middle.

"Explain to me why that goat is wearing a tutu," Goldie whispered to Tiffany.

"That's more surprising to you than the fact that he's wearing a damn door?" Tiffany replied.

"See?" Maxine said as they got closer. "Every time I try to get to him, he runs off, and I'm afraid he's going to hurt himself even more."

"We'll have to catch him to treat him," Goldie said. "Surely we can do that between the three of us."

Maxine turned to Goldie. "So you're the new doc everyone is talking about?"

"I guess," Goldie said, smiling at Maxine. "I'm Goldie McKenzie."

Maxine looked Goldie up and down and said, "You're just a little thing, ain't ya? Sure you can handle it?"

Goldie wasn't exactly sure what "it" was, and she wasn't entirely sure she could, in fact, handle "it" at all. She looked at Tiffany, who only shrugged. "Um, I'm sure I can."

"All right," Maxine replied. "Let's spread out and see if we can get him to come to one of us or faint trying."

"Wait a second," Goldie said, bending down and opening up her travel kit. "I brought a mild sedative. I figured it would help if we needed to get him out of—"

"A kitchen door," Tiffany finished.

Goldie pulled out the vial and the syringe and filled it with a small amount of the sedative. "Okay," she said. "Let's see if we can free Edgar."

The three women spread out on the back lawn and attempted to close in on Edgar. With the circle tightening, and Edgar admittedly not having much in the way of a line of sight, it looked for a moment as if he might actually faint.

Edgar faced Goldie, as Maxine and Tiffany closed in on him from either side. Edgar swung this way and that, letting out several displeased goat noises in the process.

"Why isn't he fainting?" Maxine asked.

"I don't know," Goldie called over to her. "Maybe he's all fainted out!"

"That doesn't sound very scientific!" Tiffany replied.

They all took a step closer to Edgar.

"I'm going to try to grab him," Maxine yelled.

"Wait!" Goldie said, but it was too late.

Edgar began to zigzag toward Goldie, head down, in a classic goat stance. There was no way for Goldie to avoid him now, and so she braced for impact.

Edgar knocked her over, and they both went crashing down onto the ground. The impact ripped the screen further, freeing Edgar and leaving the screen door right on top of Goldie.

Before Edgar could escape, however, Goldie reached up through the giant hole in the screen and stuck him with the needle.

"I got him!" she yelled, as Edgar, disoriented, wandered off.

Tiffany ran over and lifted the door off Goldie and helped her to her feet.

"He should start to relax in a few minutes," Goldie said to Maxine, catching her breath. "Then I can examine him for injuries."

Maxine stared at Goldie, and then she put her hands on her hips and replied, "Well, I'll be damned. You *could* handle it."

* * *

EDGAR HAD A small puncture wound in his flank, but it wasn't very deep, and it didn't require stitches. They carried the still-sleepy Edgar inside and laid him down on a blanket that Maxine spread out on the floor.

"He'll feel better when he wakes up," Goldie said. "Tiffany will bring by some medicine for him on her way home from work today."

"Stay for a minute and warm yourselves up," Maxine replied. "Sit down here at the table." She cleared a mess of tulle and sewing tools off the tabletop.

Goldie sat down. She was going to be very sore tomorrow; she could already feel it. She silently thanked every headstrong bulldog she'd ever come into contact with in Los Angeles for preparing her for that moment.

She looked around the house. It was surprisingly clean and orderly for a home that boasted so many goats. There was a faint and lingering smell of animals, but it wasn't as overwhelming as Goldie thought it would be in. In short, Maxine's house was quite lovely.

"You've got a beautiful home," Goldie said.

"You expected it to be a trash pit, didn't you?" Maxine asked. She laughed. "It's okay, everyone does, on account of the goats. But I've had goats for nearly forty years, and I've got my tricks."

"Mainly that they live outside," Tiffany replied. "Those little huts you saw on the adjoining lot are for the goats."

"Oh," Goldie said. "I didn't even notice them."

"My sister used to live next door before I bought the lot," Maxine replied, handing each of them a steaming mug. "Goats make better neighbors."

Tiffany looked at Goldie and raised an eyebrow.

"Drink up," Maxine ordered. "It'll warm you all the way through."

Goldie took a drink and nearly choked when she realized that the tea was laced with whisky. She hadn't been expecting it.

"It's all right," Maxine said, clapping Goldie on the back. "I should have warned ya. Tiff knows. It's my famous hot toddy."

Tiffany grinned at Goldie. "Whoops. Guess I forgot to mention it."

"So," Maxine said, sitting down at the table, "I guess this Christmas carnival nonsense is happening."

"We think it'll help put the town back on the map," Tiffany said. "It could be good for local businesses, Maxine. Including yours."

"Hmph," Maxine mumbled.

"What about the petting zoo?" Tiffany asked Maxine. "We've just got a few animals so far."

"That would be great," Goldie said. "Would you be interested in that?"

"Oh, and you could put them in a couple of tutus and sell your product," Tiffany said.

"So, you make tutus for goats," Goldie said. "Like, for them to wear?"

"I make 'em for all kinds of animals," Maxine replied. She stood up and walked to her windowsill, grabbed a small white card, and handed it to Goldie. "I have a website and everything."

"Is that a tiny picture of Edgar?" Goldie asked, looking at the card.

"He's my best model," Maxine said.

"So you'll do the petting zoo?" Tiffany asked. "Cohen is bringing Alice, and I've got a guy coming with a couple of miniature ponies."

"Hmm . . ." Maxine thought about it. "Who else is signed up to volunteer?"

Tiffany held out her hands and said, "I know what you're thinking, and I'm telling you right now that you won't have to worry about it. She'll be on the other side of downtown with her cat-hair Christmas ornaments."

"We could really use the help," Goldie added.

"All right," Maxine said, finally. "I'll do it."

"That's great!" Goldie replied. "Thank you so much."

"I heard you and Cohen Gable were gettin' awful cozy at Ruby's diner the other night," Maxine said to Goldie as the women got up to leave. "Heard you were all wrapped up with each other in the bed of his pickup."

Goldie tried to keep her face neutral, even though she could feel Tiffany staring at her from across the table. "Well," she said, "I'm not sure where you heard that, but—"

"Oh, don't try to deny it," Maxine said. She attempted to laugh, but it came out more like a cough. "I like you better for it. If it's not true, don't tell me. Cohen deserves a little happiness, doesn't he, Tiff? Doesn't matter if it's with an outsider."

"Okay," Goldie said, looking to Tiffany for help. "Thank you, I guess?"

"Just don't break his heart," Maxine said, pushing a finger in Goldie's face. "Edgar bites when he's not sedated."

Chapter 25

Tiffany and Goldie were halfway to the clinic before Goldie spoke. "What did Maxine mean when she said Cohen deserved happiness?"

"I don't have a clue. Lord only knows how many of those hot toddies she had before we got there," Tiffany said. "That's probably how Edgar ended up in a tutu in the first place."

"She seemed to be pretty swift on the uptake," Goldie replied. "And I think you know exactly what she meant."

"Everyone wants Cohen to be happy," Tiffany said. She wasn't looking at Goldie. "We care about each other here. I know that might be shocking to someone from the city . . ."

"Oh, give it a rest," Goldie said as they pulled back in to the clinic parking lot. "This has nothing to do with my understanding of small-town nuance. Why does it seem like everyone is protecting him for some reason?"

"It wasn't her place to even mention it," Tiffany replied. "What is it with old women and gossiping about relationships, anyway? My nana used to go to church on Sunday just so she'd have something to talk about for the rest of the week—rumors about who was dating who and who looked upset with who. I've never understood it."

"Am I going to have to go to the town library and look through old newspapers to find out what happened?" Goldie asked. "Because that's what they always do on detective shows, and I don't think I have the stamina for it."

"Do you like him?" Tiffany asked, turning to face Goldie. "I mean, do you really like him, or is this some fun fling for you while you're slumming it down here in the Midwest, because if it is, I don't want any part of it."

Goldie was hurt. She thought Tiffany knew her at least a little better than that. "I'm not slumming it," she said.

"I know," Tiffany replied. "I'm sorry. I didn't mean that."

"You know that morning that Alfie showed up here early, before we opened?" Goldie asked.

"Yeah, I still don't think you're telling me the truth about that," Tiffany said.

"Well, he wanted to talk to me about the carnival," Goldie replied. "He said he might have someone in Milwaukee to help with advertising, but he didn't want me to mention it to Cohen."

"Joshua," Tiffany said, her voice quiet.

"Who?" Goldie asked.

"Joshua," Tiffany said.

"Is that Alfie's stepson?"

Tiffany's eyes widened just a little. "How do you know about Joshua?"

"I don't," Goldie replied. "Alfie said he has a stepson in Milwaukee, but then you showed up, and he stopped talking about it. He never told me his name."

"It's Joshua," Tiffany said again. "God, I haven't seen Joshua in at least fifteen years."

"Why not?" Goldie asked.

Tiffany sighed, resigned. "Well, I guess it's not really a secret."

"What's not a secret?"

"Cohen's mama died when he was ten," Tiffany said. "It was ovarian cancer. Nobody even knew she was that sick. She hadn't wanted anyone to know. That's where Cohen gets it, you know, not wanting to talk to people about anything. Anyway, his mama died, and I imagine Alfie got real lonely after a couple of years, and there was Cohen, getting ready to be a teenager with no mama, so he took himself out a personal ad in the big Milwaukee newspaper, and a few months later, he came home with Angela and Joshua."

"Alfie got remarried?" Goldie asked.

"He did," Tiffany replied, a small, winsome smile playing on her lips. "Oh, she hated it here at first. She was a little like you—she had some trouble fitting in. But Joshua had been in some trouble in the city, and the valley was good for him. They both settled in after a while. Joshua was just about Cohen's age, and they seemed real close."

"What happened?" Goldie pushed. "Where is Angela now?"

"Everything was fine until the boys graduated from high school," Tiffany continued. "But then Cohen went off to college and Joshua didn't. He stayed in the valley and started getting into trouble again . . ." She trailed off. "There was a car wreck just outside of town, not far from Gable Farm. Angela died. Joshua, well, he didn't want to—couldn't—stay here. He took off back to Milwaukee to live with his aunt. I don't think he's ever been back. Honestly, Goldie, I didn't even know if Alfie kept in touch."

"That's awful," Goldie murmured. "How awful for all of them."

"It was awful," Tiffany agreed. "Cohen and Joshua are around the same age as my daughter, and I remember it was just . . . well, awful."

Goldie was silent then. She wasn't sure what it was she'd been envisioning as the mystery surrounding Cohen, but that sure hadn't been it. Part of her wished she hadn't asked about it at all. He'd lost two mothers. What kind of rotten luck delivers that kind of blow to a kid?

"Listen, Goldie," Tiffany said, taking Goldie's hand. "Please don't tell him you know. He'd be pissed if he knew I told you. I'm sure he thinks you'll treat him differently if you know, and it wasn't my place to tell you. He'll tell you when he's ready. I know he will."

"I won't," Goldie said, and she meant it. How would she even bring something like that up with him, anyway? No, it would be better if she kept it to herself. "I promise I won't say a word."

"Thanks," Tiffany said, finally shutting off the car's engine. "You know, Cohen still thinks the town doesn't know about his little cider business he's got. As if you can't see that cider press sitting in the barn from an acre away."

"Everyone knows about it?" Goldie asked.

"Absolutely everyone," Tiffany said. "Brian's got a big mouth. He told everyone two years ago. Cohen should have known better than to let Brian help him build that cider press."

"It is pretty good cider," Goldie admitted. "I wish he'd consider selling it."

"Oh, Dr. McKenzie," Tiffany replied. "You sure do have a lot to learn about Blue Dog Valley."

Chapter 26

As a child, Goldie had wanted a sibling. She'd wanted a sibling more than anything else in the world, and that's exactly what she asked for, for Christmas, when she was eight years old. She'd written a letter to Santa, and she'd told the mall Santa on a trip to visit her mother's friends in Santa Barbara. She couldn't see why this would be too much to ask. Surely Santa had the power to make her a sibling if he had the power to bring her a Barbie Dreamhouse the year before. Barbie houses had to be much more difficult for the elves to make, and there weren't nearly as many working parts on a human baby.

Goldie had lots of friends with siblings. Her mother's friend in Santa Barbara had twin daughters, and Goldie was jealous of them. They looked exactly like the *Sweet Valley High* twins on the cover of the books she'd seen in the "too old for her" section of the public library that her father took her to on the weekends. It seemed to Goldie that everyone had a brother or a sister but her.

She didn't ask her parents for a sibling, though. She'd over-heard them talking one night after she was supposed to be asleep. They'd been sitting in the living room, each drinking a glass of red wine.

They were editing an academic paper they'd written together for a medical journal, and her mother had said to her father, "I think Marigold is lonely in this house all alone without a brother or a sister to play with."

"I'm sure that's not true," her father had replied. "She has a great imagination."

Goldie had smiled at that. She did have a great imagination, even though it got her in trouble sometimes when that imagina-tion got away from her like it had the week before at school, when she and one of her friends had planned a party in the girls' bath-room during recess and charged everyone but their friends one dollar for entry. Her mother had been livid.

"I just wish we could have given her that," her mother said. "You're so close with your brothers, and I remember wishing I had a sister of my own when I was her age."

Goldie's father had looked up at her mother then and placed his pencil behind his ear like he always did when he was about to say something thoughtful. He reached out and took his wife's hand.

"I know," he said. "But we both know the risks better than anyone, and you nearly died having Marigold. I don't want to lose you."

"I don't want to lose me, either," Goldie's mother had said then, smiling a little. "It just makes me so sad sometimes."

Goldie had snuck back into her room and tried to understand what her parents meant. How had she nearly killed her mother? How could any baby kill their mother? She didn't know, but she didn't like to see her mother upset. That was when she decided to ask Santa for a sibling.

She was sure she'd wake up to a brother or sister, or maybe even both, on Christmas morning. She was even more sure when she rushed down the stairs on Christmas morning and saw a present underneath the tree that looked big enough for at least one baby.

She tore open the wrapping paper without waiting for either one of her parents to pour their coffee. Goldie was so excited that she prematurely cried out in delight, only to realize that she was holding in her hands not a flesh-and-blood baby, but a Kid Sister doll, a toy they advertised on television during every commercial break on Saturday mornings.

"What did Santa bring you, kiddo?" her father asked, bleary-eyed with sleep and holding a mug with both hands.

Goldie held up the doll, trying not to burst into tears, but it was no use. She threw the doll down at the base of the tree and ran back up the stairs to her room.

A few seconds later, there was a knock on her door and her mother came in, bewildered. "What's wrong?" her mother asked. "Don't you like your doll? I thought Santa did a good job this year."

Goldie sobbed into her pillow.

"Tell me what it is," her mother said.

"I wanted a *real* sister," Goldie managed to say through hiccups. "I asked Santa." She sat up and looked at her mother. "Was I bad?"

"Oh, honey." Her mother enveloped her in a hug. "Santa doesn't bring real babies for Christmas."

"Why not?"

"Because his elves make toys," she said. "Only a mommy and a daddy can make a baby."

"But you'll *die*!" Goldie said, dissolving into tears all over again. "Daddy . . . said . . . I . . . almost . . . killed . . . you."

Goldie's mother pulled her away from the hug and looked her in the eye. "I'm not going to die," she said. "But I am also not going to have any more babies. Your daddy and I have you, and you are more than enough for us."

"I wanted a real baby," Goldie said again.

"I know," her mother replied. "I wanted a brother or a sister, too, when I was your age. If I could give that to you, I would, but I can't. So we'll just have to be happy as a family of three, even though I know it will be hard sometimes."

There had been many times over the years when Goldie looked back on that memory and felt so much guilt for the way she'd made her mother feel that morning. She couldn't imagine how difficult it had been for her mother.

Once, home on break from college, Goldie had tried to apologize. The friend from Santa Barbara had just become a grandmother, and her mother was telling her how excited she was for her friend, how cute the baby was.

"I don't know if I want children," Goldie said.

"You should only have children if you want them," her mother replied. "It's very important that you know that. Being a woman does not mean you are obligated to also be a mother."

Goldie gave her mother a grateful smile. "Alex's mom says that being a mother is the most important job a woman can have, and Alex told her that passing biomedical science was the most important job she had."

"I like Alex," her mother replied, and then she laughed. "It's okay for her mom to feel that way. I always felt like being your mother was one of my most important jobs, but being a doctor was also an important job. I don't think I have to choose being your mother over being a doctor *or* being a doctor over being your mother."

"I know you wanted more kids," Goldie said haltingly. "And I'm sorry—"

"No," her mother said, cutting her off. "You don't need to be sorry for anything. Your father and I don't have any regrets about that. You are better than ten children."

Goldie felt lucky to have parents who loved her more than anything else in the world, and she was well aware of the fact that not every child had that kind of family growing up. It broke her heart to know that Cohen had suffered the loss of two mothers and clearly no longer had a good relationship with his stepbrother. She wondered what had happened between them.

There was a small part of her that hoped Alfie really would talk to Joshua and ask for his help. If Joshua had contacts in Milwaukee who could assist them with advertising, that might really make the carnival a success. She felt like if it wasn't successful, then she wouldn't be successful, either. The people in town were looking to her, and she was starting to feel the pressure. Goldie hoped that her involvement in the Christmas carnival would put her at least one step closer to acceptance. The community wanted to save their town, and Goldie was bound and determined to help them do it.

Chapter 27

Goldie and Tiffany had an agreement. Goldie would bring the coffee and cinnamon rolls in the mornings from Ruby's, and Tiffany wouldn't complain when Goldie was five minutes late for work. Tiffany liked opening up by herself, and Goldie liked Ruby's cinnamon rolls.

She also liked getting to know the morning crowd at the diner. Her favorites were two elderly men, Elvis and Jack, who sat in the same booth every day, pretending to read the newspaper but really secretly gossiping about everyone who came through the door. At first, Goldie sat at the booth in front of them to listen to them talk, but it didn't take long before they started including her in their conversations.

"See that waitress down there at the end with the coffee stain on her uniform?" Jack would ask, inclining his head in one direction or another. "She's got a boyfriend two towns over who's all hat and no cattle."

"Would you believe me if I told you the man who just walked

in lookin' like he's been rode hard and put back wet is really a rich son of a bitch?" Elvis would say.

They'd begun ordering her coffee and a cinnamon roll, so that when she got there, all she had to do was slide into the booth and listen to whatever salacious details they'd been saving for her.

The Tuesday before Thanksgiving was no different.

"What have you got for me today, gentlemen?" Goldie asked, shaking off the cold from her clothes. "I've been waiting all weekend to hear it."

"Well, Doc, we was wonderin' about you this morning," Jack said. His tone was very serious.

"What about me?" Goldie asked. She couldn't imagine there could be any new gossip about her—she'd fallen asleep with her mouth open in front of the television every night over the past weekend. Her life was hardly exciting.

"What are your plans for Thanksgiving?" Elvis asked. "Seein' as how you don't know nobody here and all."

Goldie hadn't thought about it. Honestly, Thanksgiving had completely snuck up on her. She'd been so busy preparing for the carnival, seeing patients, and hoping she might run into Cohen that the November holiday hadn't even entered her mind. She had, at least at one time, considered flying home, but she didn't want to leave Airport and Kevin alone, and her parents were planning on going to her uncle's house a few hours away. Thanksgiving hadn't been much of an event for her over the past several years. She usually ordered Chinese takeout and watched old movies, and with business picking up at the clinic, she didn't want to leave and run the risk that she'd be needed.

"I don't know," Goldie replied, finally. "I'll probably just stay home and order takeout."

"You can't order takeout on Thanksgiving Day," Jack said. "Everything's closed."

"Everything?" Goldie asked. "Really?"

"Except the gas station," Elvis said. "You don't want to eat there. Trust me. Nobody is really sure what those egg rolls are made out of."

The door chimed and they all looked up to see Alfie walk inside. He smiled at Ruby and began greeting nearly everyone.

"He's early today," Jack said.

"Alfie!" Elvis hollered, motioning to him. "You're early! Everything all right?"

Alfie ambled over to them, removing his brown Carhartt hat and gloves in the process. "Hello, boys. And Miss Goldie."

"You all right?" Elvis asked again. "You're early."

"Oh, I'm fine," Alfie replied. "I had to get into town early today to pick up the tent for the Christmas carnival. Cohen wants to set it up beforehand to make sure we can get it working properly."

"I'm gonna bring my great-granddaughter to see that alpaca you've got," Jack said. "Cohen told me he asked Maxine to make her a new cape."

"Did he?" Alfie asked. "Well, he's been pretty ate up with this whole carnival. He wants to make sure he does it right." Alfie turned his attention to Goldie. "I expect you're to blame for that."

"I didn't even know he was planning to participate until Tiffany told me," Goldie replied, trying not to appear too pleased with Alfie's comment. "I'm sure it was someone else."

"I'm sure it wasn't," Alfie replied with a grin.

"Did you know this girl doesn't even have a place to go for Thanksgiving?" Elvis asked Alfie, jabbing his thumb in Goldie's direction. "Says she's gonna watch TV and eat at the gas station!"

"Well, that won't do," Alfie said.

"I don't mind it," Goldie replied. "Really. Thanksgiving isn't a big holiday for my family back home. I won't even notice I'm missing anything."

"What about the pie?" Elvis asked.

"And the turkey?" Jack added.

"Just so long as you don't flash fry it," Elvis said. "Remember that year Roger Dale damn near caught his trailer on fire doin' that? The whole town smelled like turkey for a month. Every hungry dog in three counties was roamin' the streets."

"Why don't you come and have Thanksgiving dinner at the farm?" Alfie asked. "I promise there will be no fires."

"There is never a one hundred percent guarantee of no fires," Elvis replied, solemnly.

"Even so," Alfie said. "We would be delighted to have you."

"Thank you," Goldie replied. "But I'd hate to impose."

"Hell, we'll all be there," Jack said. "Half the town comes to the Gables' for Thanksgiving dinner."

"Not quite half the town," Alfie corrected. "Mainly the old fogies and Ruby."

"Will Ruby be bringing her cinnamon rolls?" Goldie asked.

"Yes, ma'am!" Ruby hollered from behind the counter.

Goldie smiled. "Okay, then. I'm in. What time should I be there?"

"Four o'clock," Alfie said.

"Should I bring anything?"

"If you'd like," Alfie replied. "But we'll have plenty of food. Don't feel obligated."

"Nothing from the gas station," Elvis said. "Remember that, kid. Nothing from the gas station."

Chapter 28

Goldie stared at the tiny stove in her cabin. She hadn't even turned it on since she moved in. For the most part, she'd eaten takeout from Ruby's, or she'd made salads, and once in a while, she'd throw something in the microwave. She couldn't imagine any of her friends back home, especially Alex, knowing what she'd been eating since arriving in the valley. It wasn't really that she'd eaten terribly, but she sure hadn't been eating the way she had in L.A. It was the soda—the Coca-Cola—that she could never tell anyone about.

She'd never been a very good cook, but she didn't want to go to the Thanksgiving dinner empty-handed. Goldie had seen how these dinners went on television, especially in holiday movies. Everyone brought something. People arrived with their casserole dishes, knocked on the door, and they were greeted with open arms. Nobody without a casserole dish was ever welcomed.

After doing a Google search for "traditional Thanksgiving dishes," Goldie settled on sweet potato casserole. Looking at the ingredients sitting on the kitchen table, she wondered if maybe she'd gotten a little overambitious. She didn't know the first damn thing about sweet potatoes. Why couldn't she just offer to examine a cow or something once she got there?

Airport jumped up on the table and began to examine the contents of the grocery bags, promptly sneezing on the sweet potatoes. She looked over at Goldie.

"Don't judge me," Goldie said. "The internet says it'll be good once it's all put together."

Airport sneezed again.

"You believe me, right, Kevin?" Goldie asked the furry lump snoozing in front of the fireplace.

Kevin looked up lazily and then promptly fell back asleep.

"You two are no help."

Goldie peeled the sweet potatoes, cubed them, put them to boil in a pot she found in one of the bottom cabinets, and started in on the topping for the casserole. She found the topping was fairly easy to make, since it was basically just oats, brown sugar, salt, and butter combined in a bowl.

Once the potatoes were done, she took them out of the pot and threw them into a bowl to mash, promptly realizing that she didn't have anything to mash them with. There was no hand masher or mixer, so she grabbed a fork and tried to mash them. By the time she was finished, she was out of breath, and she wondered if anybody in L.A. had thought of this as a new kind of workout. It seemed just weird enough to be expensive and popular.

Once Goldie put the casserole in the oven, she had just enough time while it baked to get ready to go to the farm. She'd just gotten out of the shower when Alex called.

"What are you doing?" Alex asked when Goldie answered. "You sound weird."

"I just got out of the shower," Goldie replied. "I'm soaking wet."

"Sounds kinky," Alex replied.

Goldie rolled her eyes. "You know I love you, but I'm kind of pressed for time. Can you call me back later?"

"Ooooh, do you have a hot date?" Alex asked.

"It's Thanksgiving Day," Goldie replied. "No, I don't have a hot date. Is that why you called?"

"No," Alex replied. "I actually called to tell you that we're cutting the trip short. I'll be home in a few weeks."

"Did something happen?" Goldie asked.

"There was some miscommunication about the flight schedule," Alex said. "I guess a flight got canceled for our return trip, and this was the only way we could get it fixed without having to stay longer."

"Well, I'm glad you're coming home," Goldie replied. "Maybe you can come and visit me after Christmas."

"In Wisconsin?"

"No, on the moon," Goldie said.

"I'd rather go there."

"Listen," Goldie replied, hurrying to the bedroom still wrapped in a towel. "I've got to go. Will you call me as soon as you get back in L.A.?"

"Of course," Alex replied. "Go get ready for your date."

"It's not a date!"

* * *

It had started to snow by the time Goldie got into the Jeep to head to Gable Farm. Goldie couldn't quit looking at the snow as she drove, not just because she could see it from the window, but because it was the first real snow she'd ever seen. It was the kind of snow that stuck, the kind that kids made a snowman out of, and it was the kind that, living in California, she never even knew she missed until that very moment.

She was nearly there, looking at the gorgeous snow, when Mrs. Lucretia Duvall came to mind. She wondered what the older woman was doing for Thanksgiving. Clearly, she had some help around her house, but did she have anybody, *really*?

Goldie turned the Jeep around and drove into town, this time pushing open the giant gate and driving right up into the yard. This time, it took Lucretia a minute to get to the door, and when she answered, she looked utterly confused.

"Dr. McKenzie?" she asked. "What on earth are you doing here?"

"Are you doing anything today?" Goldie asked. "I mean, for Thanksgiving?"

"I'm making a tuna casserole for my Amos."

"I have a better idea," Goldie said, entering the house when Lucretia stepped back to let her inside. "Why don't you come with me to Gable Farm?"

"Why would I do that?" Lucretia asked.

"Because your cat is very, very fat, and he doesn't need a tuna casserole," Goldie replied. "Speaking as his veterinarian, of course."

"I haven't been invited," Lucretia said.

"Everyone is invited," Goldie said. "According to the old men at Ruby's diner. Please come. It will be nice having another outsider with me so I'm not the only one."

Lucretia smiled. "Well, all right then. Just let me grab my coat."

Chapter 29

"It's snowing!" she said when Cohen opened the door to greet her and Lucretia. She thrust the casserole dish into his hands. "It's snowing a lot!"

"It does that here in Wisconsin," Cohen replied. His eyes slid from Goldie to Lucretia. "Well, hello there, Mrs. Duvall. It's a pleasure to see you."

"I should have baked a pie," Lucretia said, worried. "I apologize for my rudeness. I didn't know I was coming until fifteen minutes ago."

"We've got plenty of pies," Alfie called from the hallway. "Come on over here, Lucretia, and let me find you a seat in the living room."

"You're such a gentleman, Alfie," Lucretia replied, taking his arm and allowing him to lead her away.

"How on earth did you get old Mrs. Duvall to leave her house?" Cohen whispered once they were gone. "I don't think she's left since 1994."

"I'm very persuasive," Goldie replied, grinning.

"I bet you are."

"I seriously cannot believe this snow," Goldie said, unable to stop herself from talking about it. "How long will it last?" She walked back out onto the front porch.

Cohen set the dish down on the table by the doorway and went outside. "For a day or two, maybe a week. Depends on if it stays cold enough to keep."

"And it'll snow again?"

"It will snow more than again," Cohen said, grinning. "This is the first snow, but it's not the last by far."

"Don't you love it?" Goldie asked, facing him.

"Have you never seen snow before?" Cohen replied. "You sound like my cousin Grace's kid when they come up to visit from Florida. He's four."

"I don't care how old I sound," Goldie said. She took off one of her gloves and reached her hand outside the porch to catch a snowflake on her fingertip. "I don't think I've ever seen anything so pretty."

"Haven't you ever seen snow before?" Cohen asked again.

"I have," Goldie replied. "Just not like this. Not so much of it."

"Come on inside," Cohen replied. He grabbed her gloved hand. "Everyone is waiting on you to eat."

Goldie allowed him to lead her inside. "I thought the dinner started at four?"

"It's ten after," Cohen replied.

She handed Cohen her coat and looked around. The house was old, but it was well maintained, with dark hardwood floors and a large staircase not too far from the entryway. It was clear Cohen and his dad—or someone—had done a bit of remodeling. The large family room was bustling with activity, and Ruby grinned when she saw Goldie.

"Hey!" she said, hurrying up to her. "We thought maybe you'd stood us up."

"I took a detour," Goldie said. "And then got distracted by the snow."

"It's gorgeous, isn't it?" Ruby asked. "I've lived here my whole life, and I still get excited to see it."

"Cohen doesn't seem to think much of it," Goldie replied. She waved at Jack and Elvis, who were sitting in the recliners at the far end of the room.

"He's never impressed with anything," Ruby replied. "He's an old fuddy-duddy like your two buddies."

"I heard that!" Jack hollered.

"Good!" Ruby replied. "I meant for you to hear it!" Then she turned to Goldie and said, "I can't believe Mrs. Duvall is here! Nobody can believe it. Everyone is smiling and offering her a drink, but inside, they're dying to run home and call their neighbors. It's like seeing Big Foot!"

Goldie laughed. The atmosphere was so cheery. Everyone seemed to be having a good time. She recognized several of the people there, and overall, there were about a dozen. There were two women talking with Alfie whom she didn't recognize. They were older, about his age, with matching white bowl cuts.

Alfie had been right about the age of the people present—the only people near Goldie's age were Cohen and Ruby.

"You're wondering why we're the only young people here, aren't you?" Ruby asked. "I can see it all over your face."

Goldie crinkled her nose, embarrassed. "Yeah, kind of."

"Well, they're mostly Alfie's friends," Ruby replied. "Jack is my grandpa."

"What?" Goldie asked. "How come neither of you told me?"

"Everybody knows," Ruby replied, shrugging. "I didn't even think about it until you got here, and then it occurred to me. My grandparents raised me and my sister. She's the mom of the great-granddaughter he's always talking about. They live in Michigan. Anyway, they raised us, and I guess you could say the Gable family helped."

"Alfie seems like the kind of guy who would do that," Goldie replied. "So you've always come to Thanksgiving dinner here?"

"Since I was in high school," Ruby said. "Cohen is a couple years older than me. I guess it really started that Thanksgiving after Angela died."

Goldie, who'd been watching Cohen pick up her casserole dish from the table by the door and look at it curiously, snapped her attention back to Ruby. "Angela?" she asked. "Was that . . . was that Cohen's stepmother?"

Ruby nodded. "I didn't know you knew about that."

Goldie bit her bottom lip. She shouldn't have said anything, but the truth was, she'd been hoping to find out more about it without asking Cohen, which she knew she was absolutely not supposed to do.

"Who's ready to eat?" Alfie asked. "Time we waste in here is time we could be eating turkey!"

Inside the dining room was the longest table Goldie had ever seen. There were at least three tablecloths spread out on top of it, and a collection of mismatched chairs sat beneath it. Goldie waited until nearly everyone was sitting down and then found an empty seat in between Elvis and one of the white-haired women from the living room.

"You must be Dr. McKenzie," the woman said to her, smiling. "I'm Sharon."

"It's nice to meet you," Goldie said. "Please, call me Goldie. I'm still getting to know everyone from Blue Dog Valley. Do you live here?"

The other white-haired woman, sitting on Sharon's other side, leaned forward and replied, "Oh no. We live in Florida."

"Goldie, this is my wife, Linda," Sharon said, sitting back in her chair so Goldie could see Linda. "We're both *from here,* but we retired about a decade ago and moved to Florida to be with Linda's kids. I'm Alfie's third cousin on his mama's side."

"And I'm no relation to Alfie at all," Linda replied. "Just in case you were wondering."

"She wasn't wondering," Sharon said, jabbing her wife in the ribs.

"So you came all the way up here just for Thanksgiving?" Goldie asked.

"We come and stay through Christmas," Linda said. "The grandkids are teenagers now. They don't care if their old granny is there or not on Christmas morning."

"We still own a house here," Sharon interjected. "We try to come a few times a year, and Christmas is just a whole lot more enjoyable when it actually looks like Christmas."

"I grew up in Los Angeles," Goldie said. "I've never seen snow like this before today."

"Oh, you're in for a treat, sugar," Linda replied. "It snows and snows here in the wintertime."

"You'll be sick of it by March," Sharon said. "That's why we leave by New Year's. Then we have nearly a year to forget about hating it."

Goldie grinned. "I can't imagine hating it," she said.

"I haven't seen a meal like this in decades!" Lucretia said. "What a lovely table you've set, Alfie."

"I did most of the work," Jack replied, pointing to himself. Then he winked at Lucretia.

Lucretia blushed, and Goldie and Ruby shared an amused smile.

"I'm starving," Elvis said, quieting the group. "Somebody better pray before I commit a sin against the mashed potatoes."

Alfie stood up and cleared his throat.

Goldie watched as everyone at the table folded their hands in their laps and bowed their heads. She did the same, but she couldn't help sneaking a peek around the table as Alfie began the Lord's Prayer.

Her family didn't pray over their dinners. She couldn't really remember a time when they'd prayed at all. Once in a while, her lapsed Catholic parents would get a wild hair and take her to a service that wasn't on Christmas Eve or Easter Sunday, but Goldie still didn't know the nuances of family praying.

Looking around, it seemed to come naturally to everyone else. Some of them were mouthing the prayer to themselves, and on the opposite side of the table, Ruby held her grandfather Jack's hand. It was such a sweet gesture that Goldie couldn't help but smile.

As she continued her cursory look around the table, she stopped short on Cohen. His head was bowed, but he wasn't mouthing the words. He didn't even have his hands folded. His dark hair was a bit tousled, and Goldie wondered if that was on purpose or if it was that he just didn't care about the way it looked. She hadn't met very many men who didn't care about their appearance, but even living in California, she'd not met very many men who were as beautiful as he was, either.

The memory of their shared evening at the diner ran through her mind, and she couldn't help but fantasize about what might've happened had they not been interrupted. She doubted very much it would have gone further, since they were out in public and clearly people had seen them together. Still, she might've let his hands wander . . .

Cohen looked up and caught her eye before she could look away. She hoped everybody else's heads were bowed, because she couldn't have looked away from him even if she'd wanted to. She wondered if he realized that while his hair didn't show that he cared about much, his eyes betrayed him. His eyes were hungry.

"Amen," Alfie said, plopping back down into his seat. "Now dig in!"

Goldie averted her eyes to take a platter of asparagus and shovel a bit onto her plate. By the time all of the food had been passed around, including her sweet potato casserole, her plate looked like no more than the base of a food mountain. She didn't think she'd ever been so excited to eat in her entire life.

"How are you enjoying your first real Thanksgiving?" Elvis asked. "Sure beats the gas station, don't it?"

"Yesh," Goldie replied, her mouth full of turkey. "Sho good."

Jack, who was clearly not happy about being left out of the conversation, shouted, "Goldie! How do you rate Thanksgiving in the valley?"

Goldie held up all ten of her fingers.

"She's too busy eating to reply to you!" Elvis said to Jack.

"My kinda gal," Jack said. "You better save some room for pie!"

An hour later, Goldie was miserable. She'd never eaten so much in her entire life, and the apple pie that Ruby made, with a scoop of Alfie's homemade ice cream, had not helped matters any. She didn't understand how she could be so full and still unable to say no to any food that was offered to her.

She leaned back in her seat and stretched, involuntarily yawning in the process.

"Now, that's the mark of a good dinner," Sharon said, patting her stomach. "I'm about there myself."

"I'm not carrying you home," Linda warned her. "This will not be a repeat of Key West in 2009."

"That was beer, not turkey," Sharon replied.

"Either way, I'm not aching to relive it."

"Do either of you know where the bathroom is?" Goldie asked.

"Go back through the kitchen, and there is one off there to the right," Linda said. "You can't miss it."

"Thanks," Goldie replied, pushing her chair back and standing up.

She wandered out of the hum of conversation and into the kitchen. There was even more food there. Every countertop was covered with something, and Goldie wondered how anyone, even the dozen or so people in the dining room, would ever be able to eat it. Maybe, if she was lucky, they'd offer to let her take some of it home with her. A little late-night turkey sandwich was going to sound pretty good in a few hours.

Goldie made her way into the hallway. There were a few framed pictures hanging in the narrow walkway, and she stopped to look at them. There were several of a young Cohen that made Goldie laugh, especially one that had to be of him in middle school, with braces and a shaggy haircut. There were others of another boy that Goldie assumed was Joshua. He was blond, with a round face and watery, blue eyes.

The last photo on the wall was of the whole family—a much younger Alfie, Cohen, and Joshua with a woman with the same blond hair and eyes. They were wearing matching flannel shirts and jeans and standing in front of a tractor. They all had huge smiles on their faces.

Goldie didn't think she'd ever seen Cohen smile like that. It wasn't pained or forced or small. It was genuine, and it was a little unsettling to see him so happy. In all of the house, at least the parts she'd seen, this was the only wall that had pictures.

When she came out of the bathroom a few minutes later, the table had splintered off into little groups, all talking among themselves, chairs scooted together. It was a cozy scene.

She thought about going back over and sitting down next to Linda and Sharon, but her chair was currently occupied by Ruby. Goldie knew that no matter where she sat down, someone would include her. She didn't feel left out, not exactly, but she realized she was a little jealous of their relaxed communion with each other. They'd all known one another for years. They'd all known Cohen for years. They'd known him when he smiled like he had in the picture, and they all knew exactly why his smile had been damaged. He didn't have to tell them, and they, unlike her, didn't have to guess.

Goldie stood there for a few seconds, awkwardly trying to

decide what to do, and then remembered that it was snowing out-side. She pulled her jacket, gloves, and hat down from the coa-track by the door and slipped outside.

It was colder than it had been when she arrived, and the snow was coming down even harder than before. She wrapped her coat tightly around her body and began to slog through the white pow-der, enjoying the crunch it made beneath her boots.

After a few seconds, she dropped down onto the ground and made a snow angel. Then she got up, dusted herself off, and started to hop around, amused by the footprints. No wonder kids on television had always been so excited by a snow day. Now all she needed to do was get a sled. She was so engrossed in what she was doing that Goldie didn't realize there was anyone else outside until she felt a soft *thwack* on her back.

She turned around just in time to see Cohen aiming a snow-ball square at her chest.

Thwack.

"Hey!"

Cohen broke into a loud guffaw, nearly doubling over.

Goldie bent down and picked up a handful of snow, shaping it into a poorly constructed snowball. When she tried to throw it at him, it disintegrated into snow dust at his feet.

"You're gonna have to try harder than that, California!" Cohen taunted.

"I'm sorry that I didn't spend my whole life up to my ass in snow!" Goldie shot back. She bent down again and grabbed more snow, this time working harder to pack it together. She launched the snowball at him, and it narrowly missed his face.

"That's better!" he called back. "Try again!"

Goldie ran behind the Jeep to escape the onslaught of snowballs advancing in her direction and began to build up an arsenal of her own. It didn't take long before they were both covered in shattered snowballs.

"Okay!" Cohen said, finally. "Okay, I give up! Truce!"

Goldie peeked out from behind the Jeep. "I don't believe you!"

"Look!" Cohen said, holding up his mittened hands. "I don't have any snowballs to throw at you."

"What about your pockets?" Goldie asked. She was squinting into the darkness.

"There's nothing in my pockets!"

Goldie stood up and walked toward him. "If you throw a snowball at me right now, you won't live to throw another."

Cohen didn't respond. He was crouched down, forming a mound on the ground a few feet away from the porch steps of the house.

"What are you doing?" she asked. "That's too big to pick up."

"I'm not going to pick it up," he said.

"What are you going to do with it?"

"I'm building a snowman," he said. "If you don't build a snowman on the first real snow, you'll have bad luck for the whole winter."

"That's not true," Goldie replied.

Cohen looked up at her. "Are you willing to take that risk?"

Goldie knelt down beside him and began to help him pile the snow onto the base of the snowman. She was freezing, but she didn't want to go inside. Not if there were snowmen to be made.

After a few minutes, Cohen said, "Okay, now we just need to roll a couple of bigger snowballs for the middle and top. The middle one needs to be bigger than the top one, though, or it'll fall over."

"You have some kind of a degree in snowman building?" Goldie asked, following his lead and rolling a much smaller ball of her own.

"Nah," Cohen said, slightly out of breath. "But I have built more snowmen than I can count. It's been a long time, though."

"My friends and I built one out of wet sand at the beach once," Goldie replied. "It didn't stay together very long, though."

"I never would have thought of that," Cohen said. He picked up the large snowball and set it gingerly on top of the base.

"You have to improvise when you live in a place that doesn't get all four seasons," Goldie said.

"Do you miss it there?"

"A little." Goldie looked over at the middle part of the snowman and then back down at the ball she was rolling. "I miss my parents a lot. I miss my best friend, Alex. I miss my old clients at the clinic. Sometimes I miss all the action, but I don't know if it's the actual city I miss or the idea of it, you know?"

"Yeah, I know what that feels like." Cohen walked over to her. "Here," he said. "Let me get it." He picked up her snowball and placed it on top of his.

"Have you ever lived anywhere else?" Goldie asked. "I mean, besides Blue Dog Valley."

Cohen nodded. "I lived in Ithaca, New York, for three years," he said.

"Really?" Goldie asked. "Why there?"

"Cornell has one of the best ag schools in the country," Cohen replied.

"You went to Cornell?" Goldie stared at him. He was looking

at her as if it were no big deal, as if attending an Ivy League school on the East Coast was just something anyone could do.

"Oh, so you don't think I'm smart enough to go to Cornell?" Cohen asked. "I think my dad still has my acceptance letter stashed away somewhere if you want to look at it."

"No, I believe you," Goldie replied. "I just . . . didn't expect that to be your answer."

"Nobody ever does," Cohen said. He gave a short, rough laugh. "Sometimes I even forget it happened."

"I haven't ever been that far north," Goldie said. "I've only ever been to NYC, and that was for my senior trip in high school."

"I hated it at first," Cohen said. He walked over to a naked tree and grabbed a couple of small, broken branches. "I wanted to come home, but my dad said it was important I stayed and gave it a shot. Then, after the first year, I wasn't sure I even wanted to come home."

"Why did you?" Goldie asked. She watched him place the branches on either side of the snowman's middle. "Come home."

Cohen's eyebrows furrowed, and for a second, it looked like he might not answer. Finally, he said, "I had responsibilities here."

Goldie desperately wanted to ask what he meant by that, but she didn't, because by then, Cohen was walking toward the barn.

"I've got an old scarf and hat in here," he called to her. "Come on. We can warm up while I find them."

Goldie let the warm light of the barn wash over her, and she took off her damp coat, hat, and mittens. "It feels so good in here," she said. "My nose is starting to thaw."

"Do you want to try the cider I was working on the last time you were here?" Cohen asked.

"Absolutely," Goldie replied. She took the glass bottle he held out to her.

"That'll warm you right up."

Goldie tipped the bottle back once and then a second and third time. "I like this," she said. "It's sweeter."

"It'll get you drunk a lot faster," Cohen said. "It tastes better, but the alcohol content is higher."

"Sounds like it would be popular, then," Goldie replied. She handed the bottle back to Cohen, who also took a swig.

"I like my cider with more of a bite," he replied. "But this'll do in a pinch."

"Hey!" Goldie said, her eyes lighting up. "You could bottle this and sell it at the carnival. I bet you'd sell it all."

"I'd need a cider license for that," Cohen replied.

"There's a liquor license just for cider?" Goldie asked.

"In Wisconsin there is," Cohen said. "But even if I could get the license in time, I'm not interested."

"Why not?"

Cohen handed Goldie the bottle. "This is my hobby. It's just for fun, and nobody but my dad and you, because you were spying on me, know about it."

"I wasn't *spying on you*," Goldie said. "I was trying to find you so I could do the *job* you asked me to do."

"Is that why you tried to hide when I saw you *spying on me*?" Cohen asked.

"I was startled," Goldie replied. "Besides, it's not like I knew you were listening to classical music in your barn while smashing apples to bits. You can't blame me for watching. It's weird."

"I can be as weird as I want in my barn!" Cohen exclaimed. "It's *my* barn!"

"That doesn't make you sound any less weird," Goldie said. She took a drink from the bottle, finishing it off.

"That's pretty rich coming from a woman who stole a cat from an airport," Cohen replied.

"How did you know about that?" Goldie asked. "And I didn't *steal* her. She was *abandoned*. I saved her."

"Tiffany told me," Cohen said. "That first week or two you were here. She said the crazy West Coast vet that Doc had called in to replace him had to bring her ugly cat in to be vaccinated. Naturally, I asked why a veterinarian wouldn't already have their cat vaccinated, ugly or not. That's when she told me that cat I found you talking to in the airport was catnapped. You made me an accessory."

"I couldn't just leave her there," Goldie said. "She was alone, and you know what, at that very moment, I knew exactly how she felt."

Cohen took a few steps closer to where Goldie was standing and looked down at her. He reached one arm around her waist and pulled her to him, so that their bodies were flush. "You're not alone right now."

"No," Goldie said. "I'm not."

All she could think about was that their bodies were so close together that she could feel him breathing, and his eyes were two dark storms, like they'd been the first night she met him.

When he finally leaned in to kiss her, Goldie kissed him back with everything she had. She didn't even know it was possible to want something, someone, so much. His lips were soft, but they weren't gentle.

She let him kiss his way down her neck to her collarbone and allowed his hands to wander down past the small of her back. Goldie wanted him to pick her up like he'd done that day on his front porch, but this time, she wanted him to carry her someplace soft and lay her down. She wanted Cohen to do more than kiss her.

Cohen groaned when Goldie slid her hands underneath his shirt, running her fingertips along the ridge of his jeans around to his back. "This is a bad idea," he muttered in between heated kisses. "But I . . . You make me . . ."

Goldie pressed herself farther into him in response, and he groaned.

"Cohen!" someone yelled from—what seemed to Goldie—very far away.

There was noise coming from the house, people dispersing.

"Goldie! Where are you guys?"

Cohen broke apart from her reluctantly, releasing her back into herself, and Goldie had to regain her balance and her sense of reality. She looked around for her coat and pulled it back on. It was still damp, and so were her hat and mittens.

"We better get back outside," Cohen said. "I, uh, I should help my dad get cleaned up."

Goldie nodded. "Okay," she said. "I should probably go home, anyway. I didn't think I'd be gone this long."

Ruby peeked her head into the barn and eyed them suspiciously. "What are you two doing in here?"

"Getting a hat for the snowman," Cohen replied. He held up a frayed baseball cap. "We need a scarf, too, but I can't find one."

"Everybody's looking for you," Ruby replied. "Linda and Sharon want to say goodbye before they leave."

Cohen sighed. "Like we won't all see each other tomorrow," he said.

"Not to you," Ruby said, rolling her eyes. "To *Goldie*." She stepped inside the barn and grabbed Goldie's hand. "Come on."

Goldie followed behind Ruby, still more than a little lost in what had just happened before Ruby interrupted them. She turned around to look at Cohen, and he was staring at her, a small, satisfied grin on his face.

Goldie grinned back. This hadn't exactly been the way she'd imagined her first Thanksgiving in Blue Dog Valley ending, but she had to admit that so far nothing about this place was like she thought it would be. And as the snow continued to fall down all around her, she knew that, at least tonight, that was just fine with her.

Chapter 30

The Christmas carnival committee meeting was not going well. There were nearly twenty people crammed into the back of Ashley's shop, and so far, the only thing they'd managed to agree on was that Ruby should bring breakfast to the next one.

"All I'm sayin' is that you can't have a Santa Claus whose Mrs. Claus is in jail!" Roger Dale said. "Besides, Roy, you're too skinny to be Santa, anyway."

"Betty Ann won't care if I find me another missus for one night," Roy replied. "And I've got the white beard already! Come on!"

"You findin' another missus for the night is how Betty Ann ended up in jail in the first place," Roger Dale said.

"Boys, I don't think Santa is our biggest issue," Ashley cut in. "So far, we don't have enough food and drink vendors, and we've had three floats cancel on us because the Millersville parade is the same weekend. We've got to figure out a way to get the word out about the carnival so people don't think it's the same boring parade as every year."

"What kind of advertising do we need?" Tiffany asked.

"Well, the rotary club has paid for some signs up on the interstate," Ashley said. "That takes care of signage on the highway, which I think will help. But we still need airtime on the radio and on television closer to Milwaukee, if we can find it."

"My cousin at the radio station is gonna run an ad every hour," Roy replied. "He ain't exactly in Milwaukee, but he's closer than us."

"That's a good start, Roy," Ashley said. "But you still can't be Santa. That's Mayor Rose's job. He's been Santa for the last five years at the parade."

"Sounds like ne-*po*-tism to me," Roy grumbled.

"Who taught you that word, Roy?" Roger Dale asked.

"Yer mama, that's who," Roy said.

"Don't make me whoop your ass like when we was kids," Roger Dale replied, halfway standing up.

"I kicked both of your asses when we were kids," Tiffany said, rolling her eyes.

"Go ahead and try it now," Roy said, sneering at Tiffany. "This time I won't be so distracted by a pretty face."

"You better watch how you talk to my ex-wife!" Roger Dale warned.

"Would you two sit down?" Ashely said, her voice rising to a volume just below yelling. "Have you forgotten why we're here? This is an attempt to save the valley from becoming a ghost town. We're trying to keep our kids from moving off and never coming back, to make people believe that we have something to offer other than foreclosed farmland. If you two want to act like schoolyard bullies, go do it somewhere else."

"Sorry," Roger Dale and Roy said in unison.

Goldie snuck a glance over at Cohen, who was sitting in the back of the room, his chair leaned back on two legs against the wall. He'd come in late with Alfie. When Cohen caught her eye, he gave her a lopsided grin.

"Okay," Ashley continued. "Goldie, what do you and Tiffany have so far?"

"Goldie?"

"Huh?" Goldie felt Tiffany kick her under the table. "Ouch!"

"Where *are we* with the layout for the carnival?" Tiffany asked, pointedly.

"Uh, oh, right," Goldie replied, clearing her throat. She looked down at the town map she had spread out in front of her. "Well, you're right, Ashley. We don't have nearly enough food and drink vendors. The Bushy Beaver is going to have a beer garden, and the Girl Scout troop is going to have a lemonade stand—"

"Not next to each other, right?" Ashley asked.

"No," Tiffany replied. "The Girl Scouts are going to be inside the gym with the Boy Scouts. They've got popcorn, and two of the den mothers are making popcorn balls, too."

"So, beer and lemonade?" Cohen asked. "That's all we've got?"

"We also have four food trucks signed up," Goldie replied. "There's a Greater Milwaukee food truck group on Facebook, but I haven't been approved to join. I thought I'd ask if any of them wanted to drive down for the event."

"We need more vendors," Ashley said. "No offense to you, Delores, but I'm not sure if your cat-hair Christmas ornaments will draw the biggest crowd."

Delores waved one of her hands in the air. "No offense taken," she said. "I guess I could start using my neighbor's dog hair if you think that would help."

"Let's keep that in mind," Ashley replied. "I have a few Milwaukee contacts from going to market to buy clothes for the shop, and I've reached out to them."

"We're running out of time," Mayor Rose said. "Maybe we bit off more than we can chew this year. Do you think we should reschedule for next year instead?"

Ashley looked over at Goldie.

Everybody looked over at Goldie.

Tiffany kicked her again.

"No," Goldie said. "No, of course not. We can do this, can't we? We've got time. The carnival isn't scheduled until the weekend of the twenty-third, and we might only have a few out-of-town floats signed up, but the parade is essentially taken care of. We won't have to do much for that."

"We've ordered trophies for the floats this year, in addition to the small cash prize," one of the board members said. "They're really nice, and they're made by a local shop."

"How much did that cost?" Ashley asked.

"They donated them," Mayor Rose replied. "Free publicity."

Brian, who was standing in the doorway of the packed room with Layla, spoke up. "I've got a buddy in Milwaukee who has a great Whitesnake cover band. They said they'd come down and play at the Beaver for free. He thinks he might be able to get a couple other bands to come down, too, as long as I'll provide free beer. And Marcy over at the lodge says they can stay there for one night on her."

"That's great, Brian!" Ashley replied, scribbling something down with her stylus on her iPad. "See, this is all going to come together in the end."

"We still need more advertising," came a reply from the crowd. "Cheap advertising."

"It doesn't do us any good to advertise here," Tiffany said. "We all *know* about the carnival. We need to reach a bigger audience."

"Who has advertising contacts in Milwaukee?" Mayor Rose asked.

This time, all eyes, including Goldie's, rested on Cohen and Alfie, who seemed to be having a silent argument in the back of the room. Their faces were tense, and Cohen was now sitting straight up in his chair, arms crossed over his chest.

"Anyone?" the mayor asked. His gaze flicked around the room, but even he couldn't help it. "Alfie?"

Finally, Alfie sighed. "Joshua said he would help."

There was a collective gasp, and Goldie felt like, in that second, all of the oxygen had just been sucked out of the room.

Cohen cleared his throat, and Alfie continued. "He says he'll set up an interview at Channel 27 Milwaukee."

"That's fantastic!" Mayor Rose said.

Ashley looked worried, and she was staring at Cohen much the same way Goldie was, to gauge his reaction.

"Will you be going up to give the interview?" the mayor asked.

"Aw, heck no," Alfie replied, blushing a little. "I couldn't be on the TV. I figured we'd let one of our young people do it."

"I could . . ." Roy began.

"No!" came the collective response.

"Ashley could do it," Mayor Rose offered. "She's been on the old boob tube once or twice."

"I can't this weekend," Ashley replied. "The girls have a basketball tournament."

A murmur went around the group as everyone talked among themselves about who should go up for the interview.

"What about Dr. Goldie?" Delores asked. "She could do it."

"I think it should probably be someone local," Goldie replied quickly. She absolutely did not want to be on television. She'd been in a commercial once for the clinic in L.A., and it had taken more than fifteen takes for her to get her one line right.

"You live here, don't ya?" Roger Dale asked.

Goldie nodded.

"Then you're a local!"

Goldie felt more than pleased with this, but she still didn't want to agree to an interview. "I've only been to Milwaukee once," she said. "And that was at night and in the airport. I don't know my way around."

"Cohen can take you," Alfie said, speaking up for the first time since he'd mentioned the interview. "He knows where the station is."

"Dad," Cohen began. "I don't think—"

"He'd be happy to do it," Alfie said, cutting him off. "I'll call Joshua and let him know we've found someone."

The remainder of the meeting was spent with Roy and Roger Dale arguing about the benefits of a skinny Santa, and as soon as they adjourned, Cohen got up and left without saying a word to anyone, and Goldie couldn't help but feel a little deflated. She told herself that this was because he didn't want to go to Milwaukee to see his stepbrother for some reason and not because he didn't want to be stuck in his truck with her for a four-hour round trip. She wasn't entirely sure *she* wanted to be stuck in his truck with him. The last time they'd done that, it hadn't exactly gone well.

After the meeting, Goldie got up and followed Tiffany outside.

"I can't believe you don't want to be on TV," Tiffany said to her. "Doesn't that run in your blood or something? Hasn't everyone in California been on TV?"

"No," Goldie said. "I'm terrible in front of a camera. I'm not going to sleep at all this week worrying about it."

"I doubt Cohen will, either," Tiffany replied. "He didn't look too pleased with the arrangement."

"I know," Goldie agreed. "Do he and his stepbrother not get along or something?"

Tiffany shrugged. "Cohen never mentions him."

Goldie got the distinct impression that there was something Tiffany wasn't telling her, but before she had the chance to ask, Delores caught her by the arm.

"Dr. Goldie," Delores said, tapping Goldie on the shoulder. "Can I have a word with you in private?"

"Sure," Goldie replied. "I'll catch up with you," she said to Tiffany.

Goldie and Delores watched Tiffany go.

"I heard that Maxine is going to bring some of her goats to the petting zoo," Delores said.

"She is," Goldie replied. "But your booth won't be anywhere near the petting zoo, I promise."

"Good," Delores replied. "I don't want to be able to see her *or* smell her damn goats while I'm tryin' to make a sale."

"I don't think that will be a problem," Goldie said. "We've put you in the gymnasium, up at the front with a few of the other crafting ladies."

"I hope that will work," Delores replied, her tone doubtful. "But I'm not making any promises."

"Delores?" Goldie asked, unable to stop herself. "Why don't you and your sister get along?"

Delores gave Goldie a small, sad smile, a far-off look in her eyes, and Goldie could see in the older woman the beauty queen she must once have been, because, for just a moment, a much younger, happier woman took hold.

"Oh, child," Delores replied, clasping Goldie's hand a little tighter. "That was a whole lifetime ago, and I don't go back to that. Not anymore."

Chapter 31

Goldie stopped by Ruby's after the meeting, before heading back to the cabin. She'd recently learned that biscuits and gravy could be a meal at any time of the day, and it was her absolute belief that biscuits and gravy were better than any other dinner option on the planet.

Besides, Ruby always threw some kind of sweet surprise into the bag for dessert. Goldie could never wait, though, and tonight, the surprise was a chocolate chip muffin. There was something uniquely cozy about returning to the cabin at night, away from nearly everyone, with food in her hands and pets waiting inside for her.

Kevin went outside regularly, and sometimes he disappeared for an hour or two, but he was always back by dark, and most nights, he was waiting for her when she got there. Goldie had asked around about his "real" owners, the farm and farmer Tiffany had mentioned, but she found out that the farm had gone into foreclosure a week before she'd arrived in the valley. The livestock were sold off or given to neighbors, and the land and house both to be sold at auction. Kevin, with his wandering tendencies, had simply been overlooked. The neighbors thought he'd gone with the former owners, and the former owners probably thought he'd found a home somewhere else.

In a way, Goldie guessed he had.

Tonight, Kevin was on the porch, his tail *thump, thump, thump*-ing against the wooden planks. He was so large that Goldie didn't notice the wooden box nestled on the doormat until she opened the door and Kevin loped inside.

Goldie set her food down on the kitchen table and went back out to inspect the box. It was filled with hay and a corked glass jug. Goldie knew immediately that it was from Cohen. She held the jug up to the light, the amber liquid swirling around, and read the handwritten label: "Goldie: A California Sparkle. Best paired with the first snow of the season."

Goldie looked around the yard, wondering if Cohen was still there, but she didn't see him. Then she heard a rustling sound coming from the side of the cabin. It wasn't until she walked around that she saw him standing near one of her windows, staring at it in concentration.

"What are you doing?" she asked him.

"Did you know that this windowpane is cracked?" he asked her.

"No," Goldie replied.

"Didn't you feel a draft coming in?"

Goldie shrugged. "It's an old cabin, and it's cold outside. Isn't there always a draft?"

Cohen nodded at the box she was holding. "I meant to just leave it and go," he said, sounding more than a little embarrassed.

"And then you decided to try to break in?"

"And then I decided that I wanted to see you."

Goldie hugged the box a little tighter. "I'm glad," she said. "Do you want to come in?"

"Yes," Cohen replied. "I mean, no. I mean, listen, I'm sorry for how I acted at the meeting earlier, just running off without a word. I just needed to get out of there."

"It's okay," Goldie replied.

"It's not, but . . ." Cohen trailed off. "I just—shit, I don't know."

"If you don't want to take me to Milwaukee, you don't have to," Goldie said. "Really, it's okay. Tiffany can take me, or I can find someone else."

"I want to take you," Cohen said. "I just don't want to . . . You know what? I just really don't want to talk about it."

Goldie nodded, and they stood there in awkward silence for what felt like forever.

Finally, Cohen said, "I want to show you something."

"What is it?"

"Come on," Cohen said, inclining his head toward his truck. "It's just down the road a little way."

Goldie went back to the porch and set the box down, then followed Cohen to the truck. He didn't say much as they drove down the road, and Goldie wasn't exactly sure where they were going. They were headed in the opposite direction of his farm, and Goldie was confused when they drove up to another cabin that was every bit as old and small as hers.

"Wait right here," Cohen said.

He hopped out of the truck and jogged up to the cabin. Goldie squinted through the windshield as Cohen knocked on the door, it opened, and a figure of a man appeared in the doorway. The man and Cohen spoke for a few minutes, and then the door to the cabin closed.

"Who was that?" Goldie asked.

"Brian," Cohen said with a laugh. "Didn't you hear Layla barking from inside?"

"I didn't," Goldie replied. "I wish I'd known. I'd like to see her."

"She's doing really well," Cohen said. "Thanks to you." He began to drive away from the cabin and toward what looked very much to Goldie like the woods.

"Where are we going now?" she asked.

"Just wait," Cohen replied. "Brian and I have been working on a little something for the carnival. I want you to be the first to see it."

A couple of minutes later, Cohen came to a stop. "Here we are," he said.

Goldie got out of the truck. All she could see in the darkness was a vast wooded area. "I can't see anything," she said.

Cohen took her hand and led her forward, using the flashlight from his phone to guide the way.

Just when Goldie was about to proclaim that she didn't appreciate whatever joke he was playing on her, a chorus of lights began to buzz—blue, yellow, green, and red—and Goldie gasped, taking in the glory of it all. She was standing in the middle of a field of Christmas trees, every last one of them clothed in a spiral of stringed lights.

"Oh," she breathed, when she'd regained her composure. "Cohen, it's *beautiful*."

Cohen grinned at her, a wide, pleased grin. "We've been

working on it for a couple of weeks. Brian and I thought we could make up some signs to mark the way, and people could drive through. There's a pretty wide gap in the middle—big enough for a line of cars."

Goldie stared at him. She couldn't decide in that moment if the trees were more lovely or if he was, and when he pulled her a little closer to him as they stood there, she didn't resist. She simply stayed right there in his arms, content with the world as it opened up in front of her.

Chapter 32

Goldie was starting to feel the pressure of organizing the carnival. So far, there had been at least four disasters around town, and they all had something to do with the carnival. First, the school gym had a leak in the roof, which dripped down onto the wooden bleachers. Not only did the roof have to be patched, but a section of the bleachers needed to be replaced, and the earliest the school superintendent said it could be finished was the day before the carnival was supposed to begin, which meant that they would have to spend nearly all of that evening decorating—decorations that they'd planned to spend several days on. Then the mayor had called to say that one of the food vendors had caused a massive bout of food poisoning the previous weekend and now their state food license had been pulled, which meant they could no longer attend the event. After that, there had been a pileup at cheerleading practice, resulting in broken bones for at least three cheerleaders. Now the cheerleading squad, who'd planned to host a dance competition for carnival-goers to spectate, had to drop out entirely. The least pressing matter was that of the petting zoo, which now had more animal volunteers than the space could accommodate, so Goldie and Tiffany were searching for another location.

"I haven't slept in three days worrying about this damn carnival," Tiffany said one evening. "I haven't even decorated my own house for Christmas!"

"You better get on that," Goldie replied. "You may not be special enough for the whole town to turn out and decorate for you."

"That was my idea," Tiffany replied. "And you can bet your ass it won't happen again next year."

"Honestly, I'm thankful," Goldie said in earnest. "I didn't keep anything that Brandon and I shared—I really wanted to just light it all on fire."

"I understand that," Tiffany said. "The year after Roger Dale and I got divorced, I burned all of our Christmas decorations."

"Like in a fire pit?"

"In his trailer," Tiffany said with a grin.

"It's a wonder you're not in prison," Goldie replied.

"It's not like he was inside the trailer or anything," Tiffany said. "Besides, I did him a favor. That trailer was junk."

"Every day I have a new reminder never to piss you off," Goldie said.

"Hey," Tiffany said, perking up. "I forgot you have that interview in Milwaukee. Are you nervous?"

"We've been so busy, I haven't even had time to think about it much," Goldie replied. "But now that you've reminded me, I'm incredibly nervous."

"Do you know what you're going to say?"

Goldie made a face. "Nope," she said. "Not a clue. I assume

that they'll just ask some questions about the carnival. I hope they don't ask me anything I don't have an answer to."

"I'm sure they won't," Tiffany replied, but she didn't look so sure. "Besides, I bet nobody watches, anyway."

"That doesn't make me feel better," Goldie said. "We *want* people to watch. We want them to come to the carnival, especially the hordes from the city. If people see how wonderful Blue Dog Valley is, maybe they'll come back."

Tiffany smiled. "I never thought I'd hear you say that back when you first showed up. Honestly, I didn't think you'd last a week."

"I'd like to be offended by that," Goldie replied. "But I really didn't think I would, either."

Just then, the door opened, and Maxine stepped inside. She was carrying three packages that were so large, Tiffany rushed over to help her with them.

"What's all this?" Tiffany asked, when she'd set the packages down on the reception desk. "Is this more stuff for the carnival? Because if it is, we're out of room."

"No," Maxine replied. She looked over at Goldie. "I heard you were headed for Milwaukee tomorrow."

"I am," Goldie said. "For an interview about the carnival, with Channel 27."

"Perfect," Maxine said, wheezing slightly from the weight of the packages she'd been carrying. "I need you to drop these off in Milwaukee for me."

"Uh, okay," Goldie replied. She looked over at Tiffany. "Where do you want them dropped off?"

Maxine produced a rumpled Post-it from her jeans pocket

and handed it over. It was slightly sticky. "That's jam up there in the corner," she said. "It's not goat's blood."

"I . . . didn't think it was," Goldie said.

"Sometimes it is," Maxine replied. "But most of the time, it's jam."

Goldie looked over at Tiffany again, who was pretending to inspect the packages.

"What's in the packages?" Goldie asked. She couldn't help herself. They were gorgeous. Each box was a variation of purple with a twine bow tied around it. They looked incredibly elegant, which didn't coincide with Maxine's jam-covered note.

"Oh, nothing important," Maxine replied. "But I don't like mailing boxes that big. It's expensive, and half the time, they arrive banged up. The customers don't like that."

"If Jay the mailman stayed sober long enough to do his job, that would help," Tiffany said. "Last week, he about took off my mailbox when he drove down the road. I could see his Coors Light can in his hand from my porch!"

"That doesn't sound safe," Goldie said.

"Safer than having to deal with him sober," Maxine grumbled. "So, will you take these packages to Milwaukee or not? If you say no, I'll just go and ask Cohen. He won't tell me no."

"Of course I will," Goldie replied, still trying to pry her hands off the sticky note. "I'll make sure they get delivered safely."

"Thank you," Maxine replied. "I'll let the girls know you're coming."

"Okay," Goldie replied.

It was clear to her that Maxine wasn't going to tell her what was in the boxes *or* who the girls were, when Maxine turned on her heel and marched out the front door of the clinic without saying another word.

"Should we open one and see what's inside?" Tiffany asked, once Maxine was safely out of the building. "They look so fancy."

"No way," Goldie replied. "She'd know. I don't know how she would know, but she would."

"You're right," Tiffany said, her voice sullen. "She would."

"Maybe 'the girls' will open one of the boxes in front of me, and I'll see what it is," Goldie replied, conspiratorially.

"You better text me," Tiffany said. "My bet is those things are full of sticky notes and goat's blood."

Chapter 33

Goldie had decided, for the interview, that she needed to wear something professional—something she might've worn back in L.A. Most of those clothes had been shoved to the very back of her closet. It felt like years since she'd worn them, and if she was being honest, she didn't really miss them. She much preferred the comfort of the Muck Boots and the incredibly warm lined leggings and the multitude of sweatshirts she'd seemed to acquire. She always dressed up a little for work, but now she'd take comfort over class any day of the week.

She picked her favorite cardigan of all time—a Gucci silk-crêpe cardigan that she'd bought herself on a whim a few years ago. She'd spent so much, she'd been embarrassed to wear it for months, until she couldn't stand it any longer. Now Goldie wore it only on special occasions, and she figured being interviewed on live television was pretty special. She paired it with navy cigarette pants and a pair of flats.

When she looked in the mirror, she hardly recognized herself.

It was clear that, as she carried Maxine's boxes out to Cohen's truck an hour later, he hardly recognized her, himself.

"You look ready for your interview," Cohen said to her. "I'd about forgotten what you looked like the first time I saw you."

Goldie wasn't sure how to take that.

"I don't feel like that's a compliment," she replied, allowing him to take the boxes.

"I like it," Cohen said. He paused. "I like . . . I like you either way."

"Thanks," Goldie said, her face warm. "Hey, aren't you curious about all these boxes?"

"Nah," Cohen replied. "Maxine called this morning to tell me we needed to drop a few things off for her. She said she was afraid you wouldn't do it."

"I don't know why she keeps saying that," Goldie replied. She got into the front seat of Cohen's truck. "I told her I would."

"That's just Maxine for ya," Cohen said. "She's a little . . ."

"Batshit?"

"Well, I was gonna say eccentric, but I guess that works, too."

"Don't tell her I said that," Goldie replied.

Cohen laughed. "I might be a country boy, but I'm not stupid, Doc."

The drive to Milwaukee was full of conversation about the carnival and Blue Dog Valley. Goldie finally remembered to ask if there were actual fighting moose. To her relief, Cohen told her there were not. She wanted to ask about Joshua, wanted to find out what it was about driving to Milwaukee to see him that set Cohen on edge. She wanted to know about his stepmother. But she was afraid to ask. She knew it wasn't her business, and the way his mouth was set into a grim line when he wasn't talking to her told Goldie that Cohen did not want to talk about it.

Still, Goldie enjoyed the drive and looking at the city in the daylight once they'd arrived. She got a little rush seeing all of the traffic and the storefronts and all of the people. She wished that they had more time to stop a few places, but if they were going to drop off the packages and then make it to the interview, they had to get to the address Maxine had provided ASAP.

"Do you know where we're going?" Goldie asked, squinting at the sticky note and then back at her phone, where she'd plugged in the address.

"No clue," Cohen replied. "I'm just turning where that robot woman tells me to."

Eventually, Cohen turned onto a tree-lined residential street. The houses were all older, but they looked well-kept. Goldie could imagine children playing outside in the summertime and parents pushing their infants up and down the sidewalks. She nearly felt homesick at the thought.

"What a cute little neighborhood," Goldie said as they drove through.

"The houses are all so close together," Cohen replied. "And can you imagine the traffic on a busy day when it's not so cold outside?"

Goldie could imagine, since that's just what she'd been doing.

"I think it seems nice," Goldie said. They pulled up in front of a house with the number 205, just like on the piece of paper Goldie held. "All the neighbors talking to each other and having barbecues. Getting to know each other. I bet it's a friendly place."

"We do that in the valley," Cohen said, a little grumpily. "We just don't live in houses on top of each other, with traffic going through all hours of the day and night."

"I don't mind the traffic so much," Goldie replied. She got out of the truck and pulled open the back door to unload the packages. "The noise reminds me that the city is alive. I like that."

Cohen gave her a sideways glance from the other side of the truck that Goldie couldn't quite read. Was it disappointment? Annoyance? She couldn't tell.

"Hi!" came a voice from behind them. "You must be here with the delivery."

Goldie turned around to see an absolutely gorgeous woman standing there. Not gorgeous in the way she thought Ashley was gorgeous, with a sort of fresh-faced, girl-next-door look. No, this woman was different. She was buxom, with dark hair piled high on her head and dark eyes made nearly feline with wing-tipped eyeliner.

She stuck out a hand with well-manicured, burgundy nails attached. "I'm Sam," she said. "Thank you so much for driving all this way. My roommates and I appreciate it."

Goldie handed Sam two of the boxes, while Cohen carried the other two to the front steps. "It's no problem," Goldie said. "We were coming into Milwaukee, anyway."

"I heard you were going to be on TV," Sam replied. "Ms. Maxine told us all about it."

Goldie smiled nervously. "If I don't pass out from anxiety first."

"You'll be great!" Sam said. "We're all going to watch it later at work. Seriously, thank you so much. Our old uniforms were getting so ratty. We couldn't have performed tonight without these."

Goldie looked at Cohen for an explanation, but he wasn't looking at her. He was staring at Sam, all six feet of her.

She didn't really blame him.

"Well, thank you," Goldie said, finally. "Um, good luck with your performance."

"You, too!" Sam replied, waving at them as they walked back to the truck. "Tell Ms. Maxine we said thank you!"

"What kind of a performance do you think she has?" Goldie whispered to Cohen when they were out of earshot of Sam. "And what do you think is in those boxes?"

"I don't know," Cohen whispered back. "I thought they were goat tutus this whole time."

Goldie turned back to Sam, who was still waving at them. Goldie didn't see any goats, but she guessed they could be in the backyard. Was it legal to have goats in the city limits of Milwaukee?

"Tiffany told me that Maxine was some kind of seamstress back in the day," Goldie said. "And Sam mentioned uniforms. So I guess that's all it is."

Cohen turned around as well to give Sam one last look before he replied, "Well, whatever it is, I sure wish we were staying in Milwaukee long enough to see it."

Chapter 34

When they got to the news station for the interview, Goldie was so nervous, she hurried inside to find the bathroom just so she could be alone for a few minutes. She was terrified she was going to forget nearly everything she was going to say. What if she forgot the name of Blue Dog Valley? What if she forgot the state of Wisconsin? What if . . .

She splashed some cold water on her face from one of the grimy faucets and realized too late that the water would ruin her makeup. Frantically, she dabbed at her cheeks where the mascara had started to run and took a deep breath. She needed a pep talk.

"I cannot believe you didn't tell me you were going to be on TV!" Alex squealed into the phone when Goldie called her. "I mean, honestly! How could you not tell me?"

"I don't know," Goldie replied. "I completely forgot that you were back in the country, and I guess I just didn't want to bother you."

"That's a bullshit excuse," Alex replied, pouting. "You've found new friends and now you don't need me anymore!"

"I called you for moral support, didn't I?" Goldie asked. "Please, chastise me later. I need you to tell me I'm not going to make an idiot of myself."

"Of course you won't make an idiot of yourself," Alex replied. "You've seen me on TV a million times. You know what to do!"

"Watching isn't the same thing as doing," Goldie reminded her friend. "What if I get up there and start barking like a dog or something?"

"Then you need to rush home and ask one of your parents to give you a brain scan," Alex said. "Because you've clearly had an aneurysm."

"I might have an aneurysm."

Alex sighed. "Okay, the interview is about the carnival, right?"

"Right," Goldie replied.

"Then that's easy," Alex said. "All you have to do is talk about the carnival. That's it. Don't answer any questions that the interviewer didn't ask. Don't offer any extra information. Answer the questions. Smile. Maybe laugh a little if the guy is cute . . . It is a guy interviewing you, right?"

"Yes," Goldie said. "How did you know that?"

"Lucky guess," Alex replied. "Seriously, you need to calm down. Reach into your purse, pull out some lip gloss, and do the thing. You'll be *fine*."

"Okay." Goldie took a breath in through her nose and let it out through her mouth. "I can do this. I'll be fine."

"Wait," Alex said. "Did you say this interview is in Milwaukee? Isn't that like, hours from where you live?"

"Two hours," Goldie replied.

"Did you drive yourself in that awful Jeep you told me about?"

"No," Goldie said. "Uh, someone drove me."

"Who?"

Goldie paused. "Just this guy . . ."

"A guy?"

"Shhh!" Goldie hissed into the phone. "Just this guy I know. His dad set up the interview. That's all."

"Is this the same guy you told me you were going on a date with on Thanksgiving?" Alex asked.

"There was no date on Thanksgiving," Goldie replied, exasperated. "Look, I have to go. I need to get out there."

"Break a leg!" Alex yelled as Goldie pressed the END CALL button.

Goldie shoved her phone into her purse and practiced her smile in front of the mirror. Her first thought was that she looked more like one of the animals she treated at the clinic than a refined, well-mannered veterinarian, but it would have to do. She could do this, because she absolutely had to do this.

She walked out of the bathroom and into the lobby to find Cohen talking to a short, bearded man with a clipboard. He looked harried and slightly annoyed. Cohen was pointing in her direction, toward the bathroom.

"I'm here," Goldie said, hurrying over. "Sorry. I just needed to . . . uh, freshen up."

The man stared at her. "Okay, honey. You're Dr. Marigold McKenzie, then?"

"Yes," Goldie said, straightening her sweater. "I am."

"Perfect." He checked something off on his clipboard. "I'm

going to lead you both back. Josh has asked that he speak with you both before we go on air, and we don't have much time."

"I'm fine to just wait out here," Cohen said, not budging from where he stood. "You two can go on back."

"No," the clipboard man replied, nonplussed. "He specifically requested you both."

"But . . ."

"Please," Goldie said, grabbing Cohen's arm, completely forgetting about the fact that Cohen and Joshua were stepbrothers and the fact that Cohen did not want to be there. "I don't want to go back there by myself."

Cohen's face softened. "Okay," he said. "Okay, come on. Let's go."

"Lovely," Clipboard Man said, rolling his eyes. "Josh is waiting."

They followed him back through several doors that could be opened only with a keycard. Finally, the last door was opened, and Goldie and Cohen walked inside to find a short, muscular man sitting in a chair while an incredibly thin, blond woman fluffed his hair.

"Cohen!" the man, who Goldie already knew had to be Joshua, said. He jumped up and disrupted the stylist, who made a tutting noise and moved away from him. "How are you, man?"

"I'm all right, Josh," Cohen said, accepting Joshua's handshake. "It's, ah, it's been a long time."

"When Dad told me you were coming up, I couldn't believe it," Joshua continued. "I told him I'd have to see you here in the flesh to believe it!"

Goldie stared at Joshua. He still looked a little bit like the photo in the hallway at Cohen's house—same light hair, fair skin, and blue eyes. He hadn't gotten much taller, either. But it was clear that he'd spent a significant amount of time on his appearance as a news anchor. His face was no longer quite as round, and neither was the rest of him. His clothes, Goldie knew, had been tailored to fit him perfectly.

"And you must be Dr. McKenzie!" Joshua said, with the same gusto he'd used to address Cohen. "It's nice to meet you."

"Please," Goldie said, trying not to be knocked off her feet by his firm handshake. "Call me Goldie."

"All right, Goldie," Joshua replied. "Why don't you have a seat here, and Leanna will get you ready for those camera lights."

"Okay," Goldie said. She was secretly pleased she was going to get a little extra oomph before she went on the air.

"Are you two spending the night?" Joshua asked Cohen as Leanna tried to do something with Goldie's hair. "Because I know this great little restaurant downtown—"

"We're headed back to the valley after this," Cohen said before Joshua could finish.

"Oh." Joshua's impeccable smile fell for a moment. "Well, hey, that's all right, man!"

There was a silence that Goldie had to bite her tongue not to fill. She knew she shouldn't interject with anything, especially not right now while she was so nervous. She was likely to say something absolutely ridiculous and make the awkwardness worse.

Leanna leaned down to Goldie and whispered, "This is the quietest I've ever seen Josh in five years."

Goldie stifled a giggle and felt herself relax a little.

"Take a deep breath," Leanna said, bouncing a powder brush

off Goldie's nose. "You cannot be any worse than the spaghetti guy we had on last week. He had actual spaghetti stains all over his shirt."

"I've got to go out and get the ball rolling," Joshua said, finally, turning around to Goldie. "I promise I won't be too hard on ya, Goldie," he said. He tried to laugh, but it was strained. He kept glancing over his shoulder at Cohen, who'd somehow managed to back himself into the corner of the room and stand there, head down, with his hands in his pockets. "I'm going to ask you a few questions about the, uh . . ." He snapped his fingers.

"Christmas carnival," Leanna replied.

"Right, the carnival. It'll take five minutes, tops. Fun answers only!"

"Okay!" Goldie replied. She had no idea what *fun answers only* meant.

"I'll see ya out there!" Joshua trotted out of the room, and Goldie let out a big breath she'd been holding.

"I'm just going to go back out and wait," Cohen said, pointing toward the door. "Where's that guy with the clipboard?"

"Hang on," Leanna said, shoving her makeup brushes down into a fanny pack on one side of her hip. *"Aaaandrew!"*

The Clipboard Guy appeared, looking annoyed. "Leanna, how many times have I told you to use the walkie?"

Leanna shrugged. "Not enough times for me to care." She nodded to Cohen. "Can you take this lady's boyfriend back out, please? I don't want him to get lost and wander into *Cooking with Crimson*. She's awful when she gets interrupted."

Andrew's eyes widened. "Oh shit. I forgot she was on tonight. Come on," he said to Cohen. "Follow me."

Cohen looked at Goldie and mouthed, *Boyfriend?* to her while raising one eyebrow.

Goldie grinned and then looked at herself in the mirror. "Wow, Leanna," she said. "I look one hundred times better already."

"That's my job," Leanna said. "I'd like to get my hands on that guy of yours, though. Damn, he's a tall drink of water."

"He's not really my guy," Goldie confessed. "He's—well, I don't know what he is."

"Do you think I could get his number before you leave, then?" Leanna asked.

Goldie slid off the chair and flattened the nonexistent creases in her pants with the palms of her hands. Her hands were *so* sweaty.

"Sorry," Goldie said to her. "He doesn't have a phone. He's Amish. And, uh, engaged to his cousin."

"Damn," Leanna replied wistfully. "Too bad."

Chapter 35

Joshua and his co-host, Lisa, were seated across from Goldie, both of them shuffling papers and making jokes between themselves. Occasionally, they looked up at her and smiled or offered words of encouragement as Goldie worried and sweat in places she didn't know a person could get sweaty. She hoped Leanna's efforts wouldn't go to waste.

"Are you ready?" Joshua asked her. He gave her a thumbs-up. "We're on in thirty."

"Great evening, Milwaukee!" Lisa said, her smile turning up several wattages. "You know what time it is! That's right! It's our human-interest fifteen minutes of fame! Tonight, we're here with small-town veterinarian Dr. Marigold McKenzie. Welcome, Dr. McKenzie!"

Goldie realized a beat too late that she was supposed to respond. "Oh yes! Thank you for having me!" she said, trying to mimic Lisa's smile.

"So, Dr. McKenzie," Joshua said. "We hear your town, Blue

Dog Valley, is having a spectacular Christmas carnival to celebrate the season."

"We are!" Goldie replied, still smiling. "On Saturday, December twenty-third, from nine A.M. to ten P.M."

"Fun fact," Joshua said, turning away from Goldie and facing the camera. "I actually used to live in Blue Dog Valley. Now, it's been nearly two decades, but it was a great town with great people. Not too long ago, an interstate bypass went in, and the town has struggled. It's my understanding that this carnival could help put Blue Dog Valley back on the map, so to speak. Isn't that right, Dr. McKenzie?"

"Yes!" Goldie said, nodding her head a bit too much, which caused both Lisa's and Josh's smiles to dim. She dialed it back and tried again. "Yes, that's true. We're hoping that people from all over the area will come to the carnival and see what a wonderful town we live in and want to come back soon for another visit."

"So, tell us more about this carnival," Lisa said. "What can visitors expect to see?"

"Well, we've got food and drink trucks," Goldie began. "And live music, which I guess is probably expected at most carnivals. But we've also got a wonderful petting zoo with the world-famous Alice the Alpaca and a whole bunch of cute little goats in tutus."

"Goats in tutus?" Lisa broke in. "Really?"

"One of the women in town makes them!" Goldie said, thrilled to see real excitement coming from Lisa. "We've also got various craft stands, and many of them have holiday-themed home decor and tree ornaments, and you're not going to believe the baked goods. Our own Ruby of Ruby's Diner makes *the best* cinnamon rolls in the entire state!"

"Who doesn't love cinnamon rolls?" Lisa enthused. "And it's free to enter?"

"Of course," Goldie replied. "Anyone is invited to come and spend the day at our winter wonderland. Oh! I almost forgot! We also have a drive-through light display in a forest of Christmas trees. I've seen it firsthand, and it is gorgeous."

"It sounds like a real treat," Josh said. "What do you say, Lisa? Should we head on up to Blue Dog Valley on December twenty-third?"

"Count me in!" Lisa said. "We hope to see you all there!" She pointed at the camera for emphasis, and then relaxed as the segment ended and the station went to a commercial.

"You did it," Joshua said to Goldie, giving her another thumbs-up. "Great job."

"I can't decide if I want to go skydiving or take a nap," Goldie replied, relieved that the whole experience was over. "I don't know how you two do that every night."

"It's not for everybody," Lisa said, a bit too pointedly for Goldie's taste. "But Josh and I make it look easy."

"You do," Goldie agreed.

"Sixty seconds!" a voice from the beyond boomed.

An assistant motioned for Goldie to get up, but before she could leave, Joshua said, "Goldie, Lisa and I will be down on Saturday for the event. I remember Maxine from when I was a teenager. I think she'd be fun to interview with all of her goats. Do you think she would be around that morning, say, maybe about five A.M. for the live recording?"

Fun wasn't exactly how Goldie would describe an interview

with Maxine, but it would for sure be interesting. "I'll ask her," Goldie said.

"Perfect," Josh said, giving her a wave. "See you next Saturday!"

Clipboard Guy was waiting for Goldie to lead her back out to the lobby. He looked no less annoyed to see her than he had before.

"Did I do okay?" she asked him.

"You were better than the spaghetti guy," he replied, suppressing a yawn. "Of course, so is everyone."

Chapter 36

They were nearly out of the city before Cohen looked over at her and said, "So how long have you known that Josh is my step-brother?"

"Well . . ." Goldie said, searching for the right answer.

"I know that you know," Cohen replied. "You didn't even flinch when he said he used to live in the valley. Did my dad tell you?"

"He said he had a stepson who might be able to help with advertising," Goldie said, finally. "I think he was just trying to help."

"Do you think I'm mad?" Cohen asked. His tone was slightly hurt. "I'm not mad, Goldie. I know I should have told you before, but I just didn't really know how."

"Don't you like each other?" Goldie asked, unable to help herself. She felt like she'd been carrying the question around with her forever.

Cohen sighed. "It's complicated," he said.

"It's okay if you don't want to talk about it."

Cohen rubbed his five-o'clock shadow with his free hand. "I haven't . . . I haven't talked about it to anyone in a long time."

Goldie had never seen this look on Cohen's face before. She'd seen him angry, and she'd seen him annoyed. Both of those expressions were pretty common, but lately, so was his smile. This look was a mixture of something Goldie couldn't quite place, but if she had to pick an emotion, it would be pain.

"Josh's mom and my dad got married when we were kids," Cohen said. "My mother, Mary, died of ovarian cancer two years before he met Angela. I really liked Angela, and you know, I really liked Josh. Then we got to be teenagers." Cohen paused. "We just kind of drifted apart. I don't know. He got into drugs and skipped a lot of school. We fought a lot. He and my dad fought a lot. Angela was in the middle. I couldn't wait to leave for college."

Goldie turned to face him as the daylight faded and they drove on past what was left of the city until they were a lone pair of headlights on the highway.

"I came home around Christmas," Cohen continued. "Right about this time, probably, and Josh was so much worse. He wasn't working. My dad kicked him out, because he kept finding drugs in Josh's room, and he wouldn't go to rehab. Nobody even knew where he was living. I went out one night to see Ashley." He looked over at Goldie. "I'm sure you've heard about that by now, too."

"A little," Goldie admitted.

"Well, we dated all through high school, and we were trying to make the long-distance thing work, but it was hard, and neither one of us were really very good at it. I went to see her hoping I could fix it, and it just made it worse. Then Angela called me. She said someone called her and said Josh had been at a party and someone beat him up pretty badly. She wanted me to go and check on him. I told her no . . . I told her that I didn't want anything to do with Josh, and I was embarrassed by him. God, I was so angry."

"I don't blame you for being angry," Goldie said.

"I shouldn't have taken it out on her," Cohen said. "My dad was out at the Rose farm helping Doc with some kind of sick horse, and I should have done what she asked me to do. Instead, I told her no, and she went by herself to find him. She was way out on some county road and it was so dark. I guess she swerved to miss a deer and hit a patch of ice. She was out there all alone, and it took three hours to find her. By then it was too late."

"Oh, Cohen," Goldie said. She was trying and failing to keep her throat from tightening. "I'm so—I'm just so sorry."

"It was my fault," Cohen said. "It was my fault, and I knew it. I knew it, but I blamed Josh. We nearly had a fistfight at the funeral, and I was too young and stupid to realize that he was grieving, too. Too young and stupid to realize my dad was grieving."

"It wasn't your fault," Goldie said. "You can't believe that. It was an accident."

"Josh moved in with his aunt in Milwaukee," Cohen continued, as if he hadn't even heard her. "She helped him get sober. He got his life together. A few years ago, he wrote me a letter as part of his sobriety program, but I've only seen him a handful of times since the funeral. I never know what to say. It ends up like it did today every time. I can't . . . I can't . . ." He trailed off.

Goldie slid over to him and put her hand on his leg. He grabbed it and held on, pulling her closer. When they got back to the cabin, they sat in the truck for what felt like an eternity, not saying anything. Finally, she leaned over and kissed him.

"Do you want to come inside?" she asked.

Cohen looked at her. Even in the dark, Goldie knew his answer before he said it. "Yes," he said. "That's all I want, is to come inside."

Goldie spent a few minutes tending to Airport and Kevin, who weren't exactly used to being alone all day. Airport hid from Cohen, but Kevin immediately went in for slobbery kisses and nearly knocked Cohen over in his excitement.

"Hey, buddy," Cohen said, giving Kevin's head a rough pat. "You sure do think you've died and gone to heaven here, huh?"

"I doubt heaven spends as much money on dog food as I do," Goldie grumbled, dishing food and fresh water into both Kevin's and Airport's bowls. "I know I'm a veterinarian, but I really didn't know how much food a dog his size could eat."

Cohen laughed. "Well, he's clearly taking advantage of the situation."

Goldie finished up and walked into the living room, where Cohen had been abandoned at the sound of the tinkling of the food landing in the bowls. She hoped that the reality of the lights and the animals and everything else hadn't made Cohen realize what was about to happen and second-guess himself.

"We don't have to," Cohen began. "I mean, you know, if you don't want to."

Goldie took a step closer to him. "I want to," she said. "If you do."

Cohen wrapped one arm around her waist, pulled her all the way in, and kissed her. It was different from the kiss in the barn.

It was just as hungry, just as longing, but it was softer. He was telling her something, but Goldie wasn't quite sure what it was yet.

When she slid her hands up under his shirt and traced her way down the dark hair of his stomach to the denim of his jeans, Goldie looked up at him, and the storm in his eyes flashed for just a second before he picked her up, this time without setting her down away from him, and carried her back into the bedroom.

There, in the quiet, everything melted away as Cohen undressed her. She tried to stay still when he worked his way down from her neck to her breasts and then to her stomach.

"Be patient," he whispered to her.

Goldie didn't want to be patient. She felt as if she'd been patient her whole life, and right now, nothing but right now mattered. She didn't want to think about what came before or what would come after. All she wanted was Cohen, right then, and waiting felt like torture.

Cohen stopped at her hip bone and peeled away her panties, sliding them down her legs and losing them in the sheets before settling between her legs. This time, when Goldie cried out, he moved up to meet her mouth.

She grabbed a fistful of his curly hair, now matted with sweat, and he brought his full weight, all of him, crashing down onto her, into her, until there was no space at all between them. Every color, every moment, every fiber of their beings met at once, and she never wanted to let go.

Chapter 37

And then it rained.

It rained every day that week leading up to the carnival. What started out as a drizzle became a torrential downpour by Friday afternoon. Goldie sat on the floor of the school gym, crisscross applesauce, staring into the abyss of decorations and equipment. This wasn't good.

"It's supposed to stop by tomorrow," Tiffany said, sitting down next to her with some effort. "The mud is what'll be the problem."

"It'll be like that scene in *The NeverEnding Story*," Goldie replied, glumly. "All our horses are going to get stuck in the mud."

"I cannot even believe you would invoke the name of Artax at a time like this," Tiffany said. "My daughter can't even discuss that scene without bursting into tears."

"That's what I feel like doing right now," Goldie said. "I hope this won't keep people from showing up."

"It won't," Ashley said, standing over them. "A little rain never hurt anything. Besides, we've got everything pretty much ready.

All we have to do is get it all put out tomorrow. *And* the gym was finished early." She twirled around. "That's pretty lucky, considering the weather."

"You're right," Goldie said, getting up. "We do have pretty much everything finished. We've also got plenty of help. It seems like everybody in town has offered to lend a hand."

"That's what we do here," Ashley replied. "A bunch of the high school kids are working on parade floats down in the ag building. Let's go and see how far along they are."

Goldie and Tiffany pulled on their boots and raincoats and followed Ashley outside, into the rain, and halfway across the high school campus to the agriculture building. It was nearly twice as big as the gym. In fact, it was the biggest building of all.

The inside of the ag building was full of teenagers crawling all over beds of at least six trailers, laughing, throwing things at each other, and decorating the floats more than a little haphazardly.

"Looking good, guys!" Ashley said, encouragingly. "Oh, hey, Jayden, stop spraying that fake snow everywhere. Mr. Hutchins will have your hide!"

"Sorry," Jayden said, clearly not at all sorry.

"Who's watching these kids, anyway?" Ashley asked.

"I am" came a muffled voice from behind trailer number three.

The women peered around the corner to see Cohen crouched down, attaching several wreaths to the sides of the trailer. He looked up and grinned at them, his eyes lingering on Goldie just a second long enough for both Ashley and Tiffany to notice.

"Well, and Peanut Butter." Cohen pointed to the sleeping dog in one corner of the room.

"I think she's more reliable," Tiffany said.

"So, do you think we'll be in business by tomorrow?" Ashley asked. "With this weather?"

"I think so," Cohen replied. "It's supposed to quit later today. The only issue is gonna be the mud."

"Don't mention the mud," Tiffany said, nodding toward Goldie.

"I'm just nervous," Goldie said. "I want to make sure everything goes perfectly."

"It's not going to go perfectly," Cohen said. "There's bound to be a few issues here and there, but I'm sure it'll be fine. We'll have the floats done today. Mayor Rose said nobody has canceled a single float yet. Everybody is still planning to come."

"Good," Goldie said, releasing a breath she didn't know she'd been holding. "That's good."

The door to the ag building opened, and Teddy poured himself inside, dripping from his head to his toes. "Oh, thank God you're here, Dr. Goldie," he said.

"Why?" Goldie asked, alarmed. "What's wrong? Is it Large Marge?"

"No, but there's a crazy lady up at the gym who says she knows you," Teddy replied. "Might as well be Large Marge."

Goldie wrinkled her forehead. "Says she knows *me*?"

"I've never seen her before in my life," Teddy continued. "Drove up, slinging mud everywhere. Said she's been calling you all day. Said she flew in from California and—"

"Alex!" Goldie exclaimed. She hurried out past Teddy and back into the rain.

Alex was standing just inside the gym, staring at a trophy case that housed state basketball championships from the 1980s. She didn't turn around until Goldie called her name.

"What are you doing here?" Goldie asked, enveloping Alex in a hug.

"You kept telling me I should come to visit," Alex replied. "So I did."

"You should have told me," Goldie said.

"I tried! I wanted to surprise you, but then you didn't answer the phone, so I had to drive all over this . . . town . . . to find you." Alex pulled away from Goldie and held her at arm's length. "What are you *wearing*?"

Goldie looked down at herself—at her raincoat, hoodie, black leggings, and Muck Boots. "Are your shoes wet, Alex?" she asked.

"God, yes," Alex replied. "They're soaking, and now my feet are freezing."

"Well," Goldie said. She lifted up one of her feet. "Mine aren't."

"So this is the famous Blue Dog Valley?" Alex asked, unbothered. "You weren't joking when you said it was small. I blinked and drove from one side to the other!"

"How did you know I was here?" Goldie asked. "I mean, here at the school?"

"Well," Alex began, "I put the vet clinic into my GPS, but you weren't there. So I drove around and finally stopped at that diner."

"Ruby's?"

"Yeah, that's the one," Alex continued. "Anyway, there were a couple of old guys sitting there who asked me if I was lost."

"Jack and Elvis."

"Two old guys," Alex repeated. "I told them that, yeah, actually, I was. Then some teenager said I looked like I was from the city and asked if I was looking for you."

"Kaitlyn," Goldie said. "Ruby gave her a job at the diner to keep her away from this guy who is really bad news."

"And then some old lady showed up, and one of the old men got up and kissed her hand," Alex said. "Like a weird old-timey black-and-white movie."

"Lucretia," Goldie said, raising her eyebrows. "Wow, Jack moves fast."

Alex stared at Goldie. "Do you know everyone in this town?"

"Pretty much, I guess," Goldie said.

"Well, that teenager—what did you say her name was again? She gave me directions, and now here I am!" Alex reached out to embrace Goldie again.

"I'm so glad you're here," Goldie said. "I can't wait to show you around, and you're going to be here just in time for the carnival."

"Great!" Alex replied. "I'm starving. Can we go back to that diner to eat? It smelled like heaven in there."

"I can't right now," Goldie said, looking down at her watch. "There is still so much to do. Give me an hour or so, though, and I'll be able to take a break."

"Go ahead," said a voice from the doorway. "We've got this covered."

Goldie and Alex turned to see Tiffany, Ashley, and Cohen standing there. They'd followed Goldie up from the ag building, and they were watching the two women with active curiosity.

"Alex," Goldie said. "These are my friends, Tiffany—we work together at the clinic—Ashley—she owns the best clothing store in town—and Cohen—he's . . ." She trailed off. What was Cohen? She couldn't really call him her friend. Even though they hadn't had a discussion after their trip to Milwaukee, it was clear he was much more than that. But she didn't want to call him her boyfriend, not in front of other people without talking to him first.

"I'm the local farrier," Cohen said, stepping forward to shake Alex's hand. "It's nice to meet you."

"It's nice to meet you, too," Alex said. She eyed Cohen with interest.

"We better get going," Goldie said, trying to shake off her anxiety at the strange intersection of her old life and her new life.

"I have an idea," Alex said, her eyes lighting up. "Why don't we go grab dinner from that diner and bring it back here for everyone? My treat! I'm *dying* to hear all about this place and what my best friend has been up to. Especially"—she grinned at Cohen—"if it has anything to do with *you*."

Cohen cleared his throat, and Goldie nudged Alex.

"I think that's a great idea," Tiffany said, ignoring Goldie's silent pleas for her to shut up. "I'll have the cheeseburger with the works. And fries."

"Me, too," Ashley added.

"I guess you better make it three," Cohen said. "We'll go finish up with the floats and meet you back here."

"Okay," Goldie said. She grabbed Alex by the arm and began dragging her away from the group. "We'll be back."

Chapter 38

"You don't seem very happy to see me," Alex said, following Goldie out to the Jeep.

"What?" Goldie asked, turning to her. "Of course I'm happy to see you! Why would you say that?"

"I can catch a flight out of here," Alex said. "I know I really should have told you first. I thought it would be a nice surprise."

"It *is* a nice surprise," Goldie said, taking Alex's hand. "I'm sorry. I've been so busy with this carnival, and it's been raining all week, and I'm just really stressed. I am so happy to see you. I swear. Please stay."

"I didn't realize this carnival or whatever was such a big deal," Alex replied. "It seems like the entire town is involved."

"They are," Goldie replied, unlocking the passenger-side door of the Jeep for Alex. "We've got billboards up . . ."

"I saw those on my way in."

"And we've got radio and even a television station out of Milwaukee advertising for us," Goldie finished. "I hope it'll be enough. Blue Dog Valley has been struggling for a long time. This carnival could really make a difference."

"Aw," Alex said. "You really care about this place, don't you?"

Goldie paused. "Yeah," she replied. "Yeah, I really do. I like it here, Alex. A lot more than I ever thought I would."

Alex stared out the window as big, fat droplets of rain rolled down the glass. "It's so cold here," she said. "I had to stop and buy a coat. Like, a real coat."

"It's not that cold," Goldie replied. "I mean, I guess it's cold for L.A."

"We aren't *in* L.A.," Alex said, wistfully.

"No," Goldie replied. She came to a stop in front of Ruby's. "We absolutely are not in L.A."

Ruby was waiting for them at the counter when they came inside. "Looks like you found her," she said to Alex.

"I did," Alex replied.

"I'll tell Kaitlyn," Ruby replied. "She was afraid maybe she gave Goldie's location to some kind of stalker. I told her she listens to too many true crime podcasts."

"Ruby, this is my friend Alex," Goldie said. "Alex, this is my friend Ruby."

Ruby wiped one of her hands on her apron and stuck it out toward Alex. "Nice to meet you, Alex," she said.

"You, too," replied Alex. She shook Ruby's hand and then looked down at her own. "Is that . . . is that cinnamon?"

"Sure is," Ruby said. "I'm making cinnamon rolls for tomorrow." She turned to Goldie. "Don't worry, Doc. I've saved you a few back."

"You're the best," Goldie said. "Hey, do you have time for a few to-go orders? We've got Ashley, Tiffany, and Cohen back at the school, and we're all starving."

"You bet," Ruby said. She took out her order pad. "What can I get ya?"

"What do you want, Alex?" Goldie asked.

"I'll just have whatever everybody else is having."

"You're going to have a cheeseburger?" Goldie asked, skeptical. "I haven't seen you eat anything that wasn't green in nearly a decade."

Alex shrugged. "When in Rome."

While Goldie placed their orders, Alex walked around the empty diner. Usually around this time of day, the diner was full of customers, just getting off work and hungry, especially on Friday. Today, however, was different. Nearly everyone was preparing for the carnival. Mayor Rose had asked everyone who lived in Blue Dog Valley to pitch in, and nearly everyone had complied. Goldie had never seen anything like it. Even Roger Dale and his band had forgone their usual sound and were working on Christmas heavy metal carols to sing in the town square. Until a couple of days ago, Goldie didn't know a heavy metal version of "Jingle Bells" could sound so good.

"It's a cute place, huh?" Goldie asked Alex, as they waited for their food.

"It is," Alex agreed. "I can't believe how cute it is, actually."

"Did you think the town was just going to be full of cows or something?" Goldie grinned. "Maybe a few goats? Because there are a lot of goats, actually."

"Maybe," Alex replied with a laugh. "I'm not sure what I was expecting. But this wasn't really it."

"I had that same feeling at first," Goldie replied.

"Hey, speaking of unexpected, that guy you introduced me to is pretty cute. What did he say his name was?"

"Cohen," Goldie replied.

"God, I'm terrible with names," Alex said. "He's got a good face, though."

"It's not too bad," Goldie said.

"What's not too bad?" Ruby asked, handing over three paper bags filled with food. She waved away Alex's attempt to pay. "It's on the house tonight."

"Thanks," Alex replied. "Oh, and that Cohen. His face. It's not so bad."

Ruby laughed. "He does have a pretty good face," she said. She stole a glance at Goldie. "I guess we'd have to ask the good doctor about the rest of him."

"Goldie!" Alex exclaimed. "Is that true?"

"We'll talk about it later," Goldie said to Alex. "Thanks, Ruby."

"See you tomorrow!" Ruby said. "Get a good night's rest! You're going to need it!"

Alex couldn't even wait until they were out of the parking lot before she was demanding Goldie tell her about Cohen.

"You have to tell me everything," Alex said.

"I like him," Goldie said. "I don't know what it'll lead to, but I like him."

"You just *like* him?" Alex asked.

"I like him a lot," Goldie replied. "I didn't at first. We didn't like each other at all when I first got here, but I don't know, Alex. I really like him."

"Well, he's gorgeous," Alex said. "*I* like him."

Goldie laughed. "I don't know what it is yet, whatever it is he and I are doing. So don't make it weird, okay?"

"Me?" Alex asked, pretending to be offended. "I would never. So other than the guy, how is everything else going? The practice?"

"I think it's going well," Goldie said. "I mean, at first nobody wanted to bring their animals to me at all, but it's gotten a lot better. I don't know that I've convinced everybody, but I think most people are coming around . . . slowly."

"That's good, I guess," Alex said. "If that's what you want."

"It is," Goldie replied, realizing that she was being completely honest. "It is exactly what I want."

Chapter 39

"Damn, Ruby makes a mean burger," Cohen said, biting into his cheeseburger.

Alex stared down at the hunk of meat in front of her, hesitant. "Do you know if the meat is locally sourced?" she asked.

Cohen, Tiffany, and Ashley stared at her.

"How many farms did you see on your way into town?" Cohen asked.

"More than I could count," Alex replied. "Pretty sure you've got more cows than people."

"Well, there's your answer," Tiffany said.

"Just eat it," Goldie said to Alex. "Trust me, you're going to love it."

"Peanut Butter loves it," Cohen said, breaking off a piece of meat and feeding it to her. "She'll eat it if you won't."

Alex looked at Peanut Butter, who seemed ready to pounce on her burger, and so Alex took a huge bite and hid the rest behind her back.

"The floats are done," Ashley said, dipping a fry into a blob of ketchup. "All the local shops are ready. We've got the tables and chairs for the outside booths that will need them in city hall. We can pull them out tomorrow morning . . . and . . ." She paused for effect. "*All* of the food and drink vendors are confirmed!"

"That's fantastic," Goldie said, her mouth half full. "I can't believe it's coming together. A few hours ago, I was sure everything was going to fall apart."

"You've done a great job, Goldie," Ashley said. "We never could have done this without you."

"It was a team effort," Goldie replied.

"Now all we have to do is make sure the weather cooperates," Tiffany said.

"I'm not sure we can control that," Goldie said. "But it does look like it's clearing off a little."

"Does it rain a lot here?" Alex asked. "I thought for sure I'd get to see snow."

"It's warmer than it usually is this time of year," Ashley replied. "But wait a couple of days. All of that could change. That's Midwest weather for ya."

"How long are you planning to stay?" Goldie asked Alex, realizing that she hadn't even thought to ask. "Are you going to be here through Christmas?"

Alex looked over at her. "I figured we'd go home for Christmas together," she said. "You're going back to L.A. for the holidays, aren't you?"

There was a long pause while everyone chewed, and then Goldie said, "I'm going home after the carnival. I don't want to leave during a busy time. I'm the only vet for nearly twenty miles. I thought I'd wait until things slowed down a little."

"Oh," Alex said. "Yeah, I guess that makes sense."

"Goldie's become pretty essential here in the valley," Cohen said. "And we didn't make it easy on her at first, either."

"You mean *you* didn't make it easy on me," Goldie replied, throwing a pickle at him.

"I didn't," Cohen said. "But I was wrong, and I'm man enough to admit it."

"I'm going to need you to say that again right into my phone," Ashley said, pretending to record him. "Nice and loud."

"Okay, let's focus on something else," Cohen said good-naturedly. "Alex, uh, what do you do in L.A.?"

"I'm a dermatologist," Alex said. "I have a practice not too far from Goldie's old clinic."

"I bet you have people walking up to you and asking you to look at their gross moles all the time, don't you?" Tiffany asked.

Alex laughed. "Sometimes, when they find out what I do."

"I bet you hate that."

"It's not my favorite."

Tiffany swallowed the last bite of her burger and then replied, "I guess I won't ask you to look at mine, then."

Goldie stood up, grabbing the wrappers that were now scattered around them on the gym floor. "Give me your trash," she said to them. "The sooner we get back to work, the sooner we can all go home and go to bed."

Alex looked down at her watch. "It's just six o'clock."

"And we have to be downtown by three A.M. to start setting up," Goldie said.

"We?" Alex stared at her. "As in, you and me?" She followed Goldie over to the trash cans in the gym lobby.

"You can sleep in if you want," Goldie said.

"You're really all in on this, aren't you?" Alex asked.

"In on what?" Goldie wiped her hands on a paper napkin.

"This," Alex said, gesturing around her. "This place."

"Oh," Goldie said. "Yeah, I guess I am."

"So you're going to stay?" Alex asked.

"I don't know," Goldie said. "But before I make any kind of a decision, I have to talk to Dr. Saltzman. Technically, the clinic is still his."

"Do you want it to be yours?"

Goldie bit her bottom lip, considering the question. Deep down, she already knew the answer. She'd known it for weeks.

"I mean," Alex continued, "are you really going to stay here and become some kind of a farmer's wife or something? Raise chickens and bake bread or whatever it is they do here?"

"Alpacas," Goldie said automatically.

"What?"

"Nothing," Goldie replied. "Look, can't we talk about this later?"

"Don't you miss the city?" Alex asked, ignoring her. "Your parents?"

"Of course," Goldie said. "You know I do."

"But you're coming home for Christmas, right?" Alex continued. "Your mom said you are."

"Yes!" Goldie replied.

"And you promise you'll spend some time at home before you make any kind of rash decision?" Alex grabbed Goldie's hand and held on to it. "You'll think about all the shopping and the food and the nightlife and everything else that you can't get here in Podunk Holler before you decide?"

"Yes," Goldie repeated. "I promise. Now can we please get back to work? I have so much to do before we're ready."

Behind them, Cohen cleared his throat. "Sorry to interrupt," he said. "But there's something going on at Maxine's. Mayor Rose called Ashley to tell her there are a couple of Channel 27 news vans over there, and Maxine was hollerin' at them like she usually hollers at Delores."

"Why would the Channel 27 vans be there now?" Goldie asked. "The interview with Maxine isn't until tomorrow morning."

"I don't know," Cohen replied. "But I think we might need to go over there and see what's going on."

"Okay," Goldie said. "Did you tell Ashley and Tiffany?"

"They're already on their way," he said.

"Where are we going?" Alex followed Goldie and Cohen toward the gym exit.

"Do you like goats?" Goldie asked.

Alex stopped walking. "Not particularly. Why?"

"Well," Goldie said, without turning around, "in that case, you might want to sit in the truck when we get there."

Chapter 40

Mayor Rose had been right—Maxine was absolutely causing a scene. By the time Cohen, Goldie, and Alex arrived, Tiffany and Ashley were standing outside the house with Joshua and a very bewildered-looking camera crew.

"What's going on?" Goldie asked. "I thought the interview wasn't until tomorrow."

"I tried to call you at least fifteen times," Joshua said. "Our producer scheduled another interview tomorrow morning with a couple of the bands performing, and we wanted to get with Maxine tonight."

"I haven't looked at my phone all day," Goldie admitted. "I've been busy with preparations for the carnival."

"So you just showed up without making sure it would be okay?" Cohen asked. "Josh, don't you remember Maxine at all?"

"I thought I did," Joshua said, looking sheepish. "I didn't think it would cause a problem. Most people don't mind, as long as we give them time to get ready for the cameras."

From inside, there was a chorus of elevated voices, and loudest of all was Maxine's.

"What is going on in there?" Alex asked.

"We knocked on the door," Joshua said. "Some half-dressed woman answered. Then Maxine came barreling out. She was waving around a pair of gigantic *scissors*."

"Shears," Cohen said. "Goat-shearing scissors. You're lucky you still have your manhood intact. I've seen her use them."

Joshua shuddered. "I wasn't trying to make trouble," he said. "We were just trying to get everything recorded so we could promote the carnival."

"You should've called me," Cohen said.

"I don't have your number anymore, Cohen," Joshua said. "I tried calling Dad, but he didn't answer, either."

"He's working on the petting zoo," Cohen replied.

"I'm going to go inside and check on her," Tiffany said.

"I'll go with you." Goldie followed after Tiffany, with Alex not far behind.

Tiffany knocked on the front door, but it was already partially open, so she went inside. There were goats, of course, with Edgar standing guard not far from Maxine, who was curiously standing in the middle of four half-dressed women. Maxine no longer had the shears in her hands, but she looked mad enough to pick them back up at any second.

"Maxine," Tiffany said, "what on earth is going on?"

Maxine sniffed. "He knocked on my door."

"It's not illegal to knock on someone else's door," Goldie said.

"You sent him," Maxine said, pointing at Goldie. "He was supposed to come tomorrow!"

"I didn't know he came early," Goldie replied.

One of the women was waving at Goldie, a huge smile on her face. "Hi!" the woman said. "Remember me? From Milwaukee!"

Goldie squinted. Sure enough, it was Sam, the gorgeous, dark-haired woman she and Cohen had delivered the packages to. "Hey," Goldie said. "What are you doing here?"

"My dress didn't fit," Sam said, shrugging.

"I told you to lay off the bread," Maxine growled. "I've gotta let this thing out two more inches." She held up an incredibly short dress that appeared to be nothing but black lace and mesh, with the exception of the bust, which was a dark red satin.

"Those don't look like goat tutus," Tiffany said.

"Nope," Goldie replied. "They sure don't. Not unless your goat is a stripper."

"Oh, we aren't strippers," Sam said, unperturbed. "We're burlesque dancers."

"The best in the Midwest," another woman said. She was wearing a similar dress, but the satin was a soft baby blue.

"Is this why you didn't want to do the interview tonight?" Goldie asked, motioning toward the women.

"That Joshua said *tomorrow morning*," Maxine replied. "I can't have the entire town knowing my business."

"Maxine," Tiffany said. "Nobody would care."

"I make Christmas and Easter dresses for the little girls in town," Maxine replied. "You think nobody would care if they found out I was also making peel-off lingerie for dancers in the city?"

"These peel off?" Sam asked. "That's awesome!"

"Go on upstairs and make sure these fit," Maxine said to the women, handing over more outfits.

The women complied, taking the pieces of fabric and going upstairs, chattering among themselves about the advantages and disadvantages of clothing they might actually be able to peel off.

"I'm so sorry, Maxine," Goldie said. "I didn't know they wanted to come early to interview you."

Maxine sighed. "I know, but it's my business. I don't have to share my business with the whole town, especially not my nosy sister, Delores."

"Delores doesn't know?" Tiffany asked.

"Of course not," Maxine said. "She'd just tell me our mama would be rolling over in her grave."

"I knew your mama," Tiffany said. "I watched her slip her number to half the eligible bachelors at the Methodist church fellowship dinner. She'd be proud."

Maxine smiled a little at that.

"What can we do to help?" Goldie asked.

"Make them go away," Maxine said. "I don't know why they're standing out there like a bunch of stalkers. I'm not doin' that in-terview tonight."

"Their producer double-booked them," Goldie explained. "If you did the interview tonight, we'd get more exposure for the carnival."

"What if you had the girls stay inside, and you agreed to give the interview outside?" Tiffany asked. "You could introduce the goats, and even put Edgar in a tutu."

"And nobody would come inside?" Maxine asked, her tone suspicious.

"Nobody would come inside."

"Fine," Maxine said, throwing her hands up in the air. "But tell them nobody touches the goats."

Chapter 41

"Wow," Alex said, when Goldie drove up to the cabin. "This is . . . quaint."

"Kevin is going to be really excited to meet you," Goldie said, ignoring Alex's passive-aggressive comment.

"Who is Kevin?"

"Oh," Goldie said, realizing that of course Alex didn't know who Kevin was. "He's my dog. Well, he's kind of the town's dog, but he basically lives with me."

"That's . . . weird," Alex said, two seconds before she was accosted by a mass of fur and slobber. "Oopmh . . ."

"I told you."

"That's not a dog," Alex replied, after Kevin had finally calmed down. "That's some kind of wild animal."

"I have a cat, too," Goldie said. "Her name is Airport."

"What?"

"I found her in the airport," Goldie explained. "She's a Sphynx cat, and she's a little shy. She's probably hiding under the bed."

"I feel like I don't know you at all," Alex replied, setting her bag down and opening the refrigerator in search of a drink. "Coke? You have like six Cokes in here, Goldie!"

"There's water in there, too," Goldie said defensively. "You didn't tell me you were coming, so I didn't have time to prepare."

"You mean hide the evidence."

"Did you come here to insult me or to visit me?" Goldie asked. She took a Coke out of the refrigerator and took a drink, enjoying the horrified look on Alex's face.

"Well, I came here to save you, actually," Alex replied. "But it looks like you've fully adapted to small-town life."

"I have," Goldie replied. "I don't need you to save me, Alex. I like it here. I like my job, and I like the people. I don't know if I want to go back to L.A."

Alex sighed and sat down in one of the kitchen chairs, and Kevin, thinking this was his opportunity for treats, sat next to her on the floor. "I'm sorry," she said. "I didn't expect to find you so happy. You didn't always sound that way on the phone."

"I really am happy," Goldie replied. "I could really use my best friend, especially tomorrow. I have no idea what I'm doing. I'm terrified everything is going to fall apart at the last possible second."

"Why do you do that to yourself?" Alex asked. "Nothing you do ever falls apart." She put her hand on Goldie's. "Okay. From here on out, I'm your friend. We'll get up at the ass crack of dawn and make the carnival the best thing this town has ever seen, and everyone will love you, especially that hot farmer of yours."

Goldie handed what was left of her Coke over to Alex and said, "Thank you, and you know, Cohen does have a best friend. From what I hear, he owns a lot of land. We might be able to turn you into Laura Ingalls Wilder yet."

Chapter 42

The morning was beautiful. The rain and gloom of the previous days were gone and had been replaced with sunshine and a record high of forty-two degrees in Blue Dog Valley. Alex had gotten up before Goldie and fixed French toast, and although it wasn't quite as good as Ruby's cinnamon rolls, it was enough to wake Goldie up and get her going for the day.

By the time the food trucks and outside participants began rolling in, everything was set up and ready to go, including the tent Cohen had ordered for the petting zoo. Inside, there was a chorus of animal noises that told Goldie she wasn't the only one who was nervous.

"Are they going to be okay in there all together?" Goldie asked Cohen. She and Alex were walking from booth to booth to make sure everyone was getting what they needed. "The piglets don't sound happy."

"Those piglets are afraid someone is going to grease 'em and chase 'em," Cohen replied. "That's usually what happens when they get put in a pen like that."

"Grease them?" Alex asked.

"Yeah, you know," Cohen replied. "For a hog chase."

"I'll have to take your word for it."

"What about Alice?" Goldie asked, reaching up to give Alice a carrot. "Is she all right?"

"Oh, she's fine," Cohen said. "Everybody's fine. Stop worrying."

"Okay," Goldie said. "I guess we'll go and check on someone else."

"You don't have to do that," Cohen replied. "We've got it covered."

Goldie looked at him, but he wasn't looking at her. There was something about the tone of his voice that was a little sharper than she'd been used to lately. She couldn't imagine that she'd done something to upset him, but she didn't have time to ask. She heard her name being called from outside the tent and went to see about it.

"There you are," Roger Dale said when he saw Goldie approaching. "I thought I was going to have to use my walkie."

"You have a walkie?" Goldie asked. She tried her best not to giggle at Roger Dale with his clipboard and badge that read CARNIVAL VOLUNTEER that he'd clearly made himself. He was taking his duties *very* seriously.

"Tiff didn't give it to ya?" he asked. "Aw, shit. I gave it to her this morning!"

"It's still morning," Goldie replied. "I'll find her and see about it. Now, what's up?"

"Well, the macramé sweater lady and the Christmas sweater lady have booths right next to each other," Roger Dale said.

"I know," Goldie replied. "I put them together, because their products are so similar."

"The Christmas sweater lady doesn't like that," Roger Dale continued. "She's afraid she's going to lose business."

"Why?"

Roger Dale sighed. "*Because* the macramé sweater lady technically comes first if you're walking counterclockwise."

"But there's no specific way people have to walk," Goldie protested.

"Tell that to the Christmas sweater lady."

"Okay," Goldie said, putting a finger to her chin. "Move the Christmas sweater lady over by Delores. She's selling cat-hair Christmas ornaments. There's room over there, and it comes way before the macramé sweater lady, if, you know, you're walking counterclockwise."

Before Roger Dale could answer, there was a crackling from his walkie-talkie, and then a voice screeched, *"Roger Dale! Come in, Roger Dale!"*

Poor Roger Dale nearly jumped out of his visor, dropping his clipboard in the process. "Tiffany!" Roger Dale said when he'd recovered. "You are not authorized to have that walkie! Your instructions were to give it to Dr. Goldie!"

"It's mine now!" Tiffany proclaimed.

"Don't worry," Goldie said, patting Roger Dale's arm. "You go and deal with the sweater ladies, and I'll find Tiffany."

"This is why we divorced, you know," Roger Dale said. "That woman can't take basic instructions."

"I thought it was because you cheated on her with her sister," Goldie replied.

"That, too," Roger Dale agreed.

"You know," Alex said as she and Goldie headed off to find the abducted walkie-talkie, "this town is a lot more interesting than I gave it credit for. You've got a lot of fascinating characters."

"You don't know the half of it," Goldie replied.

The streets were beginning to fill up with people—older couples strolling along and holding hands, families with children already sticky from caramel apples, and teenagers pretending to look bored while secretly eyeing the large bouncy castle in the far corner of the carnival. Lively Christmas music was being piped in from somewhere, even though Goldie couldn't quite figure out where it was coming from.

They found Tiffany in the gymnasium, where Kaitlyn was manning the high school bake sale.

"We've already made fifty dollars!" Kaitlyn said when she saw Goldie. She held up a stack of miscellaneous bills. "Granny's gooey butter cake sold out in fifteen minutes!"

"That's great!" Goldie replied, holding out her hand to Tiffany. "Now tell your Granny to give me the walkie-talkie before your pop has a heart attack."

"Fine," Tiffany grumbled, handing it over to Goldie. "I was having fun, though."

"Maybe a little too much fun," Goldie replied.

"I guess Mayor Rose hasn't found you yet," Tiffany said. "Otherwise, you'd be freaking out already."

"Why?" Goldie asked. "What's wrong?"

"Nothing's *wrong*," Tiffany replied. "But the city council voted to have you be the grand marshal of the parade!"

"What?"

"Yeah," Tiffany continued. "Well, you and Alice. You'll walk together at the front of the parade. Maybe wave a little. Throw candy."

"Who's Alice?" Alex asked.

"Cohen's alpaca," Goldie replied, still somewhat shocked from the announcement.

"You're going to be the parade marshal with an alpaca?" Alex looked first at Tiffany and then over at Goldie.

"Why me?" Goldie asked, ignoring Alex. "Why would the city council pick me?"

"It's usually the mayor," Tiffany said. "But he told the council he was too old and slow for it this year, and so they decided you should do it."

"And Alice?"

"Oh, she does it every year," Tiffany replied.

"Dr. Goldie! Dr. Goldie! Over," came the crackling of the walkie.

Goldie pushed the TALK button. "What is it, Roger Dale?"

"We've got a new wrinkle. Over."

Goldie sighed. "What is it?"

"You forgot to say *over*. Over."

"Just tell me what it is Roger Dale . . . Over."

"Well, we've got an outhouse race going on over on the baseball field, and we've got a guy stuck in his outhouse. Over," Roger Dale said.

"How did he get stuck?" Goldie asked. "Wait, never mind. I'll find Mayor Rose and head over . . . Over."

Chapter 43

It took Roger Dale longer to explain to Alex what an outhouse race was than it took to free the man, who actually turned out to be a high school senior, from the makeshift outhouse. He hobbled off the field to cheers and applause.

"This mishap aside," Mayor Rose said, once the teenager was off the field, "I think today is going pretty well. All of our lots reserved for parking are full."

"That's great!" Goldie replied. "I think the interviews Joshua did for Channel 27 really helped us out."

"I agree," the mayor replied. "That boy's really turned himself around."

Goldie smiled. She hoped that at some point during the day Cohen would find the time to talk to Joshua. She hadn't seen him since their conversation at the petting zoo. "So, Mayor Rose," Goldie said, "Tiffany mentioned something to me about being chosen as the, uh, grand marshal of the parade?"

"She was supposed to wait for me to tell you," Mayor Rose said.

"But there's a homemade-brew tasting happening at the Bushy Beaver, then the battle of the bands, and then we'll have the parade. You'll need to meet at the ag building by six P.M. to be co-marshal."

"And you're sure you want me?" Goldie asked.

"It's all decided," Mayor Rose replied. "If I were you, I'd go have some lunch and rest your feet."

"Can we get a funnel cake somewhere?" Alex asked. "Oh my God, I haven't had a funnel cake in literal *years*."

"The stand over by the Beaver should have them," Mayor Rose replied.

"Let's go!" Alex said, excitedly.

"Are you sure you don't need me to do anything right now?" Goldie asked the mayor. "I don't want to leave you to all the dirty work."

"Like sawing boys out of outhouses?" Mayor Rose replied, laughing. "No, I think we'll be fine. Go and have some fun."

* * *

THERE WAS A crowd gathering at the Beaver when Goldie and Alex got to the food truck that was parked nearest to it. They each ordered a funnel cake, and to Goldie's surprise, Alex ordered a Coke to go with it.

"When in Rome!" Alex said with a laugh.

They sat down at a picnic table and watched the people streaming in and out of the bar. Most of the people, clearly tourists, were taking pictures in front of the "Bushy Beaver" sign and giggling to themselves.

"You have to admit," Alex said, her mouth half full. "That's quite a name."

"I can't decide if it's really gross or really clever," Goldie replied. "Maybe a little bit of both."

Goldie felt a sense of pride at seeing the happy people buzzing around the town. She hoped lots of pictures would be added to social media, and if they were lucky, maybe a few influencers with a horde of followers would create a little bit of buzz around the valley. A yearly event, she thought, could help the town. Maybe next year, they could have a fall festival. Her brain was fizzing with so many new ideas that she almost didn't notice Cohen and Brian standing outside the bar near the side door, both of them with their arms crossed and their voices elevated a notch above friendly.

"Hey," Alex said. She nudged Goldie. "Isn't that your farmer boyfriend up there arguing with some guy?"

Goldie looked up. "Yeah," she replied. "I wonder what's going on."

"I can't hear them," Alex said. "But neither of them looks happy."

After a couple of minutes, Brian threw his hands up in the air and went back inside, leaving Cohen outside still fuming. When he caught Goldie's eye, he didn't smile. He didn't wave. He simply turned around and walked off.

Goldie stood up to follow after him, but she decided against it and sat back down.

"Did you two have a fight, too?" Alex asked.

"Not that I know of," Goldie said. "But I thought he was kind of weird to me this morning at the petting zoo."

"Maybe he's just having a bad day," Alex replied. "I won't hate him yet unless you want me to."

"He wasn't happy about the carnival," Goldie said. "I thought he'd come around, though."

"Don't let it bother you," Alex said, putting her powdered-sugar-covered hand over Goldie's. "You're a hit! This carnival is a hit! I've already taken a ton of pictures, and I'm going to record a video later to put on my YouTube channel."

Goldie's eyes lit up. "Alex!" she exclaimed. "I totally forgot you're an influencer!"

"Well," Alex said with a laugh, "it'll be a nice change for my followers. They're used to looking at gross skin stuff, but today, it's all about the funnel cake, baby!"

Chapter 44

Goldie reported to the agriculture building at the high school right on time. She left Alex with Tiffany, and the two of them promised to be good and not get into trouble while she was gone. She didn't believe for a second, though, that they wouldn't get up to something. She just hoped Tiffany left poor Roger Dale out of it this time. He'd called her on the walkie at least fifteen times after lunch.

Everyone participating in the parade was already there, including Mayor Rose in his Santa suit. He'd clearly stuffed a pillow up underneath the fur-lined red coat to hide his lean figure, but for some reason, Goldie thought it worked.

"This wasn't what I had in mind when you said I would play an integral part in the parade," Roger Dale said, coming out of the bathroom wearing a Mrs. Claus dress and white, curly wig. "I look ridiculous."

"I think you look kinda cute," Goldie said, trying her best to hold in the laugh that Mayor Rose couldn't.

"That's it," Roger Dale said. "I'm takin' this off."

"You can't," the mayor replied. "Think of the children!"

Roger Dale threw his hands up in the air. "Fine!" he said. "If it's for the kids."

Goldie looked around the building for Cohen. Alice was there, being petted and fed treats by a couple of high school girls who were taking about a hundred selfies with her. But there was no sign of Cohen.

Finally, as they were lining up, Cohen walked through the doors and took Alice's leash. He led her to where Goldie was standing at the front. She looked over and smiled at him.

"Hey," she said. "Where have you been?"

"You're not the only one who's been busy today," he said.

"Okay, people!" said a woman with a megaphone. "It's time to *move*! Be careful not to cut anyone off. Make sure to follow the person directly in front of you. When the parade marshal stops, we all stop! When the marching band stops, we all stop!"

"Will someone tell me when to stop?" Goldie asked the woman once she'd lowered her megaphone.

The woman nodded. "I'll be following you just to your left. I'll let you know. Here is your candy. You can throw it out whenever you see kids. But don't throw too much. It needs to last the whole parade."

"Okay," Goldie said. "I wish I'd had a chance to go home and change clothes."

"You look fine," Cohen said. "You don't have to be fancy. It's just a parade."

The woman with the megaphone raised it again and yelled, *"Let's go!"*

The parade lurched forward, and they moved away from the ag building and off the school grounds toward Main Street ahead of them. Goldie waited until she saw a crowd of children waving on the side of the road and threw them a few pieces of candy.

"Is something bothering you?" Goldie asked as they walked. "You're being really . . . I don't know. Weird."

Cohen gritted his teeth. "We'll talk about it later."

Goldie stopped walking when the megaphone woman held out her hand, and the high school marching band began to play "Jingle Bells."

"No," Goldie said. "I want to talk about it now. If you're going to continue being a jackass, I want to know why."

"What if I stop being a jackass?" Cohen asked. "Can we talk about it later then?"

"Are you really going to stop being a jackass?"

Cohen reined Alice in from meandering over to a child with a caramel apple in his hand and said, "*Someone* entered my cider into the tasting contest at the Beaver. It won, and now Joshua wants to do a piece on it for the Christmas special on Channel 27."

"That is amazing!" Goldie said. "Why would you be mad about that?"

"I told you I didn't want anyone to know about it," Cohen said. "I said I wanted to keep it my thing, just a hobby."

"I know," Goldie replied. "So why did someone enter it?"

"Why did you enter it?" Cohen asked.

They started marching again, and Goldie had to look straight ahead to make sure she would be paying attention when the woman told them to stop again. It was so loud, but Cohen's words were ringing in her ears.

"Me?" she yelled over the noise. "Why would I do that? I didn't even know there *was* a tasting contest until today."

"You're basically in charge of this entire thing. You're telling me you didn't even know about what's happening at the Beaver?"

"Candy!" the megaphone woman screamed.

"Brian must've forgotten to tell me," Goldie replied, reaching down into the candy bag.

"It was *your cider*, Goldie," Cohen said. "The California Sparkle. I haven't given that to anyone else but you."

"Well, it wasn't me," Goldie replied. "You have more bottles of it in your barn, don't you?"

"So you're trying to tell me someone broke into my barn and stole a bottle of cider to enter into this contest that apparently Brian didn't even tell anyone about?" Cohen asked.

"I said he didn't tell me," Goldie replied. "Clearly he told other people. Why don't you just ask Brian who entered it?"

"He won't tell me," Cohen said. "He said he promised he wouldn't tell who it was."

By now, they'd reached the town square. There were people everywhere, cheering, waving, and taking pictures. Goldie made a mental note to herself that the next time she was made honorary parade marshal, even if it was for the Macy's Thanksgiving Day Parade, to respectfully decline.

"I didn't do it," Goldie said again, stopping for the marching band to play another Christmas tune. "I'm telling you, I didn't."

"There's nobody else who could have done it," Cohen said.

"There are plenty of people who could have done it," Goldie said. "But I wasn't one of them, and I can't believe you think I'm lying to you about it."

"It doesn't make sense for it to have been anyone else," Cohen replied. "Not everything has to be shared with the world. This isn't Los Angeles. I don't want a social media following. I don't want everyone to see what I'm doing all the time."

"What are you talking about?" Goldie asked. "I'm not trying to do anything except help the town."

"Maybe *we* don't need it," Cohen said.

"*We* do need it," Goldie countered. "And if I'm going to make a life here, I want to help—"

"Are you?" Cohen asked, cutting her off. "Going to make a life here? Because the way you were talking to your friend, it didn't seem like you were."

"Is that what this is about?" Goldie asked.

They started walking again but didn't get even ten yards before stopping again. This time, Cohen turned to Goldie and said, "I heard what you said. You told her you would think about going back to L.A. and forgetting about *Podunk Holler*."

"I only said that to get her to stop talking about it," Goldie replied. "I wouldn't make any kind of a decision, not a big one like that, without at least talking to you first."

"Well, we're talking now."

"It feels a lot more like you're talking *at* me," Goldie said. "You're accusing me of doing things I haven't done and may not even do."

"Don't stay because of me," Cohen replied, bitterly. "I was fine before you got here, and I'll be fine when you leave."

Goldie felt like she'd been punched in the stomach, and she had to blink to keep herself from bursting into tears out of sheer frustration and hurt. How could he say that?

"Is that really how you feel?" she asked, finally.

Cohen relaxed his grip on Alice's harness when they stopped in front of city hall, which was the endpoint of the parade. For a moment, it looked as if he wasn't going to answer Goldie, or maybe that he couldn't answer Goldie.

Over the noise surrounding them and the deafening silence between them, Teddy rushed up to them, winded, his face red from the cold and creased with worry.

"Have either of you seen Addie?" he asked. "I can't find her anywhere. Nobody has seen her!"

"What?" Cohen asked. "Addie's missing?"

Teddy looked as if he might cry. "I just left for a second! For a second at the Beaver to grab a case of beer to help Brian inside, and when I came back out, she was gone."

"Where was she when you left?" Goldie asked.

"Outside at the picnic tables," Teddy said. "She had a balloon animal that she was playing with, and I told her not to hold it too tight or it would pop . . . Oh Christ, where is she?"

"We'll help you look," Goldie said to Teddy, stepping out of the parade just as it ended and there were more unintelligible screams coming from the megaphone.

"I'll take Alice to the trailer," Cohen replied. "I'll round up as many people as I can."

Teddy nodded and hurried away from the parade crowd at a clip that nearly forced Goldie to break into a run. "Teddy!" she called after him. "Wait!"

Teddy slowed down a little and turned back to her. "Where is she, Goldie? Where?"

"I don't know," Goldie replied. She felt a knot form in the pit of her stomach, and she tried not to think about how often, on the news, stories like this didn't end well.

Teddy scanned the crowd. "I can't see her. I can't see anything. There are too many people."

"What is she wearing?" Goldie asked, reaching into her pocket to text Alex. "That will help if we tell people what she's wearing."

For a moment, the worry on Teddy's face dissolved, and he said with fondness, "Her red stormtrooper costume. I haven't been able to get her out of it since Halloween."

"That should be easy to spot," Goldie said. She stood on her tiptoes and glanced around, and waved at Roger Dale, who was coming toward them with his clipboard.

"That was great, Dr. Goldie," Roger said. "Just great. I—"

"Roger," Goldie said, cutting him off. "Teddy can't find Addie."

The color drained from Roger Dale's face. "What?"

"I don't know, man," Teddy said, running his hands through his hair. "She was there, and then she wasn't."

Goldie put her hand on Roger Dale's shoulder and said, "She is wearing a red stormtrooper costume, you know, from *Star Wars*."

"I know what a stormtrooper is," Roger Dale replied.

"Okay, good," Goldie continued. "Can you go find Mayor Rose or someone who can announce over the speaker system that a four-year-old girl is missing? Blond hair and blue eyes, wearing a red stormtrooper Halloween costume. Then round up as many people as you can and start looking."

"Do we need to call the police?" Teddy asked, the panic in his voice rising. "I didn't think about calling the police!"

"I'll take care of it," Roger Dale replied. He reached out and turned Teddy toward him, forcing Teddy to look him in the eye. "We'll find her. Okay? We'll find her."

"Let's go back to where you saw her last," Goldie said to Teddy. "Let's retrace your steps, starting at the Beaver."

Teddy nodded, and they silently headed back over to the bar to begin their search. Surely, Goldie thought, there had to be some clue there—some shred of evidence that they could use to figure out where she'd gone. She couldn't remember seeing Addie at all that day, not early in the morning as they set up or in the afternoon around the carnival, and not on the sidelines of the parade like the rest of the children, reaching out their hands for candy. Of course, she'd spent a fair amount of time during the parade arguing with Cohen over issues that seemed, at this very moment, incredibly trivial.

"She was sitting here," Teddy said, pointing to a picnic table. "I told her, 'Stay right here, baby, Daddy will be right back.'"

Goldie scanned the area, but it was so dark that she couldn't really see anything. It was getting colder, too.

"I walked up here," Teddy continued, running up the little hill to the bar's back door. "I saw her sitting there as I went inside. I wasn't in there for more than a minute . . . two at the most."

Goldie moved away from the picnic table and walked down toward the path that led away from the carnival and out of town, toward the vet clinic. It was the path that ran alongside the main highway, beaten down from years of walking and horseback riding. It was also the path that the hayride was using to pull people up toward Brian's Christmas tree farm full of lights. There were three trailers pulled by tractors going back and forth, with frequency picking up now that it was dark and the display would be at its brightest.

It wouldn't be hard for Addie to have joined the hayride, if she'd seen it go by while she was sitting at the picnic table waiting for Teddy. Goldie followed the path farther up, and as she did, she spotted something blue and flat, mashed into the path. She bent down to pick it up and discovered that it was the remnants of a balloon.

"Teddy!" Goldie called out. "Hey, Teddy! Over here!"

Teddy rushed over to where Goldie was standing, and he snatched the balloon out of her hands. "That's her balloon animal. Oh God."

"I'm going to follow the trail up toward the Christmas tree farm," Goldie said. "Maybe she got on one of the rides."

"I'll come with you," Teddy said, and started to follow her, when Roger Dale approached them with a sheriff's deputy.

"Teddy," Roger Dale said. "Deputy Goode wants to ask you some questions about Addie."

"I need to go look for her," Teddy said. "I don't have time."

"It'll just take a few minutes," Deputy Goode replied. "I just need some basic information."

"You know all her basic information, John!" Teddy said, exasperated. "Your wife helped deliver her, for Christ's sake!"

"Teddy, please," Roger Dale said, again turning Teddy toward him. "Mayor Rose is gathering up a search party. Cohen is already out with Peanut Butter, and you know that dog has one hell of a sniffer. This will just take a few minutes."

Teddy sighed and signaled to Goldie to go on, and so she left him there with the deputy and Roger Dale and continued on the path ahead of her. After a few minutes, she passed by her cabin, and out came Kevin, wiggling with excitement to see her.

"I can't come home right now, bud," Goldie said to him, taking a second to bend down and scratch his head. "I'm sorry."

Kevin didn't seem to mind, and he loped along beside her as she walked. She felt better having him with her, especially as her mind raced with all the possibilities out there, about all the places Addie could be or would end up if they didn't find her.

As they neared the farm, a tractor pulling a trailer full of squealing children descended upon them. Goldie stood in the middle of the road and waved her arms back and forth. The man on the tractor, confused, cut the engine.

"What's the problem, Dr. Goldie?" he asked.

Goldie immediately recognized the man as Alfie. "Oh, Alfie," she said, relieved. "Does Teddy's little girl, Addie, happen to be on your hayride?"

"I don't think so, but you're welcome to have a look."

Goldie walked around the side of the tractor and scanned the rows of hay bales for the little girl. Kevin, who'd been interested at first, lifted an ear at something in the woods that only a dog could have heard and scampered off. Normally, Goldie would have called for him to come back, but she was too focused on finding Addie and was disappointed when she came up empty-handed.

"It doesn't look like she's here," Goldie said, finally.

"Brian brought another crew up and back about twenty minutes ago," Alfie offered. "Might check with him."

"Okay, thanks," Goldie said, waving to the children, who yelped and cheered when Alfie started the engine roaring again and resumed their ride down the hill.

Goldie considered following after them and making her way back to the carnival, but instead she decided to keep walking up toward the farm, just in case. Besides, Kevin had run up that way, too, and she didn't want to just leave him. At the very least, she could bring him back with her and he could aid in the search.

As she walked, she pulled out her phone and tapped the flashlight app.

"Kevin!" she called. "Come here, boy! Come on!"

There was a woof in the distance, and Goldie followed the sound. There weren't any hayrides at the farm when she entered, no laughing children. Just lights so bright she no longer needed her flashlight, and rows and rows of trees. There were so many trees, Goldie felt overwhelmed. Right now, it wasn't nearly as magical as it had been when Cohen brought her there the first time. All she could think about was a lost little girl, the darkness and cold, and what might happen if they couldn't find her.

Finally, as she was about to give up, Kevin appeared, brush stuck to his thick fur. "Where have you been?" Goldie asked. "Come on, we need to get going."

Kevin ignored her and trotted off again, barking his displeasure at her order.

"Get back here!" she called after him, picking up her pace, and eventually breaking into a run. "Kevin!"

She was moving so fast, she didn't see the slight change in landscape, didn't see the way the ground fell out from beneath her until she was tumbling down, nearly head over heels, through a small opening in the trees. She landed flat on her back, staring up at the lights, and she heard—at least she thought she heard—laughter in the distance. Or maybe it was just a dog barking. She couldn't tell, not right now, when the searing pain in her ankle was trailing up through all of her extremities, making it difficult to think or move.

Finally, Goldie sat up. "Kevin!" she yelled. "Kevin, you—" She stopped when her eyes focused on the scene in front of her—that of her huge dog sitting beside a tiny girl in a red stormtrooper costume stroking his head and giggling.

"Good doggie," she was saying. "Good doggie."

"You wonderful dog," Goldie finished. "Kevin, you wonderful, glorious dog!"

Addie ran up to Goldie and inspected her. "You fell down," she said, picking a twig out of Goldie's hair.

"I did," Goldie agreed, smiling despite her pain. "Everyone has been looking for you, Addie. How did you get up here?"

"Hayride," Addie said simply. "I jumped off cuz I wanted to play in the trees."

"Well, your daddy is missing you. We better get you back to him." Goldie pulled herself up, wincing. She attempted to put a little pressure on her ankle, and it hurt, but she could walk.

"Okay," Addie replied, her bottom lip turning outward in a pout. "I wanted to chase the doggie."

"You can chase him back to town," Goldie replied, and then added, "as long as you stay where I can see you."

Addie seemed satisfied with this and called to Kevin, who dutifully followed her. Goldie, for her part, limped after them, wishing they all could go faster so that Teddy didn't have to worry a second longer. She'd just pulled out her cell phone to call Tiffany to relay the message when Cohen and Peanut Butter ran headlong into Addie and Kevin.

"Two doggies!" Addie shrieked.

Peanut Butter, seeming to understand the situation, submitted to a flurry of pets from Addie without even the faintest hint of a growl.

Goldie waved at Cohen and limped toward him, unaware of the flood of tears streaming down her face at the sight of him.

"I've got them," Cohen said into a walkie-talkie, and Goldie could only guess that Roger Dale was on the other end. "Addie seems fine, but I think Goldie might be hurt. Send a truck up here."

"I'm fine," Goldie said, through her tears. "I'm fine. It's fine. We're both fine."

"You don't look fucking fine," Cohen replied.

"Bad word," Addie said to Cohen. "Bad word, Mr. Cowhen."

"Sorry," Cohen said to Addie. "You stay right here next to me."

"I just twisted my ankle," Goldie said before Cohen could say anything else. "I tripped chasing Kevin."

Cohen bent down to examine her ankle. "It's already swelling," he said.

"It's not broken," Goldie said, willing that statement to be true. "I can walk on it."

"You shouldn't be walking on it."

Goldie sighed. "I'm fine."

"Why did you go off on your own looking for Addie when you could have waited for someone to go with you?" Cohen asked.

"*I'm* not a lost child," Goldie replied. "I don't need permission to go anywhere or do anything. I went looking for her, and I found her. I think 'thank you' are the words you're searching for."

Cohen's jaw flexed. "That's not what I meant. I just meant— aw, hell."

Behind them a horn honked, and Teddy jumped out of the back of a trailer filled with hay and ran to Addie.

"Daddy!" Addie said as he engulfed her in his arms. "Hi, Daddy."

Teddy held her out to look at her. "Are you okay? What were you doing all the way out here?"

Addie tilted her head to one side. "I was playing."

"You can't just run off like that," Teddy replied. "You always have to tell Daddy where you're going. Daddy always has to go with you."

"Okay, Daddy," Addie said.

Teddy looked over at Goldie. "Thank you," he said to her. "Thank you so much for finding my baby."

"Kevin found her," Goldie said. "I was just following him."

"Kevin?" Teddy asked, one side of his mouth threatening a smile. "Well, I'll be damned. I guess he's a better sheepdog than we all thought."

Goldie began to hobble her way toward the trailer, when Cohen stopped her. "Don't walk," he said.

"How else am I supposed to get to the trailer?" she asked. "Fly?"

"I'll carry you," Cohen said.

Goldie snorted. "That's ridiculous. I can get there myself. It's just a few feet."

"Goddammit, Goldie," Cohen said. "Will you just—will you just please let me help you?"

Goldie nearly protested again, but when she looked up at him, his eyes were so pleading, his jaw so set that she relented and allowed him to pick her up. She wrapped her arms around his neck while he carried her, drying her cheeks on his shirt as he walked. When he sat her down, gently, onto a bale of hay, she held on a little longer than she meant to.

They rode in silence for a while, listening to Addie chatter to Teddy about the pretty lights and the nice doggies. Finally, Cohen said, "I'm sorry about what I said to you earlier. About my cider."

"I didn't enter it, I swear," Goldie replied. "I would never . . . I would never *do* that to you."

"I know," Cohen said. "I know that, and I was just angry that *someone* did and now I have to talk to Joshua about it on television."

"You need to talk to Joshua, anyway," Goldie reminded him. "Don't you?"

Cohen nodded. "I do, but not on network television."

"Promise me you will," Goldie said. "Talk to him for real."

"I will," Cohen replied. "I will in my own time."

"I know."

"I do everything in my own time, Goldie," he continued. "Sometimes I worry that you'll think it's too slow for you."

"What do you mean?" Goldie asked.

"I don't know," Cohen began, stopping to clear his throat. "I don't know if I'm ready for all of this. For you and me. And I don't know if you're ready to wait on me to figure it out."

Goldie turned her head away from him, tears stinging her eyes again.

Chapter 45

The tractor and the trailer ground to a stop just beside the clinic. Tiffany was standing outside, waiting on them. Goldie thought she was waiting to make sure Addie was all right, but the look on her face told Goldie it was something different altogether.

"Goldie!" Tiffany jogged up to Goldie, out of breath. "It's Delores's cat. She went home to check on him during the parade, and something is wrong. She won't say it, but I think poor Milton is dying. She's bringing him to the clinic right now."

"Oh no," Goldie said. "Is she on her way here?"

Tiffany nodded.

"You can't go to the clinic," Cohen interjected. "You need to go to the ER and have that ankle checked out."

"What's wrong with your ankle?"

"I'm fine," Goldie said, and this time, there was no changing her mind. "Tiffany, help me down."

Tiffany obliged, and Goldie managed to get her bearings on the ground beneath her. She knew Cohen was staring after her as she limped to the front door of the clinic, but she didn't look back. He'd said all he needed to say, and she'd heard him loud and clear. There was no point in looking back now.

"Have you seen Alex?" Goldie asked Tiffany. "She's got to be wondering what the hell is going on."

"She was with me when Delores called. I sent her to the cabin with my spare key."

"You have a spare key?"

"Come on," Tiffany said. "We'll discuss that later."

Delores arrived a few minutes later, and this time, she didn't have Milton in his carrier. She was holding him in her arms, wrapped in a pink bath towel.

"Let's get him into the exam room," Goldie said to Delores. "What happened?"

"I don't know," Delores said through sobs. "I went home to check on him, you know, because I'm not usually gone from him that long. And he was just lying there. He couldn't even pick his head up."

"Was this out of the blue?" Goldie asked.

Tiffany took Milton and laid him down on the table. "Delores, has he been having trouble eating lately?"

Delores nodded. "Well, he hasn't been wanting to eat for the last week or so. I've been feeding him by hand, you know, because he was kind of weak."

Goldie and Tiffany shared a look with each other.

"I know," Delores said before either of the women could respond. "I know it's time. He told me it's time. But I just don't know if I can bear it. He's all I have." She dissolved into tears. "He's all I have."

Goldie put her hand on Delores's shoulder. "Tiffany and I are going to step out of the room so you can have some time alone with Milton," she said. "We'll be right outside when you're ready."

"I feel so awful for Delores," Tiffany said once they'd left the room. "I hate this for her so much."

"Me, too," Goldie replied. "This is always the worst part about this job, isn't it? I've always just hated it."

"Me, too," Tiffany said. "And you know me well enough by now to know I'm not the most empathetic person."

"You're wonderful," Goldie said, honestly.

Tiffany smiled. "Thanks."

"Hey," Goldie said. "Do you have Maxine's number?"

"Yeah, but why would you call her?" Tiffany asked.

"Well, they're sisters," Goldie replied.

"Who hate each other."

"Wouldn't you still want your sister with you during a time like this?" Goldie asked.

Tiffany considered this. Then she handed over her phone. "Here," she said. "You can try it. I guess the worst she can say is no."

It took a few tries, but Maxine finally answered. "What is it, Tiff?" she barked into the phone. "I'm down here at this damn petting zoo trying to collect the goats."

"Uh, Maxine, it's actually Goldie," Goldie said. "I know you're busy."

"I am busy," Maxine said.

"I know you're busy," Goldie repeated. "But Delores is here at the clinic . . ."

"Don't talk to me about Delores," Maxine said, clearly losing her patience. "I don't have anything to do with her."

"Well, maybe you should," Goldie snapped. She felt the weight of the entire day hanging over her, and she was tired. So tired. "Your *sister* is in my clinic, and her cat is dying. She's going home without him tonight, and do you know what she keeps saying? She keeps saying that he's all she has, and that's not true, is it, Maxine?"

There was silence on the other end of the line, and Goldie realized she might have gone too far. Still, she wasn't sorry.

"No," Maxine said, finally. "It's not true . . . I can be there in ten minutes."

"Thank you," Goldie said, softening her tone. "We'll see you soon."

"Wow," Tiffany said when Goldie returned her phone. "I didn't expect that to work."

"Me either, honestly," Goldie replied. "But I'm glad it did. They need each other, don't they?"

"They're old ladies, living alone with no other family," Tiffany said. "Yes, they for sure need each other."

When Maxine got to the clinic, she didn't look nearly as defiant as she'd sounded on the phone.

"Where is she?" Maxine asked.

"She's in the examination room with Milton," Goldie said. "Don't go in there unless you can be kind."

"She has to be kind to me," Maxine said, stiffening a little.

"Aren't you her older sister?" Tiffany asked her.

"Two years."

"Then it's your job to be nice first," Tiffany said.

Goldie led Maxine back into the room. When Delores looked up, her eyes wet, she looked first at Maxine and then at Goldie and Tiffany.

"What . . . what are you doing here?"

Maxine cleared her throat. "Well, uh, Dr. Goldie called me. She said, uh, your Milton was really sick, and it might be his time."

"And you came?" Delores asked.

Maxine, who'd hung back a little behind Tiffany and Goldie, stepped forward and said, "Of course I came. Of course I did."

Chapter 46

"Do you want me to hate him now or hate him later?" Alex asked as she applied an ice pack to Goldie's ankle. "Stay still. You've got to keep it elevated, and the ice will help."

"I *know*," Goldie said. "I'm a doctor, too, you know."

"An animal doctor," Alex said under her breath.

"Hey!" Goldie said. "Rude! You're a face doctor!"

"Between the two of us, which one is an M.D.?"

"You are," Goldie grumbled.

"Exactly," Alex replied. "Now be quiet while I get you fixed up. You're lucky it's not broken."

"I just wish none of this had happened," Goldie said.

"None of what?"

"This!" Goldie used her arms to motion around the kitchen. "All of this. All of it. I messed everything up. If I'd never come here, nobody's lives would be any different—Cohen wouldn't have had to talk to his brother before he was ready, Maxine wouldn't have been caught on camera with a bunch of burlesque dancers, Addie never would have gotten lost . . ."

Alex rolled her eyes. "Goldie, you're the most interesting thing to happen to this town since . . . well, since anything interesting ever happened in this town."

"Cohen heard you call it Podunk Holler," Goldie said.

"I'd feel bad about that, except he broke your heart, so now I hate him," Alex replied.

Goldie tilted her head back and stared at the ceiling. "This is a mess."

"You're planning to leave tomorrow morning anyway, aren't you?" Alex asked.

"Yeah," Goldie replied. "I'm taking Airport with me, and Tiffany can probably watch over Kevin. But that's working under the assumption that I'm coming back. Right now, I don't know if I want to."

Alex nodded, drumming her fingers on the table. "You've got time to decide that," she said. "Don't make any rash decisions."

"You're one to talk about rash decisions," Goldie joked. "You just flew to Wisconsin on a whim."

"Nobody flies to Wisconsin on a whim," Alex joked. "I don't even think I could find it on a map."

Chapter 47

Alex managed to sweet-talk her way into an extra ticket for her flight, and Goldie agreed to pay dearly for the first-class seat. She called Tiffany and asked her to take Kevin for a few days, and Tiffany agreed, especially after she found out that Goldie and Dr. Saltzman had conspired to give her a sizable Christmas bonus.

"Don't let Kevin wander off," Goldie said to her.

"Kevin does what he wants," Tiffany said. "But I promise I'll keep him safe. The kids will love having him here for Christmas. He's as big as they are."

"Thank you," Goldie said to her. "For everything."

"You're welcome," Tiffany replied. "But you're coming back. I'll see you soon."

Goldie didn't tell Tiffany, or anyone else, that she'd considered not coming back. Her agreement with Dr. Saltzman had been through the first of the year, and after that, the decision to stay in Blue Dog Valley was completely hers. She wasn't entirely sure that the town was big enough for her and Cohen to both be there and not be together. She wasn't entirely sure that she wanted to be there without him. She didn't want to run into him at the supermarket or at the Rose farm and have an awkward and superficial conversation with him, all the while knowing what could have been.

She'd left a note on the office door asking that anyone who needed veterinary care call the vet in the next town over, but she'd simply said the clinic was "closed for the holidays." That was true, wasn't it? It was the holidays. She was allowed to take a break from, well, everything.

"What are you thinking about?" Alex asked her, once they'd boarded the flight and Airport was nestled in a cat carrier beneath Goldie's feet.

"Nothing," Goldie said. "I'm just ready to go home."

Her parents were waiting for her at the airport with a sign, and Goldie hadn't realized just how much she'd missed them until they were both embracing her.

"We missed you so much, kiddo!" her dad said. "We're so glad you decided to come home for a few days."

"Me, too," Goldie said. "Me, too."

"Is that the, uh, naked cat you told us about?" her mother asked, pointing down at the cat carrier.

Goldie nodded. "Yep. This is Airport."

"I don't know why that name surprises me," her father said. "You once named your stuffed bear Oh My, because you heard

'Lions and Tigers and Bears, Oh My!' in *The Wizard of Oz* and thought all bears were named Oh My."

Goldie laughed. "I don't remember that."

"Come on," her mother said. "Ignore your father. He's delirious with excitement. Let's get you home."

Chapter 48

Los Angeles, the place Goldie had always considered home, didn't feel quite like it had when she'd left. She knew better than anyone that L.A. shed its skin about as often as a snake, most of the time to reveal something new and shiny underneath. But to Goldie, absolutely everything felt dull when she compared it to the past couple of months in Blue Dog Valley. She found that she missed the people, the animals she'd cared for, and even the cold of Wisconsin. No matter how hard Goldie tried to get back into her California groove, it eluded her.

And then it was Christmas. It was obvious that her parents hadn't decorated at all until the last minute. The tree was a little flat, and the ornaments were thrown on haphazardly, but it was still perfect. They'd done all the things that she hadn't done with them since she was a teenager, like baking cookies and drinking hot cocoa and watching *It's a Wonderful Life*, even though Goldie's mother hated it.

Airport hadn't been sure about the house at first, but she'd settled in quickly, and more than once, Goldie had walked into the living room to see her father and Airport snuggled up together, sound asleep.

"This cat is a marvel," her father said as they unwrapped presents. "Her skin feels like velvet."

"That took us a little while," Goldie replied. "She wasn't in the best shape when I got her."

"I think we need a cat like this," her father continued. "What do you think, honey?"

Goldie's mother wrinkled her nose. "I don't know about that."

"Look at her!" Goldie's father said, holding Airport up for Goldie's mother to see. "Look at her face!"

Goldie laughed. "They've got really unique personalities," she said. "I think you'd both enjoy having a cat of your own."

Her father leaned over to Goldie and whispered, "I got her a sweater at this little shop down the street yesterday. I wrapped it up. She's going to look so cute."

Goldie laughed. It felt good to laugh. Despite the fun she'd been having, she'd be lying to herself if she said that she didn't miss the valley. She missed Tiffany, she missed Maxine and Delores, and she even missed Roger Dale. There were faces and voices she'd come to know and love.

"Here!" her mother said, handing her a present. "Open this one!"

Just then the doorbell rang, and they all looked up, confused.

"Are either of you expecting someone?" Goldie's father asked.

Goldie and her mother shook their heads.

"It could be Alex," Goldie said. "I know she's usually fed up with her own family by about now."

"That sounds right," her father said, standing up to go to the door. "I'll let her in."

Goldie's father came back a few minutes later, looking no less confused than he had before. "Goldie," he said. "There's, uh, there's a man here to see you."

Goldie's heart leaped to her throat. Standing beside her father was Cohen, looking nervous.

"Hi, Goldie," he said.

Goldie stood up and pulled at the hem of her plaid nightgown. "Cohen? What are you doing here?"

"Why don't we give you two some space to talk," Goldie's mother said. "We'll be in the kitchen. There's plenty to eat . . . Cohen, was it? You're welcome to stay for lunch."

"Thank you, ma'am," Cohen said, as her parents left the room.

Airport stayed for a few seconds, just long enough to give Cohen the stink eye, and then trotted off on the heels of Goldie's father.

"What are you doing here?" Goldie repeated.

"I'm sorry to show up like this," Cohen said. "I was afraid you'd tell me not to come if I called, and I . . . I had to see you, Goldie."

"How did you find my parents' house?" Goldie asked, still unable to believe Cohen was standing in front of her.

"I went to the cabin, but you weren't home," Cohen continued. "I saw the note on the clinic. So I went to see Tiffany. She said you'd gone. She had Kevin."

"She's taking care of him," Goldie said.

"I know," Cohen replied. "She gave me Alex's number. I called her. She told me where you were, but she didn't want to. She sure gave me a piece of her mind first."

"That sounds like Alex," Goldie said.

"You were just gone," Cohen said. "I didn't know you'd left."

"I didn't think you'd want me to tell you," Goldie replied. "You said you weren't ready, that you needed your own time, and you were right—I don't want to wait around for you to make a decision. I didn't come to Blue Dog Valley to wait on someone to figure out how they felt about me. I went there because I was . . . *am* tired of waiting."

Cohen ran a hand over the stubble on his jawline—it was obvious to Goldie that he hadn't shaved in a couple of days, at least, and he looked like he probably hadn't slept much, either.

"When I realized you left," Cohen said, "left the town, the state . . . me, well, I think I might've gone a little crazy. I couldn't stop thinking about you, and everywhere I went, even in the town where I've lived my whole life and you've only been two months, I saw you. Everywhere."

Goldie shifted her weight off her bad ankle and watched him, waiting for what he was going to say next.

"What I'm trying to say is, I don't want you to wait, because *I* don't want to wait," Cohen continued. "When I thought you might come back here for good, something inside of me cracked open, and I didn't like it. I didn't like the way it made me feel, so I pushed you away. I thought ending whatever this is between us would fix it, and it didn't. You're the only thing that can fix it, Goldie."

"Cohen, I—"

"And even if you hate me and never want to see me again," Cohen broke in, "you have to come back. Tiffany won't speak to me after Teddy told her what he overheard me saying after we found Addie. Come to think of it, neither will Teddy, considering you saved Addie's life. Mrs. Duvall said she'd burn her buildings down before she ever let the town use them again, and Kevin is so depressed he won't even eat, and everyone in town has been calling me. Ruby said she'd never make another cinnamon roll for as long as she lived, and Roger Dale said he'd run me off the road the next time he saw me if I didn't come here and get you back."

"He'd do it, too," Goldie said.

"We need you," Cohen said. "I knew it the minute I saw you at the airport, crouched down talking to that ridiculous cat. I just couldn't admit it to myself."

"I need you, too," Goldie replied, her voice shaking just a little. "I need Blue Dog Valley, but you know what I need most?" she asked, just before she leaned in to kiss Cohen's lips.

"What?" Cohen mumbled, bending down to meet her.

"Ruby's cinnamon rolls."

Epilogue

"I don't see why I had to wear a dress shirt for this," Cohen grumped, pulling at the sleeves of his crisp blue button-up. "It's making me itch."

"Hush," Tiffany replied, elbowing him in the ribs. "This is an important day."

Cohen looked past the crowd of people gathered and saw Goldie walking toward him, radiant, as the sun glinted off her shoulders. He couldn't believe that his entire world had opened up and presented him with *her*, the most beautiful woman, inside and out, that he'd ever known. It pleased him to no end that practically the entire town had turned out for today, knowing just exactly how much it meant to her, to his Goldie.

He looked down at Peanut Butter and winked. "Don't worry, old gal, you're still my best dog."

As Goldie approached him, elbow to elbow with a grinning Dr. Saltzman, Cohen prepared to tell her just how lovely she was. But before he had the chance, Kevin, in all his chaotic glory, burst through the crowd and ran up to him, settling his massive and *very* muddy paws squarely on Cohen's chest.

"Kevin!" Tiffany shrieked. "Kevin, you—"

"Wonderful dog," Goldie reminded her, taking her place beside Cohen. "Wonderful, wonderful dog."

"That's *not* what I was going to say," Tiffany replied.

Cohen, who hated his shirt anyway, laughed. "I guess this means I'll never have to wear this ridiculous getup again."

Dr. Saltzman eyed him. "Don't be so certain," he said.

Goldie turned her attention to the gathered crowd and cleared her throat. "Thank you so much to everyone who has helped to make me feel so welcome here," she said. "I don't think today would be possible without you. I am so honored you've allowed me to find a place here, with the best community a vet could ever ask for."

Dr. Saltzman handed Goldie the giant pair of scissors he'd brought for the occasion, the second pair he purchased, once he landed in Milwaukee, after nearly being arrested in Florida for trying to fly with what the TSA considered to be a lethal weapon.

"Here you are, my dear," he said. "It's time to make this clinic officially yours."

Goldie hugged him, and just as she cut the ribbon to her very own veterinary clinic in Blue Dog Valley, her new forever home, the crowd began to cheer.

About the author

About the book

Insights,
Interviews
& More . . .

Meet
Annie England Noblin

Photo courtesy of the author

ANNIE ENGLAND NOBLIN lives with her
son, husband, and three rescued bulldogs
in the Missouri Ozarks. She graduated
with an MA in creative writing from
Missouri State University and currently
teaches English at Arkansas State
University.

Her poetry has been featured in such
publications as *Red Booth Review* and
Moon City Review, and she coedited and
coauthored the coffee-table book *Gillioz:
Theatre Beautiful*. ❧

Annie's Family Snapdoodle Recipe

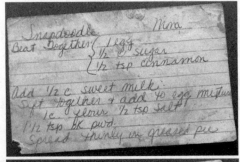

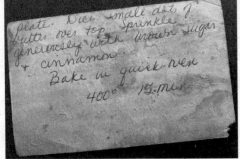

Ingredients:

1 egg
1 teaspoon cinnamon, divided
½ cup sugar
½ cup sweetened condensed milk
1 cup flour
1½ teaspoons baking powder
½ teaspoon salt
¼ cup light or dark brown sugar
Unsalted butter ▶

Annie's Family Snapdoodle Recipe
(continued)

Instructions:

1. Preheat oven to 400°F and grease a pie dish.

2. Beat together egg, ½ teaspoon cinnamon, and sugar. Once mixed, add sweetened condensed milk and set aside.

3. Sift together the flour, baking powder, and salt.

4. Add the dry ingredients to the egg mixture and mix until a dough is formed.

5. Spread the dough evenly onto the greased pie dish.

6. Cut small pieces of butter and spread over the dough.

7. Mix together the brown sugar and the other ½ teaspoon of cinnamon, and sprinkle generously over the dough.

8. Put in the preheated oven and bake for 15 minutes.

9. Remove from the oven and let the snapdoodle slightly cool before serving. ⌒

Ruby's Famous Cinnamon Rolls

Makes 16 rolls

When I wrote about Ruby and her famous cinnamon rolls, I was thinking about my great-grandmother, Pauline Roper, and the way she believed baking could solve the world's problems. I went to her house every day after school, and she always had something fantastic to eat. Her snapdoodles and cinnamon rolls were the best around, and to this day, simply smelling a cinnamon roll makes me happy.

—Annie England Noblin

Raisin-nut filling ingredients:

¼ cup Karo dark corn syrup
2 tablespoons melted butter
   or margarine
¼ cup brown sugar
2 teaspoons cinnamon
½ cup raisins
½ cup chopped nuts

Cinnamon roll ingredients:

¾ cup Karo light corn syrup
¼ cup butter or margarine
¼ cup brown sugar
3 cups sifted all-purpose flour ▸

Ruby's Famous Cinnamon Rolls
(continued)

4 teaspoons baking powder
1½ teaspoons salt
½ cup shortening
1 cup milk

Instructions:

1. Preheat oven to 425°F.

2. Make the raisin-nut filling by mixing the dark corn syrup, melted butter or margarine, brown sugar, cinnamon, raisins, and chopped nuts together. Set aside.

3. Place the light corn syrup, butter, and brown sugar in a saucepan, bring to a boil over medium heat, and boil for 1 minute.

4. Pour the mixture into a 9-inch square cake pan. Set aside.

5. In a separate bowl, sift the flour, baking powder, and salt, and then cut in the shortening with a pastry blender or two knives. Finally, add the milk and mix to form a soft dough.

6. Turn the dough out onto a floured board and roll into a rectangle ¼ inch thick. Cover with the raisin-nut filling. Roll the dough like you

would for a jelly roll, cut into 1-inch slices, and place the slices cut side down into the syrup.

7. Bake in the preheated oven for 45 minutes.

8. Let stand in the pan about 2 minutes, then invert the pan to remove buns. ∽

Reading Group Guide

1. Goldie impulsively changes her life by leaving Los Angeles and moving to Blue Dog Valley. If you could leave and move anywhere else in the world—changing your own life completely—where would you go, and why?

2. Why do you think Dr. Salzman leases his practice to Goldie? What might he see in her that he hasn't seen in anyone else?

3. Discuss some of the preconceived ideas that the people who live in Blue Dog Valley have about Goldie because she is from Los Angeles. What did they get right and wrong?

4. Do you think Goldie came with her own preconceived ideas as well? What, if anything, could she have done differently to fit into Blue Dog Valley sooner?

5. Goldie at one point realizes she's slid into an easy life with Brandon. What was it about her life with him that was so comfortable? When do forgivable faults develop into irreconcilable differences in relationships?

6. Books with animals are always so popular. What are some of your favorite novels with animals and pets?

7. Goldie comes to Blue Dog Valley without any warm clothes. Is it because she's just an unprepared city gal, or is there a deeper meaning to this refusal?

8. At one moment Goldie realizes she's lived four decades without ever "hearing quiet." What does it mean to you to "hear quiet?"

9. If you were casting the movie of *Christmas in Blue Dog Valley*, who would you choose?

10. If you have or have ever had a pet, what is the one thing about your pet that always brings you joy and puts a smile on your face? ᴄᴡ